The Rock

a novel by

JOHN MASTERS

SPHERE BOOKS LIMITED

For Barbara

SPHERE BOOKS LTD

Published by the Penguin Group
27 Wrights Lane, London w8 5tz, England
Viking Penguin Inc., 40 West 23rd Street, New York, New York 10010, USA
Penguin Books Australia Ltd, Ringwood, Victoria, Australia
Penguin Books Canada Ltd, 2801 John Street, Markham, Ontario, Canada l3r 1b4
Penguin Books (NZ) Ltd, 182 190 Wairau Road, Auckland 10, New Zealand

Penguin Books Ltd, Registered Offices: Harmondsworth, Middlesex, England

First published in America by G. P. Putnam's Sons, New York 1970
Published by Sphere Books Ltd 1989
1 3 5 7 9 10 8 6 4 2

PUBLISHER'S NOTE
None of the characters mentioned in the fictional sections of this
book have any relation to, or are intended to represent, any living person.

Printed and bound in Great Britain by
Richard Clay Ltd, Bungay, Suffolk

Contents

✖✖✖✖✖✖✖✖✖✖✖✖✖✖✖✖✖✖✖✖✖✖✖✖✖✖

Foreword

COMING in low from due east, looking through the curved perspex, it appears first as a pale cloud on the surface of the sea off the mountains of Africa. The edges fast become more sharply defined, and the whiteness intensifies as the morning sun strikes back from it. Darker areas, but still quite pale, take form to left and right of the central white, and the sky beyond silhouettes the shape of the crest. It is a great wall of rock, over 2 miles long, 1400 feet high at right and center. It falls gradually to the left—south—and seems to be a gigantic crouching animal, its head toward Africa, its paws extended. Northward the resemblance ends, for there are no hind quarters or tail: the rock ends sheer.

There is a huge straight-sided patch in the middle of the eastern slope, as pale in itself as the gray of the cliffs but appearpearing brighter from its smoothness, which more strongly casts back the sun's light. It is man made, the huge patch, perhaps half a mile long and 700 feet high; but who knows what it is? There is nothing else like it on earth.

Closer now: parts of the wall are thinly painted in green—a few broad daubs run down gullies, a fine stippling marks ledges, crevices, gentler slopes where soil can stay and plants take hold. Along the shoreline the dark mouths of caverns appear, some small, most large. The outer arch often shelters a lesser inner arch and that a lesser again, thus gradually bringing the eye from the colossal to the human scale, in the manner used by the architect of the Buland Darwaza at Fatehpur Sikri.

The upthrust rock is sliding past on the right, and the works of man command the eye. The crest bristles like a threatened porcupine. Guns, masts, directors, radar towers, range finders, antennae, guns . . . guns . . . guns . . . scattered large buildings toward the low point of the rock—not houses, but barracks or hospitals, or prisons perhaps . . . on the very point, a white and red lighthouse. Turning north, the barracks give way to houses; the houses close in on each other; trees, gardens, streets cling in parallel rows to this western slope. It is more gentle than the almost sheer eastern wall but still very steep for a town. Directly below now a big harbor opens up—long sea walls, gray warships alongside, dry docks: more sea moles—yachts, oil tankers, cargo ships: The houses condense rapidly into suburbs, the suburbs become a narrow, huddled town. Momentarily, a four-square medieval castle appears on a bluff above the town. Below it, half hidden, half ruined, there are the regular zigzags of fortifications, more walls, embrasures for cannon.

The landing pad drifts up to the wheels. On the right the sheer cliff which we had once seen as the back of the crouching lion begins to take on a familiar shape. Everyone knows it, for everyone has seen it in advertisements, and by now it is not only a place but a byword. The name evokes a geographical location, a habitation, a fortress, yes—but equally, an idea, an attitude, an attribute.

It is the Rock: Gibraltar.

Everyone knows it, but only in part, because although it is small in area, it is big in story. No place in the world has witnessed, and played a part in, so much history. It is a history not only of battles and sieges, of that defiance and resistance for which the name has come to stand, but of mankind's climb from the caves—these very caves—to the technological heights exemplified in the artifacts arrayed along this very crest. It is a story of man exploring the world and himself, of building civilizations and casting them down, of the long, eventful journey to the miracles and malaises of today. The Rock has seen it all.

It is a story of immense length and complexity, with two special problems. The first is the lack of human continuity. Except for prehistoric peoples and occasional later visitors, the Rock was uninhabited until medieval times, and since then there have been four complete turnovers of population. But except for one break, and that very short in Gibraltar's time scale, one people has always been represented here: the Jews; and it is they who provide the continuity. This is not the story of Gibraltar as seen through Jewish eyes, still less a history of the Jews of Gibraltar; but as in actual history, Jewish characters and the Jewish character—so aptly similar to the attributes of the Rock—link what would otherwise have no human connection.

The second problem is that of uneven depth, caused by the fact that much is known of some parts of Gibraltar's history, little of others; yet the importance of an event and the realness, the humanity, of the people involved in it should not be lessened by our ignorance. The two-stream plan on which this book is written has been designed to overcome this drawback.

Back then, not this time in a helicopter, nor to east or west or north or south—but back in time, to the beginnings. . . .

Book One

In the Beginning

FOUR thousand million years ago, as the molten ball of Earth whirled through space, it began to cool. Its surface solidified into a crystalline crust. Earth's atmosphere formed, and new forces began to act on the rocky surface. Ice, wind, frost, lightning, rain—storms of unimaginable fury lasting for thousands of years on end—broke up and wore away the fire-born rock, grinding much of it into sand and silt and sweeping this debris down to the plains and to the sea.

The coming of vegetation and of the first forms of life vastly increased the amount of matter deposited. In deeper seas the sediment was mostly the calcareous skeletons of marine life. Closer to the land masses, where much of the sediment was brought down by the rivers, it was mostly pebbles, grit, and mud.

In the course of hundreds of millions of years these deposits, cemented together by chemical action and compressed by their own sheer weight, formed a different kind of rock: sedimentary rock. In the Gibraltar area the sedimentary rock being formed far below the sea was limestone. It continued to be laid down during the Jurassic period (180,000,000 years ago) and was then covered by a thinner layer of shale and grit.

As the Earth continued to cool, it shrank. The crust had to

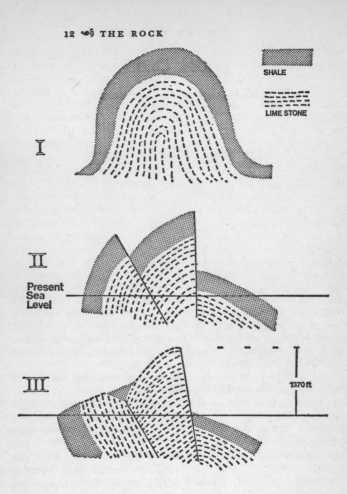

SHALE

LIME STONE

I

II

Present
Sea
Level

III

1370 ft

adjust to the new smaller size and did so by folding. The folds did not take place evenly but where the crust was thin, weak, or unusually depressed. The western Mediterranean was such an area. It is bounded by a huge circle of solid masses of igneous rock: the Spanish tableland, the Massif Central of France, the main body of North Africa. The shrinking pressure forced the earth's crust to fold up here. Inside the resistant shield behind, new mountains were formed—steep, high, dramatic, quite different from the rounded igneous hills of the containing circle. The new mountains were the Atlas, the Apennines, the Alps, the Pyrenees, and the Sierra Nevada.

At a bend in this new fold (here running north to south) appeared a special phenomenon. The surface here, the substance being folded by the pressures of the earth's shrinkage, was limestone, thousands of feet thick. On top of the limestone lay a thin deposit of shale and grit. Limestone is not cloth, and when the folding reached a certain point, it split. It might have cracked in any number of ways, but it actually split in two places: one in the top center of the fold and one halfway down the western side. The unbelievable pressure continued. The central wedge of limestone continued to thrust upward, breaking the weak tension of the shale, pushing on up, baring a vertical face scores —hundreds—thousands of feet high. The outer parts of the original fold subsided, one almost completely, the other saving itself by leaning against the towering center.

The shale, which had been lying on a fairly flat surface far below the sea, now found itself clinging to exposed and sharply tilted slopes. Wind, rain, and the upheavals of adjustment to the new form washed the shale off the steeper parts of the limestone and collected it in the hollows. Gibraltar had come into existence.

The process of settling took a long time. During these eons the earth sank and rose and the seas advanced and retreated several times, to immense heights and depths. About 12,000,000 years ago other passages between the Atlantic and the Mediterranean closed, and the earth sank south of Gibraltar. The waters passing through this strait survived as the only link between the two oceans.

The Rock guarded the north side of the new channel, looking very much as it does now—its steep white faces, of pure limestone, toward the north and east, its sloping and duller aspects, of shale, toward the south and west. It was 2¾ miles long by three-quarters of a mile wide at the widest place and was joined to the mainland on the north by a sandy isthmus about a mile long and gradually increasing from half a mile to a full mile wide where the mainland proper begins. The west side of the isthmus curves gently round in a full semi-circle 4 miles in diameter. Two rivers flow into this bay from the land behind, which quickly rises and fades to distant mountains. On the east side of the isthmus the shoreline continues almost due north, curving only very gradually toward the northeast. South, the jagged African shore is 11½ miles away, and the mountains on that side are higher than Gibraltar. Southwest, through the strait, the Atlantic ocean forms the horizon.

Limestone is a clean, hard, pale gray rock, formed mainly of calcium carbonate. It dissolves slowly under the action of water, especially if the water carries acids or alkalis. As soon as the mass of the Rock was raised and exposed, water began to eat into it. Rainwater, falling into cracks, enlarged them into clefts, then into "vertical" caves. Seawater tunneled into the foot of the cliffs to make "horizontal" caves at all levels, for during the settling period there were many sea levels (one sea-made cave is 700 feet above the present shore) .

The sheer energy of the years created tunnels, halls, passages, rooms, cells, and amphitheaters inside the Rock. And the chemical action of the water not only excavated the caves, it decorated them. As water comes out of the interior of the rock, where it has been under pressure, and enters a cave, it must give up some of the calcium carbonate with which it has been super-charged. A tiny deposit of sinter-limestone is made, and according to the other substances through which the water has flowed—e.g., iron, carbon, shell layers—or the acids which have been added to it, the deposit will have color, a limitless variety of colors, though all muted in intensity and tone. Limitless, too, are the other forces which will shape and sculpture the accumulating deposits: how the wind blows, whether the roof is flat or sloping, whether the water drips regularly or irregularly, fast or slow. . . .

Doubly limitless, then, are these formations of sinter-limestone in the caves—stalagmites rising from the ground, stalactites hanging from the roof, pillars, knobs, warts, candles, palettes, tree trunks, water lilies, straws, frills, flounces, curtains, tracery, leaves, cathedral arches and hammer beams, people, animals . . . in white, tan, rust red, blue, gray. Three of the most extraordinary forms are helectites (crazy worm casts shaped by wind action, which seem to defy all laws of gravity and reason); cave pearls, or pitholite (formed when the steady dripping of the water keeps rolling the sinter deposit around as it forms); and rimstone (thin ledges around the rim of pools and lakes, or even right over them).

The floor of the caves, if it is not "live" sinter—that is, still being formed—is an extraordinary dark brown powder, like snuff, of the consistency of fine flour. This is the deposit of millions of years of vegetable mold and, in some caves, of bat guano. It is often many feet thick.

About three quarters of a million years ago the Ice Ages began to modify the Rock into its present exact form. Each ice age lasted at least 40,000 years, and the warmer gaps between them, the interglacial periods, were generally longer.

In each ice age the north polar ice cap spread much farther south than it does now. During one it covered England solid; France was uninhabitable and Gibraltar very cold. Because so much water was locked up in the ice the sea level fell: at Gibraltar it was some 300 feet below its present level.

During the interglacials the climate was much warmer than it is now. England became tropical and Gibraltar equatorial; the sea level rose to 300 feet above the present; and the loss of the weight of the ice actually caused those areas that had been under it to rise, while bordering areas, such as Spain, sank in compensation, raising the sea level there still higher.

At each of these levels—and every ice age and every interglacial had different ones—the sea made beaches, sea cliffs, and sea caves. Some are now submerged; others are stranded far above the shore but quite recognizable for what they were.

The ice ages also continued the work of previous eons in sculpting the Rock. Ice and frost action broke off pieces of sharp-angled limestone, which rolled to the foot of the slope and were cemented together by the action of the charged water to form the limestone breccia which covers most of the lower part of the Rock. Mixed into it, and also sometimes in considerable depth in and above the shale deposits, is bone breccia, presumably from the victims of carnivorous animals.

Finally, there is sand. A large part of the eastern face of the Rock is covered by a gigantic and very steep slope of aeolian (windblown) sand. This sand—some of it cemented by the usual action—was formed in the ice ages, when for thousands of years without cease a strong east wind blew sand from the exposed floor of the Mediterranean onto the Rock.

When the last ice age ended, the east wind created another special feature of Gibraltar's climate, the *levanter* cloud. Coming across hundreds of miles of Mediterranean, it is always charged with water. When it meets the steep east face, it has to rise 1,400 feet very rapidly. It cools, and some of its water condenses to form vaporous cloud, which often hangs oppressively over the top of the Rock, also streaming out to the west, while the sky over mainland, bay, and strait is quite clear. For the rest, the climate is equable, temperately warm, and—except with a levanter—pleasant. The rainfall, concentrated mainly between September and March, is adequate.

When the land took its present shape, Gibraltar stood at the gate of the only channel linking the Mediterranean with the Atlantic. The surface current formed: strongly eastward in the center of the strait, less so at the sides. For thousands of years no one knew how the Atlantic water pouring into the Mediterranean returned. Then in the last century British naval surveys found an equally strong underwater current, perpetually westbound, which carried huge amounts of water over the sill of the strait into the Atlantic. The configuration of the ocean bed causes much of this great river to come to the surface off Cape Trafalgar, increasing the already great danger of that cape for small vessels, especially in the days of primitive navigation by sail and oar. (These discoveries solved some legendary sea mysteries, notably that of a ship sunk in collision off Tarifa about 1805. She sank in a riproaring eastbound current—and came to the surface the next day off Trafalgar, 30 miles to the west.)

The fish that inhabited these waters were, first, the tunny. The ancients believed that tunny perpetually circled the Mediterranean in a counterclockwise direction, since they had only one good eye, the right. Modern pollution, the increase in fishing, and the noise of ships' engines have driven tunny away from the immediate neighborhood of the strait. Beside tunny there are or were whale, swordfish, squid, eel, bonito, sardine, sea bream, sea bass, red mullet, perch, pollack, and gilthead.

As the land took shape, the vegetation settled on and in it. The Rock is too steep, and the surface soil too shallow or scattered over the limestone, for the vegetation ever to have been lush; but neither was it ever wholly barren. Now, its climate median between the extremes it has known, the pale limestone is overlaid with a thin-woven carpet of scrub, mainly aromatic— heather, rosemary, sage, Sodom apple, thyme, lavender, pennyroyal. In the scrub stand steeply tilted thickets, woods, or isolated trees—cork oak, carob bean, holly oak, wild olive, wild fig.

The flowers do not lie in great banks like cowslips in an English meadow, for there is no rich loam to make the bed for them. Instead they line the edges of runnels, shelter in small crevices, or hang onto tiny patches of earth exposed to the wind, high on the cliffs. Every month of the year some flowers are cautiously displaying their blossoms—clematis, narcissus, mesembryanthemum, stonecrop, ragwort, oxalis, bindweed, mignonette, borage, asphodel, marigold, autumn crocus, periwinkle, bee orchid, snapdragon, rue, mallow, gladiolus, giantleaved acanthus. In March three score varieties flower, stippling the whole Rock with color—white and yellow of chrysanthemum, jasmine, coronilla, broom, sea aster, giant fennel, freesia, campion; blue of iris, bugloss, pimpernel, scilla, wild pea; rose and pink of mallow, cistus, snapdragon; and a flower that, in Europe, exists only here—the flat white and mauve, many-petaled faces of Gibraltar candytuft.

The birds came and are as various as the flowers but in the main not as noticeable—warblers, finches, tits, wrens, orioles, choughs, jays, ravens, kestrels, buzzards, vultures, ospreys, gannets, puffins; and, as with the candytuft, one bird that in Europe is unique to Gibraltar—the Barbary partridge. It is about twelve inches long, so is a little smaller than the redlegged partridge. It is studded with small white spots, has a chestnut

collar and a metallic blue tinge in the wing coverts, and its legs
are red or pale buff. It is a noisy, unsuspecting bird, much hunted
by cats, eagles, lizards, and snakes.

After the vegetation and the birds, the animals. . . . They
came early and lived through the fluctuations and upheavals of
the Rock's formation. Bone breccia of animals was being deposited in some of the rock fissures before the great submer-
gences of more than 30,000,000 years ago. By such traces as this
breccia and the bones deep under the present cave floors, we
know that the wolf came, and the fox, seal, ibex, and chamois;
all the animals that have since been domesticated—horse, pig,
and cattle (including the aurochs); rabbit, rat, water rat—and
two kinds of rhinoceros; tortoise, bat, gecko, and leopard. Most
of these lived on the Rock for as long as the species existed in
Europe, though there can never have been large numbers
here, and the bigger, more noticeable animals soon vanished at
the arrival of the last comer—man.

In remote geological times various land bridges existed for
millions of years between Europe and Africa. One such bridge
was certainly at Gibraltar, which saw some of man's ancestors
pass in both directions, "African" types going to Europe and
"European" types to Africa.

At some time more—perhaps much more—than 50,000 years
ago, a type of man flourished in Europe, including the Rock,
who represented the biggest advance in evolution thus far. He
was big and burly and stood upright, with his heavy head thrust
a little forward. His face had a marked frontal bone, eyes deep
sunk under it, and a wide flat nose, but he was definitely a human, not an ape. He had developed only the simplest tools
and lived by hunting deer, ibex, rabbits, and water birds and
by gathering shellfish, nuts, and fruit. He may also, from need
or for ritual reasons, have been a cannibal, but probably seldom
inside his own family group.

As he had no pots, he could neither store food nor cook it, except by grilling over an open flame. The climate was colder than
ours during most of his stay, but not greatly so. With the sea bed
lower all around the Rock, those who lived here had a wider
terrain in which to hunt, and the seashore was more easy to get
at for shells and fishing in the rock pools. Two or three hundred
feet above the sea and about a mile back from it there were

many high-arched, deep caves at the foot of the huge cliffs. The cliffs gave good protection, and in these caves the people lived. In the same cave or a neighboring one they buried their dead with ceremonies and artifacts, proving that they had some non-instinctive beliefs about the nature of death and hence of life.

Not long afterward another type of man appeared. He may have been a parallel development of the first, or he may have been quite separate. He was not so powerful but was taller, and he had a larger brain. He was more agile, both mentally and physically.

The temperate interlude began to end. The ice again crept southward across Europe. Every living thing which could move fled in front of it, trying to adapt to new conditions as it went, for the "flight" was spread over thousands of years.

The old man and this new man found themselves in competition for the available game, shelter, and food. The conflict was long-drawn and widespread and took many forms. Here it went one way, there another. In some places perhaps common sense won and the two types united and interbred. In others it was not the human enemy but the changing circumstances that conquered. No one knows the details, only the result: by about 33,500 years ago, the old man had gone—vanished—become extinct.

One of his last stands must have been at Gibraltar, for the strait, perhaps 6 miles wide then, barred all further southward flight. It was the Rock's first human war, its first siege, its first fall.

The Woman

The Woman moved along the shore in a group of women and children, her baby in the crook of her arm. A snow flurry momentarily whitened the reddish hair hanging to her waist and speckled her naked body with large white splashes. She did not notice but went on turning over rocks, feeling under ledges and in crevices. When she found a shell, she cracked it carefully between two stones, poured the juice down her throat, and tore out the flesh with her teeth and strong nails. When she threw a shell down, the children pounced on it, snarling and snatching, until the winner ran a little way up the sandy slope to eat by himself.

The Woman hitched her baby around and pushed her nipple into its sucking mouth. Her body ached from hunger, and her throat hurt. Straightening her back, she glanced up the slope to the cave at the foot of the cliffs. She saw movement there, recognized the Old Woman, and growled, "It is well." The baby spat out her nipple and began to cry.

As the sun in front of them sank toward the crest of the Rock, they turned away from the water. The wind blew colder, driving sand stung her eyes, and the baby howled more loudly.

A half-formed girl, trudging in the lead, stopped suddenly with a low word—"Deer." The tracks were clear in the sand, coming from the sun, moving diagonally across the slope, and disappearing into the scrub on the flat land north of the Rock. The Woman saw from the size and spacing of the slots that it was a stag. It was the rutting season, and she could also detect the male rankness clinging to the sand.

They all stared a long time in the direction the deer had gone, then continued up the slope and onto a shoulder of the Rock, above the last low cliffs. Here the Woman just caught sight of a big bird's wing, flapping close to the ground on her right. A vulture. Vultures mean food . . . a sharp pain twisted her belly. She stopped, as though to pluck some of the weeds growing between the stones. A pair of children paused by her and groped where she groped, pulling up the weeds, sniffing them, looking at her. One said, "Nothing," and they ran on. The woman slunk away alone toward the three trees where she had seen the vulture. None of the others noticed for a time, then Big Woman cried, "What?" and the Woman with the baby broke into a run, the baby bounding on her hip. Three vultures took off heavily from under the trees, two remained on the prey. The Woman picked up a stone and hurled it as she ran. The last vultures rose, hissing, and she fell on the dead lynx, grabbed the red hole the vultures' beaks had opened into the stomach, tore out a piece of flesh, and crammed it into her mouth. She had her hand on another when the rest arrived. The other women grabbed and snarled, and the children reached between and under them.

When they had torn out what they could, Big Woman took the bloody carcass and slung it round her neck. They went on down to the lake in the gully. The Woman with the baby felt good, and her belly had stopped aching. In the gully there were trees and another cave. No one lived in it, but there was a trickle of water and shelter from the wind. The Woman knelt, cupped her hands in the lake, drank, and then held water for her baby, but it would not drink. The low sun shone full on her, and she pushed back her hair to let the warmth touch her body. Yawning, she reached slowly out toward one of the little green cucumbers that grew among the rocks. The children leaned close, expectant. As her fingers touched the outermost of the cucumber's thousand tiny hairs, it sprang free from its stalk with a sudden pop and jumped into the air, squirting her finger and face with liquid white seed. The Woman laughed, the children laughed. A small boy ran round screeching with laughter, found another cucumber, and reached cautiously out to touch it. But it was not ripe and did not explode.

The Woman leaned over a rock where rainwater lay in a flat shallow pool. She saw her face there and moved her head, and the face moved. She touched the water with her finger, and the face broke up, crushed, but slowly came back again. It was her, and it was not her. She scratched herself, and soon they all started back for their own cave, looking for nuts as they went.

It was good also in the cave, the low fire red and hot. The Old Woman had scraped the last of the rotting flesh off the ibex skin the men had killed many days ago. Bent Brother was striking a flint with a stone. Big Woman began to skin the lynx with a sharp flint burin. Soon she had worked one thigh bone free, and thrust it into the fire. Now Small Woman came to the Woman and they squatted face to face near the cave mouth, searching for fleas and lice in each other's hair. When they found one they squashed it between their nails, and licked off the remnants.

Later the Old Woman in the cave mouth muttered, "The men. They have nothing."

The Father came in first, the two young men behind. Their hands were empty and clean and they had nothing on their backs. The Father threw down his spear and seized a lynx bone from Big Woman. She growled and for a moment held to it, and he jerked it free and sent her flying across the sand with a blow of his arm. He cracked the bone, sucked out the marrow, then threw it down. One of the young men picked it up.

It was almost dark, and the Old Woman lay down in the mouth of the cave. She wore a long tooth on a thong round her neck. The tooth came from a great magic animal killed long ago and far away, and it belonged to them all, but the oldest woman wore it. Big Woman came back to the fire and warmed her feet. She told the Father of the deer tracks they had seen. The Father grunted and told how the men had seen a female bear and wounded it, but before they could kill it, Others had come and frightened it away.

A shiver crept across the Woman's skin at the mention of Others. She had never seen one but she knew they were not animals, yet they were not us. They were Other. Her baby was sucking, half asleep, at her nipple. She put her arm around it, and a low purring growl throbbed in her chest.

One of the young men held his spearpoint in the fire and began to sharpen it with a flint blade. The Father's spearpoint was a sharp flint tied on with sinew, and he took Bent Brother's round stone and struck the flint to make a better edge to the point. Snow flurries whirled past the cave mouth, and a cold wind blew sparks from the fire. The Woman went toward a far corner, past the pile of chips where Bent Brother worked. He was there, squatting, and grabbed her and put his hand between her legs. She knelt, waiting. He felt her and in a moment mounted her and thrust into her. Her loins throbbed, her knees weakened. She moaned aloud and jerked, so that her baby rolled free in the sand under her breasts. When Bent Brother had ended, he pushed her over so that she lay on her side and he behind her, huddled together. She took her baby to her breast again. Big Woman curled up with the Father. The children huddled together in groups and the two young men with Small Woman. The Old Woman crept in from the cave mouth, snow on her shriveled breasts, and put more wood on the fire.

In the first dawn the Woman awoke, stretched, and went out onto fresh snow. The young men were at the place, and as she squatted beside them she watched them pick up snow, and one suddenly threw it at the other, then they both laughed and threw snow at each other. When the sun rose out of the sea, far away, the Father went to the cave mouth, stretched and scratched, and said, "Come." They all went with him except the Old Woman, who kept the fire. The Father led down the slope to the beach. The sky was a pale blue, and the wind had sunk, but the snow and the wind of the night had destroyed the marks of the stag, nor could the Woman smell any trace of it.

They worked north along the beach. At a big pool they surrounded it, then all ran in together and caught six little fishes, which the men ate. Later the Woman found a few limpets and ate them quickly. Later, after the sun had passed its height, one of the young men in front crouched, his spear raised. Everyone stopped. The Woman put her hand over her baby's mouth, listening, but heard only the splash of the waves. The men ran forward and crouched behind a point of rocks.

Three upright animals came round the corner of rock, and Big Woman muttered, "Others!" There were two males and a female cub. They were all tall and stood upright. The bigger male carried a spear and the other a heavy flint set sideways on a short stick.

The Other cub, picking up an empty shell, saw them first. It screamed, and at once the Father, Bent Brother, and the two young men rushed out at them. The Others turned and ran, but Bent Brother threw a big stone which hit the cub on the head, so that she fell. The young men leaped onto her, and she snarled and bit one's hand, but the other pushed his spearpoint into her throat, then quickly held her up and drank the blood while it was still running.

The Woman looked along the beach at the male Others. They ran fast; none could catch them. The children were pulling the Other cub about, turning her over and sniffing at her. The Woman saw that she looked like a woman of their own, but she was not, she was Other—thin, the teeth far back in her mouth, and smelling dangerous. The Father threw her over his shoulder and started back toward the cave, shouting, "Food, food, food!" and everyone shouted regularly with him.

In the cave Bent Brother hacked with the flint edge, and the men broke her bones and twisted them apart. Some ate her flesh raw and some put chunks onto the red-hot wood, and the little children pulled out the entrails and searched in the carcass for pieces the rest had overlooked. The Woman sank her teeth into a roasted piece of flesh. The juice ran down her chin, and her baby sucked contentedly at her nipple.

The Man and his young companion, Feetborn's Son, saw their fire from a long way off through the trees and moved a little faster, for the wind blew colder as the sun sank, and the winter time was coming. The woman Feetborn was tending the fire, and the Man went directly to her and said, "We met Others by the sea. They killed Red Girl."

Feetborn was Red Girl's mother, too, and she raised her face to the sky and began to howl. Tears ran down her cheek. When the Man stroked her arm, she turned and hid her head in his shoulder. He touched her back and stroked her long hair and then left her. Feetborn's Son was telling the other women, Cryer and Snowborn, and the children about their meeting with the Others. He told how the Others had been lying in wait behind rocks on the shore, how they rushed out screaming: many, many Others, one with a twisted hip. He imitated the way the Others stood, his head sunk into his shoulders and stuck forward, his mouth pushed forward and all his teeth showing and sticking out forward and his hand over his eyes where the Others had a big bone and the eyes deep-sunk under it. Then he walked like the Others did, shambling, his knees always a little bent. The women and children listened eagerly, with low cries. They were all huddled together around the fire, against the cold. Snowborn had sharpened a small deer bone and was putting it into her hair and twisting her hair around it, her arms raised above her head and her breasts raised and rounded. The Man's loins thickened as he looked at her. But Cryer's baby was very silent and blue in her arms. And he kept thinking of the Others. When he first saw one, years ago, he had called, "Friend," mistaking it for a man. For a moment he thought it had understood, but then it snarled and ran away. So they were not men. But they were not animals.

He shook his head, unsure, and growled at the children to get more wood for the fire. Lefthand, the tall young man whose mother was dead two snows past, sat beside him. They talked about the bear the Others had frightened away the day before but decided not to hunt her again. Lefthand told the Man about a stag that had passed, and they decided to hunt that the next day.

The children came back with wood and set it by the fire. Feetborn laid a long bough on a long bough, and the flames blew higher. Even close to the fire it was cold, though, and sleet began to fall, slanting down, so that for a time the Man could not see the trees across the river. Cryer began to whimper over her baby.

Snowborn came to the Man and sat by him. Gently she bit his ear. He held her breasts, and she lay back, singing, and pulled him down into her arms.

When he rolled away, he saw Lefthand by the fire, curled up in a ball, no one by him. The Man lay down in the thin shelter of a tree, women and children around him, and slept.

In the first light he went carefully to the running water, watched the forest on the other side, felt the wind—it was less now, but touched with cold rain—drank, and rubbed water on his face and body. Cryer was moaning quietly, her head bent. Feetborn and Lefthand were by her, but she cried, "No. No. No." The Man went close and thought that Cryer's baby was dead. He touched it and found it was cold and stiff. Cryer bent her head and took his wrist in her teeth, but gently. He stroked her shoulder with the other hand, kneeling beside her, and slowly she opened her mouth and let go of his wrist. He took the baby from her, and Cryer let it go. Red Boy took its foot and pulled, as though to play, but the baby did not move, and the little leg stuck out stiff.

The Man looked down at the baby in his arm. He felt again the hurt in his chest and behind his eyes that was common but strange, for it hurt you, but you could not hurt it. He set the baby down, straightened its legs and arms, and told them they would put it away the next day. Then he picked up his spear, looked well at the point and the fastening of it, and started out, Lefthand and Feetborn's Son at his heels.

They went through the forest toward the Rock, keeping the running water on their right, until they came to the place where the water was shallow and animals crossed. There they looked at the marks in the mud and saw that the stag had crossed the day before. They waded through, shook themselves on the far side, and cast around until they again found the trail of the stag. The Man could not smell most animals, but male ibex and some cats that sprayed the leaves he could smell for hours after they had passed; and the stag in the time of rut, for days.

They loped along all the morning and all the middle of the day, the tracks becoming clearer in the damp ground and half-melted snow. The stag was moving north, and when the sun was high, they came out of the forest onto a bare hill, where the snow lay white on the ground. From here they saw the Rock small in the distance. They found the stags' droppings and a yellow stain in the snow. Now the tracks led west along the ridge but after an hour swung left again, down the hill and back into the forest. All afternoon the three ran with the sun in their right eyes, and every time they came to a break in the trees the Rock was closer. The rank scent grew stronger and the marks of the stag's passing more recent. They came to mud where the water was still running back into the new-made slots. The Man paused and turned his head this way and that. The wind was from behind, so the stag would smell them coming. They must get ahead of him.

Lefthand said that the stag was heading for the thick brush under the north of the Rock to make that his stand for the rutting. The Man thought so, too, and the three turned left and ran faster, though they were tired, for they had run from the rising to the setting of the sun and had eaten no food but a few mussels since the day before yesterday. After half an hour swinging around through the forest and five minutes crawling through the dense scrub closer under the wall of the Rock, they came to an animal walkway.

The Man was looking for a place to lie in wait when he heard loud calls and barks. He shrank down and looked, wondering, at Lefthand. Lefthand whispered, "Others. They are killing the stag."

The men crept through the tangle toward the sounds. The Man thought furiously, the Others again! There was no respite for them. Invisible in the undergrowth, he watched them. Four males—the same four who'd killed Red Girl yesterday. One big female was with them. The stag was dead at their feet, the body out of sight but the huge antlers towering up above the bushes. They had already drunk blood, for their faces were red-splashed.

Beside him Feetborn's Son pointed his spear and wanted to kill the Others, but the Man knew that he was tired, and they were many and strong. He shook his head. The big Other female hurried off alone and a long time later came back with more Others—four more females, one with a cub at her breast, and many bigger cubs. They gathered around the dead stag, and instead of tying it to a pole as the Man did, they all took hold and like ants with a fly pulled it through the bushes and onto the slope below the cliffs. When they were well out of sight, the Man said, "Go to the women. I will come later."

Lefthand hesitated, questioning, but Feetborn's Son feared the dark and was already running back through the forest. "Go," the Man said to Lefthand—"Go, and see that all the spears are sharp."

When Lefthand had disappeared in the trees, the Man went cautiously after the Others. The wind still blew gently from behind, but he did not think they would detect his scent while they were all so close to the dead stag. They were dragging it slowly along at the foot of the cliff, and he could hear them calling and grunting together as they moved. He stole behind in silence.

When they reached their cave, it was quite dark. The Man made a wide loop and came up to the cliff again the other side of it. There he was safely downwind; but he smelled ordure and thought he must be in the place where they dropped their dung. He moved cautiously closer to the cave and up the rocky slope. He could see a little way into the cave. There he stopped.

The Others were cutting up the stag, but their flints were not sharp. The big male was strong, with powerful teeth and neck, for he ripped at the meat like a leopard or bear. They had built a great fire, and watching it made the Man feel colder, for it had begun to snow. There was no snow in the Others' cave. Soon they would be heavy with eating. Tomorrow they would be stronger from the food, but for tonight they would be heavy. His jaws were clamped tight against cold and hunger, but slowly he managed to open them and put out his tongue and let the snow melt on it. Then, moving stiffly at first, he crept back and down, circled around well below the cave, and headed for his own fire, in the forest.

Cryer heard him first and called, warning, but Lefthand was up at once, saying, "It is the Father. Hold, hold!"

He came in, and they were all on their feet, yawning and

stretching. He told them how the Others were eating the stag, how heavy they would be, how warm and dry was their cave. Then he told them they would all go now to kill the Others.

Feetborn's Son growled, "Food!"

But Lefthand's brow wrinkled, and he said, "For tomorrow?"

The Man nodded. They would eat the Others, yes, but it was not for food that he meant to kill them, but because they were where he wanted to be, where the mussels were, where the water was, where the warm was.

He told them there were four male Others. Someone had to bring them out of the cave so that he and Lefthand and Feetborn's Son could kill them. He looked at the women. Cryer was the fastest runner of them. He motioned to her and Snowborn to come, and Red Boy as well. Then he looked to the spears, and felt that they were sharp. He wound a length of twined hide thong around his waist and was ready.

They left the fire, the three men with spears in front, then Cryer, Red Boy, and Snowborn last with a flint ax. They heard sounds of animals in the forest, and Feetborn's Son whimpered until the Man hit him; for they all knew, Feetborn's Son too, that no animal would attack them when they were so many unless it could not run away.

They stopped by a bush near the Others' cave. They saw a small glow of fire on the roof of the cave but heard nothing. The Man muttered, "Some sleep." They went on toward the cave, but lower down the slope. When they were directly below the cave, the Man stopped. He told Cryer and Red Boy to stay there until they heard an owl call. Then they must walk up toward the cave until the Others ran out at them. Cryer whispered, "Yes," and Red Boy's eyes glowed in the hazy dark.

The Man led the rest—Lefthand, Feetborn's Son, and Snowborn—very carefully up the slope. The moon was making a little, soft, blurred light, and snow and sand and bush and rock all looked alike. He judged the distance as he climbed. When the Others saw or heard Cryer and Red Boy, some would run out at them, and some would not. He must trap those who ran out far enough from the cave so that those who stayed inside could not help them until too late. But he must not be too far. Above all, he must not be heard.

He came to a place he had noticed earlier, a stone's throw below the cave. There was a little cliff, too high to jump down. The Others would run down the gully the far side of it. He went in under the little cliff and looked up. He could not see the mouth of the cave, so a watcher there could not see him.

He brought the rest close, unwound the long thong from his waist, and gave it to the young men. He showed them where to crouch, the thong lying along the ground between them. He did not have to tell Snowborn where to go, for she knew that the woman's task was to kill any wounded or fallen animal.

Now he was ready. He put his cupped hands over his nose and mouth and made the owl's call, quavering slow, twice. Then he picked up his spear and stood, tautly strung, pressed against the rock.

Cryer and Red Boy would be starting up the slope. When the Others heard them, would they ask themselves why they were coming? They would be too heavy and sleepy to wonder. Small stones rolled away under someone's feet, and then he heard Red Boy's breathing. A moment later there was a tiny movement above. An Other had heard it, too.

And in that instant the Man saw, six inches from his right foot, a crouched bird. His heart nearly stopped, for if it flew up now . . . The Others would be creeping to the cave mouth . . . the bird did not move . . . they would be looking down, gathering . . . the bird moved its head, no more. Another five steps and it would not matter: four, three, two . . . Cryer and Red Boy were level. The Others meant to let them reach the cave itself and kill them there.

He muttered, "Look up. See. Scream. Run."

As he spoke, Cryer obeyed: stopped—looked up—then she really saw them crouched in the cave mouth above, for her mouth opened in a rising shriek, and she turned and hurtled down the slope, Red Boy beside her. The bird shot up drumming from the Man's foot with a loud squawk. Above there was a bellow and the pad of running feet. Two young males crashed past down the gully, and the Man let them go. A moment later the big male came, running at full speed, and the Man cried, "Now!" His young men jerked up the thong; the Other tripped over it and went flying head first far down the slope. As he landed, Snowborn crashed her ax into his head. By then the three men were racing after the young Others. Below, Cryer and Red Boy turned, snarling in the moonglow. The others slowed and drew back their spear arms. Neither looked around as Feetborn's Son and Lefthand struck, hurling their spears between their shoulder blades from a few feet away. The Others fell, coughing, and the men pounced. "Kill, kill, quick!" the Man cried. He stabbed once, pulled his spear free, and started back up the slope, all the rest with him. There was only one more male Other, the twisted one.

The six of them reached the cave mouth together, all armed now. The old female was there, keening and screaming, the big female behind, and many cubs, all staring, snarling, backing up into the darkness. Where was the bent one, the last male?

The Man saw him on the left. He pushed Snowborn and said, "Kill the big female!" Snowborn grunted and ran forward, her ax held high, the Man close behind her. The big female stabbed out at her, piercing her shoulder, but the Man, leaning over Snowborn's bent body, passed his spear through the female's throat. Then he turned and ran at the twisted male. He was waiting, crouched, bent. As the Man feinted a thrust, he too feinted, and as the Man struck, he stabbed upward with his short spear at the Man's belly. The Man felt a burning pain under the ribs but laughed aloud, for the spear was blunt, and it had not entered his bowels. As he stabbed down at the exposed back, Snowborn hit the Other on the ear with her ax, and he fell. The Man thrust his spear into his throat, waited while the jerking stopped, then turned around.

Now all were running about, screaming. In the cave mouth Lefthand and Feetborn's Son struck regularly so that none passed, and beside them Cryer and Red Boy stabbed those who fell. The female with a cub at breast rushed suddenly out of the depths of the cave and brushed past the Man, taking him by surprise. He grabbed at her but missed. The men at the cave mouth were both engaged, and the screaming female ran past them and out into the snow.

Now they searched the cave and found a female hiding behind a pillar, and several cubs, and killed them all. The saliva began to pour from the Man's mouth, for it was almost done now. There was only the old female left, crawling by the entrance, and her Cryer killed and took a big tooth that was hung around her neck and put it around her own.

The Man looked at the bodies and the blood and brains and scattered ordure, and he smelled the pieces of the stag that were still roasting by the fire and raised his face and cried out in triumph, again and again. Feetborn's Son and Red Boy sang with him; of the males only Lefthand did not sing but knelt looking wonderingly into the open eyes of a dead female cub.

The Man told Lefthand and Cryer to go and bring the rest to the cave at once. Then he walked slowly about, chewing a piece of deer flesh. Feetborn's Son began to saw off the head of the big female. Red Boy was stuffing deer meat into his mouth with both hands. Snowborn's shoulder had nearly stopped bleeding. The Man looked curiously at the chips of flint in one corner. The twisted male had had a flint-head spear, but it was blunt. The young males only had hardened wood spears. These flints were not sharp. He picked one up and made a scratch on the cave wall, then another and another. Now he had made the mark of a bird, like the red-legged bird that had stayed silent by his feet even at the owl call. They were fat and good to eat and easy to kill, those birds, but none of his should ever eat one again, except as a blessing, for now it was his brother.

Snowborn had set the big female's head in the coals, and the smell of roasting brains rekindled his hunger. Soon Lefthand and Cryer came back with the rest, Cryer carrying her dead baby. They all stood close, and the Man put a piece of flesh into the baby's mouth, then carried it back far into the cave and pushed it into a high crevice, where no animal could reach it. Cryer wept a little, for her breasts still hurt, but one of the boys drank milk from her, and then the Man told them of the bird, his brother, and all began to talk excitedly.

The Man looked about him and began to smile. He jumped up and down and grabbed Snowborn and Feetborn together, one arm about each, and danced with them, twirling round and round around the fire, shouting at the top of his voice.

The Woman crouched by a bush far from the cave, under the steepest cliff of the Rock, where the sun never shone. It had begun to snow, and her baby was cold. She had fallen in her flight, landing on top of it, and it had not cried or moved or sucked since. Her throat itched to wail, but she dared not. Bent Brother she had seen killed, but where was the Father? The young men? Was there no one? She began to whimper softly, uncontrollably.

Late in the morning two young male Others came, with their tall, straight-up walk. They would have passed below, but her skin prickled, and before she could stop herself, she jumped up and ran away. Then they saw her, and she heard their shouts behind her. She ran with all her strength, but they closed fast. She threw her baby away and dived into the thick brush at the foot of the cliff. She ducked and twisted through thorn and creeper, but they were very close. A cleft in the rock, narrow and low, showed black before her, and she slipped in, dropped to her knees, to her belly, wriggling frantically forward. Soon the cleft widened. She turned and waited, her hands like claws and her lips drawn back from her teeth.

She heard the Others at the cave mouth, and the thin light was blocked. They growled and hissed for a time, and then they too waited. They made no sound, but the Woman smelled them. When the sun set, they went. The Woman lay without movement of hair or muscle until no light at all came down the narrow slit. Then she began to unwind and wriggle toward the entrance. As she moved her left knee against the side of the cave, a mass of rock broke free, fell, and crushed her leg. It was a big block, sharp-edged, and however hard she tried, she could not move.

Book Two

◊◊◊◊◊◊◊◊◊◊◊◊◊◊◊◊◊◊◊◊◊◊◊◊◊◊◊

Out of the Caves

To the Jewish year 3188, which was
AUC 180 (180 years from the founding of the city of Rome)
573 B.C.

THE loser in the encounter and in the general struggle for existence was Neanderthal man; the winner was Cro-Magnon man (both named after the places where their remains were first identified). Europeans of today, however, are not direct descendants of Cro-Magnon man but rather the result of a further 30,000 years of interbreeding, movement, and evolution in particular environments. These movements were accelerated and extended by each advance in human technology, but until food-growing took the place of food-gathering and hunting (an advance which had to await the passing of the Ice Ages), the caves of Gibraltar were as good a place as any to live and better than most. Most of the big horizontal caves were again at sea level, and in the floury earth of their floors man began to leave the pottery, basket work, stone tools, shell amulets, ornaments, metal weapons, and coins which trace his progress.

When we reach the dawn of history, about 5,000 years ago, Spain was occupied by tribes of people since called Iberians. They came from the northern flanks of the Caucasus, but before that from the Middle East. Their language was of Hebraic origin. The word *iber* itself derives from *eber*, meaning "ultimate, beyond" in Hebrew; *Iberia* is thus "the last land." The

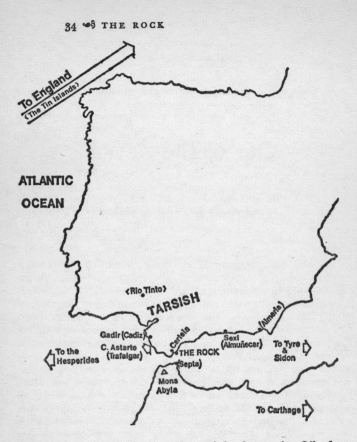

Iberian tribe which lived on the mainland opposite Gibraltar
was called the Turdetani; and some Spanish scholars claim that
this is from an old Hebrew word meaning "region, country."

Southern Spain was known to the ancients as Tarshish; and
in it there may or may not have been a great capital called
Tartessos and a great king called Argantonio. If it did exist, no
one has yet found a trace: if it did not, the "city" was probably
a symbol used by Greek and Phoenician poets to personify all
the wonders and marvels of the far west.

Tarshish is mentioned several times in the Bible. Jonah met his misadventure with the great fish while on his way there:

> But Jonah rose up to flee unto Tarshish from the presence of the LORD, and went down to Joppa; and he found a ship going to Tarshish: so he paid the fare thereof, and went down into it, to go with them unto Tarshish from the presence of the LORD.
> —Jonah 1:3

And, as we know, there were whales in the strait.

Solomon had commercial dealings with it:

> For the king had at sea a navy of Tharshish with the navy of Hiram: once in three years came the navy of Tharshish, bringing gold, and silver, ivory, and apes, and peacocks.—I Kings 10:22

> The kings of Tarshish and of the isles shall bring presents . . . .
> —Psalms 72:10

The reference to peacocks and ivory shows that there was a trading link between Tarshish and Africa, and this is not strange, for the Egyptians later sailed right around Africa (it took them three years). The truly revealing reference is the mention of gold and silver, and again, "Silver spread into plates is brought from Tarshish" (Jeremiah 10:9), for these coasts had long before Solomon felt the first thrust of the civilizations beginning to flower in the Near and Middle East. The Egyptians began to use gold, silver, and copper very early, and soon after 3000 B.C. they were getting some of it from Tarshish—specifically, from near Almería and from the Rio Tinto region, which is west of Gibraltar. An Iberian on the Rock, then, tending goats perhaps, must have seen vessels of the most ancient design creeping past, westbound with oil and cotton and blue beads for the natives, eastbound with sheets of copper and silver.

The Greeks came to share in the trade; and about 2800 B.C. the Minoans, who brought with them and left in Spain a deep-rooted belief of their religion: bull worship. The trade went beyond Spain to England and beyond copper to tin, and soon copper and tin were being melted together to make a new harder and tougher metal—bronze. The Age of Bronze was born close to the Rock, and the Iron Age followed from the same womb, for Tarshish contributed large iron ore deposits, too.

Several peoples traded past the Rock, but it was the Phoenicians who dominated these western waters for over five centuries and, through the colonies they planted, for another three
after their own decline. They were the Canaanites of the Bible,
who occupied the coastal strip of Palestine north of Carmel—
the land allotted to the tribes of Asher and Zebulon at the
Exodus, though the Jews were unable to turn the Canaanites
out. They were a Semitic people as old as the Jews and closely
linked with them by many ties. The Hiram of the quote from
I Kings was king of Phoenicia and a close friend of David and
Solomon. When, after the death of Solomon, the ten northern
Jewish tribes broke off to form the Kingdom of Israel in 975
B.C., Phoenician friendship with the southern kingdom of Judah
cooled but with Israel increased; for the people of the north,
largely renouncing the Jewish God, took to sharing the
worship of the Phoenician gods—Baal, Adon, Moloch, and the
chief ones, Melkart and Astarte; and in many other ways began
to blend with the Phoenicians.

The ancient world held the Phoenicians in awe for their industry and intelligence—they invented the alphabet—and at
the same time in aversion for their custom of burning small children as sacrifices to Moloch. Their temples enjoyed the services
of religious prostitutes of both sexes, but this was not uncom-
mon in other religions.

They are remembered now not for their vices or virtues
but for their skill as sailors and merchants. Their own capitals
were Tyre and Sidon, but in 1100 B.C. they founded Gadir
(Cádiz) and in 814 B.C. Carthage (near modern Tunis on the
North African coast). They had already founded a town on
Gibraltar Bay. . . .

Or had they? There are doubts.

North and west from the Rock around the head of the bay,
a river empties itself into the sea. Often, and appropriately
called First River, its true name is Guadarranque. On the left
bank there are the ruins of an ancient town. Everyone agrees
that the town was called Carteia; the doubt is, when was it
founded? Some modern scholars tend to believe there was no
town here before Roman times or perhaps only an Iberian village; but the Greeks had a word for it—Heraclea; and if the

river and beach were properly shaped for a port, as everyone agrees they were, it is a perfect site, with better natural shelter than any other in southern Spain (except Gadir). On balance it seems probable that Carteia *was* founded by the Phoenicians in 940 B.C. to exploit the tunny fishing and the beds of murex. The murex is a shellfish from which was extracted the famous "Tyrian purple," the color which later became the fiercely guarded prerogative of Roman nobles and emperors. It was never in fact a true purple but something between rose and dark violet. The dye was made by extracting the shellfish and dropping them into large vats or tanks, often of stone. When they rotted they secreted a yellow liquid, which was the dye. The vats were always placed downwind for obvious reasons.

The colony's full name was Melkartcia, after the god, but that soon became abbreviated. A thousand years before Christ, therefore, the Rock looked down upon, and was surely regarded as the sacred mountain of, its first real town.

These are all facts, as best they can be traced through the deceptive and evershifting curtains of the years. The ancients, with ancestral memories sharpened by tens of thousands of years when all knowledge, experience, and wisdom had to be passed on by word of mouth, recorded them differently. They did not have modern tools of discovery and analysis and, having been actors rather than spectators, were more interested in transmitting emotion than fact. History was recorded and handed down in myth and fable. One such is the story of the opening of the Strait of Gibraltar. Although it is inconceivable that thinking man could have been present on Earth when it actually happened (at least 30,000,000 years ago), yet the most ancient voices of the past seemed to find it necessary to explain that it *had* happened within human ken. The act is attributed to a god or demigod, in the Greek version called Herakles and in the Latin Hercules; and this figure was probably the same as Tubal. Hercules tore the mountains apart and set up pillars inscribed *Non Plus Ultra* (Nothing Beyond) to mark the end of the earth. From the very beginning all men knew that the Pillars of Hercules were the mountains called Abyla on the African shore and, on the European side, the limestone block which the Phoenicians called Alube and the Greeks Calpe, meaning "urn, hollowed out." This

was the Rock, Gibraltar, and it was called "hollowed out" because of its innumerable caves, especially one very large one
high on the west face, the Great Cave.

About 1100 B.C. one or several Greek poets called Homer began to compose the *Iliad* and the *Odyssey*, which are, in fact,
history and geography books, respectively. In them the bards set
out in metrical form (so that it could more easily be memorized)
all that was known of their own past and of the outside world.

In the *Odyssey* Homer's archetypal wanderer, Ulysses or
Odysseus, passes through a narrow strait. Here is the relevant
passage in the lucid translation of S. O. Andrew:

> *Of the two other rocks, the one reaches up to the sky*
> *With sharp-pointed peak, and a cloud encompasses it*
> *That never disperses, nor clear air ever reveals*
> *Even in summer or autumn its heav'n-soaring crest.*
> *No mortal that perilous summit could scale or descend*
> *Though with twenty hands and with twenty feet he were born,*
> *For its surface is smooth, like polish'd marble, and sheer.*
> *Midmost the rock is a cavern, misty and dim,*
> *Turn'd toward the region of darkness where Erebus lies,*
> *And beneath it, O noble Odysseus, your bark ye must steer.*
> *Not even an archer of power with a shaft from his bow*
> *Could shoot from a hollow ship to the depth of that cave;*
> *Therein has yelping Scylla her secret abode,*
> *Her voice like a newborn whelp's, no greater, yet she*
> *Is an evil monster indeed, nor would any that pass'd*
> *Rejoice to behold her, not though an Immortal he were.*
> *She has twelve feet, which she dangles down in the air,*
> *And above, six necks, very long, and on each of the six*
> *A hideous head which is arm'd with a triple array*
> *Of teeth set thickly teeming with black-venom'd death.*

And nine lines later:

> *But mark thou, Odysseus, that other rock which is low,*
> *Quite near to the first (thou coulds't shoot with an arrow across),*
> *And on it, in full leafage a fig tree there is,*
> *Whereunder the mighty Charybdis sucks down the tide.*
> *Thrice in the day she disgorges and thrice in the day*
> *She sucks it again; mayest thou never be near when she sucks. . . .*

These passages have sometimes been taken to refer to the Strait of Messina between Sicily and the Italian mainland, but the description fits the Strait of Gibraltar much more closely. Gibraltar was also very far off, and its links with the fabulous Hercules and the hardly less mysterious Tarshish would make it a more attractive location for marvels. The cloud hiding the Rock's head is the most telling evidence, for the levanter cloud is unique in the Mediterranean; and in this poetic version of returned seamen's tall tales one can easily trace the Great Cave, the sheer eastern and northern cliffs, the giant squid with its black ink "venom," and the dangerous race which forms off the point of Septa on the African shore. The only factors against this identification are that the African pillar (Charybdis) is in fact not lower than Gibraltar but considerably higher, and the distance between the two is a good deal more than a bowshot; but the dramatic isolation of the Rock so dominates the strait that several later travelers fell into the first error, and the bowshot distance is a liberty required by Homer's plot.

To return to the harsher yet still breathtaking light of history. This is Gibraltar about 600 B.C. . . . The trees grow thick on the lesser slopes, and sailors often go ashore but do not tarry unless they mean to worship at a shrine of Hercules, for the demigod inhabits the place and is not mocked. Above all, none but the very devout, or the very blasphemous, enter the Great Cave, though it is known to the whole civilized world—it goes into the womb of earth; it holds armies and is not filled; it is dark, but a torch held high shows pillars and walls and steps wrought and decorated and colored beyond the power of mortals to describe. . . .

The small town by the First River flourishes. The colonists have increasingly close relations with the hinterland, where the Iberians are being diluted by successive waves of another people from the Syrio-Turanian region—the Celts—to form the Celtiberians (this particular influx goes on, in dribs and drabs, for about 800 years, for Julius Caesar records some 6,000 Celts, with women and children, entering Spain in 49 B.C.).

In the basin of the Mediterranean the peoples, having developed and spread, begin to fight for empire. Phoenicia is attacked by the Assyrian Shalmaneser V in 721 B.C. and much weakened:

The burden of Tyre. Howl, ye ships of Tarshish; for it is laid waste, so that there is no house, no entering in. . . .—Isaiah 23:1

Carthage breaks free of the mother country, as colonies will, and from now on it is Carthage, not Tyre, which controls the Phoenician settlements in the west.

The Babylonian Nebuchadnezzar besieges Tyre in 587 B.C. The following year he destroys Jerusalem, sacks the First Temple, and takes some of its people captive. From both the Assyrian and Babylonian invasions many inhabitants of Phoenicia and neighboring countries, including Judea, escape for refuge to Gadir, Carthage, Sexi (modern Almuñécar), Carteia, and a dozen other settlements at the far end of the Mediterranean.

It is nearly 3,000 years since Mediterranean man first deliberately sailed past the Rock to trade with the wider world his restless explorations kept uncovering. These explorations have kept to the coasts, north and south.

The kings . . . of the isles shall bring presents. . . . Britain, the Tin Islands, he has known for a thousand years. But in the evenings, faces lit by the flaring lamps, the bards tell of other islands, other continents . . . the Isles of the Blest, the Hesperides, Atlantis. Is the Rock, then, a pillar to mark the limit of this world? Or the hinge of the gate which will open to another?

The Talisman

The man Pendril stood in the prow of the galley, steadying himself with one hand on the buttocks of the carved figurehead. He was square-built and strong, as though rough-hewn from a hard reddish wood, with curly red hair and deep blue eyes. He did not seem to note the heave and shudder of the vessel under his feet, nor to feel the spray dashing regularly onto his cheeks, nor to hear the rhythmic grunt of the rowmaster's chant to the rowers. The gray mountain in the sea loomed close now. For the past hour its cliffs had cut off the westerly sun. Pendril stared at it somberly, like a man watching a woman whom he has never possessed but dreams of above all. He knew every cleft and crag of those cliffs, every stone and bush and flower. The wind began to slacken, cut off by the sea mountain. The man stared on.

The girl Tamar stood in the stern, holding with one hand to the gunwale beside her. The wind molded her cotton dress against her thighs and breasts and whipped tendrils of her black hair about her ears. Beside her, two bare-chested sailors held the steering oar, their feet braced strongly against slats set in the deck.

The girl's husband, Daniel, came up from their cabin and stretched and yawned. He looked over the side and called, "Pendril, it is calmer. We can round the point after all."

The man in the bow did not seem to hear, and Daniel repeated his remark louder. Pendril turned then and came aft, rolling easily with the motion of the galley. "It is only calm here because we are in the lee of Alube," he said. He spoke a strangely accented Phoenician which Tamar found harsh and unpleasing.

"I disagree," Daniel said. "It is calm. Keep them rowing."

Tamar nodded approvingly. The new boatswain was a rude man, experienced, of course, but uneducated. Daniel was too gentle with him. Such men as he only understood force.

The boatswain said, "Look, you can see the waves off the point from here. That's a dangerous race in this wind."

Daniel stamped his foot. "I am the owner and the captain! We will not anchor. We will round the point and go into Carteia!"

Tamar caught the boatswain's blue eyes glancing at her under raised eyebrows and scowled fiercely at him.

Pendril said, "You are the captain, but you are not the god Melkart. The rowers are exhausted. The race prevents the oars' getting a good bite. We will not get around the point, however long we try."

"Go farther out into the strait," Daniel said. "There is no race there."

"No," Pendril answered. "But the current against us is over a knot faster than we can row."

"Oh, anchor then," Daniel cried and strode up to the bow and stood there with arms folded.

Pendril shouted below, "Stand by to anchor." The rowmaster stuck his head through the hatch, where he could hear the deck commands and bob down to give the necessary orders to the rowers below. One sailor stayed at the steering oar; the other five went to the bows, thrusting Daniel out of the way with little ceremony. He came aft, and Tamar went to him.

"The gods have turned the wind against us," he said gloomily.

"Or perhaps it is Pendril who makes us go so slowly. I wish you had not hired him."

Her husband shrugged. She knew he had had no choice, for the real boatswain had deserted at the last port, Sexi. It had been a stroke of good fortune to find a qualified man ready and willing to take the long journey to the Tin Islands, and without one they could not go, for Daniel had never sailed beyond Gadir.

"Come," she said. "The cook is making a savory smell." He brightened and rubbed his hands together gleefully, for his moods were never deep or long held but like a child's.

She slept badly that night, partly because the motion of the ship was different from when it lay in harbor, partly because dreams disturbed her. She had hoped, after supper, that Daniel would take her as a man had a right to take his wife, though he so seldom did. She had yearned toward him, caressed him while they ate, pressed her body against him when they lay down, sent him messages of love and desire from her eyes. But he did not respond, only slept.

Sleep did not come to her for two hours, and when it did, images of lust filled it. Unknown men held her, and she welcomed them one after another. Daniel shook her at last where she lay beside him on the wolf skins and said she would awaken the whole ship, she was making so much noise. But though she tried to soothe the trembling void of her womanhood, she could not sleep again.

In the morning the wind still blew strong from the west, and broken white water extended far out from the point of the Rock. She was pacing the deck by dawn, tired but unable to rest, biting her nails, patting her hair, looking at the sailors asleep by the mast. Daniel came up, followed by Pendril.

"This wind will hold all day," Pendril said.

"We shall stay here till tomorrow then," Daniel said at once, as though to forestall the boatswain's suggesting the same thing.

"Aye, captain," Pendril said. "Then I shall go ashore to Carteia. It is Midsummer's Eve, our most important feast day."

"Very well," Daniel said.

"I shall be back before dawn tomorrow. It would be safe to let half the sailors and rowers ashore, too. They will . . ."

"No," Daniel snapped and turned his back.

"I want to go, too," Tamar said suddenly, astonished to hear herself saying the words. "Take me to Carteia, Daniel. There must be an inn where we can stay."

"But, Tamar, we will be there tomorrow. . . ." her husband said.

"I want to go today, now," she cried. "I am tired of being caged in this ship. I want to see the feast!"

Daniel said, "I am tired, wife. In truth, I do not feel well. . . . Would you go with Pendril, if you must go? She can stay with your family, I suppose?"

Pendril said, "I have no family. There is the inn." He launched the little horse-prowed dinghy over the side. Tamar hesitated, frowning. Pendril and a sailor dropped lightly into the dinghy. He called up roughly, "If you are coming, come."

"Wait," she commanded and rushed to her cabin. Quickly she tidied her hair, put it up with her silver pins and comb, donned her best robe, fastened the neck with a little bronze scarab brooch, and made up her eyes with antimony.

Pendril waited, tossing alongside in the little *hippos*. She was a spoiled Judean brat but pretty in a wild way and brave. Not many rich women would be going to the Tin Islands when they might be entertaining lovers in comfort at home.

She came on deck, and his eyes widened. She looked like an Egyptian whore now . . . albeit a beautiful one. That husband of hers was a pleasant fellow but not built for the sea: or for women perhaps.

A sailor helped her into the *hippos*. "Careful now," Pendril growled, "Kneel. I cannot save you if you go over."

"There would be no need," she snapped. "*I* can swim."

"Enjoy yourself," Daniel called from the deck, as the sailor started paddling the *hippos* toward the cliffs. In a few moments they reached the small waves in the shallows. Pendril swung himself overboard and held out his arms. She ignored him, lifted her robe above her knees, stepped over the side, and waded ashore. The sailor paddled back to the *Kedesha*.

Ahead, a great cave opened at the foot of the cliff, a steep slope of sand and earth leading up into it. Pendril started up into the cave, and Tamar followed, wondering. Deep in under the overhang of the arch she found Pendril on his knees, digging with his hands in the powdery earth. He did not turn round or speak.

"What are you looking for?" she asked at last.

He did not answer, and she began to turn the dark powdery earth over with her foot, not knowing what she might find. Sailors had been sheltering in this cave for a long time.

Pendril's hands touched something hard; he scraped away some more soil and pulled out a stoppered jar. "Strong wine," he said briefly, broke the seal, and poured some of the colorless liquor down his throat. She was gazing at him, and she seemed lonely and unsure for the first time. He handed her the jar. "Take some."

She drank cautiously, gasped, coughed and spluttered, and gave him back the jar. Smiling, he reburied it. He had hidden his first jar here eighteen years ago, when he was twelve, and had kept one buried ever since.

He led back down the sand slope. The blue and yellow *Kedesha* rocked gently on the swell two hundred feet offshore. Tamar stopped and gazed at the ship. Everyone on board seemed to have gone back to sleep. Pendril said, "Are you coming, or are you going to wait here, hoping that your husband will come after all? Because you will wait a long time."

"Hold your tongue," she snapped. "Lead me to Carteia."

"This way, this way," he said with burlesque obsequiousness and led on fast, deliberately forcing the pace; but he heard her sandals keeping close behind, and there was no sound of heavy breathing. After a steep climb he stepped out onto the rough ground above the flat point. The west wind blew hard, shaking the grass and wild flowers about his feet. The sea was gray green, shimmering under wind-driven spume. Over there the African pillar towered out of a glittering sea haze about its feet.

It was here that he had lain with the girl Menesha and, her hair spread in the flowers, asked her to be his wife; and she had laughed up in his face, saying, "Be a sailor's wife? You are mad, Pendril!"

A red-legged partridge ran out from a bush ahead. Tamar cried out behind him, and he turned to see her pick up a stone. He struck down her arm as she threw. The bird flew away with a hard clatter of wings.

"Why did you do that?" she said. "Partridges are good eating."

"Because . . . ," he began and stopped. Why should he explain to her that this kind of red-legged partridge was sacred to him? Here on his Rock was the only place on the northern side of the sea that he had ever seen one. Other birds he loved to hunt with bow and arrow and sling, but this one, never.

"It is of no importance," she said, tossing her head. "Lead on." He was a boorish half-Iberian, half-Phoenician sailor, wholly beneath her notice.

"You throw well for a woman," he said. "And swim, you say? Perhaps you should have been born a man."

She sniffed angrily. They came to a patch of forest, and Pendril said, "Up there is a great cave and a shrine to Hercules."

"What does it look like?" she asked, interested in spite of herself.

"I have never entered," he said.

"What are you afraid of?" she asked. "There is but one God, Jehovah. . . . Shall I escort you in?" she mocked.

"No, no," he said sullenly. "The gods of this Rock are not to be blasphemed." He led down past the forest and around the skirt of the mountain where a path ran a hundred feet above the sea. Looking past his broad back she saw the sandy curve of a beach and, a mile away, white houses and the mouth of a river, heavy trees on each bank. She ran into him, for he had stopped without warning.

"What is it?" she asked.

"Nothing," he said and strode on.

"It must be something," she snapped. "What were you staring at?"

"The land," he said shortly. "Here, this corner of Alube,

where the sand meets the Rock. On this slope, looking west across the bay at the mountains there, where the sun sets. This is where I want to build my house. I have wanted to all my life."

"Why do you not build it, then?"

"The Rock belongs to Astarte, and her priestess will not permit me."

She did not laugh, for he spoke seriously; and she knew, in her own religion, that YHWH kept a close grip on his own.

They came to the town, and Pendril said, "This is Carteia. A small place, but some of us would not trade it for Carthage itself. . . . Here is the inn. It is clean, and the host is not a robber."

"Where are you going?" she asked in sudden fear of being left alone in this strange place under the frowning Rock.

"To attend to my business," he said. "I will return here before dusk, when the rites begin."

He turned his back and strode away up the river front. The host of the inn came out, bowing courteously, and showed Tamar to a small room. Soon she went out to explore the town. It was a place of many smells, of fresh fish and oysters rotting in the dye works, of cooking spices, oil, garlic, seaweed, and the sea. The river slid by, blue-green and fresh, and she saw many fish in it. The air was clean, and birds sang in the woods at the edge of the river. Fishing boats big and small passed in from the sea, and the Rock stood as a sentinel over their comings and goings. Along the docks she saw great blue-backed tunny strung on hooks and men cutting them up and women rubbing salt into the flesh. One woman wore a silver brooch with the open Torah represented upon it, so Tamar asked, "Are you from Judea?"

The woman rested, her hands on her hips. "Yes. From Jerusalem."

"I, too," she said eagerly. "My father was a priest. The Babylonians killed him and all the family except an uncle, who took me to Carthage."

"You were lucky," the woman said. "You must have been only a child. You had nothing to lose. Some of us . . . everything."

"There are more here?"

"About twenty," the woman said. "We all work today because most of the heathen do not, since this is their great feast of the year. . . . Did I not see you walking into the town with Pendril?"

She nodded, and the woman continued. "Are you his woman?"

"God forbid," she snapped.

The woman looked at her strangely. "There are some who would agree with you," she said, "but most would not. Only, he will have nothing to do with any except the temple girls. We thought a foreign woman had caught him at last." She laughed pleasantly.

"No," Tamar said. The woman returned to her work with a nod, and Tamar walked on. Carteia was the boatswain's home, of course. It was strange to find a place where he was of more account than she or Daniel. . . .

Pendril, meanwhile, was seated on a low stool before the high priestess of Astarte in her private chamber at the back of the temple. The light filtered in through gauzy curtains of purple and white, seeming to cast stripes of those colors upon the woman's high-boned, high-nostriled face. She was tall and slender. The lines under her huge eyes and the fine wrinkles in her brown skin showed her age—she was forty. She had permitted Pendril to make love to her since his fourteenth birthday.

"I have come about the land," he said.

She raised her hand, the long nails black-lacquered. "The land *first?*" she asked.

Pendril hesitated. He did not want to make love to her at this moment. Later, yes, but not now while his corner of the Rock filled his thoughts and dominated his desires.

She rose and pulled him slowly to his feet. Her arms went around his neck. Her bare breasts pressed into him. Her tongue began to search his ear, and her breath came quicker.

Two hours later he began to pull on his short, coarse seaman's robe. The high priestess sat before a mirror, reapplying black around her eyes and red to her cheeks. "Who is the girl you brought here?" she asked.

"The wife of the shipowner," he said.

"Is she a passionate lover?"

"I do not know. I have not touched her. . . . About the land. The goddess does not use it. No one else wants it. I would build a shrine to her and pay for a great feast to all of you priestesses once, twice a year. I would dedicate to the goddess a tithe of whatever I make from the oysters. I would . . ."

She turned on her stool. Her nipples stood up like little towers, red-tipped. Her flat belly glistened with oil. She laughed up into his face. "You are a man among men, Pendril," she said. "The best lover I have known, and that is among some eight thousand— If we let you have that land, you will marry some plump cow. Instead of performing the divine rites to Astarte with me you will be seeding her fat belly. No!"

"Please permit me to buy the land," he said doggedly. "I will always come to you, as I do now. All our women know that marriage cannot alter the worship of Astarte."

She stood up and pointed her finger at him, the jewels jangling at her neck. "You shall have the land. . . ."

He started toward her. "Queen!"

"Hold! The price is an apple. A golden apple of the Hesperides."

"But where? How?" he asked miserably.

"A naked woman sends you," she mocked. "And only another naked woman can lead you, a third pluck the apple from the tree, and a fourth bring you safe back home to claim your corner of the Rock!" Laughing high and loud, she disappeared through the curtains.

Pendril stood a long time staring at the purple and white stripes. A golden apple of the Hesperides. The islands where the sun goes down to lie with the sea. The sacred trees guarded by the daughters of the Creator. *A naked woman sends you.* He started violently. *And only another naked woman can lead you.* Kedesha was the name of Daniel's new galley; a *kedesha* was a priestess such as this Irauna whom he had known so long. The figurehead of the galley was a *kedesha,* a naked woman facing the waves with breasts upthrust, arms back, and legs twined around the stem of the ship, which disappeared into her body.

Pendril turned and hurried out of the temple.

Early in the afternoon the host at the inn stewed a fat dog with herbs, olives, onion, and wine; then Tamar rested and waited impatiently for Pendril to return. Toward dusk the people seemed to be wearing finer clothes, and there was an air of expectation to their movements. She heard distant shouts and orders and the tuning of stringed instruments. Men carried great wine vessels to and fro, and women set earthenware pots around the houses and lit the rope wicks in them so that they gave out a smoky reddish light. At the edge of the river and in the open place outside the temple to Astarte, boys lit fires. The fires grew larger, the dark beyond more dense and impenetrable. Shapes passed, embracing, and still Pendril did not come.

When at last he came, she saw that he had been drinking. He had a small wineskin which he held up at arm's length, squeezing a jet of wine into his mouth, then, although she protested, into hers.

"Come," he said thickly. "Come to the feast, the dance. . . ." His gold earrings shook, glinting in the red light.

She went with him then, to the rites of Midsummer's Eve. The time, like the people, passed with gradually increasing pace and passion. For the first hour she felt like a sleepwalker, gliding very slowly, one of a race of sleepwalkers. Then she moved more briskly and they, too, and the songs grew louder and louder, and faster the twanging of the plucked strings from the temple, and taller the fires, tall as men, and the young men began to jump over and through them, running, calling to each other, then leaping, and afterward shouting again in triumph. The wine splashed in her face, and a string snapped in her head. Her feet moved, faster, faster the drummer pounded, sweating, and suddenly there were women in serpent headdresses of gold and silver and with necklaces between their breasts dancing in front of the temple. They were naked, silver belling on their ankles, breasts jerking, bellies pulled in, mounds of love thrust forward. They sang, the fires roared higher. With a shriek a naked man ran by her and leaped like an antelope through the top of the fire. The people gasped, a priestess wrapped herself around him, and in a moment, as the dancer slowly swung, her feet spread wide, her body arched far back, Tamar saw that the man had entered her. They shuffled thus, locked, the man's face straining.

The priests came out, chanting. She heard snatches of Hebrew, the sacred names of Jehovah, other languages, other names, other gods. There was kneeling and bowing before images of Sun, Moon, Stars, Winds, Clouds. The Golden Calf gleamed inside the temple, its doors now flung wide. The child that would be sacrificed at dawn sat enthroned in gold and silver finery, its eyes feverish and bright, its lips parted in excitement. All around her there was dancing and lovemaking. She stood pressed against a house, her palms damp against the wood. The fire burned her face, and the sweat poured down her body. She trembled with the sounds about her—the groans of women, the chant of the dancers, the shriek of a boy missing his leap and falling into the fire, the smells of flesh, wine, lust.

The high priestess appeared before them, legs widespread. Her eyes shone into Tamar's, worming down into the secret parts of her body. "Greetings, Jewess," she said softly. "What do you seek here?"

"Nothing," Tamar muttered.

"A man, I think? You are an empty vessel, quaking to the touch. There is a strong man beside you. Take her, Pendril. Show her how the children of Astarte serve the goddess. Go!"

Pendril's voice was thick and deep. "You want me?"

"She does not want you," the priestess said. "She *needs* you."

"No," Tamar cried. "I have a husband."

Pendril said, "In name. I lie too close, with only the canvas curtain between us. He never touches you."

"Why do you think he sent you here with Pendril?" the priestess said. "Because he wants another man to calm you, that he may sleep in peace. . . ."

"Yes!" Tamar burst out. Then, aghast at what she had learned and said, she turned and stumbled away. It was dark by the river, and she heard him running behind her. She slowed and, at the edge of the wood, turned, her back to a tree, her hands clutching it. She waited, her heart pounding.

He came slowly to her, and she closed her eyes. Her skin trembled, and there was a sudden warm wet release at her loins.

He said, "I spoke ill. I am sorry. The high priestess does not understand such as you. Come. Let us go back to the ship."

Gradually her heart stilled, the trembling stopped, and she felt cold and alone. She began to cry. He said gently, "Walk. You will feel better."

Now clouds obscured the moon, but a little light filtered through. She walked at his side in a gusty wind along the sand toward the milky loom of the Rock.

"Where did you meet your husband?" Pendril asked.

"In Carthage," she said, sniffling. "I was seven when Jerusalem was sacked. His father lived close to my uncle, and they were rich. They are of the tribe of Zebulon but do not keep the Law. We grew up together. . . ."

"And married—how long?" he asked.

"Three years."

"And you are—twenty-one?"

"Twenty."

A flash of lightning lit the Rock, thunder boomed around the bay, and he broke into a trot. The lightning grew more frequent, more thunder rolled in through the strait. Pendril gabbled prayers under his breath as they passed under the sacred grove and the magic cavern of Hercules, and Tamar felt better, even smiling to herself at his superstition. As the first huge drops of rain began to fall, they reached the western beach.

"Up into the cave," Pendril said. "They will never hear me calling in this."

They sat down deep inside the cave while the rain poured down outside and lightning flashes momentarily painted the *Kedesha* a more livid blue against the greenish sea.

Pendril said, "I was going to say, before the thunder began, stay in Carteia, Tamar. Tell your husband you do not want to go to the Tin Islands. He will be pleased and relieved. I know it."

"But I *do* want to go," she said. "I am weary of staying at home, caged like a pet bird alone. We have no child. I insisted that I come on this journey, and I shall go to the end."

"There is nothing to see in the Tin Islands," he said. "The savages there eat pigs! Their temples are nothing but circles of great stones. There is always fog and rain. The sea between here and there is always rough."

"I go!" she said.

"Very well," he said. "So be it. It will rain all night. All on the *Kedesha* are below and asleep. Take this—" He gave her his cloak. "Sleep there. Have no fear of me."

She thought she would lie awake all night with the thunder and lightning, memories of the rites, consciousness of what she had said and so nearly done. It was not her own will or virtue that had saved her from adultery but this man, strange, brutal, sometimes gentle, practical but filled with visions and dreams of this magical Rock, brave but superstitious, ignorant but skillful. And he was lying there so close to her that . . .

His hand was on her shoulder. "Wake up. They have seen me. The sun is rising, it has stopped raining, and the wind is in the east."

She stood up, yawning and stretching, and put her hands to her hair. Then she straightened her robe, but when she tried to refasten it, she found that the little bronze brooch was gone.

"I have lost my brooch," she said. "It must be here, though, because I remember feeling it when we reached the foot of the path last night."

"Look quickly, then," Pendril said. "They are launching the *hippos* and making ready to up-anchor."

She hurried about the cave, down to the beach, back up, but saw nothing. She began to dig with her fingers where she had slept.

He said, "The *hippos* is here. And they are hoisting the sail. Idiots!"

She touched something hard and cried, "I have it! No, this is not it."

"Come," he said, this time as a command. She pulled the hard thing out of the earth and followed. She held in her hand a fang, six inches long, with a hole bored through the thick end. She held it out to Pendril. "What animal is this from?"

He turned it over curiously. "None that I know. It might be a boar's, but they are more curved than this. It is much too small for those great beasts I have seen in Egypt. It has been used, worn around a woman's neck perhaps?"

The *hippos* danced and sidled to the galley, the sun warmed her, the rut and shame of the night passed into dream.

Pendril pushed her up on board and followed. As soon as his foot hit the deck, he shouted, "Down sail! This wind will blow us straight onto the cliffs, Daniel. We can hoist when we have cleared the point, not before. Rowmaster, ready? Stand by the steering oar. Row, starboard side. . . . Row all."

The *Kedesha* began to move through the sea, at first as heavily as a pregnant woman, then gliding like an oiled dancer. Pendril watched the cliffs and caves pass. Soon Irauna would see the figurehead and realize that two of the four parts of her prophecy had already come to pass. As to the rest, that he must leave to the goddess. He had his own work to do, and since he was only a human, it would be more difficult and more liable to failure. But he could only do his best.

Two days later, heavily loaded with amphorae of water and barrels of flour, dried fruit, salt meat, and pickled fish, the *Kedesha* swam away from the jetty of Carteia and headed into the bay, bound for the Tin Islands. As they passed the towering northern cliff of the Rock, Pendril murmured a prayer to Astarte to help him possess that gray-green corner by the blue water. A cloud began to form over the crest as soon as he had finished, and he muttered to the new man at the steering oar, "An omen, Tregan." Tregan and another called One-Eye were men he had hired in Carteia to replace two Carthaginians he had dismissed for drunkenness and insubordination.

The great pillars fell astern, and at last the rise of the land hid all but the cloud over the Rock. Soon that too sank below the hills. They were on the ocean. Night fell

Soon after dawn the man at the steering oar called down, "Cape Astarte abeam, Pendril." Pendril was already wide awake and now rolled quickly up the ladder to the poop and called, "All sailors aft, and Rowmaster, you too."

They shuffled aft, rubbing sleepy eyes. The slaves awoke and stretched on their benches. Tamar came up with Daniel, her hair streaming to the breeze. Pendril looked east and saw the stone building that was the temple of Astarte on the point. The cape was low and sandy, a hill covered with trees set behind it. The waters always ran steep and disturbed off this point, and strange fish often came to the surface here. It was a place inhabited by the gods, and Pendril muttered another prayer and threw a piece of bread onto the water.

"You have called us all here to say prayers?" a sailor cried, laughing.

"No," Pendril said. "It is more than that." He saw that Tregan was at the poop ladder, the lower part of his body hidden. One-Eye was here, rummaging in an old crate beside the steersman. All was ready.

Pendril stepped behind the steersman, took the knife out of his belt, and tossed it overboard.

"Hold!" the steersman said.

"Mind your oar!" Pendril snapped. "Hear me, all! We are not going to the Tin Islands. We go to the Hesperides. . . . Do not move! Tregan is at your back, an arrow fitted to a bow. One-Eye, take all knives and spikes and throw them overboard."

"You are stealing the ship?" Tamar burst out.

A sailor said, "It is all the same to me where I go as long as I am paid. But where are these Hesperides? I have never heard of them."

Daniel said, "The Hesperides are islands in the western ocean where the heavens swallow the sea. Though they may not exist."

"They exist," Pendril said. "And we go there."

"How far?" a sailor asked. "No one has ever gone more than three days west of the pillars, and then only because they were blown out by an easterly. And they had a hard time getting back."

"Enough!" Pendril shouted. "We shall go as far as is necessary. One of we three Carteians will always be awake and on watch here at the poop. Anyone who tries to thwart us will go over the side. Now, steersman, steer two points to port. Put the sun dead astern. There! Clear the poop!" The sailors slowly went forward. "Let the rowers rest while the wind holds," Pendril told the rowmaster, "and give them an extra ration of meat. They will need it later."

Daniel said, "You can die for this, Pendril, when we get back . . . if we do. Why have you done it? What are the Hesperides to you?"

"That is my affair," Pendril said.

The rowmaster stuck his head up through the hatch. "The slaves want you to speak to them, Pendril. It is not my doing," he added hastily.

Leaving One-Eye on the poop with the steersman, Pendril ran down the ladder and faced the galley slaves.

"We shall starve!" one cried.

"We have food and water for three months," Pendril said. "The ship is sound. Have no fear."

"We shall fall over the edge of the world," another cried.

Pendril hesitated. Lying on the bare, bleached rocks at the summit of the Rock, gazing through the strait at the Western Ocean, he had often tried to see the edge of the world, to imagine it there where the water poured over in an endless cataract mightier than any fall on any river. But then there would be a current, and here there was none. . . .

To the waiting slaves he said, "There must be a rim to keep the water in. Or perhaps the sea is not flat. You, as I, have seen ships coming over the horizon. From all directions they rise up, wherever we are. It is as though we were always on top of a round ball."

A slave said, "The sea cannot be round, master. The water would all roll down."

"I know not why it does not fall," Pendril said. "But it does not, and it will not." He surveyed the banked, gaunt faces. These men had nothing to live for; they could be his allies. He had been a boatswain ten years and knew sailors and galley slaves as well as he knew the corners and crannies of the Rock. "In the Hesperides," he said, "the ripe fruit falls into your mouths from the trees! Women more beautiful than goddesses, more lustful than *kedeshot,* crowd to serve you."

The slaves set up a ragged cheer and rattled the oars in the tholes with a low thunder.

Pendril raised his voice. "And you rowers, strong men all, there is a marvel there above aught else on earth. The women are slit across, not up and down!"

The rowers had all heard the old fable when they were children and set up another laughing cheer. Pendril said, "Rowmaster, a ration of wine to all."

He left to more cheering, went straight to his cabin, and lay down. He would need all the sleep he could get while the sailors were still surprised and disorganized and perhaps a little excited with the idea of the Hesperides. So far, so good. But the naked women? The apples? How? Where? He fell asleep.

Tamar and Daniel came down later. Tamar sat at her husband's side in the gloom, staring at the canvas curtain. Pendril was there. Pirate! She caught Daniel's arm, pointed at the canvas, and made a gesture of strangling. Daniel shook his head wearily. She felt in the little box where she kept a few jewels and knickknacks, pulled out a small knife, and showed it to him. He shook his head again, but she hefted it in her hand and looked longingly at the canvas. Daniel glanced uneasily at her and mumbled, "I am going back on deck."

She stayed where she was, holding the knife. She felt taut and on edge. When Pendril had called them to the poop at dawn, she had been fondling her husband, trying to arouse him to make love to her. He had seemed to welcome Pendril's call as a last-minute reprieve. She frowned, picked the big fang out of the box, and began to scrape at it with the knife. The ivory was very old, but gently, carefully, with this sharp knife it could be worked. What should she make of it? It was a thing such as men liked to handle. Smooth to the touch, rounded, waiting. Should she make a dagger of it? She stared at the ivory, trying to bring the shape hidden in it clear to her eyes.

On the third night out of Carteia the wind dropped and on the fifth turned contrary. The sailors struck the sail, and from that moment the sea began to rise, slowly but inexorably, more each day. At first Tamar crouched in the cabin, feeling the ship rise giddily, then drop, leaving her stomach behind. Later, when she was not carving the ivory fang, she spent her days on the poop, clinging to the gunwale and watching from there. Gradually, as the ship kept rising to the endless waves, a sort of exhilaration began to mingle with the anxious fear in the pit of her belly. Half the oars were unshipped now and lashed under the benches. That gave four men to each of the remaining oars, three always at work and one resting. The white foam rose higher on the waves, and every now and then she felt a sense of miracle as a mountain slope of blue-black water marched by, lifting them to its summit, and for a moment the wind blew salt into her face and the horizon was the end of the world and all between a continent of waves, water, tossing spume, with no living thing on it but themselves and the gray and white seabirds. Tamar found herself unwillingly grateful to Pendril for showing her these marvels of creation, but Daniel became sick and pale, could barely eat, and lay all day in the cabin, shivering with fear. On the twentieth day he muttered to her, "I can bear this no longer. Go to Pendril and beg him to turn back, for assuredly we shall all die if he does not. Offer him anything. Gold. Half our land in Carthage. Your body."

"My body?" she cried.

"For all our sakes," he said. "Why not? Go."

She went stiffly to the poop and found Pendril there with Tregan at the steering oar. "Turn back," she said abruptly, "or you will kill my husband."

"I cannot," he said gravely.

"Why?" she said. "What will you do if we come at last to the Hesperides?"

"Bring back a golden apple," he said suddenly. "It is the price demanded by the goddess for the land I want; for that corner of the Rock where I stopped and you ran into me."

She remembered and for a time did not speak, for she had remembered too the yearning in his face and understood now what drove him. But her husband had sent her, and she must obey.

She said, "Turn back, and you shall have your price. Gold. Land in Carthage. My body. All."

He shook his head unsmilingly.

Tregan said, "Take it, for all of us, Pendril. Turn back. There are no Hesperides except in a man's dreams."

He said, "The ship rides well. We go on."

She stared at the square red man. She had offered herself to him twice, and twice he had refused her. Anger and shame tensed her like two powerful arms bending a bow. She lashed out at him with all her strength. His hand went toward the knife at his belt as her blow landed, then he turned his back on her.

She went slowly to her cabin and lay down. When Daniel asked her how she had fared, she only shook her head. She lay on her back, staring at the deck beams low over her head. If Daniel was willing to sacrifice her for his own safety, what would he not do? Where was the nobility she had once seen in him, the strength to protect her, the warmth to cherish? He crouched here trembling while the rough Carteian above faced the waves and the unknown unafraid, driving to his dream.

She took the knife and fang and began to carve carefully, for she had almost released the shape from the bone now.

The wind blew stronger, and rain slanted down from low clouds. On the twenty-fifth day the wind dropped a little, and the white water tossed less violently on top of the waves, though the waves themselves grew larger. On the twenty-sixth day the clouds built up again, and soon after noon the light began to fail. Here and there a thin ray stabbed down onto the mountainous

waste of the ocean, the water slate blue and the clouds the same
color. To the northwest deeper gray rain curtains hung from
scudding cloud to heaving sea. She went to the cabin and found
Tregan there whispering with Daniel. They put their fingers to
their lips. When Tregan had gone, Daniel whispered, "I have
won the other Carteians over. We are going to overthrow Pendril."

"Will you kill him?" she asked.

"He deserves it. Go on deck and stand in the stern. When Tregan puts his head out of the hatch and calls, 'The rowmaster
wants you, Pendril,' that is the signal. Get behind Pendril and
seize his knife. He trusts you, and you are a woman."

She found Pendril on the poop. For a moment the appearance
of the sky made her forget the fear and doubt with which her
husband's words had loaded her. Pendril heard her gasp and
said, "It is a frightening sight. Go back below, and you will not
see it."

She shook her head. "I would rather stay here with you. It is
worse if you cannot see."

Her thoughts circled dully. How soon would they come? What
would she do? There was the knife in his belt at the small of his
back, where sailors always carried it.

"Hold hard now," Pendril said.

The wind note rose like a keening bird, the bow gave a sudden violent lurch, a sheet of water surged out to either side, and
the figurehead plunged in to her neck. The sailors had often told
Tamar there was no danger until the *Kedesha* wet her breasts:
now the sea was going over them with every wave.

The black storm raced across the sea and struck. Tamar
crouched gasping under the gunwale. The wind shrieked, the
rain deluged down. Lightning split the sky directly over the mast,
thunder cracked all around the horizon. The sea was lit by
shivering curtains of light. Under the thunder she heard the
rowers howling like doomed animals below. The stern sank, and
the figurehead's back-thrust shoulders shook against the lightning in that same obscene dance she had witnessed at Carteia.
The stern rose, and the *Kedesha* plunged her face into the sea.
Sheets of water surged along the deck and poured onto the rowers below.

As suddenly as it had come, the squall passed, fleeing eastward down the wind. Pendril turned to Tamar with a smile. "So! That one, at least, is past!"

His face was red, cold, streaming wet, happy. She said suddenly, "They are going to seize you. Tregan will tell you the rowmaster wants you. I am to take your knife. . . ."

Pendril's expression did not change. He glanced at the steersman, but the man could not have heard. He said, "It is well. When they come, take my knife, but go behind the steersman there, and if he moves, stab him hard." He opened the chest that had stood on the poop since leaving Carteia, got out the bow and arrow, and went to the very stern of the vessel. To the steersman he said softly, "Hold her head to the sea. Nothing else. Make no sound, neither cry nor call."

Almost at once Tregan's head appeared over the poop ladder as he called, "The rowmaster wants you, Pendril."

Tamar took the knife from Pendril's belt as Tregan ran up the ladder, followed by One-Eye, the other three sailors, and the rowmaster. She held the knife at the steersman's neck, and Pendril aimed the bow, the arrow notched and the string drawn. The giant waves marched slowly on, the *Kedesha* rhythmically rose and sank.

"Hold!" Tregan cried. "The woman has betrayed us."

They were gathered like snarling dogs, those behind trying to crowd forward, Tregan and One-Eye holding back. She did not see her husband but heard him calling from below, "Go on! There are only two. Go!"

"How much did he pay you to betray your promise?" Pendril said. Tregan charged with an oath, his knife blade flashing. The bow twanged, and he sank to the deck spurting blood, the arrow through his throat. At the same moment Tamar heard Daniel scream. His hand appeared, reaching up, clawing, then vanished.

Pendril said, "What happened?"

The rowmaster, at the back, stammered, "A slave threw a knife. He must have had it hidden. The captain is dead."

"And that was not the only knife we have," a voice called. "Free us, Pendril, and we will kill them all."

"Well?" Pendril said, staring at One-Eye, the bow again drawn. Sullenly One-Eye threw down his knife.

Pendril said, "Back to your posts all. The storm will return. We must work together or . . ."

A bolt of lightning and a close chord of thunder drowned the rest of his sentence. A savage jerk of the vessel flung Tamar to her knees. "An extra man to the steering oar," Pendril called. "And you two, say a prayer and throw the bodies overboard."

Tamar went down to the rowers' deck. Daniel lay face down, the knife in his back. Two sailors picked him up as she knelt. She bit her lip, but she knew the rule of the sea. She bowed her head and closed her eyes and prayed. She had not wished this fate on him. When she looked up again, she was alone.

After an hour lying in her cabin she rose and went about the ship, giving the rowers food and wine and the sailors water.

It was the opposite of the night of the ritual orgy at Carteia. Then the hours had started slowly and gradually moved faster; now they went fast and gradually slowed, though there was no minute, no second free. The roaring and groaning and creaking and crying were continuous. There were always three sailors at the steering oar. Pendril was always moving, from bow to stern, from upper deck to lower, exhorting, cursing, encouraging. In the reflected lightning she saw oars smashed and new ones put in the rowers' hands. She saw three rowers rise together from their bench and stumble like blind men toward the ladder to the deck and Pendril run at them, his knife drawn. One man fell in the gangway, a lurch of the ship flung another like a stone against the bulkhead, and the third, when he stumbled back to his oar, could not control it. The end kicked up under his chin, breaking his neck. Pendril pulled in the oar and lashed it down.

As time slowed, her bones ached, her head throbbed, and she did not know where she was or what she was doing. Once lightning fell slowly from the sky and in it, like a held lantern, she saw Pendril's face, his teeth bared, the water held on his skin, not falling down. Then darkness again. Out of the darkness he said, "I love you."

Light spread, and all was gray where before it had been black or violet or slate. Low clouds raced across the sea, but the waves were becoming less. After two hours a yellow tinge came to the day, and watery rays of sunshine began to lighten the color of the waves. By noon the storm was past.

"Take in four more oars a side," Pendril said wearily to the rowmaster. "Just keep her head to the sea until dark. Let the rest sleep." To Tamar he said quietly, "Will you go to my cabin?"

She hardly heard, for something was coming slowly to them on the waves, a dragonlike shape, dark, waving thin arms. Pendril stared too and after a moment said, "A tree branch!"

Under the slow beat of the oars the *Kedesha* crept on. Tamar said, "The bough is gnarled. It is a fruit tree." The bough drifted closer. "With fruit on it," she said. "Two . . . round . . ."

"Golden apples," Pendril cried. "But they are not gold."

"I will get them," she cried. "Tie the end of that rope around my waist!" She raised her arms, pulled her robe over her head, and stood naked. His hands shaking, his soul drunk with her slender, full beauty, Pendril fastened the rope, while the steersman gaped like a man dumbstruck. Pendril gave the rope a turn, then she slipped into the sea and swam powerfully to the bough. She plucked the fruit and started back.

On deck she stood a moment pressed close to him, and he repeated, "Will you go to my cabin now?"

"The fruit!" she said, pulling on her robe. "Are they apples?"

"Later," he said. "We shall learn later."

She lay shivering, eyes closed, until she heard his step. She felt him slide her robe gently over her shoulders and head. She waited. His warm face came down on hers, still cold from the sea. Her lips parted, her body gave one fierce tremor, then all cold was gone, all fear. She was warm, and she heard her own voice murmuring, "Pendril!" A luxurious flowering began in her body, and she spread herself to enfold him, her arms around his neck, her eyes wide, smiling up at him. She clasped her legs around him and a long thrusting began, sliding deeper to her heart. Tears flooded her eyes, and she moaned in time with the creak and heave of the ship. The *Kedesha* rose on a mighty wave, slid down, farther, farther, surely she must go under, go under . . . rose again, intolerably fast now, shaking against the sun, plunged down, faster, faster, and this time under, plunged into swirling green-blue-red depths. She heard a long cry like a seagull whistling down the wind and was gone.

When she awoke, she was alone. She lay back, her arms folded behind her head, and basked in the warmth still glowing inside her. There was no light, so it must be night. The ship seemed to have a different motion. She stretched and yawned, smiling. He would come back soon.

She heard the rustle of the canvas, and he came with a lamp. She held out her arms; he took her hands and said, "We have sprung a leak below the waterline. It is not serious, but I must lighten the ship, throw overboard all the cargo. And all the food and water we can spare. We have begun already. And the wind holds from the west. I *know* land cannot be far away, but now I dare not go on. We have turned back."

"It does not matter," she said. "You have the apple the goddess demands. But it is not gold, is it?"

Smiling, he held out one of the fruits she had plucked from the floating bough. He had cut it open, and inside the dark gray, quilted skin she saw the dried remains of golden-yellow pulpy flesh. "It was last season's fruit," he said, "not fallen from the bough. It happens sometimes with all fruit. And now we need only one more miracle for a safe return." She was about to ask him what he meant when he said, "I am sorry your husband died. I meant him no harm."

She said slowly, "I did not wish him dead. But I learned on this voyage that I could not live with him anymore, for what he did and did not do."

The lamp flickered as the ship shuddered to a bigger wave. "I must go on deck," he said. "But, oh, I am sad to be heading back. We have come so close to the rim of the world, which I have so often dreamed of, lying on the top of the Rock and staring out over this ocean."

"Will you go again?" she asked.

He shook his head. "Not I. Some other man will seek the golden apples. Perhaps he will go from Carteia. He will sail past the Rock, certainly, for we hold the latch to the west. But if we come back safe, I shall not go to sea again. I shall build a house for us—you know where."

"The Rock will be our fortress," she said. "Or will you be afraid of the spirits of the Great Cave?"

"Not if you are with me," he said seriously. "I shall harvest the shells to make Tyrian purple. We shall have goats and bees to make cheese and honey such as they have never tasted in Carthage. My phallus shall plow my soil and make it fertile." He put his hand on her belly and squeezed it gently.

"Our children shall be sons of the Covenant," she said. "For they will be born of the womb of a Judean."

He said, "Well, I shall learn to do the correct things and say the proper prayers. Anything for a quiet life in the house. Besides, I like the sound of Hebrew songs."

"Good. But you have yet to ask me to marry you. I am not a slave, to be disposed of at someone else's will."

"Do you say yes or no?" he asked.

She said, "*Verastech li leolam.* I betroth thee unto me forever."

He kissed her long and deeply, then again turned to go. "Hold!" she said. "What is the miracle which . . . ?"

He stopped and stooped under the low beams to stare at something white swaying from the plank just above. He took it in his hand and saw that it was the fang Tamar had found in the cave where he hid his strong wine. But it was carved now into the shape of a naked woman. The hole in the thick part was now part of an elaborately rolled arrangement of her hair, piled on top of her head. She was lovely, a small smile on her face, the breasts pointed, the sexual slit exaggerated. So this was the meaning of the scraping he had heard so often, so long, from this cabin.

She said, "I made it so he would have to look at me. It is I."

"It is a miracle—*the* miracle," Pendril said. "*A naked woman sends you, and only another naked woman can lead you, a third pluck the apple from the tree, and a fourth bring you safe back home!*" He hung the talisman around Tamar's neck and ran joyfully up to the poop. On the ninth day they saw the pillar of cloud over the Rock and on the eleventh ran the prow ashore on that corner of land he called his own.

Book Three

❊❊❊❊❊❊❊❊❊❊❊❊❊❊❊❊❊❊❊❊❊❊❊❊❊❊❊❊❊❊

Phoenicia, Carthage, Roman Republic

The Jewish years 3188–3831
AUC 180–823
573 B.C.–A.D. 70

The rulers of the Rock and the overlords of Carteia were the kings of Carthage. In 273 B.C. arrived Hamilcar, King of Carthage, with his son Hannibal, to extend their grip from a few coast towns to most of Spain. This brought Carthage into conflict with the Roman Republic. In 190 B.C. Carthage was finally crushed and succeeded by Rome. Gadir became Gades, and as the Romans put more men and money into the conquest of Spain, their first real colony, Gades increased until it became the second city of the later republic.

Carteia fell on bad times. It had been founded by a commercial people to take advantage of the tunny fishing and the supplies of murex to make the purple dye. In times of war and conflict the Rock goes up in importance, but a small port like Carteia goes down. By the end of the Punic Wars (Rome against Carthage) it was perhaps in ruins, perhaps vanished altogether. Its resurrection was close at hand.

In 171 B.C., the consuls for the year being Licinius Crassus and Gaius Cassius Longinus, the Praetor Lucius Canuleius found himself with a problem. His legionaries had fathered some 4,000 children on Celtiberian slave women encountered in the course of the wars in Spain. They were not allowed to marry these women, though in many cases they wanted to, as a legionary could not marry a slave. The praetor solved his problem by founding on the site of Carteia (if it previously existed!) a *colonia libertinorum* of the same name. It was the first true *colonia* in Roman Spain and soon became sufficiently important to be permitted to mint its own coins.

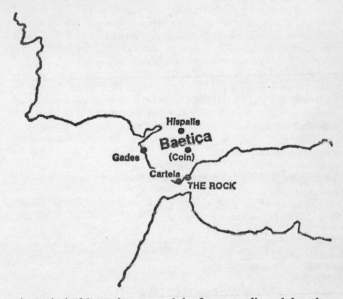

As Spain had been the scene of the first spreading of the wings of the Roman Republic, so in its soil were laid the first foundations of the Roman Empire, when Julius Caesar defeated the sons of his chief rival Pompey, at Munda (near Coin, in the province of Málaga) on March 17, 45 B.C. After the battle, while Caesar concentrated on seizing the rest of Andalusia, Gnaeus Pompey and some of his followers escaped to Carteia. Pompey was carried there in a litter, since he had been wounded in the foot. As soon as he and his party arrived, the town magistrate sent a message to Caesar offering to give him up. Caesar sent a detachment down to take him, but Pompey managed to escape in a boat—past the Rock he must have gone, past the magic forest, the Great Cave, the secret shrine of Hercules: but Caesar's men pursued, a sea fight followed, and Pompey was driven ashore. He limped away to a last fight on a hill. Defeated again, he took refuge in a cave, and there on April 12, with Caesar's relentless hounds on his heels, he fell on his own sword.

It is a grim tragedy, marching inexorable as the legions to its appointed end. But what hill? Where was the sea fight? Did they never leave the bay? Was that last scene played out in one of the Rock's uncountable caves, which have given brief refuge, over uncountable years, to uncountable other victims?

Caesar is dead. Long live Caesar.

In Judea a child was born into a time of trouble, for the unruly province and its stiff-necked people were beginning to chafe under the yoke of their new Roman masters. In A.D. 68, on the death of Nero, a series of civil wars broke out for possession of the purple. Galba, Otho, Vitellius, and at last Vespasian succeeded each other in rapid succession. An uneasy calm returned —a little war here, a little insurrection there, some expansion here, some withdrawal there—and it was to be the general condition of the empire for three centuries.

The *colonia* of Carteia, near the western limit of the empire, lived through this time, too. . . .

A Private Sacrifice

The twenty men of the town watch moved slowly across the side of the Rock, their spearpoints glistening dully, loose stones rattling under their sandals. Julius, their honorary commander, was in the center, carrying a sword and wearing his old centurion's helmet with the transverse crest. Fifty paces behind him the aedile Octavius led a dozen volunteers of all ages, who had come out to join in the manhunt for the pleasure of it. It was a close and airless day, for the east wind was blowing, and its oppressive cloud hung over the Rock.

Julius saw that all his men were sweating heavily, and they looked tired, though they had been on the go barely three hours. Everyone was too young or too old, that was the trouble with watch-and-wards everywhere. In a legion the men would hardly have been damp by now, just smelling a little acid as the wine leeched out through their leathery skins. His helmet felt intolerably heavy, and he discovered he was walking like a turtle, his head thrust forward under its weight. He swore and straightened up; but age was one enemy not even a retired centurion of the Twentieth could hold at bay forever, he reflected gloomily.

He stubbed his toe on a sharp stone and swore again. This was a bad way to be celebrating the first week of a new year—it was the sixth of Tishri—hunting down poor devils of escaped mine slaves. Work in the mines upcountry was enough to drive a free man to drink even with the good pay. That's why the only free men were overseers. The rest were slaves, captives of war, criminals, and such as these Turdetani, local tribesmen rounded up by a press-gang for the mine management. "Run them down like dogs," Marcus the duovir had said before they started out.

From behind, one of the volunteers called, "Straight ahead. A hundred paces!"

Julius looked up sharply, for it was his son's voice. The young man ran up to his side, calling, "There, father!" Ahead he saw several human shapes flitting in and out of the wild olives. Now they were in the open, running away along the slope toward the south.

"Well done, Fidus. You have sharp eyes." The aedile's voice was languid, as always.

Julius plodded on. His eldest son, Barak—or Fidus, as he preferred to call himself—would go a long way. Any father should be proud of such a son. But—Julius frowned—he was a little too eager to please, a little too eager for blood. It was all very well for the duovir to talk of these Turdetani as dogs, but they weren't; they were peasants of the soil, mountain men, goatherds, players on the oaten pipe and the bagpipe. In their own village they wore roughly worked jewels and coarse-hammered armlets of gold. Their women were beautiful and for great occasions twined their long hair around long rods set on top of their heads and then draped a veil over all.

Dogs? If they were dogs, then so were the Judeans, his own ancestors, whom Rome was chastising at this moment. As a legionary he used to think that all the people he fought were ignorant savages; but the police action in Judea, which seemed to have started last year, made him think again, and deeply. His father used to pray for Jerusalem every day. His mother had wept on her deathbed because she was going to die without seeing the Temple. If Jerusalem meant so much to him and his people, then all these others, the barbarians, must surely have their own proper loves and prides, which ought to be respected.

A man to his right said, "Here they come!" It was just below the Great Cave. Perhaps the six Turdetani had thought to shelter in it, but they were out now, running, with a high, trembling scream. They came straight at Julius, and the watch closed in. The aedile called, "Try not to kill them, men. They're worth good money!"

But the fellow running bare-handed at Julius seemed determined to be killed, a wild-eyed, tall man with reddish hair and eyes as blue as Julius' own, naked but for a rag around his loins. Julius made to lunge with his sword, and as the man dodged sideways, snarling, he stepped back and hit him hard on the temple with the pommel of the sword. The man stumbled, and Julius jumped on him, hit him again, and cried, "Lie still, fool. You want to live, don't you?" For a minute the fighting was general, and Julius saw his son kill a tribesman with a neat spear thrust: but it had been necessary, he gave him that. Then suddenly it was over, and they had five battered prisoners and a corpse.

Julius took off his helmet and mopped his forehead. The watch began to rope the prisoners together. The aedile Octavius said, "For a moment I thought they'd gone around to the Eagle's Nest cave at the back of the Rock. It's a bad place to have to get them out of."

"Nearly impossible, aedile, I think," young Barak said importantly. "But there's no escape, either. They'd either have to surrender, starve, or jump. Seven hundred feet!"

"There's no escape anywhere on the Rock," the aedile said,

"except perhaps in the Great Cave. No one's ever explored that. Some say it goes on forever."

"There's no escape from Rome anywhere, now," Julius said. "The Rock at least looks like a place where you can die with honor."

Then they started back for Carteia, the prisoners carrying their dead comrade, and the watch and the volunteers surrounding them.

"Walk with me, Julius," the aedile Octavius said. "They can look after themselves . . . especially with your Fidus among them. A very capable young man. You know, if we spend a little money, I believe we have influence enough between us, with Marcus' help, to get Fidus appointed to the Seventh as a tribune, direct."

"He would be overjoyed," Julius said formally.

"I will speak privately to Marcus," Octavius said.

The two men fell silent and walked on together without more words. They were both near fifty; both had served over twenty-five years in the Twentieth Legion, *Valeria Victrix;* both had now been settled six years in Carteia, which special privileges and exemptions to veterans made a particularly desirable place of retirement; they were friends, liked and admired each other well, and in the years of campaigning had saved each other's lives and got drunk together more times than either could count and in the long British wars had shared several snub-nosed English whores. Both were married—Octavius recently and officially, Julius in Rome twenty-three years ago to a slim girl of his own faith; but as private soldiers were forbidden to marry, he had had to pretend through the rest of his army career that the woman who trailed along behind the legion as and when she could was only a concubine, like the rest of them.

For the rest, they were different as men could be: Octavius —Roman-born, cynical, immoral, brave only when he had to be but then amazingly debonair—the perfect camp prefect and politician; Julius—Carteian-born, son of a Judean ex-legionary, direct, courageous, devout, dutiful above all—the perfect centurion, farmer, and honorary, incorruptible head of the town watch.

Striding easily along together, as they had done so often, they turned the last angle of rock and passed from under the cloud into sunlight. The sandy isthmus curved away like a golden finger crooked below them. The sun shone on rippling blue water, and white clouds traveled like lambs across the mountains beyond. They could see the river mouth, a score of jetties thrust out into it, palm trees and the masts of ships; and in the town, houses of white and marble, the green of gardens, and all around golden wheat, rusty vineyards, gray-green olive groves.

The aedile sighed. "Peace, plenty, bliss. Or so it appears on the surface. . . . What do you hear of Horatius Naso?"

"The man who some of us hoped would succeed Galba?"

"Yes."

"Nothing. Why?"

"Well, as you know, Vespasian succeeded Galba and is our undoubted emperor. Nevertheless, it seems that many are still not content and are working in secret to elevate Horatius Naso to the purple. You know I went to Gades last week. . . . It was to learn more of this movement . . . to decide whether it would be wisest to denounce it or join it. I learned that it is strong, but not strong enough. It is supported by a number of discontented or jealous men and by the people of this new blood-drinking sect, the Nazarenes . . . and by many of your co-religionists."

"Jews? Why?"

"Because of the severe campaign Vespasian's son is waging in Judea, I suppose."

"By God, in that case I could join this Horatius Naso myself," Julius said.

"And lose your land and your head! Listen to me, my friend. First, Naso cannot win. Understand that, grasp it! *He cannot win.* Second, the loyalists will use the conspiracy for their own advancement. To be safe, you must act on the winning side, and you must do it publicly. This is doubly important for you, as a Jew. . . . The conspirators are not quite ready yet, and we are going to strike first. In Carteia there are some thirty of us, all men of influence. Marcus is our leader, and though we hope we shall not have to shed blood, we are quite prepared to do so. We shall seize the chief places and people of Carteia—as our friends will be doing in Gades and Hispalis and other towns—in order to make sure that no local authority can declare for Naso. At the same time we'll imprison the local conspirators until it is clear that the rising has failed all over Hispania . . . or, if it *should* perchance succeed elsewhere, then they will be useful to us as hostages."

Julius said, "Why are you telling me this? I don't want to take part."

"You are the commander of the watch, are you not?" Octavius said gently. "Does it not strike you that you would be one of those we would have to seize unless you were on our side? Besides, your son is leading the assault group. He will be the one to take the other magistrates prisoners."

"Barak?" Julius cried. "He didn't tell me."

"Join us," Octavius said. "Marcus detests all Judeans as insolent rebels. And he's been trying to get your vineyard ever since you planted it."

Julius strode on along the sand, his head glumly bent. It was like the army again: will you have bread for dinner or bread? He said, "I'll come. But . . ."

"Midnight then, the third night . . . We meet in your back garden. Fidus suggested it."

They were at the gate of the town and soon afterward parted. When Julius reached his house, his son Barak was not yet home. He'd have to talk to him tomorrow about this idea of getting a tribuneship right away. It was a great responsibility for an inexperienced youngster. Besides . . . His wife Gavrielah put her hand on his arm and said, "You look worried. What is it?"

"I wish I could tell you," he said. She seemed older than her forty-one years. It had not been an easy life, following the legion and trying to raise a family on soldier's pay. She was almost as tall as he, frail now, some of her teeth gone, her hair gray and her skin wrinkled, but the eyes—deep, large, dark—had never lost their first magic for him. He looked solemnly into them now and saw that his worry had infected her. "Is it about Barak?" she asked.

"No," he said, then, "Yes. In a way . . . And about Jerusalem."

"We'll be able to go next year, as we planned, won't we?" she said anxiously. "Surely the war will be over by then."

"It'll be over," Julius said grimly.

"You promised your mother you'd go to Jerusalem and celebrate Passover in the Temple and make the sacrifices."

Julius did not speak. The Temple at Jerusalem was a dream to him, yet as real as the Rock outside there. He was a Roman citizen, but his body and spirit shared two homes, mysteriously unified—the Rock and the Temple.

"I don't know," he said finally. "I'll have to do my duty, that's all."

The Naso conspiracy was not much of an affair, and two hours after the loyalist group had moved out from Julius' back garden, the forum, curia, temples, baths, and mint were secured and a score or so prisoners safe in jail, including two of the other magistrates and the quaestor. Julius himself had held the jail with six reliable men of the watch and received the prisoners as they were brought in. His son Barak came early with the magistrates, went off, and returned half an hour later with half a dozen other dazed and frightened men.

Most of the prisoners started clamoring of their innocence before they were through the gates, but Shmuel Ben Zion, a short, fat old lawyer and the head of Carteia's small Jewish community, was defiant. "Stop whining!" he snapped at the others jammed into the little cell with him, as Julius bolted the door. "We should have struck earlier, that's all." He glowered at Julius through the bars in the smoky lantern light. "And may the plagues of Egypt afflict you and your fine son and all your family for what you have done tonight."

"I have only done my duty to my acknowledged and lawful emperor," Julius said angrily, for he felt guilt over the business. "He is your emperor, too."

"No more," Ben Zion said. "He is no emperor, but abomination."

"Hush, hush," the other prisoners hissed nervously.

"Abomination," Ben Zion repeated. "Every stone of the ruined Temple cries out, 'Abomination!'"

Julius' head began to ache. "The Temple?" he said. "Of Jerusalem? Ruined?"

"Utterly destroyed, razed, not one stone left upon another. The ground plowed and sown with salt. The Ark of the Covenant taken to Rome for a triumph. All this by your Vespasian's son, Titus, in *his* name and with *his* approval."

"But, when . . . ?" Julius began.

The lawyer said, "Go, Julius Cohen-ki. No true Jew has anything more to say to you."

In the public baths next day Julius lay naked on the marble slab of the caldarium, his eyes closed. His son Barak occupied the next slab. They were sweating heavily as attendants scraped their skins with strigils.

"The Temple was destroyed, Jerusalem sacked, and all the Zealots killed on the ninth of Ab in your calendar," Barak said. "Nearly two months ago. The news was suppressed to give the authorities throughout the empire time to take measures against possible uprisings. Marcus and Octavian knew some time ago. . . ."

The heat burned Julius' eyeballs through the closed lids. His hair was scorching, his very fundament burning. What law said a man had to suffer such torture? He sat up to go.

"They told *me* a week ago," Barak said proudly.

Julius sank back. It was willpower that had to be practiced and maintained. It was a man's duty to face the caldarium and the frigidarium. YHWH did not intend life to be one long doze in the baths under the hands of skillful catamites.

"Barak," he said, "do you feel ashamed that we helped, even so little, to keep Vespasian in power? I do."

"Finished," the attendants said. Julius and his son staggered into the next room and stepped down into the huge hot bath.

"I do not," Barak said. "And I am going to give up the practice of your religion. I no longer believe in it, and it will be a handicap to me in my career. Please call me Fidus from now on, as my friends have been doing for some time now."

It was strange how this very hot water felt quite cool after the caldarium, Julius thought. For a time, that is; soon the effects wore off, and you began to wish they'd pour some cold in.

"Marcus promised me last night that he'd get me a tribuneship in the Seventh," Barak said.

No, it was Fidus now. *Fidus,* faithful. Faithful to whom? To what?

"I had to worship Divine Caesar, of course," Julius said. "Everyone does. That's forbidden by our Law, but our priests wink at it. Otherwise I never found being a Jew any hindrance to me. Rather the opposite for people like us, who are not Ro-

mans of Rome. Jerusalem and the Temple were strongholds—
places of refuge—home for the spirit when it was oppressed."

"Time," the attendants said. They moved to the unctorium
and lay down on two marble slabs. The perfumed attendants began to rub perfumed oil into their skins.

"*My* spiritual home is Rome," Fidus said. "And you were only
a centurion. Higher up, I think, to be a Jew would be a severe
hindrance, even danger, to me."

He's twenty-two, Julius thought, and in a few months he'll be
higher up in the army than I reached in twenty-five years of service. At the same time he'll gain equestrian rank. Then there'll be
no limit to what he might become—tribune, governor, legate
. . . Caesar. Yes: do your duty, guard your back, obey orders,
look out for the main chance, kill rivals, and any citizen could
become Caesar.

He shook his head and muttered, "Impossible."

"What is, sir?" the attendant said.

He said, "Nothing. I didn't mean *impossible*. I meant *wrong*."

He must talk to Gavrielah. He got up and headed for the apo-
dyterium, where his clothes were. "Sir, you've missed the frigidarium," the attendant cried reproachfully. Julius swore under
his breath, turned, and went to the frigidarium.

When he reached home, the younger boys and girls—there
were five of them—seemed subdued, and Gavrielah's eyes were
damp. He beckoned her to follow him up to the roof. He sat
down there under the rush awning, and she stood before him,
arms folded. "Marcus has ordered the execution of four of the
chief conspirators tomorrow. Cneus the quaestor. Sextus. And
two Jews—Jochanan the wine merchant and Shmuel Ben Zion.
The rest he has fined and released."

Julius nodded. "Is that all?"

"No. He has taken the menorah from Jochanan's house and
Ben Zion's Torah and thrown them down before the statue of
Vespasian in the Temple as offerings."

Julius stared dully at the great Rock face a league away to the
south. No refuge there. No refuge anywhere.

"It must not be," he said.

"No," his wife said. "It must not be."

Refuge was the wrong word now; he thought it was no longer
a matter of refuge but of duty or sacrifice. Whose sacrifice?

"I am ready," Gavrielah said. "With the Temple gone, which all my life I had dreamed of, I do not feel that I am really alive. Yet I love you." She put her hand on his head and stroked his cheek.

"Our people will be dispersed all over the world," Julius said. "They will have no home now. Nor will we, for Jerusalem was our home, too."

"Perhaps we should bow our necks, so that they of the dispersal will have places to come to," Gavrielah said.

"Perhaps," Julius said, "but what if bowing the neck only makes it easier for them to cut off your head? . . . And there are the children to be considered. Ophira's only eleven. . . . Leave me, wife. I must think."

It was the ninth day of Tishri, harvest time. From his roof here near the edge of the town he could see the woods across the river. The hills beyond were full of great bustard and succulent partridge. Along the sea the orchards groaned with the quilted custard apples. All around stretched the wheat. On the threshing floors mules trotted out in circles, drawing sledges, and children rode the sledges, threshing the wheat. Men threw up the grain on long shovels, winnowing, and the wind blew the chaff away in a golden haze. He could see the paved road and the warehouses piled with wool and the long sheds of the tunny-pickling factory. The wind blew from the west, cool with a freshness from the great ocean. There was a smell of autumn flowers and ripe corn in the air and over all fields the gold of the threshing. They would have been harvesting in Judea, too, when the legion went up against the city. He could see the auxiliaries out in front making their short rushes, shouting their shrill war cries that made the legionaries laugh and imitate them. Behind, he saw the steady tramp and clink of the legion, the optios on the flank measuring the pace for each century, the eagle riding steadily on above the dust. . . .

Near sunset there was a purple light on the bay, and he could think that it was not a reflection of the sky but the dye itself, leaking from the vats to the west to stain the sea. It was the color of the Judean priests, that purple. Men wore it in stripes on their prayer shawls, and often the wrappings of the Law were dyed the same purple. Two years ago the community here had bought an especially good amphora of the dye and sent it as a gift to the Temple treasury at Jerusalem. It would all have been used up before . . . the end.

The Rock stood up like a strong man, bareheaded, neck unbowed, shadowed gray face turned square to the land. It was a strange Rock, joined to the land but not part of it. Many grazed their flock on it, but none owned it, not even the colonia. The idea of owning it seemed sacrilegious, as to say, who owns the TZUR YISRAEL, the Rock of Israel? It was a good place to make a sacrifice, even as the pagans and the tribes did.

The sun set. The tenth day of Tishri, the Day of Atonement, had begun. He got up, sighing and shivering. Then he squared his shoulders. It couldn't be any worse than facing the frigidarium.

Two hours after he lay down to sleep, he awoke, because he had set himself to do so. The little naked woman of ivory, his family's heirloom and love charm for the marriage bed, gleamed pale where she hung on the wall above his head. He knew that Gavrielah, beside him in the alcove, was awake. Probably she had not slept at all. He said, "I must go now, my love. I may not come back."

"I know. What do you tell me to do?"

"Know nothing. Rely on Fidus."

He bent and kissed her long on the mouth, then left her, went to the outer room, and dressed as though for a legion ceremony —tunic, breeches, cuirass, cloak, woolen neck cloth, sword, dagger, boots, and his centurion's helmet. He hooked his shield onto his left arm and faced the alcove where the gods would have been kept in a pagan household. He bowed three times to the menorah set up in it, then left the house and marched slowly up the street toward the prison.

He met and saw no one. A cloud passed over the moon as he neared the prison and he approached the sentry's post in almost complete darkness. The man was half asleep, pacing slowly in front of the main gate, his drawn sword resting flat on his shoulder, his head nodding. He was an old ex-soldier of the Seventh. He turned as the cloud passed away from the moon and saw the centurion striding toward him, the cloak billowing, the great helmet glowing. He straightened, bringing the hilt of his sword to his mouth. Julius raised his own right hand in salute and stepped straight in behind the short dagger in his left. It struck under the ribs, and the sentry toppled silently, blood gushing from his mouth. Julius lowered him to the ground and quietly opened the main gate. As he had thought, the rest of the watch on duty were asleep in the guardroom. He pulled the corpse inside the gate, hid it behind the guardroom, and closed the gate, bolting it from inside.

With the dead man's sword in hand he entered the prison building and went to the cell where the five Turdetani were awaiting an escort from the mines to take them back into slavery. They were awake, and he whispered in their tongue, which he knew almost as well as he knew Latin. "I am going to release you, on one condition. That you take four other prisoners, Romans, with you and see that they escape to Hispalis, or wherever in Baetica they want to go."

No one spoke. Then a voice from the dark muttered, "Who is it? Why do you do this?"

Julius said, "I am a Jew. The Romans have done worse to my people than to you. I do this . . ." He searched for the right words, which these men would understand and appreciate: ". . . to make peace with myself."

"You are he who saved my life when you could have killed me on the Rock," the voice said. Julius remembered the man well for his red hair and blue eyes, though he could not see them now. "I am called Pendreth," the man went on, "a leader among my people. We will do as you ask. I give my word."

Julius pulled back the double bolts and said, "Take this sword. Use it if you have to. Come." At the end of the prison he found the four condemned conspirators in a single cell. One muttered, as he worked the bolt, "Already?" but Julius answered, "Quiet! I have come to release you. The Turdetani will take you to the hills and hide you until this blows over, as I think it will soon. Or you can start life again in another city and send secret word for your families to join you. . . . Follow me now, all, but make no sound."

He led the way out of the building. The watch snored in the guardroom, and when he was outside, he bolted them in. Then he pushed the tribesmen and prisoners into a rough file, and, at their side as though in charge, sword drawn, he marched them to the wicket gate in the town wall, near his house. It was unguarded except in times of war or tribal unrest. "Farewell, Ben Zion," he said in a low voice. "If I do anything for the Covenant tonight, it is thanks to you. . . . Farewell, Pendreth."

The chieftain clasped his hand. "Where are you going? Come with us."

Julius said, "I have more to do yet. None of you should know of it, in case later you are interrogated." He raised his hand, closed the gate, and went back into the town.

The Temple of Jupiter and the Temple of the Divine Caesar stood next to each other in the Forum. Votive lamps burned in each, shining on garland-hung busts of gods and emperors. Before the busts there were offerings of food in earthenware bowls and wine in rare jars.

Julius threw down the images, so that they broke. He scattered the flowers, overturned the food and wine, and set fire to the curtains with the votive lamps. It only took two minutes, then he gathered up the menorah and the Torah that had been cast before the bust of Vespasian and went quickly toward the house of Marcus, the chief magistrate. Putting down the sacred objects at a little distance, he went on. A servant lay asleep across the threshold, but Julius' dagger quieted him before he could stir. Julius went through the atrium to the side room where he expected that Marcus would be sleeping. He was there, a low oil wick smoking, and his wife beside him on the couch. He started up with a cry as Julius entered the room, snatched a torch, and dipped it in the flame. He stumbled back, fumbling for the sword on a table behind him, the red flames bursting high, his wife's face frozen.

"Julius the centurion," he cried.

"Julius the Jew," Julius said. "Come to make amends for what I did . . . or didn't do . . . last night. And to punish a needless sacrilege."

"You'll never escape alive," Marcus said. "And killing me won't help the Jews in Judea or anywhere else."

"There are times when a man can't afford to be reasonable," Julius said. "Otherwise he finds himself walking meekly into the slaughterhouse."

Marcus snatched the sword from the table, but Julius struck first, plunging his sword straight through the other's body and a hand's width out behind, to the left of the spine. The duovir fell back across the couch. Julius put his foot on his neck and jerked out his sword. To the woman he said, "I am alone. Tell them, when they come." He strode out of the house, gathered up the menorah and Torah, walked to the wicket gate, and left the town. At the beach he turned left and walked along the sand toward the dim bulk of the Rock. When he reached it, he found a patch of grass, wrapped his cloak about him, put his shield under his head, and slept. After a time dreams troubled him, but not of his wife or children, whom he could never see again, nor of all the dead in all his battles; but of a naked woman, terrified, running, a low-browed woman, ugly but with deep, lovely eyes, who cried to him for help.

He awoke then, and it was dawn. He continued south, moving diagonally up and across the west face of the Rock, past the Great Cave but lower, until he reached a flat place half a mile from the southernmost point, where the mass of the mountain ended its first severe southward fall. Here he sat down, facing the way he had come. He felt hungry for a time, but that passed.

He waited there on the edge of the escarpment until nearly noon. Then he saw the party working along the edge of the sea below. There were six horsemen, including some dignitary in a purple-lined cloak, and twenty men of the watch on foot, led by the aedile—he recognized Octavius' gray stallion. He smiled slightly to think what a compliment they were paying an aging centurion to bring so many against him.

At last one of the men saw him—the sun may have glittered on his helmet or touched the red of its horsehair plume—and pointed and called out. Julius stood up and, without hurrying, crossed the escarpment toward the eastern side. A goat track led from the corner along the eastern cliffs. For a hundred yards it was four or five feet wide and flat. Then the cliff swept down vertically from above and dropped again vertically below, and a narrow ledge snaked between, sharply curved round the beak of the mountain. Beyond, the path ended in a big cave—the Eagle's Nest. There was no other approach.

Julius put away his shield—he would not need that there—and, with a brief prayer, threw the menorah and Torah into the sea eight hundred feet below. Then he waited behind the angle of the path, looking out over the water shimmering far below. The autumn crocus were in bloom, stems sprouting like tall pink girls from the crevices in the limestone. A red-legged partridge saw him and flew out from the cliff, but a falcon stooped, striking it with a great burst of feathers.

Julius was looking toward the east, toward Rome and, beyond Rome, toward Jerusalem, which was no more. The wind was from the west, so he was in shelter here, but eddies sent whorls of dust down the cliff and shook the tiny flowers in the crevices.

He heard the clink of metal on stone and took up position, pressed into the cliff, sword raised. From round the corner Octavius spoke. "Are you there, Julius? Alone?"

"Yes."

"We came here once together, didn't we? The year we settled in Carteia. We were looking for wild pig and ate bread and onions and wine in the cave. It was the first time I'd ever seen a squirting cucumber. And Fidus talked of the cave the other day. A place of no escape, he said. . . . Now that Marcus is dead and another duovir fled, our chief magistrate is Plinius—a friend of yours. Things might have been arranged, but you chose a bad day. The procurator of the province arrived on a surprise visit at sunrise. He has come out with us to see that we do our duty. He has ordered that you be taken at once, at all costs."

"And then . . . ?"

The voice from around the angle of the cliff said, "Crucifixion, in front of the temple. But you have a sword. I'll give you five minutes, then we'll have to come."

"It'll be an expensive business, Octavius."

"I know. I shall lead. In five minutes."

Julius waited. Time passed. Another partridge, forgetful of the fate it had just witnessed, whirred out over the gulf. No falcon struck. It was warm, the sun blazing along the cliff, Africa shimmering beyond the sea, the gusty wind laden with the smell of hot stone and lavender.

Octavius came fast, crouched behind his shield. Another man was on his heels, spear arm drawn back. Julius stooped and stabbed at Octavius' legs below the shield. The spearman thrust, the point entering Julius' left shoulder. He hurled himself bodily against the shield, and Octavius fell. He struck left-handed with the dagger. The aedile rolled over and vanished over the cliff. The second man turned and ran.

Julius waited. He heard murmurings from along the path. Then, after a quarter of an hour, leather creaked close by.

"It is I," a voice said, and Julius stiffened. "Fidus."

"My son."

"A tribune of the Seventh Legion. The procurator has confirmed it."

"Your career may be short."

"I am not afraid."

He came round the angle of the rock then, spear in one hand, dagger in the other, and no shield. Julius waited for the spear thrust, then seized the haft, jerked it out of his son's hand, and thrust it between his legs. Fidus stabbed with the dagger as he fell. The blade struck Julius low on the right side under the ribs, and he knew he was badly wounded. Fidus fell, one leg over the edge. Julius pulled him back, his sword point at his son's throat.

Julius was bleeding heavily now. His son stared up, his eyes cold. The Day of Atonement was near its end. Julius said, "Remember you owe your life to a Jew—twice."

He stood and leaped out over the edge, his legionary's sword flashing. As he dived through space he shouted, "Shalo-o-om!" The wind began to press against his eyeballs, and the light went out on the sea.

Book Four

≈≈≈≈≈≈≈≈≈≈≈≈≈≈≈≈≈≈≈≈≈≈≈≈≈≈≈

Roman Empire

The Jewish years 3831–4178
AUC 823–1170
A.D. 70–417

THE sacking of Jerusalem and the destruction of the Second Temple in A.D. 70 were only single strands in a larger pattern. Although Rome had from early times turned one face east, now it bent its whole attention in that direction. From Spain the tide receded. Cádiz began to lose its wealth and fame. Instead of prominent Romans making their name in Spain, intelligent Spaniards made their name in Rome—for example, Pomponius Mela the geographer, born in Carteia under the Rock, and two of the greatest emperors, Trajan and Hadrian, both born in Italica, near Seville.

Life continued. At Belo (beyond Traducta) citizens worshiped at a famous temple dedicated to Jupiter, Juno, and Minerva. Trafalgar was then Cape Juno, and on it there was a temple dedicated to the goddess. Calpe-Carteia (so called to distinguish it from another Carteia near Seville) was one of the stages on the official military march route between Málaga and Cádiz. The tunny fishing and preserving again flourished, and the Carteians retained their skill in making the necessary pickles and sauces. There was enough prosperity to enable some people to hoard coins in large quantities. (One such hoard was discovered on a farm near Jimena de la Frontera in the nineteen

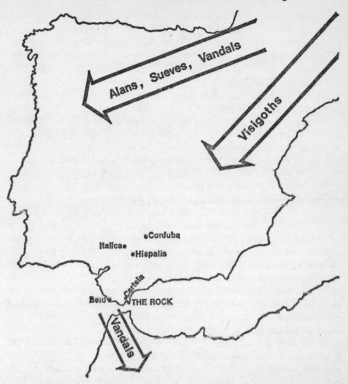

thirties, and there must have been many more.) But the hoarding of gold is not a healthy sign in any time or place. The tide of empire began to ebb, not only in the west but everywhere. Rome became a bauble squabbled over by the Praetorian Guard. Justice fled, and respectable citizens, oppressed and insecure, followed the idle and the criminal into outlawry. The Rock itself suffered an extra blow from nature: about the year A.D. 300 an earthquake threw up a sandbar which ruined the harbor of Carteia. The town and colony began to decay, though the process took centuries, and even today foundations, lines of walls, and one tall tower, the so-called Tower of Cartagena, still stand from the Phoenician and Roman colony.

For several centuries the Rock had watched over Carteia. They had been years of growth, of increase, of expansion in material achievement and in man's concepts of the universe and of his place in it. There had been violent change—that had come to Neanderthal Man, too—but now, for the first time, the Rock was to witness regression and rot.

It was not all bad, for as man suffers, the rest of nature rejoices. The carob tree and the wild olive and the wild fig would flourish, and if fewer men enjoyed the windblown scents of the Rock's rosemary and thyme and lavender, nature did not care. There would be more lynx, wildcat, pig: and the Barbary partridge, the Rock's own bird, would learn once more that its chief enemies were snakes and lizards and eagles, not man.

In the empire the milestones began to pass with increasing speed. In 323 Constantine made Christianity the official religion of the empire. Jews were already specially taxed, but now persecution increased until another emperor, the great Julian the Apostate, restored paganism and abolished the Jews' tax. Beyond the frontiers—indeed, inside them—the wolves gathered. The Rock was about a thousand miles from the nearest barbarians in Scotland and on the upper Rhine—but the ones who finally reached and passed it did not come from either of these places. They came from much farther away.

Until 376 the Visigoths (Western Goths) lived in what is now Rumania. Then they entered the empire and for a few years inhabited Bulgaria. In this period some became converted to Arian Christianity. (The difference between Arianism and Catholicism centered on barely comprehensible metaphysics about the nature of the Trinity, but that did not prevent the sects slaughtering each other in enormous numbers.) Only half pagan now, and all officially labeled as guests and allies of Rome, the Visigoths moved on west across northern Italy and Gaul.

In 409 three other barbarian groups—the Vandals, Alans, and Sueves—crossed the Pyrenees and entered Spain. In 415 the Visigoths followed. Finding the others unwilling to give up or share possession, in 416 they marched south to the strait, gathered boats, and made to cross over to Africa. Their boats were wrecked, and those in the first wave drowned. The rest decided it would be safer to fight the Vandals than the sea and (still ostensibly acting on behalf of Rome) set about their new enemies with a will.

While barbarians from the ends of the earth fought and marauded, sacked, pillaged, raped, and murdered, what of the ordinary people, caught in the death convulsions of the huge organism which had formed and sheltered them? How did *they* live in these times? *Could* one live . . . ?

Into the Dark

The goats heard the sound first and stopped, heads cocked, listening. Then the dog barked, and a man strode up out of the gully ahead. Rachel saw with surprise that it was Theophilus. He was totally naked, as always, his white-streaked gray hair hanging like a mane on his shoulders, but she had never seen him anywhere except squatting in the mouth of his cave in a gully at the far end of the Rock, a bowl beside him. Now the bowl was in his left hand and a new-peeled staff shiny white in his right. She remembered she had brought a hardboiled egg for him, as she usually did. She found it in her scrip and held it out.

He said, "The wrath of God is at hand. Say the Holy Creed after me, and though you will die, your soul might be saved, perchance."

She said, "You know we are Jews."

"Aye, aye, murderers, drinkers of Christian blood . . ." He passed on, muttering to himself. His body smelled like the goats, who had fled when he appeared but gathered again as he talked, some leaning forward to sniff his knees.

Rachel whistled and called, the dog ran to and fro, and the goats moved on around the side of the Rock. She was eighteen, slim, full-breasted, black-haired and blue-eyed. She walked barefoot on rock and thistle, and all her clothing was a black kirtle to the knee, the waist pulled in by thirty feet of coarse cord, wound round and round into a sash. Above, the kirtle swelled out to hold her breasts, and in there she could put a kid or take bread to her father when the scrip was full.

She moved the goats slowly along, watching them pluck sustenance from holes in the rock and climb up thin trees to eat the young shoots. In the gully near Theophilus' cave a spring of fresh water gushed from the earth. She drank, then shooed the goats on to the flat land by the point. They spread out to graze. It had rained much the past week, and the grass was lush. Rachel sprawled on her belly on top of a rock, her chin in her hands. She remained aware of the goats—she had been guarding them for twelve years now and did what was necessary by instinct—but her thoughts were elsewhere . . . the other pillar of Hercules, there across the narrow sea, a little cloud upon it: how near to see, how far to attain! The pale scent of a yellow flower growing in a crevice of the rock under her nose. The wind in her hair. Two partridges, red-legged, bright-eyed, oblivious of her in the act of love, bodies pressed down like her own against the earth. Warm rock firm against her belly and between her thighs. She was betrothed. The marriage was for next month, when the sowing of the fields would be done. Not long to wait.

She thought again, shall I bring Avram to my cave, or shall I keep it secret, inviolate? He will enter my body, so should he not know the other, too? But if he had done the one, would it not be all the more important to preserve to myself alone, virgin, the cave?

She got up, stood on a tall rock, and looked all round. No one. The wolves did not come to the Rock by day. The dog knew to stay with the goats and not follow her. She could safely leave them for a few minutes.

She ran lightly up a runnel in the low cliffs behind her. On the plateau above there was a tall standing stone—a magic stone, men said—and close to the stone she crawled into a thicket, and out of sight. Then, sliding sideways into a narrow cleft in the ground, she entered a tunnel. After twenty steeply down-tilted paces, she knew she was in the cave, *her* cave, Rachel's Secret. She closed her eyes tight, dropped to her knees, and waited.

After a long time she opened her eyes. Now the thin light streaming in from a crack in the roof of the cave showed the glistening walls, the shallow pond beside her, and, hung directly in front of her—herself, the goddess, a little naked woman of ivory, her hair coiled up on her head to make a loop, and by that loop Rachel had hung her on the wall of the cave.

"Give her love," she whispered. "A child of Israel. A man. Peace." The ivory woman was herself, and so was she herself. It was for both of them that she prayed. Her father and the Wise One would upbraid her bitterly if they knew, for the Lord YHWH was a jealous god. But they never would know.

"Give her goats, sheep," she prayed. "Land. The Rock. This place, Rachel's Secret, forever."

She closed her eyes again and a little later rose, scrambled back up the steep dark tunnel and out into the open. The dog was barking, and after creeping carefully through the trees until she was far from the mouth of the cave, she broke into a run.

The goats had scattered, and the dog was barking at a man throwing stones at them. It was James, the father of the Christian family in the other part of their house. He saw her and called, "This land is not to be grazed until next week, Rachel. It was agreed between your father and me and the others."

She said, "My father sent me this morning."

"He is wrong!" A flung stone hit one of the goats in the head, and Rachel said, "Stop."

"Take your goats, then. Go."

She called the flock, tears in her eyes, and led them back. There was no other free grazing this side of Carteia, so she took the flock back very slowly, letting them search along the shore, and did not reach the town much before the usual time. Her family lived in part of a ruined marble palace. All the livestock shared the great hall, where part of the mosaic floor was still intact; but they had had to block up the spaces between the pillars with brush and thorn, and the grand staircase to the upper story now ended in midair, so there was a ladder instead. Upstairs there were pictures painted on the walls—black and red women in long pleated robes, gladiators, a woman being covered by a swan. Part of the roof had gone, but it was repaired with straw. Another ladder led up there, and it was a pleasant place to sit in the evening.

Her mother called to her to bring the milk vessels, and she went to help her with the cooking. In another room she heard her brother Yakov's wife whining and the baby twins crying.

After they had all eaten and the dishes were cleaned and she had gone twice to the river, bringing back jars heavy with water, she told her father how James had turned the goats off the Rock. Yakov's wife cried, "Shame!" and Yakov, who was twisted and lame from birth, snapped his fingers and said, "Dogs . . . Christian dogs!" The three men argued—her father, Yakov, and Akiba, who was a year younger than she; and the women listened —her mother, Yakov's wife, and herself—with the baby twins and the infant son Isa, whom her mother had borne in her old age.

Yakov said, "Father, I was there when we settled this matter. It was *you* who said that none should graze on the Rock until the aedile gave word and *James* who said, 'There is no aedile, nor has been for years, so let us start at the time of the spring festivals.' . . . Send Rachel back tomorrow, but let us all follow, hidden and armed."

After a long hesitation her father said, "Be it so, but we will take no arms. Let us argue, let us persuade them." There was no gray in his hair, but he looked old, his brow always furrowed and his narrow shoulders bent, like a thin crow.

Akiba said, "What has come to Theophilus? He walks the town naked, preaching doom to all."

Yakov said, "His name means 'Lover of God' in Greek, but he loves no one. The Christian bishop has come from Asido and reasoned with him, but he will not hear. He is mad, madder than our Prophets."

"Speak not so, son," her father said. "Perchance the Lover of God is mad, but as to preaching the end of the world, in that he is right. I was born forty-four years ago, and all was bad then— our river silted up, the docks of our ancestors sticking out of the sand a hundred yards from the water, fine houses empty and falling into ruin, bribery, oppression. I believed it could not get worse. I was wrong. It has been getting worse all the time . . . wolves roaming the town in winter, outlaws infesting forests and mountains . . . and they are not escaped slaves, murderers, deserters—as such used to be—but men of substance, family men— all driven to turn outlaw because their land is seized without cause, their business infamously taxed, their rights trampled on by the rich, by every petty official."

"And since *I* was a boy," Yakov said, "the barbarians . . .

Alans, Sueves, Vandals, Visigoths. But that one who was washed up on the Rock last year, the day of the storm, said that they were fighting *for* Rome, against the others."

Her father cried, "I don't know their tribal names, nor what they claim to be doing. In fact they sack and burn and kill. . . . It is my turn for guard upon the Praetorian Gate tonight, so I must go. Woman, it is the Haggadah night tomorrow. Do you have all that you need?"

Her mother said, "All save the kid. Pick and slaughter one for me before Rachel takes them out in the morning. . . . And there is no wine."

"Yes, there is," her father said. "There are two small flagons behind our couch hidden from those who might make over-free with it. They are properly sealed." He looked meaningly at Yakov and went out.

Sighing, Rachel took down the bronze menorah from its niche, began to polish it with the end of her dress, and thought of Avram.

The next morning early, after her father had ritually killed one of the kids, she herded the remaining dozen into the street, out of the eastern gate, and through the fields to the shore. She moved them smartly along, whistling and crying and running to head them off if they tried to break into the fields, for they were mischievous and cunning as devils.

At the place which she called, for herself, the Woman's Stone, for it was here, under the stone, that her dog had turned up the ivory woman, a man now stepped out of hiding, his arms spread. It was a narrow place between the cliff and the sea, and the goats stopped. She saw it was Peter, James' son, a young man little older than herself but much taller, for all that family were tall, slender, and graceful. "No farther, Rachel Cohenky," he said. "It was agreed. . . . What is this?" His voice changed as her father and young Akiba and Yakov, hirpling with staff, came up from the beach toward them. Then he smiled, "We seem to have had the same idea." He put a finger to his mouth and whistled. His father, James, and his younger brothers, John and Young James, scrambled down from the rocks higher up the slope. The two families met around Rachel and her flock.

"What are you doing?" Yakov shouted angrily. "We have the right."

"Not yet," Peter said.

A stone whizzed past his ear. Her father shouted, "Don't do that, Akiba! James . . . boys . . . be still! We want to talk. . . ."

But the young men were at each other's throats, snarling like dogs, rolling on the ground. Rachel saw John grab her brother Akiba from behind and ran to help him. Peter held her with ease as she struggled and spat in his face. Smiling, he drew back his head. She sank her teeth into his arm. He flung her away with a yell. As she lay half stunned, the fighting stopped. The men stood separated, breathing deeply and muttering fiercely at one another. Akiba's nose was bleeding and so, she saw happily, was Peter's arm, and there was a taste of blood in her mouth. Her father turned on his heel and called curtly, "Come." He led his family toward the town. James and his sons followed a hundred paces behind.

Yakov was crying with vexation. "Oh, why did you not bring your spear, father?"

Akiba growled, "Where is our flock to graze now?"

They tramped back in silence to the town. Outside the gate her father said, "Take the goats up the river, Rachel. There is some fresh grass on this side, less than a mile up, on land which is fallow since Terence's wife died and he ran away."

The dog began to herd the goats around the outside of the town, but she heard a startled yell behind her and looked around. James, the Christian father, was falling backward, an arrow in his throat. Then she saw men coming out of the rank scrub which reached right to the wall. Peter cried, "Outlaws!" The day watchman at the gate seized his horn and blew until an arrow thumped into his chest, and the note quavered, hiccuped, and died. Rachel ran into the town, Akiba and the goats helter-skelter behind her. She saw a ragged outlaw rip his knife across Yakov's throat, then feel in his scrip. As she ran, she shrieked, "Outlaws! Outlaws!" Women rushed into their houses, doors slammed. Most of the men are in the fields, she thought, but they will hear the horn, they will come.

Theophilus stood naked in the middle of the street, his hand raised, his gray hair streaming. "Die, die! The hour of wrath is come! Slay the Jews, slay the wicked, let evil be wiped from the earth!"

She ran into her house, crying, "Block the door! Mother!"

Yakov's wife screamed, "Mother is at the river with Hadassah. Where's Yakov?"

"Dead," she snapped. Yakov's wife sank wailing to the floor. Rachel swept up the baby twins, hurried up the second ladder to the roof, left them, went down, found little Isa playing in the kitchen, and took him up, too. Akiba had seized a spear, and Rachel took a short, strong knife from her mother's carving board. She went back up to the roof.

The shrieking and shouting that had been so loud by the gate were muted here, and she saw few people—a man running; two outlaws, recognizable by their matted hair and short, filthy kirtles, breaking into a barracaded house across the street; a woman dead in the dust directly below the corner of the house.

The ladder creaked, and Peter joined her. "It's hopeless," he said. "There must be a hundred of them, and we are . . . a hundred women and children, twenty men. John's dead. Clubbed when we were trying to close the gate. Your father's safe in our part of the house. . . . Here they come!"

She heard her name called from the street below and went to the edge of the parapet. Two score outlaws were gathered there, and out in front, by himself, Julius. The pagan who had been a lawyer and had fled to the mountains. She remembered him well.

He called up, "Let us in, and no harm will come to any of you."

She said, "Let them in, Peter. Or they'll break in and kill us all. I have children to look after."

A minute later Julius came to her on the rooftop. She heard the sounds of pillaging in the house. Peter stood back, glowering. Julius spoke in a low voice. "Your mother and little sister are dead. They saw us coming and some of our men held them under water. So is Avram. I had to kill him myself. Were you not to be betrothed to him?"

She wondered whether she would be able to sink her knife in his heart before he could raise his short, old-fashioned legionary sword.

He said, "Come with me to the forest, Rachel. You heard the Lover of God? He's right. There is no law, no government, no god."

"We trust in the Lord God of Israel," she said automatically.

He said, "I love you, Rachel. When I left, you were—what? thirteen?—and I loved you then."

She thought Avram dead. Now she had no man to be her husband. Julius was strong and subtle and clever. He would give her babies and protect them. But where would be her home? What would be her land? She would never return to the Rock, towering there, cloud-crested. And what of her Secret, the deep-cleft ivory woman?

She said, "I must stay."

Confused shouting and curses rose from below, and Julius swore. "These people are hard to control, even for a moment, even in their own interests. Well, we shall be back when you have saved some more food." He ran quickly down the ladder and out of sight. Soon all the outlaws had gone, staggering back into the woods with their booty and driving stolen livestock.

A little later Rachel's father came to the rooftop. "They have taken everything except my special wine." He laughed wildly. His eyes glittered, and he moved with a quick nervous energy. "Your mother and sister are dead. Did you know?" She nodded. "It will be you next . . . me . . . all of us."

She said, "Father," sorrowfully, and suddenly he broke down and wept, wailing brokenly. Her breast ached, and her eyes filled. Could this be her father, the lord of the household, now weeping like her child in her arms?

Peter said hesitantly, "Isaac, we cannot stay here. There is nothing, no seed corn, little food, only one or two animals. We must throw ourselves on the mercy of Vitellius at the Villa Flaviana."

"Why should he take us?" her father said. "He already has a hundred men, all armed, most of them ex-legionaries."

Peter said, "Because if he does not, then we must join the outlaws. All together, we would be strong enough to take the villa and sack it."

"Take, sack, burn! Ai, what a world! But I fear you are right. Gather our people. I will speak to a duovir, if I can find one."

The Villa Flaviana was two miles round the bay to the west.

The estate, covering five thousand acres on the near bank of the next river, was one of the great latifundia where the very rich escaped from the duties of the towns and the supervision of the tax collectors and lived under the care and protection of a private army of field hands, guards, and servants, who were in fact almost slaves but better off in their semiservitude than as free men in the decaying towns.

Rachel thought, there would be no place but a barn or empty hay loft for them to sleep, no pots, no utensils. Yakov's wife was less than useless. She was the mother now. She called, "Akiba, here, fill that sack with . . ."

The doorman at the great house called loudly to the interior when he saw them coming. Other servants came out, swords drawn, but Isaac went forward steadily, bent under a heavy sack, and then Peter, and she after. Soon the majordomo came and then the lord of the estate, old Vitellius Flavius, fat and small-eyed, and later his son, young Gaius, plump and smooth, estimating her like a piece of choice meat. Isaac began to talk, dignified in his weariness.

She looked back. Ten more families stood behind them, patient in the spring rain. Ten more were on their way, and as many would come tomorrow. The rest had decided to stay in Carteia. Vitellius stared nervously at them from the porch, the twilight fading fast and his servants lighting lamps along the outer arcade. "They look dangerous to me," he said to the majordomo.

"We must take them in, master," the majordomo muttered. "There's that band of Vandals to the north and, I hear, Visigoths coming down from the east. We may need every man we can muster."

"Very well," old Vitellius said. "Put them in the barns. Give them something to eat. See that they work for their living and fight, if need be."

The majordomo motioned them around to the side, to the scattered buildings of the home farm. He showed them into a huge stone-built barn, nearly empty now of the hay which the cattle had been eating all winter. "Here and in the next barn," he said. "But no fires inside. Food will be distributed in ten minutes."

Isaac's family settled in a corner of the barn and Peter's close by. More families moved in and spread out until the barn was nearly full, but there was very little noise. Servants brought bowls of pease porridge, but Isaac took cakes of unleavened bread from his sack and gave a piece to each of his family. Next he opened a flagon of wine and mixed it with water in his brass cup. He bowed his head over it, and said, *Baruch atta adonay elohenu melech ha-olam borey peri haggafen*—Blessed art Thou, O Lord our God, King of the Universe, who createst the fruit of the vine."

Then over the unleavened bread, "Blessed art Thou, O Lord our God, King of the Universe, who bringest forth bread from the earth."

They drank and ate. The rain beat louder on the high roof. Isaac turned to Akiba, for his youngest son, Isa, was only two. "Akiba," he said, "do you remember the questions boys asked of their fathers at the Haggadah night?"

Akiba intoned, "Why is this night different from all other nights? For on all other nights we eat either leavened or unleavened bread, but tonight . . ."

The ritual of the Haggadah continued, with Isa asleep in Rachel's arms and Yakov's fatherless twins sprawled in the hay. When Isaac had finished retelling the Passover story, Peter came over to them and said, "We wish you a happier Passover next year than this."

"And a happier Easter for you," Isaac answered gravely.

Peter's chest was wide and flat, crossed with smooth bands of muscle. His eyes were wide-set and his nose short and straight. He was looking at her now, and she remembered how close he had held her . . . could it have been this same morning? She remembered the taste of his flesh in her teeth and lowered her eyes.

Soon they settled themselves to sleep.

The next day they sent for her to work in the big house. She protested that she had little Isa to care for, but the servant said Yakov's wife must do that. Peter looked unhappily after her, but she had to go.

At the villa they had a swimming pool and a heated bathhouse and tinkling bells and everywhere a subtle perfume. They gave her clean clothes of fine linen and wool and told her to wait upon the lord's youngest daughter. She ate their leavings and even so ate more, and better, than she had ever known. Young Gaius smiled lazily on her and after a week said, "Come to my couch tonight, Rachel."

She made to pass by, but he said, "Otherwise, back to the barn and work in the fields."

She hurried on, frowning. But as the hours passed she knew she would go. It was too cold, too wet out there. With him she would never feel hungry again. He was not as handsome as Peter or even her dead Avram, but he was a man. He would give her children—and the Rock was still there within reach.

In the big house everyone slept for a couple of hours in the middle of the afternoon. She awoke to a scream. "Up, up! To arms!" She scrambled up, rubbing her eyes. A trumpet began to call. She ran through the villa to the front door. A ragged mob of barbarians was sweeping up from the river, shrieking, screaming, waving spears and clubs. Ahead of them, in the center, pranced the Lover of God, a flaming brand of wood in his hand. She heard his strangely accented Latin above the din. "Kill, kill!" Rachel ran to the barn.

The Flavian men-at-arms and the male refugees from Carteia hurried together out of house and stable and granary, short swords drawn, buckling on light armor, helmets awry; but more barbarians came from the river, and they were not such a rabble as they seemed, for groups of them wheeled in blocks, one such taking Vitellius' servants in the flank with a mighty shout.

Yakov's widow had vanished with the twins. Rachel picked up Isa, grabbed her short knife in the other hand, and went back to the door. More barbarians were coming down through the olive groves, and the women who had fled that way ran straight into them. She saw a sword rise. Yakov's widow fell, cut almost in two. Peter's mother and sister went down under clubs, and a man with a wolf's-head hood picked up the baby twins and swung them by the heels against an old olive tree.

Now they were coming from the big house toward the barn, the Lover of God in the van. Her father and the young men were trying to hold them. Her father drew back his spear arm, and a tall barbarian stepped in under the throw and rammed a knife under his ribs, so that he jerked, coughed, and fell. Peter killed one barbarian and stepped back quickly, his sword flickering out again. At his side his brother Young James died, felled by a spear thrust in the knee and then clubbed on the ground. Akiba the Jew and Peter the Christian fell back slowly, side by side. Rachel waited, her knife ready.

Now, with no apparent reason, the blocks of barbarians began to eddy and break up. Some ran this way and some that, until the actual attackers here were reduced to eight men, led by one as tall as Peter but older and stronger, with reddish hair. His face was wide, square, and flat, his eyes pale gray. This man rested his heavy sword and called in a guttural Latin, "Hold, Romans! No need to die. We want slaves."

Rachel saw Peter's back muscles tighten up and called out quickly, "No, Peter!" And then, in the tongue of Hispania, she added, "Tomorrow is another day. Put up your swords." To the barbarian leader she said, "We have nothing. We are in flight here ourselves from Carteia. The outlaws took all that we had a week ago."

"All? Priest say all man's rich here," the leader spoke, glowering.

"He is wrong. There was plenty in the big house, nowhere else."

The barbarian followed her eye. A group was dragging Vitellius' body out of the front door of the great villa. Another half dozen ran by, hurling the head of young Gaius from hand to hand in a boisterous game.

The barbarian slipped his sword back into its hanger and pushed past Akiba and Peter as though they did not exist. To his men he threw a dozen words over his shoulder, and they hurried off toward the big house. He said, "I am Wildigern, Visigoth. You are surprised I talk Latin?" He glowered down at her, "I live near Romans all my life. Romans . . . *poof*." He blew into the air. "I kill many. Come." He laughed and led the way to the barn. Rachel went with him, little Isa holding tight to her hand, and Akiba and Peter followed doubtfully behind. The barbarians were strange, she thought: all the killing seemed no more than a passing storm, and now the sun was out and all was forgotten. This Wildigern was quite without fear, going alone now into the darkened empty barn with Peter and Akiba, armed, at his heels, their kin lying slaughtered under the olives.

Wildigern looked about. "Rich. Rich land. Farmers?" She nodded. "Your land, where?"

She pointed over the arm of the cork woods that separated the Villa Flaviana from Carteia. Wildigern gazed. "H'm . . . by the white mountain. What call?"

"Calpe," she said. "The Rock."

Wildigern made up his mind. "This place here"—he waved to the great estate—"this for our leader Wallia. For me—your house, land, all. You cook, make babies for me. You"—he jerked his chin at the two young men—"you work fields, teach me. Together we fight Vandals, kill outlaws. Together—eat, drink! . . . Come."

He strode out of the door and raised his voice in a great bellow. His eight men tumbled out of the villa, staggering under loot. Four Roman servant girls and a couple of wounded men-at-arms followed, also heavily loaded.

Peter muttered, "If he touches you, Rachel, I shall kill him. I love you. I learned that while you were away from us in the big house."

She said, "See that plenty of wine and brandy are brought to Carteia from the cellars."

"But . . ."

"I can't talk now. Or think. Later."

Theophilus, the Lover of God, was seated cross-legged outside the gate of the villa, his eyes closed, his hair and beard splashed with blood. His begging bowl lay beside him, and as they passed, the Visigoths threw rings and coins and gold ornaments into it with a curious defensive gesture, as though they feared the fanatic might turn them to stone. She thought, they might call themselves Christians, but it was the gods of their forests and magic and madness that they really feared. She made sure her knife was in her waistband and followed the others into the cork forest.

Two hours after dark the Visigoths lay dead drunk all over the house—upstairs, on the roof, and sprawled in the goats' droppings below. The captive Roman men-at-arms, all Spanish-born, had fallen into the service of the new masters as easily as the old. After the first flagon of wine the servant girls had abandoned themselves to the barbarians' lust with no shame or hesitation, so that there had been a singing and coupling and grunting all evening. Once Wildigern dragged Rachel to him, but she held him off, smiling, fearful for Peter's life, for he was close by, white and shaking. Later another Visigoth tried to rape her, and Wildigern cracked his skull with such a blow from the butt of his sword that the man lay unconscious for an hour.

Now it was quiet save for the snores and drunken mumbles of the sleepers. She went to a dark corner of the first floor, near the head of the ladder to the street, and Peter and Akiba came to her. Peter said, "We must go—now. But where? To the outlaws?"

"No," she said automatically. If they went to the outlaws, Peter would not live long; for Julius the Pagan wanted her, and he would not tolerate a rival. But more important than that, the outlaws promised no home, no children, no peace, only the opposite—a return to the way of the hunter, a descent from house to cave, from tilling fields to gathering nuts . . . and surely, soon, back to holes in the ground.

"Where, then?" Peter said. "Hispalis? Corduba? But the barbarians must have taken and ruined those cities on their way here."

Akiba said, "I know! . . . We will go to Africa. I know where there is a boat hidden in a sea cave of the Rock. It belonged to Simon the merchant, and he used it to smuggle salt. No one else knows. I . . . I helped him sometimes."

Rachel did not hesitate. Perhaps they would go to Africa; perhaps they would not; perhaps she could stay here—for Wildigern was no worse than many other men, only less subtle in his cruelties, and as her mother had told her often enough, *"What is born of a Jewish womb is a Jew"*: But the plight of the young men tugged at her heart, so she said, "Very well. Think now what we will need. Pots. Water vessel. Tinder. Knife . . ."

They passed over the isthmus onto the Rock before the middle hour, with Akiba ahead carrying Isa, and Peter behind, and all heavily loaded. By the goat track along the lower western slopes a pack of wolves bayed around and tried to attack Akiba but fled before Peter's sword. From the Lover of God's gully they crossed to the east side, going close by Rachel's Secret, and then turned north, as though to continue the circuit of the Rock. Here Akiba led slowly down the steep slope, Isa asleep on his right hip. After a careful, almost vertical descent, they stood on a tiny sandy beach. Starlight gleamed on wet rocks, and small waves regularly washed their feet. "It's up there," Akiba muttered, "pulled up into the cave."

He gave Isa into her arms and disappeared into the gloom of the overhanging cliff. He was gone a long time, and then suddenly he was back. "It's broken," he said. "Two planks smashed and the oars gone." His voice cracked.

Peter said, "That storm a week ago must have sent the sea up to it. We're lucky it was not swept away altogether, like the oars. Let us see it. Perhaps we can repair it."

She followed them up the sand slope. She thought that the boat, which she could feel but barely see until her eyes became used to the darkness, would be very small for the three of them and Isa. The holes were not large. A pair of smooth short planks, well nailed down over felt or canvas and caulked with pitch, would make the boat watertight again.

They stood some time in the end of the rock cave around the boat, not speaking. Then Peter said, "We must have oars. . . ."

She said quickly, "They might be in this little cove somewhere. We can look by daylight." She knew what Peter was going to say next, and he must be stopped. Two or three hours of the night remained, Isa slept, and Akiba was very tired. Tonight, as soon as Akiba slept, Peter would come to her. There might never be a tomorrow.

Peter said, "Perhaps . . . But we must have planks, nails, canvas or, better still, thick wool, pitch. . . ."

"Get it tomorrow night," she began.

She saw the decisive shake of his head. "Now no one knows we have left Carteia. I can find what we need and be back here before dawn. Tomorrow there may be a hunt up for us. Tomorrow they will not be drunk. There will be sentries, guards. No, Rachel, I must go now." He took her quickly in his arms and kissed her. "Stay hidden. Look after them, Akiba."

She did not weep until the same hour the next night, when he had not come. Then she sat by the boat, folded her arms on her knees, and wept. Akiba muttered, "Perhaps he was seen and driven inland. . . ."

She had hoped that, too. That was why she had waited until this later hour to weep. Now she knew he would never come back.

Akiba said, "I'll go tomorrow night if he doesn't come. We only need to mend the hole." She nodded, for they had found both oars as soon as they began to look around the cove by daylight.

They lay down, but Rachel's eyes never closed. In seven days she had lost three men who had wanted to put their seed in her that children might grow in her womb. She had fled from the Rock and returned. Now what? Who could tell her what she must do?

At once she knew; and as soon as Akiba slept she climbed the cliff, went to the thicket, and for half an hour knelt in total darkness in her Secret, holding the ivory figurine between her breasts. Then, her questions answered, she returned and fell asleep.

Next night Akiba left the cave at dusk. Rachel waited till he had gone, then began to gather the collected driftwood close around the fire and cut herbs into the pot with salt and water. She sliced some of the tender lamb they had stolen from Wildigern, and he from the Villa Flaviana. She kept Isa awake running about and playing with some bronze baubles she had found. When his eyelids drooped, she gave him wine from the flagon, laid him down carefully in the high back of the cave, and covered him with Peter's cloak, which he had left behind.

Akiba returned early, put down his burden, and sat by the fire. His face was taut. "I knew where Simon kept his materials," he said. Then, suddenly, "They have flayed Peter and nailed his skin to the house where Theophilus sits." He shuddered and buried his head in his knees.

She stroked his hair. "Think not of it, Akiba. It is all done. All gone. Except us."

Akiba was seventeen and healthy. He sniffed the air. "That is a savory stew, sister. But we must not waste food. It will take me two or three days to make all ready. Then we must await calm weather."

"There is enough," she said gaily. "Tonight we eat well and drink wine."

"How can you smile?" he said. "If you had seen him . . . Your eyes glitter like stars, Rachel. Have you taken wine?"

"Not yet. Here. Drink. Again. Forget. But say the blessing, that the Children of Israel may never die from the earth, for surely we are the last."

He spoke and drank. She watched to see that he took enough to wipe what he had seen from his mind, but not too much. Herself, she ate sparingly and kept the fire burning. As Akiba neared the end of his eating, she began to sing love songs, which the young men sang to the girls on summer nights by the sea. Akiba beat time with one hand, holding the wine flagon with the other. "I wish father were here with his lute," he said.

His eyes clouded, and Rachel jumped to her feet. "Remember last year's spring festival?" she cried. She danced now as the wild Turdetani of the Ronda hills did when they came down and danced at the festival. She bent her body back, clapped her hands, thrust out her breasts, and stamped her feet. She saw her brother's eyes on her swelling breasts, on her legs, visible under the thin linen. As she danced she raised her arms, slipped free of the dress, and let it slide down her body to the sand. Akiba licked his lips, and she danced closer to him. He pressed back against the wall of the cave. Little Isa lay asleep above, the firelight playing on his face and his fat, dirt-stained cheeks.

Rachel sank down by Akiba's side, took his arms, and whispered, "Come. Be a man to me!"

"Rachel!" he cried. "It is a sin, an abomination."

"We are the only Jews left in the world," she said. She put her hand to him and found him upthrust and hard, against his will.

"Sister, sister!"

She spread herself and pulled him down on top of her. As she grasped him with her legs he entered into her, for she was slippery to receive him. She cried out at a sudden pain and held him tight as his body began to move. In a moment it was he who held her, crushed her, rammed into her as though to bury her in the sand. Soon he lay still on her, moaning, "Oh Lord God, what have I done?"

She said, "You have preserved our race, even as we are *all* children of Lot and his daughters."

He said, "There must be other Jews left alive somewhere in the world."

"Why?" she said.

He got up and went out of the cave. She lay back, as though carefully guarding the seed that he had left in her.

On the evening of the seventh day since her brother had first lain with her, he came up from the little beach and said abruptly, "We are going. Tonight."

He was always constrained with her now, though he had made love to her every night since the first night and many times by day also. His phallus swelled and stiffened whenever he looked at her, and he took her with ever-growing lust and sureness, so that she too began to look forward to the act for itself . . . yet when it was done, he was withdrawn and hostile.

He had made the boat ready by the third day. She had forced him to stay four more. Her period would not come for another seven, but she could hold him no longer. The old women said that if a woman's husband came to her in the middle of the month, she was the more likely to conceive. She had done her best.

Now she said, "I am not going. I will keep Isa. Go alone, if you must."

Again his voice cracked, "Not coming?"

She said, "The boat is very small, Akiba. When you tested it, the water dashed in even from the little waves here. I do not think it can reach Africa. Stay here, brother. It is our home. Under the shadow of this Rock."

"What?" he said violently. "As a slave of the Visigoths, who murdered our father? As a louse-ridden outlaw? No, I go to Africa. . . . I go," he repeated almost happily. She saw what she had not expected, that he wanted to get away from her. "And you to Julius the outlaw, I suppose?"

Rachel nodded. There was no purpose in explaining. She watched Akiba put some hard bread into his scrip and drape a blanket on his shoulders. Turning, he pulled her to him, his face blind with the familiar lust. Her loins ached for him, but she said softly, "It is enough, brother. I am sure I am with child."

The desire dissipated slowly from his face. He went to kiss the sleeping Isa, then held her hand and for the first time since he had taken her maidenhead seemed unconstrained. "God be with you, sister. If I can ever come back, I shall, to look for you."

He ran down the slope, and in a moment the little boat set out, dimly seen in the twilight, Akiba rowing and the boat rising valiantly to the waves. She watched until the darkness hid them.

The next morning, when the sun was yet low, Rachel came to the main gate of Carteia, carrying Isa in her arms. A sentry of the Visigoths, lounging against the wall, waved her in before she could speak: No one feared a woman with a child. On the way to her father's house she passed the Lover of God, squatting against a wall, dozing. Peter's skin and mask were pegged out on the wall behind him.

She went into the house and found Wildigern on the roof. His face registered astonishment, pleasure, anger. He seized her arm and shook her. "You . . . where you go? I kill you!"

She said, "The men forced me."

His grip softened. "That one, the dead one, your man? Lover of God saw him, gave alarm. My men made double eagle of him. I said no, but Lover of God said yes. . . . Where is other man?" he asked, again suspicious.

"My brother? Gone to Africa."

"And you . . . why not you go with?"

Perhaps these barbarians would stay, perhaps they would move on. Other barbarians might come. But the Rock would remain. She watched a pair of partridges, like those she had seen mating, burst up out of the scrub and fly toward the gray cliffs. Her goats would graze there. Her son would explore the Great Cave high on the west face, which was bigger than the Christian basilica in Carteia. Her daughter, when her first blood of woman came, she would take into the Secret and to her give the ivory woman, the other, eternal Her.

She raised her chin. "I have come back to bear your children . . . if I am allowed."

"Allowed? Who not allow?" He frowned. "I am Wildigern. This Carteia mine, under Wallia."

She said, "The Lover of God will have me killed because I am a Jew. You will not be able to save me. You could not save Peter."

"No, no," Wildigern said. "He do nothing. He priest. I lord."

Rachel put her hand to her waist and slowly drew the short knife. She held it under her rib cage on the left side, pointing in.

She said, "Wildigern, I want the Lover of God's head here, now. I will not belong to a man afraid of a priest."

Wildigern stared at her with the same fearful wonder that she had seen several times in Akiba's face. Then he seized his great two-handed sword and ran down the ladder.

Book Five

∞∞∞∞∞∞∞∞∞∞∞∞∞∞∞∞∞∞∞∞∞∞∞∞∞∞∞

Visigothic Kingdom

The Jewish years 4178–4471
AUC 1170–1464
A.D. 417–711

RACHEL may not have been allowed a long domesticity with Wildigern, for the following year the Visigoths were summoned by their nominal masters in Rome to leave Spain and settle in Gaul around Toulouse. Although they were winning their fight against the Vandals, they obeyed and marched north. (Perhaps Wildigern deserted to live with Rachel under the shadow of the Rock.)

The Vandals stayed in southern Spain only long enough to give it the name by which it has ever since been known—Vandalusia. Then, in 429, they succeeded in doing what the Visigoths had failed to: they took ship and crossed to North Africa, where they stayed. The Celtiberian-Romans regained possession of Spain—rather, they shared it with the outlaws and the other barbarians—until 507. In that year the Frankish king Clovis attacked the Visigoths, killed their leader, and expelled them from Gaul. They recrossed the Pyrenees and set up the Visigothic kingdom, which soon held rule over all the Iberian peninsula. (A century later one of their princesses went back north to become a Frankish queen and quite famous in song and story: her name was Brunhilde.)

Gibraltar remained uninhabited. Carteia's ruin became com-

plete. Over the bay, as over all of Europe, darkness descended. . . . Yet the Visigoths were not "barbarous" in the modern sense. They were more dangerous than that, both to the
world and to themselves. They were savages, advanced and
retarded at the same time. They came to wear long cloaks, robes
of fine wool, and richly worked jewels—but they used neither
shoes nor stockings; and while the king's head rested in his mis-
tress's lap, she hunted it for lice. Their laws were usually wiser
and more humane than the Roman laws they replaced—but they
could not prevent the election of their kings from degenerating
into anarchy. They had conquered by the sword—and neglected
either to keep it sharp or to replace it with some other form of

security (if any such existed in that time). At their core was a cult of personality rather than of organization—and then they failed to produce the personalities. Finally, they were disunited. They already distinguished between themselves and their Roman or Celtiberian fellow citizens; and in 589 King Reccared formally changed the "official" religion from Arian to Roman Christianity, which was, as we have seen, a much less tolerant form. From 617 on king and Church waged an ever more frenzied persecution against the Jews.

The state went downhill, not violently, except at the upper levels, and not rapidly, but steadily. For over a century Gibraltar was a dinghy tied to a ship whose sails were rotting, whose captain spent his time with wine, women, and worse, and whose multiracial crew of many faiths and of none, near starvation, had no incentive, no knowledge, and no share in the vessel's fate.

In the normal course of history such a situation worsens until it becomes intolerable; then there is a revolution, and a new leader takes hold—as Charles Martel was to do in Frankish Gaul, for instance. But the Visigoths were not to be given the chance to reshape their own history. Three thousand miles to the east, in Arabia, an obscure caravan conductor began to preach a new religion—that there was one God, Allah; and he, Mohammed, was the Prophet of Allah. In 622 the Prophet was driven from Mecca to Medina, and from this flight, *the year of the Hegira,* the Muslims soon dated their events, using a lunar calendar. Mohammed died in A.D. 632 (A.H. 11), but by then the new religion was well on the move, and every day the word of Mohammed's successors, the caliphs, Commanders of the Faithful, became law over new lands. Very early in the eighth century the Muslims reached Morocco. In Morocco, across the Strait from Gibraltar, lies Ceuta, the Roman Septa (for its situation on seven hills). The governor of Ceuta at this time was a man called Count Illan, Julian, or perhaps Olban. Some historians think he was holding Ceuta for the Byzantine Empire, which seems very unlikely; some, that he was a Christian—of Vandal descent, perhaps—who was holding it for his own people; and some, that he was governor on behalf of the Visigothic king Wittica in Spain. His problem, faced with the sudden arrival of the all-conquering Muslims, would not have been much different in any of the three cases, but it is more rewarding to assume the last theory to be the correct one, as upon it has been built a lovely fabric of myth, legend, and history, complete with heroes, villains, high life, sex, and debauchery.

In 709 one Roderick murdered Wittica and usurped the kingship of Spain. Wittica was dead, but many bitter supporters still lived, including two sons; a brother, Oppas, who was the powerful Archbishop of Seville; and a daughter, Faldrina . . . who was the wife of Count Illan. Their daughter, Florinda, was a maid of honor at Roderick's court.

Tales of the richness of the Spanish soil and of the dissensions of its rulers crossed the narrow strait and were eagerly heard by the caliph's ambitious and able governor of Africa, Musa-ibn-Nusayr. In 710 he sent a lieutenant, Tarif, over into Spain on a reconnaissance. Tarif landed at Traducta and marched inland. After an extended excursion he returned to Musa with the news that Spain was ripe—overripe, rotten. About the same time Florinda sent a message to her father, Count Illan; King Roderick had foully seduced her.

The scene is set for the first known incursion of Gibraltar, as actor rather than spectator, into history. The year is A.D. 711, the ninety-second since the Hegira. . . .

Brother Aethelred's Story

TRANSLATED FROM THE LATIN

In the name of the Father, the Son, and the Holy Ghost, Amen. Obeying the command of the Holy Abbot, I set down here all that befell me, Brother Aethelred of Glastonbury, on my journey from Isca to Rome in the year of Our Lord 711.

Early in that year the Holy Abbot summoned me, I being then in my twentieth year, and told me that the Bishop of Rome had bidden him send a young man to the city that he might study there for a period of years, and when he had learned all he could, return to Glastonbury. As I was somewhat more intelligent than an ox, the Abbot said, and there was no other young man, he would send me. I set forth at once in a Byzantine vessel, for Gaul was infested with outlaws.

At sea I suffered from a revulsion of my stomach, so that I became weak as a child, though I was strong and tall in those days, with a beard and tonsure of gold and blue eyes. (I write this not to boast, but that all may be made clear.) After many weeks the vessel came to a narrow place, and the master said these were the Pillars of Hercules. Our sail was set, and a strong wind behind blew us speedily on, bearing close to the northern pillar, when we struck a piece of floating wreckage which ripped a mighty hole in the bow. The master put up the tiller and steered for the point of the headland, but the wind pushed the bow round, a great following wave fell upon us and cast us over, and in a moment we were all in the sea. By the chance of spending my childhood swimming in the river when I should perhaps have been watching my father's swine, I was able to swim out from beneath the sail which threatened to smother me, but I was alone. I swam hard and crawled ashore near the point of the headland. Arrived with difficulty at the top of the cliff, I looked seaward and saw that the vessel was gone, borne to the bottom by the sea and the weight of her cargo. None but I had survived. I wandered and climbed about the rock, and it began to rain. As darkness fell I saw a huge cavern and hurried into it for shelter. It was a place wrought by God, full of marvels of shaped stone, but I was tired and soon fell asleep. Next day I saw a goat girl, who pointed out to me the path off that Rock and showed me where was the nearest castle and village, which she called Torrox. I walked near three hours to Torrox, passing first, on the bay, the ruins of a city such as we have in Wessex and the Holy Abbot says are the work of the pagan Romans. As I reached the gate of Torrox, a red-faced young nobleman in a white tunic with a gold and green mantle rode out, followed by servants. The nobleman reined in, frowning, and spoke sharply to me in his tongue. I told him in Latin who I was and what had befallen me. He answered in Latin, poor but easily to be understood, "God be praised, for my clerk has just been drowned. I am Count Anseric, with my brother lord of all this country. Until all my letters are written and answered, you shall be my clerk. . . . You are a well-formed man, Aethelred . . . and if I cannot persuade

you to stay, then I shall arrange your onward passage to Rome."
He smiled at me, spoke to a servant, and rode on.

The servant led me into the castle. Torrox was greater than
anything I had seen in Britain, though small compared to the
mighty works I later saw in Rome. It was of two stories, all of
stone, of which there is an abundance of all kinds in that land,
made in the form of a hollow square, with only one gate. The
roof was not of straw, as in Britain, but of tiles. Many servants,
men-at-arms, and women resided there, perhaps to the number
of two hundred souls. The village lay down river and contained
about fifty houses. The servant showed me to a small cell on the
second floor, facing southwest and furnished with a bench, table,
and pallet. Through the arrow slit I could see that great gray Pillar of Hercules which, though three leagues distant, seemed to
frown down directly upon all that country. The servant gave me
to eat and brought fine robes, which may have belonged to the
drowned clerk, then led me to the great hall and introduced me
to the nobleman dispensing justice there. I started, for this
Count Theodomir was the twin of Count Anseric—they were indeed twins, twenty-five years old, and at first glance I thought it
was Anseric returned; but this Theodomir was grave and calm,
his skin pure and his gaze straight, whereas Anseric's skin was
red and mottled, his eyes bloodshot and always moving, his lips
loose.

Count Theodomir's Latin was better than mine, and he welcomed me warmly. "I hear there is much correspondence to be
dealt with," I said.

"Yes," he said, adding somberly, "Though it is the Holy Spirit
we need from you, Brother Aethelred, more than we need your
learned pen. . . . Come to me at any time, ask what you will.
You will be heard."

"Or come to me," a woman's voice said behind me. "You will
be even better received. Unless you are of brother Anseric's
faith." Count Theodomir's face went cold and tight, and he said,
"My wife, the Lady Hildoara. This is Brother Aethelred, from
Wessex."

"A monk," she said, eyeing me as though I were an animal at
market, "but more of a man between the legs than you, I'll be
bound."

He snapped at her in their tongue and turned away. She

shouted rudely after him. I suspected that all was not well between them.

A month passed. I prepared and answered correspondence for Count Anseric, who was usually drunk but showed himself most generous toward me; for though I was but a penniless monk, he lavished small gifts upon me, embraced and kissed me, and stroked my beard in wonder at its fairness. Of Count Theodomir I saw little, for he was always out upon the king's business in that province. His wife, the Lady Hildoara, spent many hours each day closeted with servants, captains, knights, and passing travelers upon her Lord's business and once even sent for me. When I entered, she was lying naked on her couch, so I knew she had forgotten her summons and slipped out quietly to save her shame. For the rest, I passed two hours each day with the priest of the church, learning the Visigothic tongue. Of the language I learned something, of the state of the kingdom and country much more.

All Hispania was rent by fear and hatred. Many believed that King Roderic had murdered the previous king, Wittica, and some now planned to slay him in his turn. The mountains were full of outlaws, the roads of brigands. In Africa a new and terrible army of men called Moors, who denied Christ, had come from the east, wading in blood, and possessed themselves even of the Pillar of Hercules upon that side; and no man knew what they intended to do but each looked fearfully over his shoulder, for the strait between the two pillars is very narrow.

As if these perils were not enough, in every court and palace of the Visigoths flourished all manner of abomination. No vice was too obscure or too bestial, the priest told me, but that it was practiced by one and by many, not in secret and alone but together and in public. I asked the priest to describe these abominations to me, but he said I should ask Count Anseric and the Lady Hildoara; and yet, he said, our people—for he too was a Visigoth—have made good laws and can live close to God's will, if they wish.

At the castle the state of the kingdom was laid before me in little, as though in a picture—for Count Theodomir lived like a saint, and his brother Count Anseric, my master, like a swine.

On a day in the middle of April Count Theodomir left on a long journey to carry reports of the province to King Roderic,

who was in the farthest north. That night the castle was filled
with carousing and revelry. The next day Count Anseric sent for
me, and I thought perhaps I should speak to him of my wish to
continue my journey to Rome, for Torrox had begun to oppress
me, more heavily now that Count Theodomir would be absent
for many weeks.

But when I came to Count Anseric's chamber, he said, "We
make a sea voyage tonight. Bring parchment and pen. Tell no
one."

The count himself came to my cell soon after dark, and we
rode with two grooms to that ruined town on the bay below the
Pillar of Hercules which men called the Rock. There a vessel
waited, we went aboard, the sailors cast off, and the rowers settled to their oars. The moon was high, and the face of the Rock
shone very white on the left hand. Then Count Anseric said,
"We go to Septa. We will talk to Count Illan, the governor, and
others about helping our king make order here in Hispania.
What we agree, you write in Latin, we sign. You understand?"

My task was plain enough and very usual, for only we of the
Church can write, and until swords are drawn, our help is necessary for every act of policy. Many had spoken of this Count Illan
in Torrox. It was said that King Roderic had violated his daughter Florinda while the maid was at court; but the count had for-
given the king his sin and only taken his wife and daughter away
from the court that no more temptation might befall. So forgiving and Christian a nobleman I much looked forward to meeting.

God afflicted me with vomiting the rest of the journey across
the strait to Septa, which we reached in the last hour before
dawn. A man in a white cloak, which concealed his face, awaited
us on the shore, and led us quickly through the city to a great
villa set behind a high wall. A strange music, as of plucked lutes,
filled the air even at that hour, and I heard water tinkling. I was
shown to a large room full of cushions, where I soon fell asleep.

The man who aroused me wore a gray robe and a black cloth
wound many times around his head. He was dark of skin, but his
hair was the color of dull copper, and his eyes were blue. He was
near thirty years of age. He spoke to me in excellent Latin, calling me by my name, which much surprised me. He said, "I am

David ha-Cohen, secretary to the general Abd-al-Malik. We meet in the center chamber at noon."

He bowed and made to leave me, but I cried out, for a shrunken man, hairy and misshapen of face, ran in upon four legs from the garden, screeching and gibbering. David ha-Cohen laughed and said, "That is an ape. The owner of this palace keeps a dozen here, well fed." He waved his hand, and the beast ran out, chattering.

Then he left me, and young boys waited upon me with spiced food, and sweetmeats in silver dishes, and wine, and iced sherbet. When all was done, one boy stayed, an affectionate lad who curled up against me as a son or brother might and showed me a wound upon his thigh, but I saw no wound and gently bade him go and play at balls outside as I must prepare myself for the conference.

When I joined Count Anseric in the center chamber I saw that the boys had served him, too, for he was very red of face and sat down most heavily upon the cushions. In that place there were marble pillars, and many spread cushions, and a pool of clear water, and mosaic figures dancing under the water. Now came a tall, thin, gray man in a Visigothic tunic, like Count Anseric's but more splendid, and this was Count Illan himself. His eyes were deep-sunk and envenomed, his mouth wide and thin. He did not look at all forgiving.

We three Christians waited, not speaking, and suddenly a mighty blast of trumpets almost in our ears set us on our feet. The silk curtains shivered, and three Moors strode in, followed by David, the scribe. He in the center was a dark prince, with a forked beard and a cunning eye, dressed all in black, and he came on alone. Count Illan muttered, "It is Musa-ibn-Nusayr, governor of Africa for the caliph."

The governor spoke sharply, pushing his hand flat toward the floor. I dropped to my knees, for his meaning was clear, and Count Anseric with me. Count Illan hesitated, but at the governor's frown he too knelt. Then the governor smiled and embraced us all and introduced the other two Moors with him: Tarik, who was dark and wide and short and wore a green robe; and Abd-al-Malik, David's master, who was tall and young and fair and wore white and gold.

Musa spoke a few sentences, then turned upon his heel and left, all bowing again. David translated. "The governor of Africa bids you make speed with your talk as he must leave in the morning. Let no foolish splitting of hairs delay agreement."

The talking began. I had little to do, for David's Latin was better than mine, and beside Arabic he also spoke Visigothic. However, I listened diligently and learned that Count Illan and Count Anseric meant to invite an army of five thousand Moors to help King Roderic make peace in Hispania. The counts would have to pretend to fight against the Moors at first, it was agreed, though I did not understand why. And if, as some said, the king was the prisoner of Arian heretics and other evil forces, then his army must be attacked, and Count Illan would be regent until the king could be released. The wages of the Moors was soon agreed, this to be freedom to sack Asido and two other towns, together with ten thousand pieces of silver. This Tarik of the green robe was to be the general, with Abd-al-Malik under him. The counts swore to obey Tarik in all that pertained to waging war, and the Moors swore to return to Africa after they had been paid, whenever Count Illan asked them.

In Hispania the Moors would land in the shelter of that Rock where I was shipwrecked. For the journey across the narrow sea they had four big boats. Each boat held one hundred soldiers and should be able to cross the strait once coming and once going each day. So it should take two weeks to transport the army to Hispania if the weather remained fair.

When we ended our talking, it was arranged that we should return to Torrox that very night, bearing with us Count Illan and his family and also Abd-al-Malik, who would make arrangements on the very place for the arrival of the army.

Then the lords went away, and David and I worked together to prepare the agreement in four copies. When all was done, and we had read each aloud, that none might differ from another, we took the parchments to our masters, and our work was done.

I returned to my chamber and David with me. He lowered himself to the cushions, sitting cross-legged in a manner I never learned to follow, for it made my knees ache, also it is ill-suited to the damp floors of Wessex. David said we had some hours to pass, and since he had heard I did not care for other entertainment, we would do well to converse together. Time spent in acquiring knowledge is never wasted, he said. He asked me many questions about Torrox and about Count Theodomir—he seemed relieved when I told him I had seen the count leave with my own eyes—and about the Jews. When I said I had never met a Jew, he answered shortly, "You are talking to one. Did you expect us to have horns and a tail?"

I apologized for my ignorance, and he said, "Aethelred, I don't know why, but I like you. Listen to me. You are in danger. Now, slip out through yonder arch. Across the street there is a blue door. It is the synagogue. Enter there, cover your head, and pass the time in meditation until tomorrow, when I shall come for you. Count Anseric will think that you have run off with one of the boys. He will not worry, as long as you stay in Africa."

I said, "I do not understand."

David walked up and down several minutes. Then he spoke slowly to me. "Aethelred, only seven people know of the agreement just made: the governor, the two Muslim generals, the two counts, we two secretaries. Of those, we four Moors are obeying the command of our caliph. None of us stands in any danger should the agreement be revealed. Think you the same is true of the counts? Think you that their king, Roderic, knows of the agreement?"

I thought that David was trying to warn me, but though I was troubled, what could I do? I said, "Count Anseric sheltered me when I came in, near drowned, from the sea. I cannot desert him. As for the king, he is a prisoner of Arian heretics. The counts plan to free him from that thrall. It is so written."

David struck his clenched fists upon his temples and cried aloud in his own tongue and then said, "What must be, must be. . . . How do you like the Lady Hildoara? The scent of her doings carries across the straits even against the wind."

I told him of her summons to me and how I had saved her embarrassment, and he fell on the cushions and lay there a long time, struggling and gasping for breath. He rose at last, weeping, and said, "Farewell, Aethelred . . . farewell." He embraced me and in a moment was gone.

The rowers thrust our vessel from the shore after dark that night. Abd-al-Malik stood silent in the stern, wrapped in a cloak. Count Anseric fell asleep at the mast. Count Illan's lady sat in the waist of the vessel, her arm around their daughter, Florinda, she whom the king was said to have defiled. The wind blew hot from Africa, and clouds hid stars and moon. Faint light seemed to come from under the water.

I heard a tread behind me on the creaking deck and turned to see Count Illan. He peered at me and said, "Ah, it is the Saxon. . . ." He seemed then to speak to himself, as though forgetting that I was at his side. "What do they know, who have never left Europe? *I* have been to Damascus. I have spoken to the Caliph Walid. It is three thousand miles to Damascus, and all the way the banner of Islam waves over city and village, field and forest, desert and shore. And beyond Damascus, three thousand miles more. And all this in ninety years, since their Prophet launched them upon the world."

"A mighty people," I said wonderingly. "And of a surety, if anyone can restore King Roderic to the peaceful possession of his throne and his rights, they can."

The count muttered a prayer and left me. At dawn we landed by the ruined town and went at once to Torrox. Count Anseric announced a great feast, and all day the castle and village bustled with preparations. By the fourth hour after noon all was ready. Soon after, the feast began.

It was as though I slid from the top of a mountain, where it was cool and clear, ever faster down a slope, the air growing thicker, the light more lurid. At first musicians played, men and women bowed and spoke politely one to another and ate daintily. Soon the platters of lamb and fowl and boar, of fish and mussel and oyster, passed more quickly, and more quickly emptied the wine flagons. From music it passed to singing, and from that to shouting. The Lady Hildoara's robe was but ill-fastened, so that unknowingly she displayed her breasts to the Moor, Abd-al-Malik. All around, men began to fondle women. By the time darkness came, scores of the Visigoths were lying on the floor in their own vomit. Others pulled servant wenches to their laps, threw up their skirts, and shamelessly stroked and entered upon their privy parts like rutting animals. Count Anseric, Lady Hildoara, and Abd-al-Malik were not to be seen, and soon I left, too, for the sights of that place were an abomination. But in the courtyard I stumbled upon Count Anseric engaged in vile concourse with a stable boy. Running in horror away from them toward my cell, I opened a wrong door by mistake and found Abd-al-Malik and Lady Hildoara, naked, watching a great wolf-hound that was mounted upon a servant girl.

I ran out then, blind with terror, past the sentries, out of the courtyard, into the village, for God must surely be preparing his lightning against such people. A man stepped out of a dark door-way in front of me and held my arm. "It is the Saxon," he said. "God be praised!"

I stared. "Lord Theodomir! The Lord be praised, indeed! What I have seen . . ."

"I know," he said abruptly. "Their punishment will come. But you have been on a journey. I must know what passed. For the sake of our country, for our very Faith, Aethelred . . . tell me!"

I collected my wits. "You must ask your brother, Count Anseric," I said humbly. "I am sworn to secrecy."

"They will kill me, fool!" he snapped. "Why do you think I creep around dark alleys under my own castle walls? In the name of our Saviour, tell me."

My heart was ready to burst, for Count Theodomir was a saint among men. But I was his brother's servant. I could not break faith. I wrenched free, and before he could recover from his sur-prise, I was gone.

I ran out of the village, ran across moonlit fields, I knew not where. Then a white light shone in the sky, and I ran toward that, believing it was a sign from Christ, until, coming at last close to it, I saw it was the Rock. Then I slowed to a walk, and the sand under my feet changed to sharp stones, and the moon hid itself. Careless of what might befall, I crawled under a great rock and curled up, shivering like a fevered animal. Sick and sore afraid I was, for in my marrow I felt the coming wrath of God. Ever more bright in the night I saw God, towering in al-mighty anger in the clouds, brightness about Him, to destroy this world and all of us upon it. Then I prayed, gabbling words without sense, until at last, being very tired, I seemed to see a woman, long-haired and naked but with no lewdness, who cried for help; but I could not help her, and after a while she left me, or I fell asleep, I know not which.

I awoke in the morning, feeling very weak. I began to think what I should do, for now I wanted nothing but to escape and go on to Rome. But before long Abd-al-Malik rode up with two Visigothic captains. I remained hidden until at the hour of noon I saw, half a league distant, four ships coming toward the land. I watched them without thinking what they might portend. Then I saw that each was crowded with men, and I saw the flash of spears, and horses I saw and knew that these were the four ships of the Moors. It was a bright morning, the cloud gone from the Rock and the wind fresh and clean from the ocean beyond the pillars. Green banners covered in strange writing floated from the mastheads. I held my breath, for these were they who had come thousands of miles across deserts and rivers, all-conquering. Now they were treading the sea and would set foot in Europe here under the great Rock. Where would they stop?

I saw David ha-Cohen in the third vessel, and he seemed then the only true friend I had in the world. Heedless of all else, I jumped up and ran along the shore to meet the boats where they would come to land.

I was close as the bows ran up the sand. I saw General Tarik jump down and wade toward Abd-al-Malik, and behind him many soldiers splashed ashore, some with those strange apes on their shoulders, and then the horses were whipped so that they jumped into the sea and came with their teeth bared to the shore. As David came up the beach, a big leathern satchel over one shoulder and a sword slung by a baldric from the other, a dozen black Moors ran upon me, curved swords flashing, and I fainted.

I awoke cold and wet. David was casting sea water upon me. He cried, "I never thought to see *you* again, Aethelred! Was it luck, or are you not so innocent as you pretend?"

The vessels were still unloading men and baggage. General Tarik, at the head of a score of horsemen, had just set off along the sand toward Torrox. The other Moors, mostly foot soldiers, had begun to carry stones, under Abd-al-Malik's direction, to make a wall.

I said, unhappily, "I want to go to Rome."

David said, "That is impossible, I fear, until what will come to pass here has come. You must stay with me. I have told my master that you surrendered to my mercy. You are therefore my slave, which puts my protection over you, for what it is worth. . . . Come, let us put up a shelter. We may be living many weeks on this Rock."

I knew nothing of war and listened with amazement, while we worked, as David explained to me the meaning of what I saw going on under my eyes but, to my ignorance, without purpose.

It was Abd-al-Malik's task to make a corner of this Rock where vessels could unload, secure against attack, so that the army coming from Africa could land whatever the Visigoths did, either the counts or King Roderic. The counts were supposed to pretend a resistance and then flee. General Tarik had gone to see that they kept their word.

The coming of the Moors was, therefore, simple treason by Count Illan, helped by Count Anseric, to make himself king in Roderic's place. I wondered if Count Theodomir had been able to learn anything of this and if he had escaped to carry the word to the betrayed King Roderic. Yet Roderic had murdered Wittica and defiled the lady Florinda. The thought that they all pretended to share my Holy Faith shamed me.

So that evening, being the slave of David the Jew, who was servant to Abd-al-Malik the Infidel, I slept under a tent on the ground and drank fresh water and ate a fruit the Moors had brought, called "dates," and felt almost that I was cleansed from the sins of the Visigoths.

The days passed. Numerous citizens, many of them Jews, came from far and near to offer their thanks and help and to beg the Moors to advance with all speed. Abd-al-Malik's soldiers built their stone walls higher and dug a well and made a rough stone jetty into the bay. The vessels traveled back and forth from Africa, and now nearly all the soldiers who landed marched at once to join the general in Torrox. I went with him, as a slave, and saw his falcons strike down many of those red-legged partridges which abound on the Rock. At night we ate of the partridge, and they were very tender, but each time I saw one between Abd-al-Malik's fierce, bearded lips, I thought it was a little Christian.

After a month, I asked David why the Moors did not now march out upon the Visigoths, since all was ready. He said, "King Roderic is in the Pyrenees. Think you we are going to march all that way and fight six hundred miles from our boats? No, no, the king shall ride six hundred miles to us. The governor of Africa has promised to send us more men. When we fight, it will not be far from here."

Another month passed. As I had learned a few words of Visigothic before, now I learned a little Arabic, and, without meaning to, found myself laughing as they did, with a high-pitched loud sound, and David taught me to greet them properly, saying, *"Ia ilaha ill Allah, Muhammadur rasul Allah!"* which pleased them mightily. And David told me that though the Moors were strong, yet might the Christians win the day, for the Moors had a most fatal weakness. It was their feuds, he said, which they took everywhere with them and cherished above women, above gold. The governor of Africa, Musa, was of one party, Abd-al-Malik of another, and only common allegiance to the caliph made them speak to each other. But Musa and Abd-al-Malik were Arabs while Tarik was a Berber from this western Africa—and they despised each other. All this and much more David ha-Cohen explained to me while we walked and climbed together all over that great Rock, and discovered many caves, and came upon dens of wild pig and lynx, and saw wolves, and found a big fallen stone, marked by the hand of man but far from the shore.

At last word came that King Roderic had passed Hispalis with a host of 90,000 men. The trumpets sounded, and the army gathered by the ruined city, being now 12,000 men. I rode out by David's side, I on a small gray donkey and he on a fierce horse with wide nostrils and turned-up nose and long tail and red eyes. As we rode round the bay upon the traces of an ancient road, such as we have in Wessex and the Holy Abbot says were made by the Romans, I looked back at the silver Rock shining in the sun and wondered if I would ever see it again.

The banners over us were green and black and covered by that strange writing. Five times a day every man of the host, from the generals to the trumpeters, knelt down and prayed toward the east, striking their heads on the earth. Such devoutness I have never seen among Christians, saving a very few holy monks. But I was Christian, and we went to fight a Christian king, however deep in sin his people had fallen, and I was sore troubled in spirit.

We marched six days by forest and mountain and along the ocean shore. We marched among great trees whereof the bark may be cut off and is indeed that cork used for shoe soles. The boughs cast a pleasant shade, and bards of the host sang wild songs. At camp and on the march spies came to tell General Tarik of the Christians' movements and of fords and water and hidden food. In a thunderstorm of lightning and rain we came to a ridge, with a great marsh full of wild duck and wading birds to the right and to the left a wide, fast-flowing river which curved out of the marsh, passed round the ridge, and flowed by more marshland to the sea. Here General Tarik planted his standard, saying, "Here we conquer." To engage us King Roderic must pass the river, and the narrow ridge between the great marsh and the river would prevent him extending his host, much greater than ours, past our wings. And, as David muttered to me that first night, that place was as far as it was prudent for the Moors to go from the Rock, and their boats in shelter under it, until they had defeated King Roderic.

It was a purgatory to wait and hear every hour of the advance of King Roderic's host, and I dared not pray for fear the Moors would kill me. Nor did I know what I should pray for. On the second day in that place, which was the sixteenth day of July, the army of the Visigoths came down to the river from the north and began to cross. The Moorish horsemen rode out in readiness, but the Christians made camp and set up their standards. "Tomorrow will be the battle," David said, "and victory will be ours. A spy has just brought word that Count Illan commands the right wing of the Christians and Archbishop Oppas the left. They are both sworn to us."

While the soldiers began to whet their sword blades, I walked away down the river, oppressed by my thoughts. I came after a time to the beach, where the river flowed into the ocean hard by a sandy cape, with a hill behind. I lay down and slept, and dreams came, for I saw the sand covered with dead men and others rolling in the waves. I awoke with a cry, hearing my name called.

I got up and saw Count Theodomir across the river. "Aethelred," he said, "my brother Anseric is dead, choked in gluttony. You owe him nothing more. Come over the river, join us, and tell us all you know. Otherwise, I fear for the Cross in Hispania—aye, in all Europe, the world."

I went to the river and walked a little way in. Then I remembered that I was David's slave and he had saved my life. I stepped back.

"Aethelred . . . we are *Christians!*" Theodomir called.

Again I went into the water, a little farther this time. The current tugged at my legs to overthrow me, and suddenly I knew I could not go. I struggled back to the shore and hurried to the camp and the tent I shared with David. I did not speak but lay shivering on the ground, my eyes closed.

The next morning the trumpets sounded early, and I rode out at David's side, and the army took its stand on the ridge between the marsh which is called Janda and the river, and the Christians came against us. Behind the center of their host I saw a domed litter drawn by white donkeys, gold and silver glittering in the sun, and David said that was the litter of King Roderic. Then the battle began.

For a time I sat upon my donkey held in thrall by the spectacle before me—so many thousands of warriors under the bright sun upon the grass beside the marsh—the army of the infidels silent under the green banners, steel casques on their heads, their horses light-footed and flecked with nervous foam; the army of the Visigoths under banners of boars and lions and eagles and here and there a Cross. Their horses were mighty and strode ponderously upon us, and their leaders wore long floating hair and carried two-handed swords and wore horns or wolf masks upon their helmets, like to the sea raiders who pillage our shores of Wessex. As the armies met, I saw that on the right the Visigoths stopped many paces short of the Moors and rested upon their swords, and to the left the same. Only in the center did King Roderic's host fall upon us. It was all I could do to keep out of the warring, for great horses reared over me and swords whistled, with a mighty shouting upon the summer air. I saw David smite a bishop so that his arm flew free of his shoulder, then a blow from behind knocked me off my ass, but David helped me again to the donkey's back, shouting, "Not yet, Aethelred, such as you are immortal!"

Then the commanders of our right wing and our left wing, seeing that Count Illan and the Archbishop stood idle before them, swept round like the horns of a crescent moon and fell upon King Roderic from left and right and behind. His men became affrighted and fled, like an army of mice set upon by cats, and I saw many horses galloping away riderless, and the domed litter of King Roderic was abandoned upon the field, but none saw the king.

Then the soldiers of General Tarik again gathered together and fell upon Count Illan's host. The count rode toward us, his hand raised, but the Moors flew by him like greyhounds unleashed, and in a moment a wailing arose in his host as the Moors rent them, and soon they too broke and fled. On the other side Archbishop Oppas' men did not wait but turned and ran, only the Archbishop coming forward to make obeisance before Tarik.

The battle was over, though for several hours more the Moors cut and hacked at the Christians as they tried to recross the river, until the ground and the bank squelched with blood and the water ran deep, dark red into the lower marsh on its way to the sea. Then Tarik's trumpets sounded a halt, and the Moors gathered their prisoners—to the number of 20,000, David said—and at the same time lit fires, set up spits, stripped a score of Christian corpses of their clothes, and set them to roast over the fires. The dusk was falling, and never have I heard, since, or hope to hear, such a wail of fear and horror as arose from the massed prisoners. Tarik gave an order then, and the prisoners were marched away.

I turned, blind, to run. I had betrayed Christ for this! David's arm stopped me with a jerk. "It is only to spread terror," he said. "When the prisoners are out of sight, the bodies will be decently buried." Then Tarik called, and David hurried to him, I following more slowly. Count Illan and the Archbishop were there, and Tarik had just finished speaking. David translated: "King Roderic is dead—or fled. I take possession of all this land in the name of the Commander of the Faithful, the Caliph Walid."

He stooped, gathered a handful of dust, and threw it in the air. Every Moor's sword flashed, and a great shout arose, beginning with those close by who had heard what the general said, and spreading as ripples on a pond so that there was still a distant shouting when David said, "'Thank the general's magnanimity for your life. Then go. He has no further use for you."

Count Illan walked away, like a man dreaming, and disappeared in the dark, blood-soaked field. To the Archbishop, David said, "Bring hither all those of quality who have surrendered, and all the women and baggage of the Visigoths. The general will give you his commands tomorrow."

Gradually the space about the general's tent cleared. I had seen the wrath of God, and I still lived. Now I longed, I prayed, only for . . .

David ha-Cohen was beside me. "My master, Abd-al-Malik, has been appointed Lord of Torrox and Guardian of the Rock," he said. "I am to be his chief minister. Stay with me. Be my friend, my companion in work and play, for I have come to hold a great love for you, Aethelred—and not such a love as Count Anseric's!"

The words rushed from my mouth, from my heart. "I cannot stay, David. I am sick at heart, for I have seen more than my spirit can encompass. I must to Rome to learn the Word and take it back to Wessex."

"Back to the land of fog and bog," he said bitterly. "You are a bigger fool even than I believed, if that is possible." He walked away and around, then came back. "Take this." He pressed something hard into my hand, and I saw the glint of gold by the starlight. "Go now, down this valley to the sea, then follow the strand north to a little village of fishermen on an island called Gades. Ask there for Timothy Opadianus. He is of my faith. He will find you a vessel going to Rome. When you pass the Rock, think of me." He embraced me suddenly and cried, *"Shalom!"* and was gone.

It came about as he had said. A month later I passed the Rock at high noon on a stormy day. The cloud streaming from its crest seemed to be green, like the standards of the Moors, and to have the words of that faith hidden in it in their long, slender writing. I gazed at the Rock until darkness hid it.

After five years in Rome I returned to Glastonbury on foot and never saw David ha-Cohen, or the Rock, again.

Book Six

Caliphs, Emirs, and Kings

The Jewish years 4471–5222
AUC 1464–2215
A.D. 711–1462
A.H. 92–866

AFTER the great battle, without waiting for Governor Musa's authorization, Tarik swept on northward and was only halted by the arrival of the furiously jealous Musa, who publicly whipped him in Toledo. Musa then took up the pursuit and within a few years had conquered all of Spain except the mountainous Asturias in the extreme north. The Pyrenees did not stop the Muslims' victorious advance, and they were not finally turned back until 732, when the Frankish king Charles Martel defeated them outside Tours, in France. This was one of history's most important battles, for it decided whether Europe would become Muslim or remain Christian.

All the leaders of the invasion have their memorials. The Roman Traducta, in the gut of the strait, was now named Tarifa, after the man who had made the first reconnaissance in 710; and from the taxes levied there on goods from Africa came the word *tariff*. Abd-al-Malik, one of the few Arabs in the invading army (most were North Africans), was given the castle of Torasch or Torrox (since vanished; it was on the Guadiaro, about nine miles north of Gibraltar). The eighth in direct descent from him was Almanzor, the greatest ruler Muslim Spain ever knew.

The African Pillar of Hercules, known to the Romans as Mons Abyla, became Djebel Musa. The man himself paid the penalty of his success and of a certain folly in marrying his son to Egilona, the widow of the lecherous but now vanished King Roderic, and then appointing him governor of Andalusia. From

Damascus this looked as though Musa were setting up his own dynasty in Spain. The caliph recalled him, stripped him of his wealth and honors, and soon afterward, as a token of appreciation for all that he had done on behalf of his lord and his religion, sent him the head of his son.

In honor of Tarik, the leader who had actually taken the Rock, the old name of Calpe, though still known and used, was overshadowed by the new one of Tarik's Mountain, *Djebel Tarik*—Gibraltar.

Besides bringing their faith into Europe, the Muslims were also responsible for introducing the famous apes. These animals, Barbary apes, are in fact tailless monkeys, macaques (*Macaca sylvana, magus,* or *inuus*). They cannot be descendants of the monkeys whose fossil bones have been found all over Europe as far north as England, for they are of a quite different species. Nor can they have come from Africa by a secret tunnel (the geological faulting under the strait rules that out, even without the abstruse arguments of common sense). The Moors brought them, and the true oddity about them is that they have never spread into southern Spain but have remained confined to Gibraltar; also that though there are plenty still wild in North Africa, there are none in their original country of origin, Persia— where they have become extinct.

They are odd beasts, grayish brown, not very large, not very attractive. Their numbers have probably always fluctuated considerably. Throughout Moorish times they were strengthened by the infusion of fresh blood from Africa. Then after two centuries of neglect and inbreeding under the Spanish they found themselves pampered and superstitiously nurtured as the alleged symbols of British power on the Rock. But they are there, with the Gibraltar candytuft and the Barbary partridge, an exotic and irrational part of the Gibraltar background, stealing fruit, fouling rooftops, grabbing baubles from children's hands, watching the bustle below from their fastnesses on top of the Rock and at the head of the eastern cliffs (a place here has long been called the Monkeys' Alameda, or "garden walk").

For the rest, the story of Gibraltar during these years is part of the story of Spain and particularly of Andalusia. Spain remained subject to the Damascus caliphs until the Omayyad family was overthrown by the Abbasids. In 750 a refugee of the Omayyads, Abd-er-Rahman, grandson of the Caliph Hisham, arrived in Spain and declared that he, not the usurper in Baghdad, was the true Commander of the Faithful. Thus began the independent Caliphate of Córdoba, which lasted, in great magnificence, until 1031. Córdoba became the intellectual capital of Europe and one of the most civilized cities in the world. There was considerable religious tolerance, and many Jews reached prominence as scholars and statesmen. For these three centuries Gibraltar was either totally uninhabited or nearly so.

When the Córdoba caliphate collapsed, it first broke up into a number of independent emirates until in 1080 these vanished under a new invasion from North Africa by the fanatic Almoravides. The Almoravides lasted until 1145, when they in turn succumbed to the weakness of power and went under to the Almohades, also from Africa. All this time the Visigothic-Celtiberian-Romans (that is, the Christians), starting in the unconquered Asturias, were slowly working their way southward, reconquering, uniting, consolidating, so that each successive wave of Muslims ruled over a smaller piece of Spain. The Almohades lasted until July 16, 1212, when they were defeated in the climactic battle of the whole 700-year reconquest at Navas de Tolosa in the Guadalquivir Valley. King Alfonso VIII's victory was largely due to a shepherd, Martin Alhaja Gontran, who led the Christians by unknown tracks and unguarded paths to the attack. After the defeat the Muslims broke up into small kingdoms, of which the only one to affect Gibraltar was the Kingdom of Granada.

Although Tarik's invaders had landed at Gibraltar, it was at Algeciras and Tarifa that they made their first ports and fortresses. The provincial capital under the Visigoths had been Asido, and it remained so under the Moors, but now called Medina Sidonia. In spite of the remarkable incorporation of "Asido" in this name, the title comes from the fact that new Muslim immigrants were allotted to that part of Spain most like their homeland; the ones who came here were from Sidon, and the whole area was known as Filistin (Palestine). Gibraltar was dependent on Algeciras during all the early years.

Meanwhile, in 844 the Norsemen pass by in their longships, after having sacked Cádiz. . . . In 1003 a great battle is fought on the River Miel, by Algeciras, between rival claimants for Almansor's power (he had died the year before). . . . After the fall of the caliphate the Wali of Algeciras (Gibraltar's overlord) sets himself up as independent . . . but soon falls under the Emir of Málaga . . . who soon falls under the Emir of Seville.

This last, hard pressed by the warlike King Alfonso VI, asked the Almoravid king of Morocco to come over and help him. Many, including his own son, warned him that one needed a long spoon to sup with the Almoravides, but the emir made a famous answer: "I would rather be the King of Morocco's camel herd then a vassal of the Christian dogs." He had his wish, for King Yusuf came, seized Tarifa, Algeciras, and Gibraltar as bases for his invading armies, and soon ruled all Muslim Spain. The foolish emir died in 1088, a beggar in exile in a Saharan oasis.

The Almoravides persecuted Christians, Jews, and other Muslims alike, and large numbers of all religions, especially Jews, fled into Christian Spain. For a time in the thirteenth century it looked as though Spain might forge the first free or open society of modern times, and a Castilian king was proud to call himself King of the Three Faiths; but Navas de Tolosa so crushed the Muslim power that Christian bigots were able to say, "We need no help," and turn Spain upon the opposite and fatal course of "unification," that is, exclusion of all but the official race, religion, and way of thought. Laws forcing Jews to wear distinguishing yellow patches were approved in 1370 and 1405. In 1412 savage edicts were promulgated excluding Jews from many trades, defining what they must wear, and forbidding them to employ Christians; and worse. Anti-Semitism was encouraged, and in 1391 over 4,000 Jews were murdered in Seville alone.

When the Almohades came from Morocco to overthrow the Almoravides, they landed at Gibraltar, seizing it in 1146. The Almohade emperor, Abd-al-Mumin, was the real founder of Gibraltar as a city and fortress. He decided that the Christians were now so strong that neither Tarifa nor Algeciras could be relied on to stay out of their hands much longer. A third and final strongpoint was needed. Gibraltar was the obvious place, and he called in a famous mathematician and engineer to fortify it. This man was Al-Hajj Yaish, who built the great mosque of Seville, now part of the cathedral.

At Gibraltar the foundations were laid on May 19, 1160, and all essential work finished in six months, which is very fast work indeed. Abd-al-Mumin did not stay long but came back in November to see the completion of the building and then stayed two months listening to poets, holding council with the Muslim governors of Andalusia, and presumably dallying with houris in his harem, though it is hard to associate such gentle activities with the Rock.

It is also hard to disentangle Yaish's city from the one built after the Moors had lost and regained Gibraltar in 1333; but there was certainly a complex system of walls, keeps, and towers at the northwest corner of the Rock, dominated by a fortified qasabah and that by a Tower of Homage. Most of the town huddled under this, though there must have been a settlement far to the south at Europa, for there was a Muslim shrine near the Point, and close by there was—and still is—a remarkable underground reservoir, the roof supported by Moorish arches, later known as the Nuns' Well. Yaish also put in an aqueduct from the Red Sands to the town and probably designed the Moorish baths under the present Gibraltar Museum. The "Moorish Wall" which runs straight up the west face of the upper Rock is Yaish's, but the Moorish Castle is not. Yaish's Tower of Homage was destroyed in the siege of 1333 and the present one built by Abu 'l Hassan, "King of Gibraltar," in about 1340. The Spaniards called it "La Calahorra," and the British, the "Moorish Castle." The attribution of any works to the original Moorish invaders of 711 is an error due to misinterpretation of an inscription which was once over the gate of the qasabah.

Abd-al-Mumin's forethought in fortifying Gibraltar bore its first fruit when Navas de Tolosa ended the Almohade power fifty years later and they began to disengage from Spain. Tarifa did not fall until 1292, and the then King of Morocco took the opportunity to get out of Europe altogether by selling Algeciras (with Gibraltar) to the King of Granada.

There now steps into the story the founder of a remarkable family which became the most powerful grandees and the largest landowners in Spain. This man, Alonso Pérez de Guzmán, was a knight from León in the north, who so distinguished himself in the taking of Tarifa that the king made him *señor*, or squire, of Sanlúcar de Barrameda. Guzmán *el Bueno*, "the Good," as he was known, soon expanded his power and in 1309, partly from ambition and partly from genuine outrage that the Muslims still held parts of Spain, he attacked Gibraltar. He landed on the Red Sands, south of the wall that protected the town, and took up a position on the steep slope above the castle. There he erected catapults and war engines and started battering the defenses. Near the end of August the Moors surrendered. This was the first of Gibraltar's fifteen sieges and the first of its four major turnovers of population, for nearly all the Muslims left.

Now that Guzmán el Bueno held the Rock for King Ferdinand IV of Castile, the problem was to repopulate it and hold it. Being in the forefront of a never-ending war, and subject to raids, sieges, and attacks, it was not a desirable place of residence, and King Ferdinand had to take extraordinary measures to attract a population. He gave Gibraltar a charter which in effect made it a sanctuary for thieves, murderers, and runaway wives: all would be pardoned if they would just come and live in Gibraltar for a few months. Prisoners were also sent there from the jails and released to be free citizens. Gibraltar became, and must have resembled, a frontier fort town of the badlands, complete with loose women, ne'er-do-wells, remittance men, and, in place of the U.S. Cavalry, such knights and men-at-arms as Guzmán could find for its defense.

The Moors tried to regain the Rock in 1315 (Second Siege) but failed. In 1333 the King of Granada instituted the Third Siege. The governor of the fortress was then one Vasco Pérez de Meiras, a nobleman from Galicia in the northwest. Meiras had ambitions of founding a mighty family and had spent the funds allotted for the defense of Gibraltar in buying himself estates around Jerez, already rich and long since famous for its sherry wines. On June 17, after four and a half months of siege, in which Meiras' heroism somewhat redeemed his venality, Gibraltar fell once more. The Christian convicts, strumpets, and knights marched out, and the Muslims marched in, making the second population turnover. The King of Granada did not retain overlordship for long, as the Moroccans, whom he had called in to help during the siege, decided to keep it for themselves—but few of the Muslim people would have left on that account.

Alfonso XI was now King of Castile, and the recapture of the Rock became his obsession. Indeed, with this second loss of it to the Moors the place became, in Spain, not just a port and fortress, but a holy cause. Alfonso at once began the Fourth Siege and came very near to success but in the end had to march his army away, defeated. Seven years later he inflicted a crushing defeat on the Muslims at Salado, just west of Tarifa. In the aftermath he could easily have retaken Gibraltar, but an unaccountable lethargy overcame him, and he did nothing until it was too late. When he did begin operations once more, it was against Algeciras, a famous siege which began in August, 1342, lasted eighteen months, and brought down, as volunteers, the flower of Europe's chivalry, including King Edward III's grandson from England. During the siege the King of Morocco gathered 12,000 troops in Gibraltar to help drive away the Christians. Nevertheless Algeciras did at last fall, was later razed to the ground, and ceased to exist as a town for four centuries. Gibraltar was now the only port on the north side of the strait left in Muslim hands, and in 1349 Alfonso XI returned to the attack, in the Fifth Siege. His army soon began to suffer from the Black Death (bubonic or pneumonic plague) then ravaging Europe, and on March 26, 1350, the king died of it. The principal Moors went out from Gibraltar in mourning to pay their respects to their dead adversary.

At this time Gibraltar was visited by the famous Moroccan traveler Ibn Battutah. He went, he said, because he wanted to take part in the Holy War against the Christians. Of Gibraltar, then under the Moroccan king Abu Inan, he wrote: "I walked round the mountain and saw the marvelous works executed on it by our master [the previous king] and the armament with which he equipped it, together with the additions made thereto by our master Abu Inan, may God strengthen him, and I should have liked to remain as one of its defenders to the end of my days." But he did not stay: he visited Málaga and Granada and then returned to his home in Tangier, probably convinced that nothing could save the Muslim cause in Spain.

The rotations of Gibraltar from the hands of the kings of Granada to the kings or emperors of Morocco and back again make a dizzy story; but it is not important. The grip of any central Muslim authority was fast slackening; indeed, the man whom the Emperor of Morocco appointed wali, or governor, of Gibraltar in 1350 at once declared himself its king—this is the "king" Ibu Battutah refers to—and no one seems to have cared very much.

Apart from the Sixth Siege, a confused civil war between Granada and Morocco factions, Gibraltar relapsed into comparative quiet, and for eighty years the only other mention of it in the records is the visit of a Castilian admiral, who dropped in on his way to sweep Castilian pirates out of the western Mediterranean and was received with much courtesy and feasting, including plenty of *couscous*.

But if the kings were no longer very interested in Gibraltar, some private citizens were. The heirs of Guzmán el Bueno were now counts of Niebla and owned all the fishing rights from Gibraltar to the Portugal border, about 150 miles. Muslim raiders were poaching in the count's seas, attacking his pickling and salting plants and causing him loss of revenue. When pursued, the pirates took refuge in Gibraltar. For glory and profit, therefore, the count decided to retake the Rock. In August, 1436, he began the Seventh Siege by landing at the Red Sands, south of the town wall, with the intention of following time-honored precedents—advance up the hill, install engines of war above the castle, batter and starve the defenders into submission.

Alas, no one had noticed that in the years between, the dastardly Moors had extended the wall southward along the sea front. When the count's forces landed, they were still under it, with no way up, a murderous current strengthening, and the tide rising. . . . Many were killed and drowned in the debacle, including the count. The Moors recovered his corpse, put it in a box, and hung it over a gate of the castle. As a Spanish historian disdainfully remarked, the social level of the Moors in Gibraltar had sadly deteriorated since the days of their noble homage at the bier of Alfonso XI.

The Rock remained in Muslim hands. The defenses cannot have been strong or the population numerous, for the Kingdom of Granada had neither the will nor the means to make them so. Muslim pirates still raided Christian fisheries. The count's son, who soon afterward added the Dukedom of Medina Sidonia to the family's titles, looked hungrily at Gibraltar from across the bay. So did others, both noble and simple. It could not be long now before some small event, some man's single-handed action, precipitated the next conflict. . . .

A Jewel for the King

The captain of the *Gaditana* lashed down the tiller and looked at his owner. "Start unloading at once, Judah?" he said. Judah nodded, glancing at the sun; it was past noon, and they would have to make haste to be finished when the gate closed for the night. Well, they could finish tomorrow—the Moors were not very strict about Christian boats staying overnight these days.

He went forward to his two passengers and put an arm round

each, for they were also his friends, all three of an age—between twenty-five and thirty—and had grown up together in Tarifa. "There," he said, "*el Peñon*, the Rock."

At the end of the jetty the town wall began, pierced by the Water Gate. Behind, roofs and minarets, thickly jammed together, rose to the towers of the castle, aflutter with the green and black flags of the Kingdom of Granada. Above the castle the slope steepened, gray rock gleamed in great tilted slabs, and far above, a gray cloud hid the crest.

Manuel Barrachina said, "I wish we could take that box down from the tower. I think the Duke would reward any servant of his well who brought him the remains of his father for proper burial." Manuel was slight and stooped and fair-skinned; he was clerk to the Duke of Medina Sidonia's agent in Tarifa.

Pedro Santangel said, "I wish we could put the flag of Castile up there instead of the Moorish banner. I think the king would knight a man who did that. . . ." He was tall and fair, with dark eyes, willowy, swooning handsome to the girls. His father was trying to make him follow the practice of the law, but all his desire was to be a knight and fight for Castile, King Enrique, and the Holy Catholic Church.

Judah said, "I wish it were settled one way or the other, so that we know where we are. Sometimes you can bring a cargo in here peacefully, sometimes they fire a cannon at you. Sometimes you can wander all over the town, sometimes guards prevent you stepping off your ship. For trade we need peace and security." He was short and square, with a wide mouth, a broken beak nose, and two fingers gone from his left hand; big ears and hands, thick curly black hair, and startling blue eyes. He had run his own ship out of Tarifa since he was twenty, and now owned three, which plied in trade along the coast, up the Guadalquivir, and, when conditions allowed, over to Africa. He was a Jew. In 1399 his grandfather's sister, Beulah Conquy, had married a young man called Jacob Azayal in Córdoba; the following year Jacob Azayal was converted to Christianity and became Luis Santangel—grandfather of the eager young would-be knight of the Church now at Judah's side; Pedro Santangel was therefore a *marrano*, a New Christian, and Judah's second cousin—a fact which both knew but never mentioned.

"Can we go ashore now?" Manuel Barrachina asked. "I must get to the Governor's audience as soon as possible."

Judah let down the gangplank. The sweating sailors were already passing sacks of wheat up from the hold to the deck, and Moorish laborers were waiting to take them ashore. At the Water Gate the Berber guard was talking to a fat, turbaned merchant and did not look up. The young men passed into the city of Gibraltar and, at once, into Africa. Donkeys loaded with brass jars trotted down the narrow alley toward the harbor, to load there with oil and wine from the ships. In the gutter lusty-voiced women sold fruit by the single stem, spices by the pinch, sherbet by the thimbleful. In all the shop fronts the merchants sat, with carpets and baskets and bolts of cloth and mounds of flour. Cobblers banged on their lasts, blacksmiths on their anvils, tinkers on pots, beggars on drums. The knife grinder made tunes on a bamboo pipe, and from the minaret of the mosque the muezzin chanted the call to prayer.

Manuel Barrachina left them to go to the castle, for his business was to deliver a note from the duke's agent informing the governor that a fishing boat from Gibraltar had been taken poaching off Tarifa and would be released on payment of the fine.

The levanter made the day close, and Judah and Pedro walked slowly, left hands resting on the hilts of their daggers. Judah had no business—his captain was in charge of the unloading—but had come because he wanted a change of air. Pedro only wanted to see Gibraltar while it was possible. So they strolled together toward the square block of the castle and then southward along shelflike streets. They paused where a flight of steps crossed, going down toward the harbor, and looked out over the bay and pointed out to each other the new aspects of hills and valleys which they knew well from the landward side. As they turned to walk on, Judah bumped into someone, hard. It was a Moorish woman, and he knocked her over. As she fell, the black veil dropped from her face, and Judah looked into startled dark green eyes under strong, straight black brows. On her forehead hung a silver ornament in the shape of the Star of David. Her lips were thin, but perfectly curved in an oval face. Judah's jaw dropped. He had never seen anything so beautiful. He stared into the green eyes, stunned. The girl lowered her lids, and he recovered his wits. He knelt quickly beside her, muttering, "Are you a Jewess?" She was fumbling for her veil. "Yes," she whispered.

"Woman!" an old voice was yelling in Berber, "What doest thou, shameless?"

"It's the duenna," Pedro said, laughing. "Shall I hold her off?"

The girl was slight, her skin like an olive's, her hair blue-black —and she was pulling her veil up now, rising to her feet. The green eyes glowed above the black cloth. "Are you a slave?" Judah whispered. The old woman panted up, screeching. The girl nodded. The old woman grabbed her by the wrist, pulled her away. "I shall find you," Judah said in Ladino, the Hebrew-tinged Spanish which was the *lingua franca* of the Sephardim. Then she was gone, hurrying down the steps beside the old scold, the black robe fluttering behind her.

"Let's follow them!" Pedro said, still chuckling. They started down the steps but had not taken three strides when heavy hands fell on their shoulders and a deep voice growled, "Slow, there." Three large Negroes, naked from the waist, curved scimitars stuck in their sashes, fell in beside them. "Do you think our master sends out his women without protection?" one said. "Such as they are not for Christian dogs. . . ." They were passing a large stable, and without warning the three seized them, threw them inside, and slammed the door shut. They heard the scrape of the bolts and the Negroes go on laughing down the steps.

They scrambled out of the dung-littered straw and leaped at the window—but it was barred. They began to batter at the door with their fists. At last an old man came, mumbling, and let them out—but by then the steps were empty, and when they ran down to the street next below, so was that.

Pedro took Judah's arm and led him into a coffee shop. "Sit down, friend," he said. "You look as if you've been hit on the head with a mace."

Judah sat sipping his coffee, staring at the wall, seeing only those green eyes. He'd traversed the Mediterranean three times, gone once to England, and knew the stews of every port from Cadaqués to Pasajes. He'd enjoyed scores of women of every color, size, and quality, but he had never fallen in love. And now, at first sight! It was impossible, he told himself. Worse, it was ridiculous. But it was so. There was no escape from it.

"I shall find and buy her," he said at last, "even if I have to come and live here and become a subject of the King of Granada."

"I guessed somehow you wanted to see more of her," Pedro Santangel said dryly. "If she weren't a Jewess, I might challenge you myself—"

"I'll kill you if you do," Judah said.

"—but she is, and, well . . . for such as me, that makes her impossible. But I have an idea. . . ."

An hour later a burly, broken-nosed man passed slowly along the street below the wall of the castle. He wore a dirty old brown djellabah with the hood up and a pair of battered Moorish slippers. A big basket of green vegetables hung on his left arm, and as he shambled along he seemed to be chanting his wares; but in truth the tune that he sang was a phrase from the Song of Songs:

> "Shuvee, shuvee Hashulamit
> Shuvee, shuvee v'necheze bach.
> Return, return, O Shulamite,
> Return, return, that we may look upon thee."

There were a few Jews in Gibraltar—one, indeed, the banker Chaim Uziel, was a distant relative of the Santangels; but though they would understand what he was singing, they would be unlikely to betray him. Judah trudged on.

> "Return, return, O Shulamite. . . ."

It was hotter than ever inside this accursed stinking garment, he thought. Pedro Santangel, back on the ship, must be ill with laughing.

Up and down, along and across, all through the city Judah passed; and even into the fortress to cry his vegetables in the empty square under the Tower of Homage until a sleepy soldier came, cursing, to drive him out. The walls of the narrow streets seemed to give off heat like ovens. On the south walls the awnings were out to keep the glare from the barred windows, and under the north walls dogs slept and men snored. Judah tramped on, chanting:

"Return, return, that we may look upon thee. . . ."

His sweat soaked the djellabah. From the houses now and then a voice cried angrily, "In the name of Allah, hold your tongue now, and let us sleep." Once a woman came to her door and spent five minutes picking over his wares; fortunately she did not buy, as he had no idea what price to ask.

He reached the height of the town, above and to the south of the castle. Half a dozen apes played, dozed, and scratched each other for fleas nearby. He picked a cabbage out of his basket and threw it at them, crying, "Lead me to her, shameless ones!" An old dog ape grabbed the cabbage and retreated with it. All the others dropped what they were doing and followed him. Judah's shoulder throbbed, and he thought his left arm would drop off. She'd never hear him, or if she did, she'd only laugh. What would she want of a thirty-year-old man with half his fingers gone, broken nose, big ears . . . ?

He got up, hitched the basket into place, and started along the path. Something white gleamed at his feet, and he stooped to pick it up. He turned it over curiously—an ivory statuette of a naked woman, her hair piled up to form a hole so it could be worn as an ornament; but what Moorish woman would wear a naked woman, her slit clearly showing, dangling round her neck? Still, it was well made. The apes must have been playing with it. He put it into the inner pocket of the djellabah and started back down the nearest flight of steps.

"Return, return, O Shulamite . . ."

Almost at once a girl's voice answered with a cradle song that he remembered his mother singing to his youngest sister.

He listened, pressed close under the wall. The singer was inside a three-storied house, with a walled garden below and the open mountain above. The tower of the castle was a quarter of a mile to the north and at the same level. Steep steps, interspersed with sections of ramp, led down on either side of a deep gutter and water channel into the town, houses becoming thicker all the way.

Then he saw her at an upper window, behind bars. He called softly, "What is your name?"

"Tova is my name. Tova Hassan they call me," she answered in the lilt of the song.

"I will buy you. I am not really a seller of vegetables."

"I did not think so."

"I love you," he said.

"How do I know what love is?" she sang. Her voice faded as she moved away from the window. Judah stared longingly for a moment more, then called, "I will be back soon," hitched the basket higher on his arm, and hurried down the steps.

The sun was sinking over the mountains across the bay when Judah presented himself again at the house on the hill, this time at the main door. He wore a richly embroidered Moorish robe of blue and gold, with a thick gold waistband and blue silk turban. He had never worn Muslim clothes before, but nothing else of quality was available in Gibraltar. Pedro Santangel stalked ceremoniously at his side, elegant as always, with a long sword added to his costume.

Judah knocked on the door with the hilt of his dagger. Two minutes later it opened suddenly, and one of the large Negroes who had thrown them into the stable appeared. Judah spoke in his sailor's Berber. "I am Messer Judah Conquy of Tarifa. Is your master, the honorable Suleiman Qureshi, in?"

"What has that to do with you?" the Negro growled. He stared at the two of them suspiciously, as though trying to remember where he had seen them before.

Judah snapped his fingers, and Pedro dropped a coin into the Negro's hand. "Important business," Judah said. "I am a shipowner and merchant. It is urgent."

The Negro disappeared. The door slammed. They waited.

"Perhaps she is like one of those loud-voiced partridges men put out as decoys to bring other game down," Pedro said cheerfully. "We shall get our throats cut."

After five minutes the door opened, and the Negro reappeared with a brief "Come." He led them down a passage and round an inner patio, where a fountain played, flowers grew in blue and yellow pots, and caged birds sang. There was also a red-legged partridge on a long tether, pecking for corn upon the grass. Pedro nudged Judah and muttered, "See?" In a cool room the other side, under a gently waving palm fan worked by a young girl—black, lovely, unveiled—a thin man sat on a pile of leather cushions.

Judah bowed. "The honorable Suleiman Qureshi? The great merchant, whose fame has spread to Fez and all the coasts of Africa?"

"I am Suleiman Qureshi," the man answered. He was bald and gray-skinned, with a pendulous lower lip. His eyes were small, dark, and alert. "You are the Jew shipowner of Tarifa. But how can you benefit me? We are rivals, not collaborators."

Judah bowed again and came to the point. The worth of a fe-male slave, young and in good condition, was about 120 dinars here or in Morocco, rather more in Granada. He must offer more, because the fact of his coming proved that he badly wanted the girl. He said, "You have a slave of my faith here called Tova Hassan. She has not betrayed you, but I chanced to see her. I wish to marry her and will buy her from you for two hundred and fifty dinars."

There was a long silence. The black fan girl's eyes rolled, and her teeth flashed. The bodyguard moved his bare feet on the tiles. The water tinkled more loudly in the patio. A reflection from the sky glowed red on Qureshi's bald head.

"No," he said.

Judah snapped a finger. Pedro pulled a silk purse out of his fob, opened it, and poured a torrent of heavy ten-dinar pieces onto the low table in front of Qureshi. Judah knew that there were fifty of them, five hundred dinars in all, borrowed from Chaim Uziel the banker.

"No," Qureshi said.

Pedro scraped up the coins, poured them back into the purse, and put the purse away. Judah said stolidly, "You must love her very greatly."

Qureshi smiled thinly. "No, Jew, it's not that. Do you remem-ber buying a number of singularly excellent carpets in Larache two years ago? In spite of being warned that they had been promised to the wazir of the King of Granada?"

Judah remembered at once. The man who had threatened

him had obviously not expected any competition, and when Judah had bought the carpets at a fair price, he had gone off scowling and muttering about Jewish dogs. He must have been an agent of this Suleiman Qureshi. If Qureshi wanted revenge, it was no use offering him money, so Judah bowed and said, "I recall the occasion perfectly. Now, with your permission . . ."

The thin man's eye glittered in the failing light. "Are you sure you won't bid higher, Messer Conquy? She is small, but between the thighs, aiiih, what a fire burns!"

Judah stepped forward and pushed the merchant backward off his piled cushions. Pedro drew his sword and pointed it at the Negro. "We go," Judah snapped. "Do not hinder us." The merchant began to shout and rave; footsteps and answering shouts echoed high in the house. Judah and Pedro ran across the courtyard, down the passage, and out into the open.

The sun had set, and in the town a few lamps showed against the twilight. "That was a bold answer," Pedro said, "though it may lead us to the bastinado."

"I couldn't help myself," Judah said. They hurried on toward the harbor, walking now, but fast. The Water Gate was still open, and they went out onto the jetty. At the gangplank of the *Gaditana* the captain said, "We've just finished unloading, Judah."

Judah saw Manuel Barrachina on the deck. There was no reason to wait. "Sail at once," he said and ran aboard.

A sailor was hauling the gangplank in when a figure appeared out of the gloom and called, "Stay! Where are you bound?"

"Tarifa," the captain answered.

"Allow me passage, please. I will pay well," the man said. He was richly dressed in black, his face hidden.

"Come on, then. Five dirhams."

The man stepped on board and paid the money. The captain pointed to the hatch, and the passenger went below. Five minutes later, the sail billowing, the *Gaditana* slid past the end of the jetty, eastbound.

Judah called for wine and sat down on a coil of rope. "What in the name of St. Thomas were you doing all day?" Manuel Barrachina asked. "The sailors have been telling me all manner of strange tales. What is the truth?"

"I'll tell you in a moment," Judah said, "but first what of you?"

"Nothing," Manuel said. "They kept me waiting two hours, then told me to come back, and when I did, said the governor was sick and asked me to give my message to an assistant. I refused. I think the governor's not in Gibraltar at all. So I have wasted my day."

"Except that you've seen el Peñon, which your master the Duke swears he's going to get back one day," Pedro said. "Now, *I'll* tell you what mad pranks this Judah Conquy, whom we all thought was just a rough merchant, with no thought in his head beyond trade, has been dragging me into. . . ."

Judah drank and watched the bulk of the Rock fade into the darkness, and the dim point of light on the southern point vanished while his friend, with great animation, told of their adventures and misadventures. But he was not listening. His mind was full of her, of how he could free her.

An oil lantern burned day and night on the end of the stone jetty at Tarifa. Shortly after it came into view, the passenger appeared on deck and walked aft. He peered at them in the dark. "Who is the principal authority in Tarifa, gentlemen?" He spoke a poor Castilian, but easy to understand.

"The Duke of Medina Sidonia's agent," Manuel said.

"The alcalde, the mayor," Pedro said. "For he is a servant of the king."

The Moor looked from one to another. "The alcalde," Judah said, "Don Alonzo Arcos, a most respected and honest gentleman. I'll guide you to his home."

Shortly afterward the captain brought the *Gaditana* alongside. Judah took the Moor to the Casa Consistorial—Don Alonzo lived behind it—and went back to his own rooms above his warehouse on the waterfront. His housekeeper tried to make him eat, but he would not. For hours he paced the floor, thinking of one plan after another to gain Tova Hassan and, one after another, rejecting them. An hour before dawn he flung himself on his bed. Before his eyes closed someone knocked on the door, and a voice called, "Judah Conquy!" He leaned out of the window. The man said, "Come at once to the Casa Consistorial."

A dozen men were already gathered in the hall of audience upstairs, with lamps lit and curtains drawn. The alcalde sat in his big chair, a tall, fork-bearded Moor beside him—the passenger from Gibraltar. Gathered around them were other shipowners, captains, a few knights, Manuel Barrachina, and the parish priest.

The alcalde said, "Come close, Messer Conquy. Pray silence, gentlemen. . . . An affair of great moment has come upon me. This Moor, Ali el Curro, is a nobleman of Gibraltar. Wronged by the governor, the wrong not redressed by their king, he fled secretly today from his post as deputy commander of the fortress. He wishes to become a Christian. . . ."

"The Holy Ghost be praised!" the priest cried, crossing himself.

". . . and he says that if we act before the day after tomorrow, two hundred men can seize Gibraltar."

A dead silence suddenly fell, louder than any noise. It lasted long seconds, then everyone spoke at once—*Impossible! . . . A miracle . . . A trick . . . We must go at once . . . Wait!*

The alcalde raised his hand. "The governor of the fortress, all the knights except one, and most of the soldiers have gone to Málaga to pay homage to their king, who is visiting there. Gibraltar is almost without defenders."

The clamor broke out again, some arguing for and some against the idea, but the alcalde, a man who imposed by dignity rather than force, said quietly, "A state of war exists between our king and the King of Granada, even though there are many peaceful exchanges. So we will not be committing any treachery in making a surprise attack. We have good reasons . . . we all know of the losses suffered by the duke and many other citizens. But there is an object greater than gold here, gentlemen. Two jewels are missing from the circlet of Don Enrique's crown— Granada and Gibraltar. I cannot sit idle here when the chance is offered to me of winning back one of them. I will therefore go to take Gibraltar, either tomorrow night or the next. I call upon you to provide men, for as you know, I can command no more than fifty of our own here. How many will each of you give, and when can they be here? And from you, shipmasters—how many ships, and how many men and horses will each carry?"

"I'll go!" Judah cried. "I have two ships in port." Here it was, the answer he had sought for in vain, presented to him like a gift from God! He jumped with excitement.

The alcalde smiled, raising his hand slightly. "Thank you, Messer Judah. But let us talk of the soldiers first. . . ."

Manuel Barrachina spoke up at once. "The duke has forty horse and forty foot here in his castle. In the absence of my master the agent, who is with the duke, I pledge them all. But I must add that Gibraltar is, and will be, a part of the duke's domains, not of His Majesty's."

"That is not for such as you and me to settle, Messer Barrachina," the alcalde said gravely. "I have your promise of the soldiers. That is all I need."

The old knight Don Carlos Fuentes then promised twenty men-at-arms, and the young knight Don Fernando Ponce de León, a nephew of the Count of Arcos, as many; and others promised horsemen until the total stood at eighty horse and one hundred and eighty foot.

"That will be enough," the alcalde said. "But I shall send messengers galloping to the king, the duke, the Lord of Jerez, and the Count of Arcos, entreating all to send more men immediately. For once we have taken the fortress, we must be prepared to hold it against a counterattack by the Moors."

Young Ponce de León said, "My uncle the count will not weaken himself by sending more soldiers unless the duke sends as many."

"The Lord of Jerez will say the same regarding the count," old Don Carlos said.

"For this jewel of Gibraltar, these feuds must be forgotten," the alcalde said. "So, gentlemen, do you go to it, that men and horses with their arms and food for three days may be gathered here by nightfall. And let no word be spoken abroad of this matter or the reason for the movements. . . . Shipmasters and captains, pray come close. . . ."

Six ships sailed before midnight, having waited an hour for the wind to veer sufficiently into the southwest. The *Gaditana* led the little flotilla, with the alcalde on board, also Ali el Curro the renegade Moor, Judah Conquy, and Pedro Santangel, full of excitement at the prospect of knightly action. The *Sevillana* followed with Manuel Barrachina and many of the duke's men. Behind came the *Santa Cruz, Santa Fe, Tiburon,* and *Angula* with the rest. The Atlantic swell steadily lessened as the vessels passed into the gut of the strait, but several soldiers were already seasick, and the horses on deck kept stamping and shifting their hoofs, unhappy with the constantly changing balance. The ships carried no riding lights, only a small lantern, shielded from the front, on the poop. The moon slid irregularly in and out of low, luminescent clouds. It was a hot night.

Judah stood in the bow so that he could be nearer to Gibraltar and Tova Hassan, and though he knew he would not see the light on the point for two or three hours, he kept staring into the darkness until when he did see it, not one but two lights wavered before his eyes. Gradually then the bulk of the Rock took shape, a black lion crouching against the sky. Three hours after leaving Tarifa, that is, at two o'clock on the morning of August 20, 1462, the captain of the *Gaditana* ran her up onto the sand of a cove on the western side of Gibraltar, near the southern point. The others followed to right and left, the sailors put out the improvised ramps, and men and horses began to splash ashore. An hour later, having scrambled up the steep slope out of the cove and mustered on the flatter ground above, the little force started north for the town and fortress. The alcalde strode ahead, Ali el Curro as guide at his side, Judah and Pedro following, then the men-at-arms, the horsemen last.

After half an hour Ali el Curro said, "We are close to the southern wall now, Alcalde, and it is near dawn. Let us stop here in the woods, for at the first light three soldiers come out of the town—one high up the hill, one opposite here, one near the sea, to search the ground and report that no enemies are concealed close to the walls."

The old knight Don Carlos said, "Lay an ambush, Alcalde, and take these scouts prisoner. Torture them separately, as to the truth of what this Moor says. Then we shall know whether this tale of the few soldiers and one knight is true or false."

"I speak the truth," the Moor said stiffly, but the other knights and Manuel Barrachina all agreed with Don Carlos. So it was done; men-at-arms went up and down, outside the wall, ready to seize the scouts when they came out. Then the light slowly spread, and Judah and the rest, hiding in the trees, saw in front of them the red wall climbing from the sea to the mountain, and gates in it, minarets and roofs beyond, and at the far side of the town Judah saw the house of Suleiman Qureshi, where Tova Hassan was, and gazed at it as though he could pierce the wall just by looking.

The Moorish soldiers came out, as Ali el Curro had said, and were taken prisoner and tortured a little. All separately swore, weeping, that there were no knights but one and few soldiers in the castle, and none in the town. Then the alcalde marched his army out of the woods and ordered the standards to be set up—the flags of Castile; of the house of Medina Sidonia, borne by a soldier at Manuel Barrachina's side; of the Count of Arcos, borne by the squire of Don Fernando Ponce de León. The light glittered on iron helmet and cuirass, sword and mace and halberd. The alcalde drew his sword and carried the hilt to his lips. "For God and Castile," he cried. "Advance!"

The captured scouts ran to open the center gate, and the army marched in, though at the last moment the squire carrying Ponce de León's banner galloped ahead so that he was the first to enter the town. Once inside, Manuel Barrachina, his face dark with anger, sent the duke's horsemen galloping pell-mell through the narrow streets toward the castle. The other knights followed, and in a moment the alcalde and his fifty men, the king's standard over them, were left alone.

"Folly!" the alcalde muttered as he marched steadily on.

When Judah reached the castle wall at the alcalde's side, the knights and horsemen were riding up and down outside, flourishing their swords and shouting war cries, but the gate was closed, the drawbridge raised. A few Moors peered down from the battlements, and a trumpet was sounding from inside. Don Carlos Fuentes muttered, "Treachery! A great host is hidden inside, preparing to rush out upon us. . . ."

The alcalde ignored him and advanced with the king's standard to the edge of the fosse. There he cried up, "In the name of Don Enrique, King of Castile, I call upon you to surrender."

An old man with a bright turban appeared in an embrasure, and Ali el Curro said, "That is Mohammed Caba, the only knight left here."

The alcalde repeated his call to surrender, and old Mohammed Caba quavered, "We have no choice. I have but forty men-at-arms here. But the people will need four days to take out what they can carry."

"Take it by storm!" young Ponce de León said. "Why should we wait four days?"

For once Manuel Barrachina agreed with him, and a new clamor arose, while the old Moor looked down with amazement from the embrasure. Then the alcalde raised his voice and shouted sternly, "Silence! I speak for the king! . . . Come down, Messer Moor, and we will settle the details. Meantime, I grant an armistice."

Then the gate creaked and slowly opened, the drawbridge clattered down on its chains, and the old Moor tottered out, bent and slow, unarmed. As he came, Judah, a little to one side, heard Ponce de León muttering to Manuel Barrachina, "Now is the moment! Don't heed the alcalde. What honor will there be for us in a tame surrender?" Manuel nodded, and they looked around and caught the eyes of their soldiers and horsemen. Suddenly Manuel shouted, "For God and Guzmán!" and Don Fernando cried, "Arcos! Arcos!" and both charged toward the drawbridge with many of their followers. Judah drew his dagger and ran to stop them, and the alcalde cried, "Stop! Shame, shame!" but all would have been in vain except for Pedro Santangel. He must have heard the whisperings too, for when the hotheads charged, he was already there, defending the narrow bridge. They ran at him, and he pierced Don Fernando through the liver, wounded Manuel Barrachina in the arm, and stepped back, sword flickering. They surged on, and he killed another knight and a man-at-arms. Slowly the Moors inside lowered the heavy gate behind him. Slowly the alcalde's soldiers overcame and forced back the assailants.

The gate closed, and the attempt was over. The attackers slunk away, and the alcalde said sternly to Manuel Barrachina, "When I have given the king's word, to break it is high treason. The king shall hear of this. And you Messer Santangel, you shall go to the king as soon as the fortress is in our hands, with my dispatch."

Judah clapped his friend on the back, laughing with pleasure. The man chosen to convey such tidings would certainly be knighted and perhaps given greater honors. Here in Gibraltar Pedro had won the prize he wanted in life; now there was no limit to what he and his descendants might become—marquis, grandee, count, cardinal.

But for himself he wanted another prize, and now was the time to seize it. He said, "Alcalde, I have private business to attend to. May I take four soldiers with me?"

"Not for looting, I trust," the alcalde said.

"No, señor. For persuasion."

He started up the hill outside the wall, the four men-at-arms following. Near the house of Suleiman Qureshi he looked back. The alcalde, Ali el Curro, and Mohammed Caba had disappeared. The alcalde's soldiers blocked the way to the closed gate. Other horsemen and soldiers and knights stood in small groups, talking, gesticulating. The Christian banners were in disarray, some propped against the castle wall, some on the ground. The green and black of King Muley Hassan still flew from the tower. The box containing the body of Enrique de Guzmán, father of the Duke of Medina Sidonia, still dangled from its chains below.

Judah turned and walked faster toward the tall house at the head of Gully Steps. He rapped loudly with the handle of his dagger and called "Open!" The sun was high, and birds chattered in the trees overhanging the garden wall.

"Shall we break in the door, master?" a soldier asked eagerly, unlimbering a heavy battle ax.

"No," Judah said. "This will soon be my property." He raised the dagger to knock again, when the door suddenly opened. The Negro bowed low. Behind him four more, half naked, prostrated themselves and beat their heads on the floor.

The Negro said, "Enter, lord. We are men of peace."

Judah pushed through to the fountain patio and looked up at the tiers of balconies. Veiled women watched from the upper one, half a dozen servants stood bowing on the lower. The tame partridge suddenly chattered, making him jump.

"Bring me the lady Tova Hassan," he said.

No one spoke. He felt cold, and his hand began to tremble. He drew his dagger and turned slowly on the Negro. The soldier with the battle ax cried eagerly, "Shall I have his head off, sir?"

The Negro flung himself to the floor, grasping Judah's ankles. "Lord, she is not here. My master took her."

Judah grabbed the man by his hair, jerked him upright, and

thrust the point of his dagger into the skin just below the ear. "*Where* has he taken her?"

"I don't . . . d-d-don't know," the Negro sobbed. "No one knows."

"It is true," a voice called down from the second balcony. Judah looked up. A fat middle-aged Moorish woman, her veil thrown back, said, "The master aroused us at dawn when a lookout reported that the Christians were entering the city. He took Tova and Raza, the head eunuch."

"Where?" Judah called.

The Negro answered, "No one knows, lord. He loaded Raza with bags of gold and jewels and himself with other bags, some full of food, and left by the garden, ordering none to follow."

Judah looked slowly around the circles of faces—down here by the plashing fountains, on the balconies above. He turned to the soldiers. "Search the house. Every cupboard, every hole and corner. Show them," he called to the women.

He went quickly upstairs, past girls pressing themselves against the wall, past bowing servants, to the roof. From there he could see the harbor. No ship was sailing or making ready to sail, so Qureshi must have gone southward or to another house in Gibraltar.

"Lord . . ." It was the Negro, beside him. "If I may speak . . . I think he is hiding in a cave, expecting your attack to be beaten off or bought off. Then he will return."

Something in the man's voice made Judah turn quickly. "You know!" he grated. "Where are they? Tell me, or I swear I'll throw you off this roof." He grabbed the man's throat and bent him back over the parapet.

"I followed . . . but Raza turned and saw me. I fled."

Judah released his grip. "How far did you go?"

"To the flat land at the foot of the southern cliffs. They were crossing it, heading east."

"East? To the back of the Rock? Are there caves on that side?"

"Many, lord. From sea level to the topmost crags. Small and large, some easy to see, some quite hidden."

Judah groaned. "Come with me, then. Show me where you turned back." He hurried down the stairs, found a soldier, and said, "Ask the alcalde to see that no one leaves Gibraltar by land or sea until I return. Run! . . . You three, come with me."

He ran into the street calling impatiently to the Negro, "Which way now? . . . Hurry, hurry!"

They stumbled along the side of the mountain, past several groups of startled monkeys, until they reached the flat above the bay the Spanish called Caleta Laudero, where the six ships of the invasion fleet were now anchored off shore. "I turned here," the Negro said, "close by this old heathen stone. They were going that way." He pointed east, where after another hundred yards the plateau ended in a sharp line. Judah moved forward, his heart sinking. The slope was very steep down to the sea. To the left the Rock rose in buttress and crag, tower and cliff, to the sky.

In that direction a goat track led along narrow ledges between great precipices. With the soldiers at his back, he hurried along it, past a dangerous beak-nosed projection of the cliff, until it ended at a big cave; but the cave was empty.

Back at the flat place he thought despairingly, I might pass close to her and she see me, but she would not dare to cry out.

To the right the flat place ended in a low cliff, then there was another flat place, the brazier of the light beacon, a few houses, a shrine, and the point. Nothing there.

Straight ahead, the flat place ended in a steep drop to the east. He went forward carefully. There was no path here, only the jagged rock curving over and then the sea, two hundred feet below. No one could have gone down there.

As he turned away, despair gripping him, something moved on the slope he had just been looking down. He stared—it was a woman, nothing like Tova—short, red-haired, quite naked. He gasped, for she was running up the steep, straight at him, her mouth wide in a scream. She passed, and he whipped around, but she was gone. "Where did she go?" he asked the soldiers.

"Who, sir?"

"The woman—the naked woman!"

"What woman, sir?"

He stared at them, and they at each other. He muttered a prayer and turned back. If the woman could come up, where he had thought it impossible, there must be a way down. He started cautiously on down and after a few minutes found a tiny piece of green cloth caught in a projecting thorn bush. His excitement mounting, he signaled to the soldiers to follow and went on. Ten minutes later the four of them stood on a narrow strip of sand at the foot of the cliffs. The sea rolled in, in small waves, behind them. In front a vast overhanging arch led back and up, the base a steeply rising floor of sand, into the Rock. There were fresh footprints in the sand, two pairs large and one small. They started up, abreast. As the light grew dimmer, where the slope flattened and a strange, shiny column of stone joined floor to ceiling, a man sprang out of the shadows on the left and struck downward with a scimitar. Judah hurled himself sideways, putting up his arm to protect himself. The blow struck his left wrist, severing the hand instantly. His missing hand throbbed, but there was no pain, and one of the soldiers, thrusting from behind him, stuck his sword into their assailants' leg. He fell, and the soldier with the battle ax shouted, "At last!" and clove his chest in two.

Judah moved forward, his left wrist raised above his head to lessen the bleeding.

A voice grated, "Stop!"

He saw, dim in the last recess of the cave, figures—Tova, unveiled, the Star of David at her forehead, her ankles bound; Suleiman Qureshi beside her, his dagger at her throat. Leather and canvas bags were stacked behind.

Wearily Judah leaned on his sword. He held out his arm to a soldier and said, "Bind this. . . . Let her go, Suleiman. I guarantee your life."

The merchant laughed without mirth. "What use is life without money?"

"You can keep your gold, too . . . except for a hundred dinars to each of these soldiers. In return I want the keys of your house. We have taken Gibraltar."

Suleiman Qureshi said, "And you, a Jew, helped the Christians do it? Ah, they will reward you well." His knife still hovered at Tova's bare throat. Her eyes glowed with a dark green fire. Judah felt dizzy.

"Come," he said. "Free her."

The merchant's hand moved, the blade sliced, her ropes fell to the sand. She came forward slowly, and Judah waited for her. When she reached him, he said, "I brought something for you . . . gift . . ." He dropped his sword, fumbled in his inner pocket and brought out the carved woman he had found the monkeys playing with. The light was fading, growing before his eyes. . . . "A charm, to make you fertile . . ." he said thickly. She took the figurine from him and looked at it, smiling. He said, "Fertile, because . . . will you be my wife, daughter of Israel?"

She said, *"Verastech li leolam."*

His knees buckled and his strength ebbed, but her eyes were over him and her arms, suddenly strong, supporting him as he sank to the sand.

Book Seven

∞∞∞∞∞∞∞∞∞∞∞∞∞∞∞∞∞∞∞∞∞∞∞

Spanish Town

The Jewish years 5222–5465
AUC 2215–2457
A.D. 1462–1704
A.H. 866–1116

JUDAH CONQUY would have done well to have taken Tova
back to Tarifa until the situation in Gibraltar stabilized—
but he would have had to wait a long time. . . .

The original Moorish offer to the alcalde was to surrender,
providing they were allowed four days to evacuate their people
and what goods they could take to Granada. The alcalde wanted
to accept this, but by now Rodrigo Ponce de León, the Count of
Arcos' eldest son (no relation to the alcalde) had arrived with
four hundred men in response to the alcalde's call for assistance
and refused to accept the surrender. He wanted to take the fortress by storm, presumably to increase the glory and the loot.
Next, a large body of soldiers from Jerez arrived under Gonzalo
de Abila. The Duke of Medina Sidonia was on his way with
more men. And so was the Count of Arcos, with still more. The
alcalde, who had taken the initiative and deserved the credit, was
now quite outgunned and pushed helpless into the background
while the grandees squabbled over the jewel that he had won.

Gonzalo de Abila planned to seize the fort secretly with his
men. Rodrigo Ponce de León came to hear of it and, to forestall
de Abila, himself attacked but was repulsed. The Duke of Me-

dina Sidonia arrived, and though begged by young Ponce de
León to await the arrival of his father, marched firmly into the
castle, announced that Gibraltar was now his, and took his own
father's body down from its suspended box. Gibraltar was again
in Spanish Christian hands, this time to be held for much longer
than the twenty-four years after its first capture by the duke's an-
cestor, Guzmán el Bueno, in 1309.

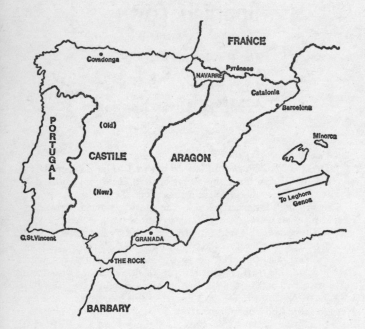

When the Count of Arcos came up a day or two later, he
found the duke in possession, the Moors all gone (the third complete turnover of Gibraltar's population), and his son Rodrigo
in such a state of passion that he tried to persuade his father to
attack the castle, kill the duke, and institute a regular civil war—
though, indeed, at this time, under a weak king and with the

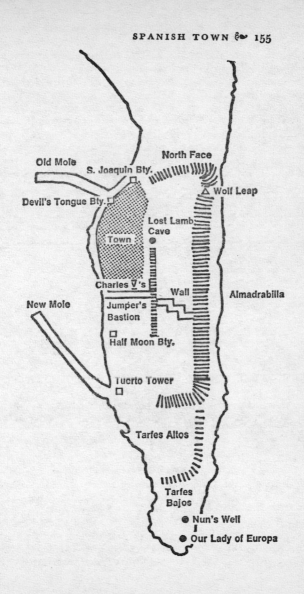

unifying threat of the Moors rapidly fading, civil war was the normal relation of Spain's barons with each other.

The Count of Arcos was as angry as his son, but he decided to accept the situation, and he and all the other contestants marched away, leaving the duke to gloat over his prize. He did not gloat for long . . . but before turning to that story it should be recorded that Alonzo Arcos, the alcalde, later became deputy governor of Seville, where he died in 1477. Ali el Curro was baptized, became Diego del Curro, and, unlike Benedict Arnold, lived happily ever after in the esteem of the people for whom he had betrayed his own.

Spain was about to enter its period of greatness, but before that could happen, it had to come into existence. Spain was a geographical entity, but politically it consisted at this time of three kingdoms: Navarre, Aragón, and Castile. In 1465 King Enrique IV of Castile's son, the Infante Alonzo, was set up as a puppet king by some rebellious barons. Fortunately for the kingdom, the prince died in 1468. King Enrique's heir presumptive was now his young sister, Isabella, and he arranged a dynastic marriage for her with Ferdinand, son of the King of Aragón. In 1474 he himself died, and Isabella became Queen of Castile. In 1479 the King of Aragon died, the crowns were united, and Ferdinand and Isabella ruled jointly over a new country—Spain. (Navarre, much smaller, was incorporated thirty-seven years later.)

Four events now took place which cast the mold of Spanish life for centuries to come and affected every inhabitant of the world. All started or were based in Andalusia. Gibraltar was closely affected by all four.

First in time was the setting up of the Spanish Inquisition. Queen Isabella was a considerable statesman except in the area of religion; here she was a maniac. The barons found her a strong ruler, but she was little better than putty in the hands of the fanatic priests with whom she surrounded herself. The Inquisition was founded in Christian jealousy of the power and wealth attained by families converted from Judaism—mostly in fear of the pogroms of a century earlier. These New Christians, or *marranos*, had become bishops, councilors, knights: for example, the Grand Master of the Order of Santiago was descended on both sides from the Jew Ruy Capon. In Aragón within a brief period the Master of the Royal Household, the treasurer, several assessors, the Chief Justice, and the president of the *Cortes* (advisory parliament) were all marranos. Marranos, or *conversos*, as they were also called, held a monopoly of the banking and medical professions. They constituted almost the whole of the small Spanish middle class.

Many conversos were devout Christians, but some secretly held their Jewish faith. On November 1, 1478, the Inquisition was founded, by order of Pope Sixtus IV at the request of Queen Isabella, to root out these false Christians. The first commissioners of the Inquisition gathered in Seville on Christmas Day, 1480, and on February 6, 1481, in that city, burned several marranos who had been surprised secretly celebrating Passover the year before. These were the first victims of an institution which blackened the name of Spain abroad and held the national intelligence in chains of fear until 1834.

If there were Christians in Gibraltar, there were certainly marranos, too, and although the Inquisition never held its inquiries in small towns, it is reasonable to suppose that some of Gibraltar's conversos were denounced by jealous rivals and dragged off to suffer for what they may or may not have secretly believed in.

From the moment the Inquisition was founded, the Church had seen the fatal flaw of such action against heretics: it could not be used against avowed Jews. But there were savage penal laws and exclusions against Jews to hand, such as those of 1412, and the Church now moved to strengthen and enforce these, with the purpose of driving the Jews out of Spain. In April, 1481, Jews were ordered to be confined to their ghettos. In 1482 and 1483 Jews were expelled from most of Andalusia and three years later from most of Aragón.

Now came the second great event, the fall of Granada, the last Muslim outpost left in Spain. Ferdinand and Isabella, *los Reyes Católicos* as they are usually known in Spain, encamped themselves before Granada early in 1490 and after various skirmishes and mishaps succeeded in bringing the King of Granada to sign terms of capitulation. These terms were wise and liberal and specifically stated that the Moors were to be regarded as free subjects of the Crown, with the free exercise of their religion. On January 2, 1492, Ferdinand and Isabella entered Granada. The reconquest, begun 774 years earlier in the remote Asturian gorge of Covadonga, was over.

Two Jews, Isaac Abarbanel and Abraham Senior, had provided the *Reyes Católicos* with most of the money they needed for the long campaign, and the monarchs demurred—just a little —when the Church suggested that now was the time to press on with the unification of Spain by expelling the rest of the Jews. Hernando de Talavera, once the queen's confessor and now the newly appointed Archbishop of Granada, soon cut off those qualms by storming into the royal presence, casting down thirty pieces of silver, and crying that they were betraying Christ's church for money, even as Judas had betrayed Christ. The *Reyes Católicos* quickly ordered the expulsion of the Jews from Spain, signing the edict in Granada on March 31, 1492. It gave the Jews four months to sell up what they could and leave.

This cruel and foolish order—the third great event—lost to Spain nearly all that was left of her professional skills, learning, and independence of spirit and thought. So on July 31, 1492, being the ninth day of Ab (the destruction of both the first and second Temples of Jerusalem took place on this date) the last Sephardim left Spain, many from Gibraltar. The total of exiles numbered over a quarter of a million. They left behind their houses, libraries, and lands but they took with them their keys (thinking that the order must soon be rescinded), such belongings as they could carry, the Ladino tongue, and a great love of a country where Jewish culture had reached its finest flower—now apparently gone mad. Many of these Jews went to Portugal and thence to Holland and England. Others went to Leghorn, Genoa, Minorca, and all parts of Barbary. Still others went as far as Constantinople, where the sultan welcomed them with pleasure, expressing his thanks to the generous sovereigns of Spain for sending him their most talented and industrious subjects.

So Judah Conquy would have had to leave Gibraltar thirty years after he had helped take it; and perhaps he would have gone with Tova and their family to Tangier, where, by climbing the hill above the old town, he could easily see the Rock on most days.

In Spain the campaign for "unification" went on. Keeping more or less to the terms of the capitulation, Hernando de Talavera set about converting the Moors to Christianity by argument and reasoning. He was having some success when Ferdinand and Isabella invited another prelate, Cardinal Ximenez, to speed up the pace. A campaign of coercion began, in direct contravention of the terms of the capitulation. A small and quite natural rising against this treatment, in 1499, was taken as an excuse to declare that the capitulation itself was no longer valid. All Moors were ordered to be baptized or leave the country. Since every obstacle was thrown in the way of their departure, most were baptized. And now the Inquisition and the greedy, bigoted aristocracy of Castile whose economic weapon it was looked hungrily at these Moriscos and began to plan how to drive them too out of Spain, making sure that they too must leave most of their wealth behind.

The fourth event, incomparably the most important, was the expedition of a Genoese sailor, probably of Catalan converso origin, financed by Queen Isabella (and by certain Aragónese conversos) to discover a new route to the Indies. Christopher Columbus discovered or rediscovered America on October 12, 1492, with incalculable results for mankind. The immediate outcome, for Spain, was to provide the nation with a new outlet for its energy to replace the reconquest. Ferdinand and Isabella's grandson, Charles V, King and Emperor, put the Pillars of Hercules onto his coat of arms, but from the demigod's original legend *non plus ultra* ("nothing beyond") he removed the first word; the new motto can be freely interpreted either as "Go west, young man," or "The sky's the limit." One of the first people to go and find out what really was "out there" was Don Rodrigo Ponce de León's son, Don Juan, the one who searched all over Florida (of all places) for the fountains of youth.

Against this background the intimate history of Spanish Gibraltar takes on a sharper focus. King Enrique was overjoyed when he heard of its fall. He at once added "King of Gibraltar" to his other titles and by a royal order transferred to the jurisdiction of Gibraltar all territories that had previously been under Algeciras. As Algeciras had not existed for a century, these territories had been quietly appropriated by neighboring towns, and the king's order was not popular with them. The king also ordered the Duke of Medina Sidonia to give up possession to his own appointed governor, Pedro de Porras. Either because the king was at the time strong or because he himself was weak, the duke unwillingly obeyed. Two year later the king visited Gibraltar in person and invited the King of Portugal (who was visiting Ceuta, across the strait) to join him there. The two sovereigns spent eight days together in Gibraltar, talking politics and hunting in the forests of Almoraima on the mainland.

Soon rebellious barons and grandees broke into revolt all over Spain, and the Infante Alonzo was set up as king, rival to his father. The Duke seized his chance, forced the pretender, then aged eleven, to acknowledge his right to Gibraltar, and in March, 1466, demanded of the new governor, Esteban de Villacreces, that he give up the place at once. Villacreces refused, and the Ninth Siege began. The defense was long and heroic, but no help came from the king, who was fully engaged elsewhere, and on July 26, 1467, starvation and weakness forced Villacreces to surrender. The duke, a vengeful man, imprisoned him with many threats of worse to follow.

Next year the duke died, to be succeeded by his legitimized son, Enrique de Guzmán, as Fourth Count of Niebla and Second Duke of Medina Sidonia. This young man, then twenty-six, was able to force the harassed king into a definite cession of Gibraltar, but—and this is most interesting, as a comparable situation holds today—the king retained sovereignty. The actual words of the grant, which is dated January 3, 1469, are *"reservando en mi . . . e para los reyes que despues de mi fueren en estos dichos reynos, el soberano señorio . . ."* ("reserving for myself . . .

and for the kings who shall succeed me in these said kingdoms, the sovereign dominion . . .")

The duke incorporated Gibraltar into the rest of his extensive domains and gave it a constitution more liberal than most, though not as privileged as the extraordinary charter of 1310. The inhabitants shared in the increase in the duke's prosperity, caused by the removal of Gibraltar's Moorish pirates and poachers. Many probably worked in his timber, cooperage, and tunny-processing monopolies. In 1477 they saw the last flurry of Moorish warlike activity when King Muley Hassan of Granada, raiding into Christian territory, was brought to battle in the forests of Almoraima, below Castellar, by two doughty warriors, Vargas of Gibraltar and Vera of Jimena. These two cordially hated each other—Vargas was the duke's man, Vera the king's; and Vera had seized Vargas and thrown him into prison when the latter was on his way to take over the governorship of Gibraltar for the duke—but they sank their differences to smite the common enemy.

The next year, 1478, the duke had himself named Marquis of Gibraltar and was also able to compel the recently enthroned Ferdinand and Isabella to confirm him in all his rights and titles, including the ownership of Gibraltar. But the times were changing, as the *Reyes Católicos* gained a firmer grip on their unified country. In the next two years they severely curtailed the power of the grandees and had several castles of the Guzmán and Ponce de León families dismantled.

Duke Enrique died in 1492, having performed valiantly in the fall of Granada. He was succeeded by Duke Juan, who went, as was customary, to the sovereign and asked for an affirmation of his rights and titles. Ferdinand and Isabella refused to give it unless he surrendered Gibraltar to them. In vain the duke protested that they themselves had specifically affirmed these rights fourteen years earlier. Ferdinand and Isabella were adamant: Isabella had a feeling for Gibraltar as strong as Mary of England's for Calais. The days of huge independent baronies were over: the duke must give up Gibraltar. After sulking for several years, he realized that times had indeed changed and yielded. On the last day of 1501 Garcilaso de la Vega arrived to govern Gibraltar for Ferdinand and Isabella. The first thing he did, being a proper civil servant, was take an inventory. Copies are still extant. It is an amusing document, starting with the second count's sarcophagus (the one that had hung from the tower) and ending with detailed lists of arquebuses (without stocks) and pikes (three with broken points).

In 1504 Isabella died and in her testament stated that Gibraltar must never again be alienated from the Spanish Crown. But the Guzmáns didn't give up easily, and in the period of confusion between her death and Ferdinand's, in 1516, the duke tried to get Gibraltar back, blockading it for four months (the Tenth Siege). It did not surrender, and under Charles V the Spanish monarchy and people stepped into their glory years.

For Gibraltar itself, the end of the reconquest meant a temporary end to its importance. In 1535, when Alvaro de Bazan arrived to take over the governorship, he found the town almost empty and the fortress abandoned. He managed to attract some citizens back, only to have them killed, looted, and pillaged in an attack by the Moorish corsair Barbarossa. Barbarossa was informed and guided by an Italian renegade, Caramanli . . . who had once been a slave of Bazan's! The raiders were caught by a Spanish admiral as they sailed away and dispersed in a sea fight. Caramanli was killed by an arrow in the chest and two arquebus shots at close range.

This occurred in 1540, but—showing how little real value was now placed on Gibraltar—Charles V did nothing until 1552, when he appointed a Milanese engineer called Calvi to design and build new defenses. The only part of these remaining or, perhaps, ever constructed is Charles V's Wall, the high wall which marks the southern limit of Gibraltar's built-up area, and which climbs from sea level to the cliff line seven hundred feet higher. Above the cliff it continues to the crest in a series of long angles rather farther to the south.

In 1556 Charles, King of Spain, Holy Roman Emperor, the most powerful ruler the world had yet seen, abdicated to a monk's cell in Yuste. Philip II succeeded him and continued his father's policy of neglecting Gibraltar, whose few inhabitants were left at the mercy of the Barbary pirates. The Invincible Armada which Philip launched against England in 1588 had two odd connections with Gibraltar. The admiral he appointed to command it was the aging but most capable and experienced Alvaro de Bazan; but he died before he could embark, and in his

place the king appointed a proud, stupid grandee, a soldier with
no experience of the sea—Alonso de Guzmán, Seventh Duke of
Medina Sidonia and Sixth Marquis of Gibraltar.

The years pass. . . . An autumn storm in Gibraltar Bay sinks
a warship preparing to escort the galleons to America. . . . A
king completes the evil work of the *Reyes Católicos* by expelling
all the *Moriscos* (descendants of Moors forcibly converted to
Christianity) from Spain; there are more than a million of them.
Many concentrate in and sail from Gibraltar, as many Jews had
done 120 years earlier. . . . The same king builds watch towers
all along his southern coast, one actually on the Rock (on what
was then called Tarfes Altos and now Windmill Hill Flats)—
this tower rather mysteriously becomes known as the Genoese
Tower—and another at the foot of the north face, on the isthmus—this one is called the Devil's Tower. . . . Another king
visits Gibraltar but has to walk in because his carriage won't go
through the gate. His courtiers upbraid the governor, who
replies coldly that the gate was not made to let carriages in but
to keep enemies out. . . . A terrible pestilence attacks the town
(it is the same Great Plague which struck London in
1665). . . . There is a lack of oil and wheat, though a surplus of
fish; and it is ordained that no ship will be allowed to load fish
for export unless it has brought in a cargo of wheat or oil. . . .
There is a steady, slow recovery from the years of neglect, and a
new large mole is built, thrusting out from the western shore beyond the old southern limit of the town.

While Gibraltar thought about its fisheries and King Philip
IV about the gold mines of Peru, some northern islanders were
thinking about Gibraltar. In 1625 a Colonel Henry Bruce—apparently with no particular emergency in mind—presented a
plan for the seizure of Gibraltar to Charles, Prince of Wales.
Charles did nothing, and in 1649 (the year of the Gibraltar
plague) lost his head on the block as King Charles I. His successor, Cromwell, was a military genius and on April 28, 1656,
wrote to Admiral Montague on the advantages to England and
the disadvantages that could be imposed on Spain if England
were to gain possession of Gibraltar. The matter was further dis-
cussed and investigated, but Cromwell never took any action.
His successor, Charles II of England, married a Portuguese princess, who brought him Tangier as part of her dowry. Tangier

was not as easy to defend as Gibraltar, but it did give England a
naval outpost at the mouth of the Mediterranean, threateningly
close to Spain, and so met some of the needs which had made
Cromwell think of the Rock. But in 1684 England abandoned
Tangier, which reverted to the Moroccan Empire.

Spain's two centuries as the most powerful nation in the world
were coming to an end. Its king, Carlos II, was a sick man with
no direct heirs. France was rising fast under the unscrupulous
and ambitious Louis XIV. England, recovered from its civil
wars, only awaited a favorable wind to spread its sails. None of
this might have directly affected Gibraltar except for the chance
of a sea fight off Cape St. Vincent in 1693. The English admiral,
Sir George Rooke, was severely handled by a French squadron
(one of the century's small, purposeless wars was in progress).
Spain happened to be allied with England in that war, and
Rooke sailed his battered ships through the strait and took
shelter under the Rock. The Spanish only had a few guns
mounted, but they fired on the French, who veered off. Rooke
was able to stay ten days, rest, and refit. The circumstance made
a deep impression on him.

Before relating Gibraltar's next and critical appearance on the
world stage, in a starring role, let us look at the Rock more
closely in these final years of the seventeenth century.

The larger wild animals had fled, though there were still wild
pig. The ape population was large, perhaps three hundred, as
they had the whole Rock to roam over except for the town itself.
The human population, about six thousand, was all white, and
all Spanish-Catholic except for a few Genoese, some of whom
lived on the east side of the Rock, round the little bay at the foot
of the great sand slope. This settlement (modern Catalan Bay)
was called Almadrabilla, as the Genoese worked a tunny factory
there. Ferdinand and Isabella had sent prisoners into Gibraltar,
partly to increase the population, but it was no longer as necessary to people the Rock as it had once been, and thieves, murderers, and runaway women no longer formed a large part of the
population.

Nearly everyone lived inside the walls in the three joined
"neighborhoods" which constituted Gibraltar—Villa Vieja to
the north, under the Moorish castle; Barcina in the middle;

Turba to the south; the whole being tucked into the northwest angle of the peninsula. The chief Moorish mosque had been converted into a church, and there were four other churches, together with a monastery, two convents, and the friars who manned the Hospital of San Juan de Dios. A public-spirited citizen had built this in 1587 in the upper part of Barcina for patients suffering from the new scourge brought back from the Americas along with tomatoes, potatoes, turkeys, and maize: syphilis.

A small chapel and shrine to Our Lady of Europa stood at the southern tip of the Rock and over the years had been richly endowed with silver crucifixes, candlesticks, and ornaments. The Nuns' Well does not seem to have been used, and there was no other settlement on the southern plateau (Tarfes Bajos, or Europa Flats).

For defense there were the Devil's Tongue Battery on the Old Mole, Tuerto Battery by the New Mole, San Joaquin Battery below the Moorish castle, facing over the isthmus, and Half Moon Battery near the foot of Charles V's Wall, plus various towers, bastions, small isolated forts, and, of course, the walls. The Governor was Diego Salinas, an able and conscientious general of artillery. To man his batteries, towers, bastions, forts, and walls he could count on 60 infantry, 6 cavalry (without horses), 140 military pensioners, and about 220 citizen militia. Many of the guns were dismounted, and for others there was no powder or shot. Blinded by the westward glare of the gold from Potosi, Spain had left its back door open.

As the unhappy King Carlos II of Spain approached his death, the maneuverings in the courts of Europe to influence the choice of his successor became more frantic and unprincipled. Carlos himself wanted to name his nephew Charles, an archduke of the Holy Roman Empire. Louis XIV wanted him to name another nephew, the Duke of Anjou, who was Louis' grandson. The wretched dying king turned to the Pope for advice. The Pope supported Louis, and Carlos gave in. On November 1, 1700, he died. Louis XIV made two famous remarks: first, to his grandson: "You are now King of Spain, but never forget that you are also a prince of France"; second, to the world at large and Spain in particular: "There are no more Pyrenees"—which, in practice, meant that Spain would be tied to the French chariot wheels for the next century, the century of England's great overseas drive.

England, Holland, and the Holy Roman Empire (its capital was Vienna) did not acquiesce in the accession of the Duke of Anjou, as Philip V, to the Spanish throne. They supported the Archduke Charles, who styled himself King Charles III. The War of the Spanish Succession began. The English and Dutch sent a combined fleet and marines to seize Cádiz. Repulsed there, they landed at Puerto Santa María across the bay and raped, killed, sacked, and pillaged the undefended town in a strenuous effort to win the Spanish people's affection for the Archduke Charles. Don Diego Salinas, feeling exposed and abandoned on his Rock, started pestering Madrid for more men, guns, powder, and money. Madrid made urgent and successful preparations to do nothing. The Archduke Charles' agent, Prince George of Hesse, supported by another large Anglo-Dutch fleet, set up headquarters in Lisbon, rather to the embarrassment of the Portuguese.

There have always been separatist tendencies in Spain, where at least two of the principal cultures, those of the Basques and Catalans, are alien to the Castilian tradition of the central power; and the Prince of Hesse thought he could raise Catalonia for the archduke if he landed in sufficient strength in Barcelona, its capital. The large fleet therefore sailed, made its landing, seized and held Barcelona, and waited for the popular rising. The Catalans' conspiracy failed to rise.

The fleet reembarked its marines and sailed away. The naval commander-in-chief must have been racking his brains thinking what he could do to wipe out the setback. He had, after all, been entrusted with some sixty warships and seventy transports for many months, and what did he have to show for it?

As the fleet headed into the Strait of Gibraltar the admiral, contemplating the gray lion-rock on his starboard bow, had an idea—for his name was George Rooke. He quickly hove the fleet to off Tetuán and held a council of war. All agreed to seize Gibraltar. The fleet sailed again, and on August 1, 1704 (N.S.), anchored off the Rock. At 3 P.M. 1,800 marines of the battalions of colonels Sanderson, Villars, and Fox (later the 30th, 31st, and 32d Foot) landed on the isthmus, cutting off Gibraltar from land contact with the rest of Spain. The Eleventh Siege had begun.

It did not last long. The prince sent a demand to the governor to surrender to him as the representative of Gibraltar's lawful sovereign, Charles III. The governor replied stoutly that they were loyal subjects of Philip V. The surrender demand was repeated and again rejected. Contrary winds prevented the fleet's moving into position until August 3, when it anchored close in and opened fire. The warships mustered about 4,000 guns and 25,000 sailors; the transports held 9,000 troops. Even if Don Diego Salinas' six cavalrymen had had horses, they could only have used them to fade more rapidly from such a bad scene.

Later that day sailors assaulted direct from the ships. Captain Jumper of the *HMS Lenox* led one party ashore inside the foot of the New Mole (the modern Jumper's Bastion). The Tuerto fort was blown up and 100 English sailors with it, but these were almost the only allied casualties, and next day the governor asked for an armistice while the terms of capitulation were worked out.

Some of the English ran amok, pillaging, looting, and raping —the worst excesses being committed at the Shrine of Our Lady of Europa. Here they raped a number of nuns and girls sent there from the Convent of Santa Clara in the town for safety from the bombardments. They also smashed the images, stole the relics, and defiled the sanctuary. They were Protestants—the Inquisition had taught the rest of Europe to translate "Spaniards" as "cruel fiends"—they had been a long time at sea, they were following a hallowed tradition of how the English behave in victory (some of them must have taken part in the picnic at Puerto Santa María): but their actions did little to advance the reputation of their country or the cause of the archduke.

On August 5 the governor signed the surrender. One of the terms was that any Spanish inhabitant of Gibraltar who took the oath of allegiance to Charles as the true king of Spain could stay and keep his house and all his possessions. Few did, and those mostly Genoese. The exodus—the fourth in Gibraltar's recorded history—began. For days the people, carrying what they could, straggled across the isthmus, past the ruins of Carteia, into the hills above the Guadarranque. Here they founded the new town of San Roque "in which is incorporated that of Gibraltar." Over the weeks the intrepid priest of St. Mary's Church, Father Juan Romero de Figueroa, smuggled church valuables and town records out to San Roque. One large image of St. Anthony is legendarily said to have been taken out on a donkey's back, clothed and supported as a sick man.

But the Key of Spain, as King Enrique IV had called Gibraltar, was in the hands of the pretender, the Archduke Charles . . . for a few minutes. At the surrender ceremony the Spanish flag was lowered (a mistake of protocol, this: if Charles claimed to be King of Spain, it should have been left flying) and Charles' personal standard, a modification of the imperial flag, raised.

Admiral Sir George Rooke looked at it and decided that it would not do. This was not what he had in mind when he proposed the seizure of Gibraltar. He ordered Charles' flag taken down and the English flag run up instead. Gibraltar now belonged to Queen Anne.

Bad feeling spread quickly. Some admirals stole guns, some stole wine, Dutch squabbled with English, sailors with marines. Admiral Rooke sailed out and met a French fleet off Málaga. It was a hard-fought day, and the French might have had a clear victory but for the "advice" of Louis XIV's personal representative afloat, who, of course, had to be obeyed. As it was, Rooke was very early able to prove the value of his capture, as he once more limped into the shelter of its guns to repair and refit. Then he sailed again, with all the warships and transports.

The force ashore, left to wait the inevitable counterattack, looted the empty houses, found hidden wine and brandy, and, sometimes, paid for the excesses they or their comrades had committed in the assault. The Spanish sprang into galvanic action to regain what, with a little care, they need never have lost. An army of 9,000 Spanish and 3,000 French soldiers (these latter under General Cavanne) began to gather on the mainland opposite Gibraltar, under the overall command of the Marquis of Villadarias. The British now had some 3,000 men in permanent garrison with many guns, all in working order. They dug inundations on the sandy isthmus to canalize any attack still more narrowly. On October 8, 1704, the Spanish started on their siege trenches.

Inside the besieged town and fortress of Gibraltar, then, the night of October 25, about midnight . . .

Weep for Jerusalem!

Rafael Santangel waited, pressed back into the angle where two houses met, outside the lower wall of the Moorish castle. It was a redcoat coming, and alone—he had seen that much as the man passed the glimmer from a lighted window lower down the ramp. It might be an officer, for few soldiers were permitted to wander round the town alone at this hour—though no one had taken much notice of the curfew while the wine lasted in the taverns.

He saw the man in silhouette against a white wall and gently put himself in balance for the thrust. It was an officer—tricornered hat, sword slung, no musket or bayonet. Quite old by the slow pace and the loud breathing. On his way up to the castle pickets probably. He passed, and Rafael stepped out, caught him under the chin with his left arm, and ripped the long knife across under his arm, opening the Englishman's throat to the bone from ear to ear. There was no cry, only a faint bubbling cough. Rafael let the body fall and stopped to wipe his knife blade on the tunic. That would show, he thought, smiling grimly. Blood was a different red.

He put on his shirt and the old jacket, glanced at his trousers to make sure they were free of blood, and slipped quickly down the ramp. He had thought once, earlier, when he began this work of vengeance, that he should shuffle to and from each murder like an old, bent man: But since the Spanish had opened their trenches any civilian caught out at night would be imprisoned and interrogated. The only hope was not to be caught.

He waited in the dark at each crossing of street or alley, then moved quickly to the next. He never stopped in the open, only in doorways. His knife was in his hand, but hidden.

The Fuentes' house was near the center of Villa Vieja. He moved quickly down the last alley, waited for a pair of patrolling sentries to pass below, then crossed the street and opened the door. This was always a bad moment, for if Amelia had not been able to open it again after Señor Fuentes had shut it for the night, or if someone had come along later and rebolted it, he would be left out all night, sure to be discovered in the morning.

But it opened. He locked it carefully and turned to go upstairs. The girl came flitting down and put a hand on his arm. She usually waited in the attic: but now she led him up and at the head of the stairs turned left instead of right. There were two tiny attics up there—the left over the room where Señora Fuentes slept, the right over Amelia's room. Ever since the day of the surrender he'd been living in the one on the right. Now he followed Amelia through the low hatch into the other attic, closed it behind him, and waited till she had lit the lamp.

"What's happened?" he muttered. He saw that she had brought his clothes, mattress, basin, and bucket from the other attic.

"The English major put a Jew from Barbary to live with us," she said. "He wanted my room. I just had time to move everything across while he went back to his ship to bring his trunk."

"What's he doing?"

"Buying and selling provisions for the English, he said."

Rafael sat down on a wooden chest, and she set out food on another chest. She was a strong-limbed peasant girl from Castellar, wide mouth and eyes, seventeen years old, the Fuentes' servant for four years now; but getting restive to find a man, marry, and return to her village—so Maria Cruz had told him, the last time he saw her alive.

"I got one," he said, drinking some wine. "An old officer. That makes twenty-four. Seventy-six to go." When he had found Maria Cruz's body out there by the shrine, the novice's habit around her neck, and all her young woman's secrets, which were to have been his, bared, bloody, defiled, her eyes open, the livid marks of crazed hands round her throat, he . . . he . . .

He put down the flagon and buried his face in his hands.

After a time he felt the girl's hand gently on his forehead. "Do it no more, master," she said. "I saw you from the window in the moonlight. Skulking down like a thief, like a rat, in the shadows. And you to be the Count of Grazalema. Man, it is not right."

"I have sworn," he said. "One hundred lives for hers."

"At first I said 'tis good," she said. "After I saw how the devils treated the womenfolk, aye, and had one up my skirt when I was kneeling, scrubbing, but I kicked him in the balls and ran in . . . But, master, 'tis not right. Your face is changing. It is not good for a great lord to want to kill."

"But it's all right for such as you?" he said, smiling, his arm round her hips.

"Aye," she said soberly. "Sometimes the likes of us has to. But not you. A lord can harm too many. . . . Besides, I think you must leave now."

"Never!" he said.

"That Jew will be coming and going at all hours," she said. "And he has a sharp eye. . . . Father Romero gave me a message to pass to you."

"What?" Rafael asked. Father Romero was the parish priest and so far still permitted to travel to and fro between Gibraltar and the new town of tents and shacks rising on the hill beyond the isthmus, where the fugitives from Gibraltar were being settled.

"Our general—I can't remember his name—"

"Villadarias."

"Yes—he is going to send many men up the back of the Rock, at night, to take the English by surprise."

"But it's all cliffs and precipices."

"Not quite, master. A few shepherds know a path. Like my uncle."

"Simeon!" Rafael exclaimed. "Yes, he'd know." Simeon Susarte was a small, wizened, forty-year-old mountain man who herded sheep and goats for their rich owners all over the Rock. Rafael remembered seeing him at a boar hunt not long before the British attack.

Amelia Susarte said, "The general, I can't remember his name, wants to send a lot of soldiers up and make a big attack, but first he wants to know what the English are doing on the upper Rock, and he wants to know whether ordinary soldiers will be able to get up the shepherds' path. So Father Romero thought you had better leave this house and live in a cave on the upper Rock somewhere where you can spy on the English. And on the fourth night from tonight my uncle will come up to the Wolf Leap with an officer, to show him that the shepherds' path is all right for soldiers. And you should meet them there two hours after midnight and tell them what you have seen."

Rafael got up and paced up and down the attic, his head hunched under the beams. Amelia shook her head and pointed down. He remembered that he was not over her bedroom now but over Señora Fuentes, who did not sleep well because she was worried about the wound her husband had received in the English attack.

He sat down again. He'd been born in his family's Gibraltar house, and as a boy, during frequent visits, he'd run all over the Rock and later hunted boar and hare and partridge. He knew it well. There were a hundred caves where a man could hide forever if he could get food and water. But he'd have to give up his campaign of vengeance for his betrothed with only twenty-four of the English gone to rot in hell for their crimes.

Amelia said, "I'll bring food and water every night."

"Once a week will be enough," he said. "But . . ."

" 'Tis for Spain," she said. "And you'll get back Gibraltar for the king and the Church."

"Not I," he said. "Your uncle Simeon. Then the king'll make him a count, and you and I could get married."

She turned away and said after a time, "Don't speak like that, master."

"I'm sorry," he said, remembering that his betrothed was not yet three months in the grave. "It was a bad joke. . . . I'll do it. I'll leave as soon as I've eaten. Now, you know the Rock, too, don't you?"

"Aye," she said. "I've often looked after the sheep with my uncle when I was a little girl." She was very subdued, her eyes red. He thought, she has run as much risk as he, hiding him, bringing him food, washing his bloody clothes, emptying the bucket that served him for a commode; and she had her normal work as well—cleaning, sewing, and washing.

"You're a good girl," he said. "I don't know how I'll ever be able to thank you for what you've done. But you'll never want as long as you live, I promise."

"Let's talk about the caves, master," she said wearily, "—and where I shall bring the food, or leave messages from Father Romero, perhaps. . . ."

The Jew was about thirty, she thought, a strong, square-built man with a long face, black jaw, and odd pale blue eyes that gave her shivers when she thought about them. She was very much aware of him, for she was kneeling on a pad scrubbing the tiled floor of the dining room, and he was behind her, sprawled in one of the master's good chairs, looking at her legs.

"So the master got wounded the day the English came, did he?" he said. "That was a long time ago. Why hasn't he gone to Spain like all the other gentry?" He spoke Spanish with an odd accent, using some words that she had hardly ever heard.

She answered him. "He had his leg shot off. He nearly died. He'll leave as soon as he can, have no fear."

"H'm." The Jew got up and wandered round, picking up things and putting them down again. "Who do you spend your nights with?"

"Alone," she snapped.

"Why do you look so tired, then? . . . But you're a woman, aren't you? You wouldn't go out stabbing soldiers at night, would you? Though you're strong enough. A good strong girl." He passed his hand over her buttock. She knocked the bucket of dirty water over his feet.

He laughed. "And good spirit, too . . . Do you know there have been no more murders since the night I arrived, three days ago? . . . What happened to Don Rafael Santangel? He was staying here, wasn't he, before the English came?"

She bent and began to mop up the mess. "He left the next day," she said.

"Why was he here?"

"He was betrothed to marry Señor Fuentes' daughter when she finished her studies in the convent next year. And now, if you will leave me to my work . . ."

"Not yet . . . Was she hurt when the English came?"

"Raped and strangled," she said coldly. "No more."

"Ah. Are you sure Don Rafael left?" She saw that her bitterness had given him a clue and resolved to keep a closer curb on herself. He was waiting for her when she came back, the bucket refilled. She knelt again. He said, "What's he like?"

"Who?"

"Don Rafael. How old?"

"'Twenty-one."

"Good-looking?"

"Yes. Tall, fair-skinned. His eyes are dark. He is heir to a great name and estate."

"Too high for you. But he used to steal a kiss now and then, perhaps." She felt the tears stinging her eyes and with effort kept to the rhythm of her scrubbing.

He said, "Where did you get this?"

She looked around and jumped up. In his hand he held the naked woman carved of ivory that Simeon had found on the Rock years ago and had given, laughing, to her, saying, "One day you'll be like that, little one." It had big breasts and a deep-cut *coño*, and she did not let visitors see it but kept it in a drawer and sometimes found herself praying to it as though it had been a sacred Virgin. But because it was not a Virgin she only prayed to it for pretty clothes and a high comb to put in her hair and such.

The Jew was saying, "This is old, my girl, valuable perhaps. See this stand and the ring on her head. They're gold."

"You stole it from my room," she cried. "You had no right to go in there!"

"I was just interested," he said. "You are a brave girl, loyal, and probably in love. A dangerous mixture." He gave her back the figurine. "I'd like to see *you* like that."

She tossed her head, and as though it had been a signal, the house shook, and a dull thudding rattled the window panes.

"The Spanish have opened fire," the Jew said softly. "They are making their next move. No more than a pawn, I think. They won't risk much for a barren rock like this."

"You talk of us as pieces in a game?" she said angrily. "We are people, not chessmen. This is our home, not a pawn."

"That is how *you* see it," he said, "But you are in minority, are you not? A very small minority." He smiled, suddenly kissed her, but gently, and went out.

From his place between two rocks, in a thorn bush, Rafael watched the English ships sweep into the bay, watched the French squadron try to escape, then the battle. The thunder of the cannon came up surprisingly loud and sonorous, though the billows of smoke sometimes hid all but the topmasts of the ships.

When the smoke cleared, the French had vanished—burning, beached, sunk. The English squadron hove to under the guns of the fortress below him.

He moved his position slightly and grimaced with pain. It was not by sea that the English would be thrown off the Rock.

It was a cool day, with occasional drops of rain from the cloud hanging low over the Wolf Leap far above him. He had been in position since before dawn and could not move till dusk, for he was almost in the middle of the upper defenses, close above San Joaquin Battery. He could easily hear the English soldiers' voices as they talked. Sometimes, as they passed along the slope, they seemed to look straight at him; but his face was daubed with mud, his clothes drab and streaked, and they had not seen him.

This was his fourth day. The English had occupied and improved all the defenses along this north face, from the water as far as the beginning of the cliff above the Moorish Castle. They put out pickets along the foot of the slope, but they were far apart, and certainly men could pass undetected between them to seize the main works, where all but a sentry or two would be asleep. The chief defense was the inundation, which left only a narrow track for approach to the Landgate; but the inundation ended below the cliff, so men could pass to the east of it to the back of the Rock. If Simeon Susarte could really guide a large number of soldiers from there to the crest . . . the English had no defenses at all facing upward except a post of a dozen soldiers close above the Hospital of San Juan de Dios.

The light began to fade, and rain fell more heavily. The redcoats scurried to the shelter of their lean-tos. Smoke of cooking fires rose. The sun gleamed once over the bay and the wreckage of the French ships, then hid, and soon it was dark. Rafael moved carefully, standing, stretching, taking the stiffness out of one limb at a time, then set off along the slope for the Lost Lamb Cave, his home.

It was on the slope, five hundred feet above the town and hidden from it by an outjutting shelf of limestone. Low holly oaks obscured the narrow sand-filled entrance. After a long crawl it widened out into a big chamber.

He went in, lay down on the bed of heather, and fell asleep.

He awoke, knife in hand, at the clink of stone and stared toward the entrance. Though there was no light, he could see her plainly, naked, her hair streaming, running, her mouth open, but he could hear nothing. She vanished. He lay sweating, afraid.

A long time later stones clinked again, and Amelia Susarte's voice whispered, "Master, 'tis I, Amelia." She came in, and he heard her put down a heavy basket. He put out his hand to feel her and touched her breast. Her breathing stopped. He muttered, "You are dressed. . . . I saw a woman naked. Running. Afraid."

"You had a dream," she said, her voice trembling.

The breast was full and round under his hand, and slowly he slid his hand round to her back. She sighed, and all the stiffness went out of her body. Her lips were warm and wet, her body trembling with love. Until the final ecstasies, when she cried out under him, he could not erase from his mind the fear in that other face, for it had been like hers but not the same. But at last, spent, the apparition and the fear faded, and it was Amelia Susarte, the shepherd's niece, beside him.

"I love thee, master," she said softly. "I always have."

He sat up but held her hand. She kissed it and held it to her cheek. "I mean you no harm," he said. "It is not that I think so little of you. It is only . . ."

"Say nothing," she said. "There is no need. . . . I have a letter for you from Father Romero to give to Simeon."

He took it. "What time is it? I shall have to go up soon."

She took his hand again. "Are you tired? Is it bad and dangerous by day?"

"Sometimes," he said. "Yesterday a partridge nearly gave me away. It was walking under the bushes, feeding on fallen berries, and stepped near on my hand before it saw me and let out such a squawk and burst up through the bushes into flight with so sudden and loud a drumming that I thought I was lost, for two English soldiers were watching, not fifty feet away. But they had no interest. They see nothing except rum barrels. . . . What of the town? Señor Fuentes?"

"Well. He threatens to leave tomorrow, but I think the señora will keep him another week. The Jew—he is called Asher Conquy—puts his nose in everything. No one can go round a corner but he is there. I am afraid of him, master."

He said, "You don't have to come up again. There's plenty of food and drink here. . . . I must go."

Outside the cave, in the rain, she turned to him and put up her face. He kissed her, found his desire and affection rising, and stepped back abruptly. What could he bring but shame to a girl such as she?

"Go," he said. "Be careful."

He turned and started up the slope. There were no English up here by day, and there would be none by night. The only paths were narrow winding tracks made by goats and sheep and wild pig. Sometimes he climbed across bare wet sheets of limestone, faintly gleaming, sometimes burrowed up on hands and knees under thorn and scrub. Suddenly, there was nothing ahead. On three sides the void opened before him. He was on the northern pinnacle of the Rock, the Wolf Leap. A few lights glimmered in the town, a few toward Spain. Cloud wraiths drifted past. He sat waiting, fearing that the naked woman would come again in her terror.

He heard the crunch of stone before he saw the men, and then Simeon Susarte was over him. "Don Rafael?" he muttered. "This is Colonel Figueroa. He will bring up five hundred men the night after tomorrow—if he found the path to his liking." The colonel was short, one-armed, and heavy-breathing. "It's the devil," he said, "But if I can get up, my lads certainly can. And you, Simeon, shall be as great in honor as Martin Alhaja Gontran, the shepherd of Navas de Tolosa. Now, my lord, what can you tell me about the English dispositions . . . ?"

Amelia went quickly down from the Lost Lamb Cave, her heart light. She was a woman at last. It had hurt, but the joy of giving had in a moment buried that pain. Perhaps even now she carried his child—though the women said it never happened the first time. Her lover could never be her husband, but that came to many girls. It was done. She was happy.

She reached the top of the town and went more carefully, for the English had increased the strictness of their curfew since the cannonading had begun. Even so, she heard roistering and shouting from farther down and thought, some of the sailors are ashore and celebrating their victory of the afternoon.

The outer door opened squeakily; she closed it and locked it and went to return the key to its proper place in the hall. Then she crept along to her new bedroom, a tiny room beyond the kitchen that had been a pantry.

As soon as she closed the door, she knew she was not alone. A man's voice said, "Have no fear, pretty."

She recognized the thick accent at once, "The Jew," she whispered. She heard the scratch of flint. A light glowed, the candle flame sputtered, towered, steadied. "What do you want?"

"You, pretty," he said. The pale eyes had a touch of yellow in them from the candle flame.

"Lay no finger on me!" she said fiercely, "or I'll . . ."

"I said, have no fear," he said, "I see you love another. It is written in your eyes, your face . . . not to mention the heather in your skirt and hair."

He was half smiling, a little grim, his eyes wandering over her figure. He said, "It's time you put some more oil on that lock. You might waken poor Señor Fuentes."

She waited, head up. He said, "An extraordinary amount of food seems to have disappeared from the kitchen. Two or three loaves. About two pounds of smoked ham. Three bottles of wine. There must be a burglar about. . . . Or a thief, like the man who seems to have lived a long time in the attics here. There are cracks in the floorboards there, over your—my—room. Do you realize that a man might have been peering down and watching you undress? . . . The question is, shall I search you?"

"No!" she gasped.

He stared straight into her eyes for a long time. "Well, you might be carrying a message," he said at last, "but I don't think so. And the murders seem to have stopped."

"Is that what you really came for?" she asked. "To find the man who was killing the soldiers?"

"Ah, so it is only one man, is it?"

"I didn't say . . ."

"I am a humble merchant, señorita, a poor Jew, buying here, selling there. . . . Sleep well. I certainly wish it was I who had pressed your pretty head into the heather." He moved past her and, as before, kissed her. She was expecting it and made no move, but let him. When he had gone, she began slowly to undress, not thinking, only remembering.

She was dozing in her little room when she heard Asher Conquy's voice saying, "It's a secret, but . . ." She sat up quietly. It was five in the afternoon, near the end of siesta time. Another man, also a Jew from his accent, was saying, "How many? We have to know if we are to bring fresh beef over." They were in the alley below the house.

"Two battalions," Conquy said. "One thousand five hundred men in two ships. They'll be here soon after dark, with this wind."

"What are they going to do with them?"

"The prince said one battalion would go to strengthen the north defenses from San Joaquin Battery to the Landport, and the other, well, he wasn't sure—or he wouldn't tell—but he did hint he might send it right to the top, where it could look down on the whole Rock. Then . . ."

"Shhh. We'd better get down to the harbor, Asher, and finish our talk there." Their voices faded.

Amelia slipped her feet into her shoes. Fifteen hundred men! And half of them perhaps going to the top of the Rock just before Uncle Simeon came up with the Spanish soldiers. And Don Rafael in mortal danger, too. She should tell Señor Fuentes. But he was still weak and knew nothing of what was happening. The señora—still less. Father Romero . . .

She hurried to the outer door and looked both ways. Señora de Fuentes called, "Amelia, where are you?" She did not answer. The street was empty, and she went out and walked hurriedly to the church. She found Father Romero in the vestry and quickly whispered her news. He threw up his hands. "What can we do, child? The English have closed all passage to and fro. They will not let anyone pass."

"Does anyone here know the way down the back of the Rock?" she asked.

"None of us," he said. "Remember, there are barely a score of us left now, and you and Señora Fuentes the only women."

She said, "I must tell Don Rafael then. At once."

"Should you not wait till dark, child?"

"That will be too late, Father. By the time he can get to them they will be halfway up the path."

She returned to the house, slipped in, and went to Señora de Fuentes. The old woman was in full mourning, her face ravaged and haggard since the loss of her daughter. She seemed relieved to see Amelia. "I thought . . . I dare not say what I thought. But now I want you to . . ."

Amelia interrupted her. "I must go, señora. It is for Spain. Say only, if the Jew or any of the English ask where I am, that I ran away to Barbary on a ship."

It was near six by now. She forgot the fearful, stricken face of Señora de Fuentes and again left the house. A few soldiers were about, but many houses stood empty, for most of the English were quartered in the lower part of the town. As she climbed, all human sounds faded behind her. Her dress was plain dark gray cotton and would not be easy to see if anyone were watching. But the English might have sent up scouts ahead to make a place for the soldiers who were to come. She must be careful not to betray Don Rafael's hiding place by carelessness.

The Lost Lamb Cave was straight above her now, over the ledge of rock and another hundred feet. Don Rafael might not be in it but along toward the batteries, where he said he spent his days, on watch. She moved left and, instead of scrambling up one of the gullies which cut through the limestone platform, kept below it and headed for the slope above San Joaquin Battery. She saw Rafael in the same moment that he saw her. She signaled urgently to him—come. No English were visible from where she was, crouched now close under a low tree, but he must be able to see some, for he did not move but kept his head turned away and very still.

A glint of light caught the very outside corner of her left eye, and she whipped around, just in time to see a man with a musket sink down behind a rock barely sixty feet from her

They were following her. In a moment Don Rafael would come back in response to her signal. She stood up and walked toward the man with the gun, shouting at the top of her voice. "Stand up, you with the gun! What do you want?"

The man jumped up, his face red with anger, and yelled at her in English. Then Asher Conquy came forward from the scrub behind her, and he was carrying a gun, too. The Englishman grabbed her by the throat and shook her violently. Conquy spoke a word, and he let her go but raised his gun menacingly. Conquy scanned the hill ahead. "I suppose he's somewhere out there. If you don't show me, I'll tell the Englishman to blow your pretty guts all over that rock you're standing on."

She shuddered involuntarily but tightened her lips.

Conquy said, "Come on down, then. We'll see if we can persuade you to talk to us in more comfortable surroundings."

He sat opposite her in the big front parlor. Señora de Fuentes had started to protest when he marched her in there, but he had silenced her with a curt, "She will either talk or hang. Leave us."

The shutters were closed and the tall candles burning. They were the last in the house, she remembered. Tonight was the Eve of All Hallows. In other years some of the children ran about shrieking of magic, and an old woman in the village said that witches rode the sky, she knew because she had seen one.

"My English friend is more used to stalking trollops in London than Spanish shepherd girls on the mountain," Asher Conquy said, "Otherwise . . . He was near, wasn't he? And it is Rafael Santangel?" She looked past him at the windows, silent.

"It does not matter much," he said. "Certainly not as to who he is. But . . ."

"Why are you helping the English?" she said fiercely. "What has this to do with you? Or do you try to betray us just for money?"

The half-smile vanished from his swarthy face, and the pale eyes snapped. He said, "Wait," went out, and came back in a moment, his right hand behind him. He thrust it under her nose and opened it. A big rusty key lay across the square, callused palm. "That's the key of our house," he said.

"In Barbary?"

"Here."

"Here," she faltered. ". . . But how . . . ?"

"We Jews were expelled from Spain many, many years ago. Without reason. Without recompense. We have not forgotten. Why do you think we speak Ladino? It is Spanish as your ancestors used to speak it. . . . Some of our forefathers locked their houses and took the key, thinking the Christian king would recover soon from his madness. But he did not. So why should we not recover our own? You robbed—now you are being robbed.

Good!" He shook the key at her. "See that Señor Fuentes takes the key of this house when he goes. Perhaps he too will wait two hundred and twelve years to come back."

He saw her look of consternation, put away the key in the skirt of his coat, and sat down. "What do you know of all this?" he said. "You are a country girl. Can you read?"

She shook her head.

He said, "I want to know what is the reason for haste. When you heard me talk about the English reinforcements, you—"

"That was a trap!" she cried.

"I fear so. . . . You rushed hither and thither like a mad thing. I had expected you to wait until dark. Why did you hurry so?"

She pressed her lips together and looked past him.

"What would you say to ten maravedis? You know, the English hang spies. Even women. Do you want me to take you to the town major? He has a gallows set up ready."

She knew, for half a dozen soldiers had dangled from it in the past month, convicted of looting.

It was a matter of time. This devil would find out or guess if he kept at her much longer. He liked her, or perhaps he liked all girls. It was her only chance. She burst into tears, only half voluntarily, and sunk her head in her hands. He had a habit of standing close, bending over her. He came now, one hand dropped gently to her shoulder, his voice was low and close. "Don't cry, pretty, just . . ." She jerked her head up and back with all her strength. She felt a smashing thump and heard a cry and sprang for the heavy candlestick. He was reeling, blood spouting like a fountain from his nose. She hit him as hard as she could with the base of the candlestick and hit him again, and he collapsed.

She flew out of the room and the house and into the stable and in a moment back with rope. She had tied up many sheep and goats, and in five minutes he was well trussed, a cloth tied in his mouth. Then she wondered if he was dead and listened. In the silence she heard his breathing and sighed with relief. She ran out and found Señora de Fuentes. "Help me drag the Jew to the cellar, señora," she said. "Then—clean the blood off the tiles. Hear nothing. Know nothing."

She went to the outer door. It was dark. She started up the street.

It was moonless and cold on top of the ridge. They were burning the heath on the sierra to the north, and a fire glowed from the fishermen's huts across the bay. Rafael Santangel sat huddled close to Amelia in the darkness, waiting. A bush stirred, and he strained his eyes to peer down the eastern steep but saw nothing. The wind soughed in the spiny grass and made a thousand tiny flutes of the pitted, holed surface of the limestone. Lights shone in the harbor, and . . .

A man stood over him, dagger gleaming. "The password!"

"All Saints," he muttered.

"Don Rafael . . . and is that you, Amelia? What are you doing here?"

Colonel Figueroa came up, gasping for breath and smelling of sweat and old wine. "Mother of sin, I wouldn't come up there in daylight for all the gold in Potosí. Lead on, Simeon, for I have five hundred men huddled like sheep on that infernal path, only they have but two legs each."

Simeon said, "I'll guide this party to St. Michael's Cave, Don Rafael. They'll all shelter there till dawn. Will you wait here for the next party and bring them along? Five hundred more."

"Very well," Rafael said. Simeon moved off, and the soldiers followed, passing in an endless line. He counted—506 men went by: then he sat down to wait. The second party should be close behind.

Half an hour passed; then an hour; an hour and a half; two hours. The wind sawed into his bones, and the thin shirt gave no protection.

"Should I go to the cave and tell the colonel?" Amelia asked.

Rafael said, "No. He will realize that something's gone wrong. We must stay here. The second party might come any moment."

This time he saw Simeon coming from fully ten paces off. "No one?" the shepherd asked.

"No one."

"The colonel asks that you join him at the cave. I'll go back down the path and see whether they are stuck somewhere. Will you come with me, Amelia?"

"I'd be afraid in the dark," she said. "I'll stay with Don Rafael."

Simeon Susarte dropped over the edge like a falling stone. Rafael led down and across the great face of the Rock to St. Michael's Cave.

There was no light, and once inside the arch, after answering a quiet challenge, they had to step carefully among men sprawled asleep all over the damp floor and propped like sacks against every stalagmite.

Colonel Figueroa seemed unconcerned at the delay. "It's five hundred French who are supposed to be following, and to tell the truth, I'd just as soon they didn't come. More honor for us, you understand? If five hundred Spaniards—and we all took the Holy Sacrament before we set out—can't beat three thousand drunken English and Dutch heretics . . ." There was a whirr of metal as he half drew his sword and slammed it back into the scabbard. Brave but stupid, Rafael thought glumly.

They sat down among the soldiers. "How was it, coming up the Rock?" Rafael asked the nearest shape.

"Ah, that? Nothing," the man answered in a strong accent. "We're from the Asturias. *Coño*, I've come up worse than that carrying a sick ewe, and in a rainstorm, man—" The voices murmured all around in agreement. "Me, too . . ." "Me too . . ." "Aye . . ." "We're shepherds, all. . . ." " 'Twas nothing. . . ."

"But this is something," another rough voice cut in. "Do you know how much ammunition we have? Three rounds each."

"Quiet there!" an officer's voice was sharp.

Three rounds a man, Rafael thought angrily. It was fortunate indeed they had all taken the Sacrament and were shriven.

The time passed. Amelia was warm beside him. He found he was holding her hand but did not let go. "You should stay here when we go," he said.

"Let me come with you," she said. "I am not afraid." He squeezed her hand.

A little later, "Don Rafael," Colonel Figueroa said, "time to go, I think. If you will be so good as to lead me to the nearest English outpost . . ."

In the first gray of dawn they passed over the ruined Moorish wall and five minutes later came in sight of Middle Hill. The bay was dull green below, the western mountains just beginning to glow with light. "The English have a guard there," he said, pointing. "They sleep under that bit of sailcloth."

The colonel drew his sword. "Ready, men?" The soldiers crowded up and around. "Charge!"

They swept past, breaking into a shambling trot and then into a full run. A musket went off, close, with a sudden nervous bang. The yell arose—"*Santiago! España!*"—more shouts, shots, confusion. Rafael found himself running forward in the middle of the pack, his dagger in his hand. Ahead, the yellow and white tide swept over the Englishmen's hill, then swirled round but did not advance.

When Rafael came up, he saw a dozen English soldiers lying about in the grotesque contortions of violent death. Colonel Figueroa was shouting, "Take position here! Captain, you go there. . . ." The Spanish soldiers formed up, marched hither and thither.

"Go on down," Rafael cried, suddenly aboil with fury. "Don't stop here, colonel! The English don't have a single man on this side. Down into the town!"

The one-armed colonel awkwardly straightened his powdered wig. "Do you look to your duty, Don Rafael, and I will look to mine. What is that girl doing here? Take her away at once. . . . Steady there, men!"

A bugle in the town began to blow hysterical calls. A couple of musket balls whistled overhead. The Spanish force gave no reply —only one or two rounds per man left now, Rafael thought. But Mother of God, if they attacked now, they could seize powder and ball from the English! He looked up the slope. Simeon came running down the mountain, bounding from rock to rock in huge leaps. He was alone.

A column of redcoats marched out of the town and began to deploy into line. Bugles blew, officers shouted incomprehensible orders. Rafael counted quickly . . . about eight hundred men. Simeon Susarte arrived, breathing evenly. "No more soldiers are coming," he said. "And no more ammunition. I have been back to the camp. General Villadarias said the French colonel refused to follow you because it was his right to go before you. Also, he thought the enterprise foolish."

"Trust a viper sooner than a woman and a woman sooner than a Frenchman," Colonel Figueroa said pleasantly. "Well then, we must die alone. *Viva la muerte!*"

"Go back, man," Simeon said violently. "Nearly all will be saved."

A storm of musket balls struck the hilltop. A dozen Spanish soldiers fell. The colonel smoothed his wig. "You go, Simeon, and you, Don Rafael, with the girl. Tell the marquis that we die like Spaniards. Give my compliments to the Frenchman. . . . Now, my chicks, face the front."

The musket balls flew thicker. Simeon Susarte's hand was on his arm, tugging. "Come, master." Then Amelia had his other arm and he began to walk, then run, scrambling up the long slope with them.

He felt no emotion until they were down the tremendous path, where they would have fallen, many times, a thousand feet to death but for Simeon Susarte's sure hand and steady voice. He felt nothing until they had hurried along the eastern beach, past the end of the Spanish trenches. Then they turned and looked at the great gray tower of the north face.

Amelia suddenly said, "Asher Conquy will take my ivory woman. . . . Let him. I owe him something."

"I'm thinking we've lost more than a little piece of bone," Simeon said somberly. "We've lost the Rock. It'll be many a year before my sheep set foot on there again. When Englishmen and Jews get together, the rest of us stand little chance."

Then Rafael felt the tears hot behind his eyes, and they flowed silently until he found Amelia's hand, and she took his and pressed it to her cheek without speaking. When they moved on, at length, she tried to free her hand, for her uncle was staring strangely at them, but he held her the tighter.

Book Eight

∞∞∞∞∞∞∞∞∞∞∞∞∞∞∞∞∞∞∞∞∞∞∞∞∞

English Outpost

Guarded by British Arms! Gibraltar Rock,
Of France and Spain, sustains the hostile shock;
See them in vain their arts and arms employ
The vet'ran fortress proves a second Troy;
Though that the Greeks by ten years' siege could gain
Here Bourbon and Iberia strove in vain.

(S. Ancell, 58th Foot)

The Jewish years 5465–5539
AUC 2457–2532
A.D. 1704–1779
A.H. 1116–1193

SIMEON SUSARTE survived to tend his sheep on the mountains of the mainland, and so did Colonel Figueroa, though he was wounded three times more in this attack—twice in the chest and once in the leg; but most of his gallant five hundred were killed. Before another assault could be made, the English had discovered the shepherd's path and scarped it to make it impassable even for mountain goats or Andalusians.

In the following month, November, vile weather, good gunnery, and starvation almost succeeded where Figueroa had failed. Food ran low, and the number of men fit for duty fell to 1,300, which was not enough to man all the guards. Then, as so often in the future, the Royal Navy came to the rescue, bringing in nine ships on December 7. Through December and January the siege continued under incessant cold rain, which was now beginning to hurt the Spanish in their encampments more than the British in their houses and fortifications. Becoming impatient, the Spanish king told Villadarias that he was to be replaced by a Frenchman especially lent by Louis XIV for the task. Since this man, Marshal Tessé, was due to arrive on February 9, 1705, Villadarias staged a massive attack on February 7. In spite of the inundation and the seemingly impregnable fortifications, the stubborn Spanish infantry nearly forced a success and probably

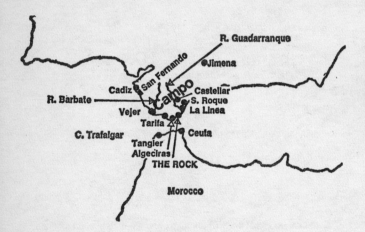

would have but for the long and heroic stand, in an isolated outpost, of sixteen men of the 4th Foot. But fail they did, and Villadarias went, and Tessé came. After he had sat under that North Face for a few weeks, he reported to his royal master that the Spanish were incompetent and improvident. On April 18, under cover of this verbal smoke screen, he raised the siege and marched his armies away, having achieved much less than the despised Spanish, in fact exactly nothing.

Late that year Archduke Charles visited the Rock which his English allies had so obligingly seized for themselves in his name, and they permitted him to appoint a loyal Spaniard, Ramos, to succeed Prince George of Hesse as the governor. But Ramos was soon succeeded by Colonel Roger Elliot, and from then on the governors were British. The war dragged on with, inside Spain, remarkably poor results for the archduke. Queen Anne of England, moved by what whim or logic has never been clear, made Gibraltar a free port, decreeing that no manner of tax or impost was to be levied there on goods whether coming, going, or in transit. This free-port status has been the source of much of Gibraltar's wealth, although from the very beginning it has been eroded, at first by the greed of the governors and later by the local administration's need to raise revenue.

The former inhabitants of the Rock waited in the "Most Noble, Most Loyal City of San Roque, in which resides that of Gibraltar" for a peace treaty which would return them to their homes. But the negotiations moved very slowly—because England was beginning to feel her rising power, because France, though financially weakened by Louis's megalomania, was still militarily strong, and because it was always to France's interest that England and Spain should not become allies; so France always tried to prevent or delay solution of the Gibraltar problem.

Then the war became more complicated. The Emperor died, and Archduke Charles succeeded him on the throne in Vienna as Emperor Charles VI. The powers which had been supporting Charles now cooled off, as success in Spain would make him almost a universal monarch. The war finally ended when Charles renounced all claim to the Spanish throne . . . and Britain insisted on keeping Gibraltar.

In the Treaty of Utrecht (1713) Spain unwillingly but formally granted Britain possession of it. Article X of that treaty, which is the basis of all Britain's claims and Spain's counterclaims, deserves to be set out here in full in the English translation from the original official Latin:

> X. The Catholic King does hereby for Himself, His heirs and successors, yield to the Crown of Great Britain the full and intire propriety of the Town and Castle of Gibraltar, together with the port, fortifications and forts thereunto belonging; and He gives up the said propriety, to be held and enjoyed absolutely with all manner of right forever, without any exception or impediment whatsoever.

But that abuses and frauds may be avoided by importing any kind of goods, the Catholic King wills, and takes it to be understood, that the above-named propriety be yielded to Great Britain without any territorial jurisdiction, and without any open communication by land with the country round about.

Yet whereas the communication by sea with the coast of Spain may not at all times be safe or open, and thereby it may happen that the garrison, and other inhabitants of Gibraltar may be brought to great straits; and as it is the intention of the Catholic King, only that fraudulent importations of goods should, as is above said, be hindered by an inland communication, it is therefore provided that in such cases it may be lawful to purchase, for ready money, in the neighbouring territories of Spain, provisions, and other things necessary for the use of the garrison, the inhabitants and the ships which lie in the harbour.

But if any goods be found imported by Gibraltar, either by way of barter for purchasing provisions, or under any other pretence, the same shall be confiscated, and complaint being made thereof, those persons who have acted contrary to the faith of this Treaty shall be severely punished.

And Her Britannic Majesty, at the request of the Catholic King, does consent and agree, that no leave shall be given under any pretence whatsoever, either to Jews or Moors, to reside or have their dwellings in the said town of Gibraltar.

Clauses follow permitting trade between Gibraltar and Morocco and ensuring that Roman Catholic residents shall be freely permitted to practice their religion. The last clause of Article X follows:

And in case it shall hereafter seem meet to the Crown of Great Britain to grant, sell, or by any means to alienate therefrom the propriety of the said town of Gibraltar, it is hereby agreed and concluded, that in preference of having the same shall always be given to the Crown of Spain, before any others.

There it is; and it is permissible to wonder what "full propriety without any manner of territorial jurisdiction" might mean. The wording has been used to assert and rebut all sorts of claims and rights, but it seems clear that the fundamental purpose of Spain's reservations was to prevent smuggling by ensuring that there should be no land trade between Spain and Gibraltar and that Spain retained certain territorial sovereignty to prevent this; that is, she wrote her terms into an infinite-year head lease.

Semantics apart, it was a bad treaty. It did not correct an injustice but legalized it. Both parties signed it in bad faith. Neither had any intention of keeping its side of the bargain. The Spanish immediately started harassing tactics which prevented Gibraltar's buying goods in Spain; the British had no alternative but to turn to Morocco, a trade which was specifically allowed in the treaty. But many of the Moroccan traders were Jews, and the rest were Moors; and the Emperor of Morocco refused to allow trading unless his subjects were given full freedom to come and go and reside in Gibraltar. Other Jews and Moors bribed the governors to permit them to live in Gibraltar. Several provisions of Article X were thus being broken before the ink was dry on the treaty . . . and the treaty itself was never considered by the European powers as a proper peace but rather as a pause for regrouping and making fresh plans.

The next spasm of the general war which took up most of the eighteenth century came in 1727, and the Spanish instituted the Thirteenth Siege of Gibraltar. This lasted from February to June of that year; vast quantities of powder and shot were fired and two or three abortive attacks made. The siege failed, the Rock continued in British hands.

The century stumbled on. The War of the Quadruple Alliance was succeeded by the War of the Austrian Succession, that is, over who should succeed our old friend Archduke Charles, later Charles VI, now dead, as Holy Roman Emperor. The Spanish king kept his country out of that one, and the Rock saw no action. Then followed the Seven Years' War, in which France finally persuaded Spain to join, with the usual calamitous results for Spain, which suffered heavily in the Americas and in trade; but again there was no action at Gibraltar.

In 1759 Charles III succeeded to the throne of Spain. Probably the best Bourbon in history, he was an appallingly ugly man (painted with ruthless sympathy by Goya) who spent his reign trying to drag Spain out of the middle ages, to modernize and reform her institutions, financial structure, industry, trade, and outlook. The recovery of Gibraltar was by no means his only aim, but it was very close to his heart. It was he who said the cardinal object of Spanish policy should be "peace with England —though war with the rest of the world, if necessary." But it was he, drawn on by the French, who was to break his own dictum and make the most determined attempt to recapture the Rock.

Before returning to the large stage of world politics and European alliances, let us look more minutely at that Rock, the object of so much intrigue. . . . When the dust had settled after Sir George Rooke's seizure, a report to London showed that some 15 single individuals and 30 families (most Genoese) had stayed, and some 60 Jews had arrived. Fifteen years later the civilian men capable of bearing arms were reported to number 45 English, 96 Spanish, and 169 Genoese: This would represent a total population of about 1,500. This dropped to 800 at the end of the Thirteenth Siege but then began to climb as England's continuing presence in Gibraltar and all that it meant, creditable and disreputable, came to be accepted. By 1753 the civilian population was some 1,800, as against 4,500 military. Of the civilians about 800 were Roman Catholic (Genoese and Spanish), 600 Jewish, and barely 400 British Protestant. From this time on the governors were continually concerned to attract more British Protestant settlers to Gibraltar; there was always the fear that a religious cause might unite the preponderant Catholic elements, which, combined with a mutiny or riot among the perpetually unruly soldiery, could mean disaster.

At first the civil population lived entirely by serving and providing the garrison. There was very little trade, as Spain kept Gibraltar in fever quarantine (a pretext for closing sea traffic as well as land traffic) almost continuously for half a century. But about 1750, with the advent of the neutralist Ferdinand VI, communications were opened, something like normal relations were established, and trade began. The chief items shipped through Gibraltar were wine from Spain and France and wine, wax, hides, and brass from Morocco—all mainly consigned to Britain and North America.

In 1777 the population was about 3,100, of whom some 1,800 were Catholics, 800 Jews, and 500 British Protestants. The Jews had established their first two synagogues, the Shaar Hashamayim and the Es Hayim. The Catholics kept the use of the churches built in the Spanish period and remained nominally under the jurisdiction of the Bishop of Cádiz; but wars were more powerful than ecclesiastical hierarchies, and the bishop and his Gibraltarian communicants saw little of each other. The Protestants could worship in the small chapel attached to the governor's lodging (it had once been the Franciscan convent), but there was no room for them on Sundays, as the available pews were taken up by the military.

This population had watched the reestablishment in 1760, on its ancient site across the bay, of Gibraltar's old rival and one-time overlord—Algeciras. It had suffered—civilians, military families, and military alike—under governors of a venality conspicuous even in that conspicuously venal age. These gentlemen regularly made twice as much as their considerable salaries in graft, known politely as "licensing"—they alone had the right to license porters, butchers, cowherds, goatherds, dairymen, bakers, chandlers, fishermen, barkeepers, wine merchants, and, I am sure, strumpets. The people had seen the state of their defenses wax and wane according to the attitude of Spain and the greed or energy of the governor; and they had come remarkably close, on several occasions, to losing their snug little home in the Gut.

Well-documented offers—secret at the time—to restore Gibraltar to Spain were made in 1715, 1718, 1721, 1728, and 1757. One of them was a personal letter from George I to the Spanish king. In each case a *quid pro quo* was, of course, required. Sometimes the Spanish thought the price was too high; once they agreed, but by then the British had raised it. The Spanish, driven on by a demonic desire to recover their territory, were always in the worst bargaining position, especially as British power grew relative to their own. British ministers, sometimes with intent to deceive but usually with genuine concern, frequently took shelter behind "Parliament" or "the people," factors which a Bourbon despot could not appreciate; but they were real enough, and anyone who gave away Gibraltar against the wishes of the British people stood in danger of losing his head. It was barely a century since the same people had proved that whether the head wore a crown or not would be quite immaterial to them.

However shakily (even the Elder Pitt at one time wanted to exchange Gibraltar as an inducement for Spain to enter a war against France), the British connection survived these perils.

And the menace of 1720, when a large Spanish force gathering

in Gibraltar Bay, supposedly to sail to the relief of Ceuta (besieged by the Moroccans) across the strait, was suddenly suspected of a closer task: a *coup de main* against Gibraltar. A hurried message brought ships and troops from Minorca (then
British-held), and the Spanish moved on.

And in 1761 when two regiments, bored, mutinous, or both,
planned to rise, kill their officers, seize the treasure chests, and
sell the fortress to Spain.

And on January 31, 1766, when a storm of fantastic intensity
struck Gibraltar; 33 inches of rain fell in 26 hours, over 50 lives
were lost, and slides of mud, rock, and stone from the upper
Rock buried houses, churches, barracks . . . and fortifications.
The commander of the Spanish forces opposite was the Duc de
Crillon, a Frenchman in the Spanish service. He suggested that
an immediate attack, before the British had recovered, would regain Gibraltar. He should, of course, have attacked first and
asked permission later, for Charles III was an honorable man; he
was not at war with England at that moment, and he refused permission; and by the time the messengers had ridden to Madrid
and back, the British would have had time to build new fortifications, let alone clean up old ones.

In 1775 the embattled farmers of Lexington and Concord
fired the shot heard round the world, but with particular dismay
by Charles III. War against England promised an opportunity
to even many old scores, in particular to get back Minorca and
Gibraltar; but to help the American rebels was almost certainly
to establish them in power as a regime, and an example which
would soon cause the loss of Spain's own huge American empire.

But reluctantly he was dragged in. In 1778 France agreed to
help the Americans and declared war against England. In May of
that year Spain offered to act as peacemaker, suggesting as a sti-
pend—Gibraltar. The brilliant French diplomat Vergennes
finessed that offer out of court and in the following April succeeded in leading Charles III over the brink. Under the secret
Convention of Aranjuez Spain agreed to declare war against
England, and France agreed not to sign a separate peace until
Gibraltar was again Spanish. The fate of the Rock was thus
linked with the outcome of the American war, which was rapidly
spreading to every place where France, England, and Spain
could attack one another's interests, that is, the whole world.

On June 4, 1779, the governor of Gibraltar, General Augustus Eliott, entertained his Spanish opposite number, General Mendoza, the military governor of San Roque, to dinner in honor of King George III's birthday. There was much bonhomie, friendship, and good cheer: the politicians had not yet told the soldiery of their secret negotiations.

On June 16 the Spanish ambassador in London suddenly presented a list of complaints and accusations amounting to a declaration of war against England. Simultaneously, orders were sent from Madrid to close all communication between Spain and Gibraltar. Information about the artificially planned break must have reached San Roque by June 19, for when Eliott made a formal call that day to congratulate Mendoza on a recent promotion, he was surprised to find himself and his party treated with marked coldness and an atypical lack of courtesy.

The courier carrying the detailed orders had been delayed on the road from Madrid and did not arrive until two days later, or Eliott might have been seized then and there. When the orders did arrive on June 21, 1779, Mendoza at once closed the land frontier on the isthmus. At sea the few Spanish ships in the bay began to enforce a strict blockade under the command of Admiral Barcello, a man with a particularly virulent hatred of Britain and her usurpation of the holy soil of his fatherland.

The Great Siege began . . . with a deafening silence.

Except at sea no one fired a shot. So, while the British peer down from their eyrie and the Spanish look for a general who owns a copy of Vauban's *Handbook of Practical Siegecraft,* let us examine the military details of the confrontation now set up. At the time no one could have forecast how the light of history would fall. We, looking back, can see that the match was between an ill-harnessed mob of dukes, counts, generals, admirals, mad scientists, and cloaked agents on one side—and on the other, the excessively John-Bull-like shape of the British governor.

There is a famous portrait of him by Reynolds, cannon smoke billowing behind him and the sacred Key of Gibraltar firmly grasped in his right hand, its chain twined twice around the hand. Apart from two factors that were beyond his control—the cession of the Rock by negotiation or the loss of all sea communication—the fate of Gibraltar came to depend centrally on this man. Seldom do those holding the highest positions at the beginning of a long campaign emerge from it with the most credit—or, indeed, any credit—at the end; but Eliott did, and it is essential to know him well.

George Augustus Eliott was born in the Scottish Lowlands in 1717, so was nearly sixty-two when the siege began and had been governor two years, long enough to show the first of his qualities, sheer military professionalism. He had already counted the stores, inspected the troops, examined the defenses, and put in hand a program to get them back into shape after the neglect, embezzlement, and incompetence normal to peacetime. His military education had included training at a French academy, volunteer service in the Prussian Army, and further study at the British military engineering establishment at Woolwich. In consequence he spoke French and German fluently. He had seen much active service, including Dettingen, Minden, and Havana. In politics he was a King's man, that is, of the Tory party, which supported Lord North, George III, and the American war. He was addicted to formality but not form: he didn't care too much what the soldiers wore as long as they obeyed orders, performed the proper salutes and evolutions efficiently, and even used a little imagination. He was strict but humanitarian when he could be, in terms of the age, the sort of men he commanded, and the general conditions of a beleaguered fortress. He was bigoted in his attitude toward all new ideas except military ones: here he was a profound thinker and a restless innovator and experimenter. He was a superb administrator and a master of logistics: supply, transport, and the administration of justice were alike rapid, effective, and sound. He had the memory of a top-grade inventory clerk and always knew exactly how much of everything there was in Gibraltar and where it was stored. He was not a good delegator of responsibility except—perforce—in naval matters, preferring, like Wellington, to make sure that he himself was always at the decisive spot at the decisive moment.

So far, so good—nothing incongruous with that great red face and beak nose of Reynolds'; but Eliott was also a teetotaler, a vegetarian, and, very probably, a homosexual—in this respect resembling his hero Frederick the Great.

The problem facing Eliott—to hold Gibraltar—was shaped by a number of factors, mostly unfavorable. The general war situation ensured that troops could not easily be found to reinforce or relieve his garrison. For several months, indeed, a huge Franco-Spanish fleet stood ready off Brittany to carry French invasion troops into England, and while that threat lasted, the British government could hardly be expected to worry much about Gibraltar. The same bad political situation could at any moment decide the Emperor of Morocco, Gibraltar's nearest source of supply and intelligence, to give up his nominal neutrality. In the immediate neighborhood of the Rock the Spanish were able to dominate, though not totally control, sea communications. Finally, the garrison was under strength (about 5,300 men against the 7,000 Eliott considered necessary).

On the other side of the ledger, the Spanish army, once the finest in Europe, was, like the country itself, in process of decline. Eliott's British and German troops were no braver, but they were much better led. The same applied with even greater force to the two navies (though Eliott's local naval commander, Admiral Duff, must be excluded from this generalization: he was weak, slow, obstinate, and fearful.

And there was the North Front, towering 1,349 feet above the only land approach; the defenses strengthened since the siege of 1727 and further improved by Eliott; the rest of the fortress out of artillery range except from the isthmus, and some of it out of range for any weapon of the time, even from there; a general air of frowning impregnability, which imposed a sense of hopelessness, of futility, in the minds of soldiers sent against it or remaining long under the gray crown of its levanter cloud.

Eliott faced six specific main dangers. Assuming normal competence, the Rock was unassailable by direct land attack, such as that of January, 1705; but a combined attack from sea and land, prompt use of opportunities that might arise in fog, storm, or night, the turning of small mishaps to practical use through a good and rapid spy service—any of these, amounting to good generalship, was the first danger.

Then there was pestilence. Minorca was soon to be lost, not by the defeat of British forces but through blockade, causing the soldiers to go down with scurvy until it was not an army but a charnel house that surrendered to Crillon. Pestilence had already struck Gibraltar several times, and a severe epidemic would obviously be very dangerous.

The third was starvation—and to this the Spanish originally pinned their hopes.

The fourth was treachery—the surrender of the garrison by its own soldiers. As we have seen, this nearly happened in 1761. Some particular discontent or grievance, aggravated by the conditions of a long siege—boredom, over-close contact, discomfort, fatigue, claustrophobia (endemic in Gibraltar at the best of times)—and by the then-current custom of leaving regiments on the same foreign station for inordinate lengths of time, could easily produce a similar situation.

Fifth, there was what might be classified as "disaster," some piece of ill luck which trumps good management. An enemy hit on one of the two major magazines could have rendered the garrison unable to resist. The magazines were well protected, but there is ultimately no protection against chance, stupidity, or carelessness. Again, a very dry winter might have failed to replenish the Rock's subterranean supplies of water, which must have led to capitulation. The chance of Spain's or Royalist France's turning up a Napoleon for command should also be reckoned under this heading.

Sixth and last, but the most likely of all, was the possibility of Gibraltar's being ceded back to Spain in return for some other piece of territory less dear to Spanish pride or more profitable to the British Exchequer.

Armed then with some 663 pieces of artillery; served and defended by 485 artillerymen, 122 engineers and artificers, and 4,775 infantry (5 British and 3 Hanoverian regiments of the line); facing an army of indeterminate size—but larger, and growing until in October it numbered 14,000 men—Gibraltar entered the siege.

Extracts from the Private Diaries
of Gamaliel Hassan

A.D. 1779

June 25: We met this afternoon in the big room of the house. All the family were there, and all tried to dissuade me from volunteering. Old Micah Benoliel said this quarrel between Christians was none of our business, but I disagreed. If Spain recovers Gibraltar, what would happen to us? My aunt Abigail said my constitution was not strong enough to withstand the rigors of a soldier's life, but I could not agree. The teacher said I would have to eat forbidden foods and disobey the Law. I said it would be for the defense of all Jews here. In the end my cousin Abraham cried, "Gamaliel's right! I also will answer General Eliott's call."

June 27: A quiet day in the house. My uncle stayed in his counting house, my sister and Abraham visiting the Conquys, only Abigail at home. She asked why I wanted to leave them all. I tried to tell her I felt it was my duty, but she would not be comforted and wept in my arms. She said she had done her best to make me happy since she married my uncle, who has really been a father to Miriam and me since our own parents died. What Abigail says is true, but now that I am a man I have found it hard to treat her as I should. She is only 8 years older than I, so barely 30 now. Abraham teases me that I love her. He does not like her. I suppose it makes some difference that she is the wife of his father but not his mother. I think it is best that I should go away for a time. I was planning to go to Lisbon to study to be a teacher, as my mother always wished for me, but now that is impossible. We are at war, but no one has fired a shot yet.

July 2: Here I am, dressed in a blue coat, surrounded by snoring soldiers. It is raining, and the only food for dinner was salt pork, which I could not eat. Two of the soldiers vomited over the gun. The sergeant banged their heads together and made them clean it up with their own shirts. They are a rough lot here, half of them still wearing the red coats of the infantry, which General Eliott transferred them from to make the artillery up to strength. The sergeant says I speak English amazing well for a Jew Rock Scorpion. I have told him that when we were young we had for a time a young Jewish lady from England in the house, who taught us the language.

July 5: Gun drill. The sergeant shouted at us like animals from dawn to dusk. He calls me Gunner Moses. I dropped a cannonball on my foot and everyone laughed. I think a bone may be broken.

July 7: I told the sergeant I ought to see a surgeon about my foot, which is most painful, but he told me foully to stick it up my a***. We are cultivating a little patch of earth beside the guns. General Eliott has ordered it, and the sergeant has told me to plant something in it that we can eat. "It's Old Von Bugger's orders," (he always speaks of the Governor thus) he shouted, "so plant something, anything, how in thunder should I know what will grow on this stinking Rock?" My sister Miriam came up to bring me a spare shirt. The soldiers spoke coarsely to her until I said she was my sister. Then they turned away, ashamed. When she had hurried off, the sergeant clapped me on the back and shouted, "No offense meant, Moses. We thought she was another Emily." He gestured, and I saw a raggety young woman with blond hair and a pretty face lying under a soldier at the back of the battery, her skirts raised. I turned away, blushing.

July 10: There is a gun at Wolf Leap at last. We have been three days dragging it up there. I never thought it would be possible, but it was done. The sergeant had a thumb crushed when the gun rolled back against the rock but only swore and wrapped a dirty kerchief about it. The gun looks down on the Spanish forts and the neutral ground between. It was the governor's idea. He came and watched us at work twice, and when I made a suggestion about working out the ranges from the top, he asked my name. I am the only man in the battery who can read or write. . . . An infantry officer has invented a shell that can burst in the air over the enemy. What ingenuity in a bloody cause. Captain Witham, our captain, has invented a light flare and struts about like a young cockerel. He has a keen face and quick eyes. He called me a damned Jew yesterday and apologized today. The sergeant says he sees I have taken my foot out of my a***.

July 13: Pointed out an error in the gun drill orders to the sergeant this morning. Received nothing but abuse from him and jeers from the other soldiers for my pains.

July 18: Had an evening's leave and spent it quietly at home. My uncle sighed to see me sunburned and my hands battered. He told me that Admiral Duff refused to provide stores to finish outfitting the Emperor of Morocco's warships, which the governor had promised him to do here. Mr. Logie, the consul in Tangier, has come over to explain to the admiral the dire consequences for the garrison here if the Emperor should turn his face against us. That country is the only source of many supplies to us, especially fresh fruit and vegetables. . . . Nahum Conquy has asked for my sister Miriam's hand. My uncle is not very pleased, as he thinks Miriam can do better than that; but she has pleaded —she is twenty-six—and he will not stand in the way. Abigail came in—she will not let me call her mother or even aunt—and begged me to tell them all about my life in the army. I talked for near three hours, and she listened most eagerly, barely taking her eyes from my face. She agrees that the sergeant is no more than a stupid ox. She is a very intelligent woman and understands much that one can hardly put into words. My uncle thinks there will be no firing here, for the Spanish will try to starve us into surrender.

August 10: The Dons are making a jetty about 50 feet long at the Orange Grove, which is just out of reach of our guns. They are also throwing up a breastwork about a mile from the North Front. Then, the sergeant says, they will make parallels, merlons, traverses, flèches, barbets, curtains, and a hundred other military devices and so creep in zigzag fashion toward us until they are very close. Then they will collect bundles of brush, fill in our ditch, and assault. "Then we'll see how you like the look of cold steel, Moses," he bellowed. But he does not say how the Spanish are to cross the inundations General Eliott has caused to be made across the isthmus, leaving only a causeway barely ten feet wide, which can be swept by grapeshot—or how they are going to climb a cliff over a thousand feet high, if they try to go round our flank. . . . Mr. Logie the consul has returned to Tangier. The Moorish vessel in which he traveled was searched by a Spanish cruiser, but Mr. Logie hid in a scuttle for 10 hours. The Governor's dispatches to England and some secret codes they had prepared for communication with each other he hid in a loaf of bread, and they were not found. The fair-haired strumpet Emily was at the battery again today. She has blue eyes and smiled at me. I turned my back. In the synagogue we are to pray for deliverance from the hands of Spain.

September 1: Saw Cousin Abraham today. He is in the infantry and says the soldiers are like animals but kind in a rough way. One relieved himself in Abraham's boots last night, liquid in one, solid in the other.

September 12: The Governor came to the battery this morning with a large retinue of officers and ladies and a band. The sergeant laid a gun on the enemy works and the Governor presented a slow match to a lady. She put one hand over an ear, closed her eyes, and somehow managed to put the match to the touchhole. The band played *Britons, strike home!* I did not see where the ball hit. It matters not. We are not going to be starved without hitting back. The governor called me out and told them all that I was a volunteer and would not be forgotten if I survived. After they had all gone the sergeant said that Old Von B. has his eyes on me for a bumboy. I can hardly believe that General Eliott, so imposing and manly a figure, should be victim to such a failing.

September 15: It is expected that the Dons will soon return our fire, which we keep up. Many civilians are moving south, where they are living in great discomfort above the naval hospital in cloth tents and brushwood shelters. The soldiers call it New Jerusalem, and many of our people have gone there, but not my uncle. Others have left for Morocco and Lisbon, and the Governor does all he can to assist such flights, for he proclaims that he wants no useless mouths in the fortress.

September 16: At work all day to take up the paving in the streets so that enemy shot and shell will bury itself in the soft earth instead of bouncing off and hurling the paving stones about with as much effect as though they themselves were shards of iron. Teams of 80 men pull the plows through the ground to turn the earth. It is the Governor's idea.

October 2: Gun drill. It is a waste of time. We all know every movement and could do them in our sleep. Soldiers are brutal people, not fit to live with, nothing fine in their nature. I wish I were in Lisbon.

October 20: The Dons continue to push forward their parallels. They have three batteries mounted, one of 7 guns and two of 14 each. A privateer has captured a shipload of rice, and the price has dropped to 8 pence a pound. Abigail says that the family eats very little and is hungry. There is no food for civilians at all except what they can buy. Everything that is captured or brought in or smuggled in is sold at auction, by General Eliott's orders, after the military rations have been made up. My uncle buys some and distributes it free to the needy members of the congregation; but Mordecai Anahori and others, Jews and Christians, buy only to hoard, planning to resell when starvation shall have increased the price. In spite of this Abigail gave me an excellent meal and gave me a basket of cold chicken and sweetmeats to take back. I have shared them with the soldiers but shall not tell Abigail.

October 30: Isaac Toledano has fallen ill of the smallpox. Captain Witham says it would be a Jew because we never wash. Then he apologized, admitting that we wash a great deal. . . . Such a pestilence can be more dangerous than the Dons. General Eliott cannot overawe a disease, though he does his best. The soldiers were all drunk this evening. Only two or three were sober enough to go to Emily and couple like dogs behind the gun. She looks sadly at me. They all drink hard and die fast here.

November 10: A child died last night in New Jerusalem, of starvation, it is said. The soldiers mutter that they will break into the food stores, damn them if they don't; but they don't. Captain Witham says the Governor has been living on nothing but 4 ounces of rice a day for the past week. He is as robust as ever, but the sergeant cries, "Let Old Von B. try feeding *me* that. . . . !" but he would obey if it were ordered, though with much blasphemy. He, indeed all the soldiers, take a strange delight in obeying the orders of an officer, however dangerous or stupid.

November 15: Great excitement as many in the town and garrison saw a British cutter, the *Buck,* fight her way into harbor through many superior Spanish ships. . . . We are ordered not to powder our queues, since the flour is needed for food.

December 28: The Spanish fired on us today for the first time. Captain Witham lost £20 over it in a bet with Lieutenant Burleigh of the infantry, for he thought the Spanish would never fire. There was a great storm the day before yesterday, and today the bay is full of wreckage and tree trunks and muddy with the swollen waters of the Guadarranque. Miriam's marriage has been arranged for next February 15.

A.D. 1780

January 13: Went home in the afternoon and fell asleep on a couch. When I awoke it was dark and my uncle had gone to bed. Abigail brought me food and warm mulled wine. She began to cry and begged my pardon. She said she is very unhappy and does not know what to do. I tried to comfort her, and she said she was so lonely. Daniel, my uncle, is 20 years older than she and no longer cares for her as a man should care for his wife. Every night she goes to bed but cannot sleep. Other men cast lascivious eyes on her, and that makes her more miserable yet. I tried to comfort her but about midnight thought it wiser, she was so overwrought, to return to the battery, though I have a permit till today. A redcoat sentry nearly bayoneted me. . . . Our weekly rations have been lessened by ½ lb. beef, ¼ lb. pork, and 1 pint pease. There is much robbery, not only of food, among civilians and soldiers alike.

January 19: I was asleep when the Rock Gun was fired (that is what we now call the gun we dragged up to Wolf Leap) to signal the arrival of a relieving fleet under Lord Rodney. All the soldiers except me are drunk, and they have forced me to drink toasts to King George III and Admiral Rodney. It is the first time strong liquor has passed my lips, and I do not feel very clear in the head. The sergeant says it will get worse before it gets better.

February 13: The fleet has sailed away but without the 73rd Foot, which was intended for Minorca, but our governor thought our need was greater than theirs. They are Scotchmen and wear colored wool skirts called kilts. Two have spoken to me, and I did not understand a word. Many civilians sailed with the fleet, for the Governor again advised all "useless mouths" to leave. Admiral Duff has gone, too, and my uncle says *Good riddance, he* was a useless mouth indeed!

February 16: My sister married yesterday. Much wine afterwards. Cousin Abraham looked strange in red coat and yarmulka. In the evening Abigail embraced me fiercely in a darkened room, everyone else gone or talking upstairs, and kissed me so that her tongue searched my mouth. She talked wildly, her cheeks glowing in the dusk, of what Nahum Conquy would be doing to Miriam now, breaking the glass of her virginity even as he shattered the glass under the awning. Then she cried passionately, "It never happens so to me now!" I know little of women, yet it is obvious she wants me to betray my uncle with her. It is vile even to think of, but I cannot put the thought out of my mind. I wish I could go to Lisbon.

February 27: Twelve more cases of scurvy in the artillery. Many more sick of smallpox, especially children, who are dying of it. The Governor will not allow the inoculation against it, as it is against his principles. What of ours? The Empress Catherine of Russia has joined our enemies. I am miserable and dare not go home. Should I try to injure myself in such a way that I will be sent away? But she would say she could look after me better than anyone else and keep me at home. Perhaps I should get drunk like the others. Emily says, "You are very handsome. I like Jews. They are so passionate." She calls me Pretty Boy and strokes my arm. The sergeant says, "It is not because you are tall and dark but because your family's rich, and you have a p**** a yard long, like all Jews, I'll be bound."

March 19: Captain Witham says that Mrs. Mainprice told him the Governor thinks the death of the children a good thing. They are useless mouths to him and nothing more. I fear that I cannot bring myself to like him, though without him we would all be lost here. Many civilians are suffering from putrid fever. A soldier of the 72nd hanged on the Red Sands this morning for attempted desertion. A year ago I would have thought him mad. Now I am not sure. Who is sane in this world?

April 5: No leather to repair my boots. I have made shoes out of an old coat, bound with twine. The sergeant asked me to read him a letter from England. It was from the vicar of his village.

His mother is dead. The sergeant cried like a child but refused rum and went to sleep in my arms. Smallpox continues, especially among the children.

May 1: Visited home today, but at noon. My uncle says that his associates in Tangier report that the British government have opened secret negotiations with Spain about the cession of Gibraltar. The Dons will not negotiate very seriously as long as they think they can get it for nothing, by conquest. The Tangier people think that the French will see to it there is no agreement.

May 19: I can scarce bring myself to write what passed today, even in the privacy of my diary. Abigail was so quiet and proper when I visited earlier in the month that I thought she must have given up her unworthy passion for me; but she came to my bedroom where I was sleeping, and under her robe she was wearing nothing. She took it off and standing there, then kneeling, begged me to take pity on her as a woman. If I did not, she would be forced to go to the soldiers and sailors in the streets, and what would the scandal be then? She is a beautiful woman, the first I have seen quite unclothed, and I had the utmost difficulty in escaping without betraying my uncle. I could not sleep for visions of her and of hell.

May 20: She must be a wicked and licentious woman to act as she does. If all women were like her, what would happen to civilization? She is not worthy of my concern. Someone should tell my uncle. His son Abraham? But that would make my uncle hate him.

June 8: The Spanish Admiral Barcello sent fire ships into the harbor last night. The wind changed in the nick of time or his ruse would have burned most of our vessels and perhaps blown up a main magazine. Even the wind bows to General Eliott's will.

June 9: Captain Witham says that Mr. Logie sent word from Tangier some days ago that Admiral Barcello would try the fire ships. Now the admiral will doubtless think of some other deviltry. Captain Witham says Lieutenant Burleigh is a coxcomb. Lieutenant Burleigh is as handsome and as dashing as Captain Witham, and the Governor thinks highly of him. That is perhaps the trouble.

June 15: Admiral Barcello has come out with his new deviltry. They are boats about 60 feet long and 20 feet in beam, with a large cannon in the bow. They have a lateen sail, but they are usually driven by oars, which makes them independent of the wind. They can move as easily by night as by day. Yesterday they bombarded South Barracks and the night before, the town. No one fired back, as no one could see them. I spoke to a sailor, and he said they are dirty, unseamanlike, cowardly inventions, beneath the notice of British tars.

July 3: The gunboats bombarded Europa Point, killing several women and children. Very hot. One soldier dead of heatstroke and rum. The riots agitated by Lord George Gordon in England will much cheer our enemies, making them think the nation is at the point of revolution. My gun did good practice this morning. Captain Witham says we are the best in the battery. Thoughts of Abigail as I last saw her cannot be put away. Spoke sharply to Emily when she approached me, smiling. She, poor thing, looked hurt.

July 24: Served bad meat today. The sergeant took a piece to show to Captain Witham. Two accidents in another battery, a man lost his leg, not expected to live. He is married, with 3 children. A soldier of the commissary tried to poison himself. Four deserters—one found drowned, the other three vanished without trace but probably dead at the back of the rock and being eaten by the apes.

August 24: Colonel Ross has called General Boyd, the lieutenant governor, a storekeeper general on a public parade of his regiment. General Boyd has let it be known that he did serve in the commissary, where the German Count Scharlberg said of him, "The British send us commissaries fit to be generals and generals fit only to be commissaries." It is pitiful that elderly men of such position should be guilty of backbiting like women. It is the military life responsible. Also our being beleaguered here, with no escape from each other's company or from our circumstances even for a moment.

September 1: Another hot day, with a levanter. One of the soldiers tried to shoot himself. Another desertion. The Emperor of Morocco must think we are going to lose the war, for he has announced that the warring nations can continue their operations against each other even in his very harbors—which means that the Spanish are now free to prevent our Moorish supply vessels from ever sailing.

September 7: The officers have rioted in the town, breaking Jews' windows and doors because, I suppose, the Jews asked for payment owed to them for goods or loans. Captain Witham says it was only "a little," but what would happen to us if we rioted even "a little"? Three more of the 72nd deserted yesterday by trying to go down the back of the Rock. They all fell. I saw one corpse being carried past, uncovered—this by the Governor's order. A horrible sight. What is more astonishing is that two Spanish deserters came in through the infantry outpost below our battery last night.

September 27: The Emperor of Morocco has now leased his ports opposite here to the Spanish, so that door is finally closed. . . . The Governor inspected our battery today. He looked grim but smiled at me. The sergeant said, "Moses, why don't you volunteer to be Von B.'s batman? He might marry you." We are at barely 30 men in the battery from 50, from scurvy. The Spanish deserters were Walloon mercenaries from Holland. I wonder the Spanish employ them here.

October 2: The Dons raided the gardens we have been cultivating in the neutral ground last night. My uncle came and told me I should visit home more often, because Abigail thinks I dislike her. She is very fond of you, my uncle said, and is unhappy when you make her think you don't care for her. What am I to do? She is advancing against me by parallels.

October 9: Yom Kippur. Many Jewish women at the cemetery, wailing and praying for peace.

October 13: The sick of scurvy are being given a medicine of lemon juice mixed with brandy (to preserve it). Captain Witham says that the navy seized a Dutch boat loaded with lemons a few days ago. What luck the Governor has—but he deserves it.

November 20: The Governor has ordered all lights out in the town and New Jerusalem at 7 of the evening so the gunboats will have nothing to aim at. The sailors say the gunboats are unseaworthy tubs. The Dons are firing at our fishing boats for the first time. They are determined to starve us. Miriam is pregnant, the child expected in April.

December 20: A terrible flood last night. Gunner Tomkins washed clean out of his battery, next to mine, and drowned. The mud is three feet deep round our gun, and in parts of the town it is over a man's head. Many streets are blocked and houses full to the second floor. England has declared war on Holland and Morocco on England. That puts us in arms against all the world except Portugal.

A.D. 1781

January 12: Mr. Logie and 110 others have arrived from Tangier, whence they have been driven by the war with Morocco. Captain Witham talked to me a long time today because, he says, I am the only *other* civilized person on the Rock. He told me that the siege is famous all over the world, but service here is not benefiting the officers professionally, and they are discontented. The army is expanding everywhere for the war, he said, and elsewhere officers are being posted and promoted rapidly for new batteries and regiments; but as no one can leave Gibraltar, officers here are not considered for these posts and promotions, however well qualified. "And some of us are very well qualified indeed," he said, stroking his chin. The officers' pay is given to them in Spanish dollars at an unfavorable rate of exchange. Old Von B. should act to better our lot, he said, or there would be trouble.

February 26: Many Jewish women sailed to Genoa. Abigail did not go although my uncle suggested she should. Saw Cousin Abraham today. He told me that Abigail is very hurt that I have not been to visit them on my leaves. I thought to tell him the truth but did not dare. He has made me promise to go with him next time he has leave.

March 21: The officers rioted in town again, throwing stones at windows. They also broke into a house and pummeled two merchants. Fortunately they did not bother us. I was at home with Abraham. Abigail was very subdued, kind, gentle. I was not alone with her but a second, when she whispered, "Forgive me, I am only a weak and wicked woman." I was sorry for her. Miriam very heavy with child.

March 25: The merchants the officers attacked were Jews, Israel and David Serruya, who had asked payment of old debts. The Serruyas complained to the Governor, who heard the case and summarily fined the officers 30 guineas each. It is the first time Jews have ever found protection in this place, and that not because they are Jews but because General Eliott will not tolerate indiscipline anywhere. The Spanish fire on us very little. It is hard to believe we are at war.

April 6: Lieutenant Burleigh of the 39th took a few boatloads of sailors last night and tried to cut out some Spanish warships becalmed under Point Cabrita across the bay; but the moon came out and they were seen but managed to return without loss. Captain Witham says Lieutenant Burleigh was only trying to puff himself up in the Governor's eyes.

April 13: A large relieving fleet arrived yesterday. The Dons seemed to take it as a sign that they will have to do something more than wait for us to starve, for as the fleet sailed in they began a tremendous bombardment—not at our batteries but at the town itself. It is still going on. Houses are being struck as I watch. The old Benoliel house was hit and knocked to pieces by the first shot, but I believe there was no one in it. Captain Witham says the naval hospital is being opened to civilians while the need lasts.

April 14: Miriam was safely delivered of a boy early this morning. She started labor the day before, when the bombardment began. They sent for me soon after I had written the above words, as she was in pain and many drunken soldiers were threatening to break into the house. The sergeant would not let me go till midnight when the battery was ordered to stand down. The town was a scene of madness, lurid flames rising to the sky, cannonballs and shells whistling in the night and bursting with terrible roars against the walls still standing. I found three drunken redcoats in the passage of our house, Abigail facing them alone and Miriam moaning upstairs. With my help we persuaded the soldiers we had nothing, and they left. More came later, but I stayed upstairs with Nahum and the midwife with Miriam while Abigail dealt with them all by herself. She was like a queen—brave, careful, never hysterical, never even rude. She must have reminded them, many of them so young, of their mothers. She certainly did to me. . . . I am back at the battery now, to find half the gunners drunk. One just tried to kill me with his ramrod. The sergeant kicked him over the parapet, where he will lie till he recovers, if he does, for it is a 25-foot fall.

April 15: The riot continues in the town, but I begin to think it is justified, for I learn that when the enemy shells knocked down walls and blew open houses, they revealed large stores of food and liquor which merchants have been hoarding against higher prices. All the soldiers—infantry, artillery, and even the engineer-artificers—are like madmen! I saw a dozen soldiers barbecuing a pig over a fire of pure cinnamon, worth near £200. I watched a corporal of the Highlanders eat 8 lbs. of beef in ten minutes. Others took the Virgin out of the Roman Catholic church and put "her" into the whirligig, as is done to loose women. I saw no officers anywhere. They are wise. Nor did I see any Germans take part in the debauchery.

April 23: The fleet has sailed, and the harbor is empty again. The gunboats fired 300 shots into the town. It has been decided to name Miriam's boy David Eliott, the latter insisted on by Nahum, in the hope of obtaining the Governor's patronage for him; but in truth it is a noble name to carry; we would all be long since in the hands of Spain without him. Four men are hanging from the beams of burnt houses. They were caught looting the king's stores. No one is punished for looting private goods.

May 3: The Governor inspected us today. We are the best battery. He was accompanied by a very handsome young navy captain. Captain Witham says he is Captain Roger Curtis, now the senior naval officer in this place. The sergeant says he's old Von B.'s new bumboy and I've lost my market. The inhabitants who had come back to their houses from New Jerusalem, after so many months of discomfort and the Dons not firing, have now fled south again, where only the gunboats can hit them. The Governor is said to be supplying them with military tentage. My uncle and Abigail have stayed at home. A provost marshal has been appointed.

May 25: Three Jews killed at New Jerusalem by gunboats. I knew them all well. Keep thinking of Abigail—not a queen, but a princess. She is only 29.

June 27: A few civilians are proposing to sue the Governor because he has knocked down their houses in the town, some for military reasons and others for storehouses. While we risk our lives they think only of their money. Captain Witham says the Horse Guards have not yet authorized the Governor to pay the staff officers who were appointed in 1779. . . . The recent rainstorm and the cannonading have uncovered many strange bones that were hidden under the rock slides. An infantry officer, Captain Drinkwater, has been around collecting them. I heard him tell Captain Witham that they were of animals, and perhaps of men, that lived before the Flood. A blasphemous idea, even for a Christian.

July 9: Miriam to the battery in a dreadful state this morning because someone has dug up part of our cemetery. Why? The president has gone to complain to the Governor. She brought the baby, David, with her; he is a sickly child. Poor Emily hangs about me more and more, but I cannot even be civil to her, thinking of Abigail. How can womankind produce two such diverse beings?

July 15: The gunboats continue their harassment. Yesterday a woman at New Town was blown dead out of her bed, stark naked. Captain Witham was on the batteries, and as soon as we heard the gunboats open fire, he directed all our guns on the enemy's camp. The sergeant says we will not let their infantry sleep, then they will petition to prevent the gunboats disturbing us. It is now known that it was Captain Witham who dug up the Jewish cemetery, to make a vegetable garden. The Governor has given him a reprimand, but not very sharp, I'll be bound, as he was trying to increase the food supplies. That means more to General Eliott than any religion. He is a very just man, it must be allowed. He treats all equally—like dogs.

August 2: Abigail sent me a note asking me to visit them. I went joyfully and spent a pleasant evening with them. I told my uncle how magnificently she had comported herself the night of the rioting. She looks very beautiful. I try to think of her as my mother, whom I do not really remember.

August 3: The Governor was here all morning while we experimented to see whether rope cleaning rods, such as the navy use, would be better than our wooden ones. Tomorrow we are to see what is the smallest amount of powder in the internal charge that will cause a shell to burst. The infantry below us have been firing their muskets with powder that has been dried, to see whether the range is thus increased. Another battery has been ordered to try firing round stones instead of cannonballs, to save metal.

September 10: My uncle has asked me to pass word to him as soon as it is known that Captain Witham is to have the batteries. He always opens fire on the Dons as soon as he arrives and fires stray shots all night, with whole batteries firing now and then, so that the Dons always become much annoyed and open fire on the town with all their guns. When our captain has the batteries, everyone leaves for the south.

October 16: A surgeon of the infantry has been found occupying a ward designed for 50 sick. He has been turned out. The sergeant says the surgeons think only of their own poxy skins and don't give a *** for the soldiers. He is away an hour every day now getting medical instruction in case of need, as there are not enough surgeons or assistants. It is an idea of the Governor's. The enemy's siege lines get closer every day.

October 23: General stand to arms last night, and at 1 o'clock all the batteries opened concentrated fire on the enemy's works. We saw some flames, and when it came light, men were trying to repair the damage, and much smoke. We continued aimed fire until they desisted, but they will finish the repairs after dark.

November 1: Last month the worst yet. Many new cases of scurvy and no more fresh fruit. The officers rioted, and many soldiers mutinied. The crew of *HMS Speedwell* tried to take their ship over to the Dons but were betrayed by a Spanish deserter who had been pressed into the navy. They will all hang. Naval discipline is both freer than ours and more brutal. I have seen two men dead by their own hands and hear of many more. Minorca is not expected to hold out much longer, and in America General Cornwallis has surrendered to the rebels. The war seems lost there. The sergeant says, "We'll never surrender here. I'd blow Old Von B. off a cannon first." Abigail sent me a cake, which I shared with all.

November 21: The Governor and Captain Curtis passed through the battery early, going up toward Rock Gun. The sergeant said they should have taken a blanket these cold mornings.

November 22: Captain Witham had the batteries, but no firing. He looked sulky and burst out 'twas not *his* will to sit idly while the enemy continued their works under his nose.

November 27: A great day. Last night after retreat, when the gates had all been locked and night guards posted, we were stood to arms and new orders read. We were to make a sortie against the enemy works, the infantry to go in three columns, and some artillerymen with each column to spike the enemy guns and blow up their forward magazines as soon as they fell into our hands. More than 2,000 men were to go out. I confess to a feeling compounded of exhilaration and fear when the sergeant named me for the sortie. We filed out through the barriers, which had been quietly opened, a little after 3 o'clock. Twenty minutes later, going very slowly, we reached the enemy's works. I heard firing close ahead and in the light of a flare saw a Highlander put his bayonet into a Spanish soldier. The Spaniard fell, grimacing so horribly I felt the bayonet in my own entrails. Yet I was not afraid, and a moment later when a Spaniard rose out of the ground and raised his musket to fire at Captain Witham, I felled him with a blow of the ax I was carrying. Captain Witham took his comrades prisoner. For a time there was great confusion there in the enemy's forward works, with some Spaniards firing at us, some in postures of surrender, some lobsterbacks charging, some firing. I saw Cousin Abraham for a moment. Then we laid the charges and blew up the San Carlos battery. Captain Witham had found the keys of the battery and, bowing, presented them to General Eliott, who was there with a sword in a sling. He is 64 but in the enemy battery, the fires and explosions lighting his face, seemed no more than 40. We started back soon after 4 and all were inside the gates by 5. I do not know yet how many men we lost, but it was very few. I have not been able to sleep, reliving every moment of the adventure. I saw many examples of bravery and sacrifice performed by these simple soldiers I have despised. They are brutal only because we make them so.

November 28: All the soldiers drunk. I spent an hour at home. Abigail is knitting me mittens so that I can work the gun in cold weather. She asked me to read the *Song of Solomon* to her in Hebrew.

December 4: Captain Witham says I am a good fellow, and he is sorry he dug up our cemetery. The sergeant says I can have his sister and be blessed. It is announced that we suffered 5 men killed and 25 wounded in the sortie yesterday and brought back every item of weapons and equipment that we took out, save only a kilt of the 73rd. Considering how much a Scotchman can do, as I have seen, without removing his kilt, it is an astonishing mishap. Over half the fit men in the garrison went out on the sortie. The Governor took a great risk for a great end. Captain Witham says that he and all other officers were forbid to fire on the works because the Governor said the Dons always fought well if attacked or kept on the alert but became careless when there seemed to be no threat. It is clear now why he and Captain Curtis were at Rock Gun, looking down upon the enemy as though studying a map, so often this last month. There is no doubt that he is a great man.

December 15: The chief credit for the sortie is now given to Brigadier General Ross, though General Boyd is the deputy governor. The Governor himself only went out "incognito" so pretends to have nothing to do with it. General Boyd is a Whig, while the Governor and General Ross are Tories. A sordid postscript to the adventure.

A.D. 1782

January 7: The siege continues, the sortie fades in memory. Last month the enemy fired 18,156 shot and shell into the fortress. The sergeant says there are 450 scurvy in hospital. Guards and fatigues increase, so that even the artillery begin to murmur. We are supposed to perform a night guard or duty only every third night, but I have been on night guards or fatigues the last nine nights and only now have a night in bed.

February 6: On fatigue duty carrying powder to the upper guns three nights consecutively. This is more than any British soldier should be asked to perform. Three boatloads of lemons arrive from Lisbon.

February 24: More lemons. The sergeant told me how they were obtained. A ship, the *Mercury*, was going to England with passengers, but the Governor gave the master secret orders to load with lemons in Lisbon and return here, while giving out that he was continuing to England. The master played his part, avoided the enemy cruisers, and returned. Some of the passengers, who expected to wake up in the Bay of Biscay, were reported to have had apoplectic seizures when they found themselves again moored under the shadow of the Rock. Nothing can stop the Governor.

February 26: General Murray has surrendered Minorca to the Spanish, because of scurvy. Another wonderful evening with Abigail. She sings like an angel.

March 7: The Spanish are up to some deviltry in Algeciras across the bay. Captain Witham looks important and says he knows what it is but is forbid to tell. I doubt it. Sixty more tents in the Spanish lines at the Orange Grove. I am distressed to find myself thinking lecherously of Abigail. How can I prevent it?

March 23: Another regiment, the 97th, has arrived. Their ships slipped past the blockade, but their wives and baggage were taken. Now our guard duties will decrease. Captain Witham says that 10 gunboats have been sent from England in parts, with instructions how to put them together. This is to enable our navy to attack the enemy gunboats, which continue to harass us, though not so much as heretofore.

April 4: It is announced that the Horse Guards have allowed the Governor's staff their extra pay for the first 6 months of 1779. It is a marvel how we survive, fighting the enemy in front and the Horse Guards behind. Lord North has resigned and Lord Rockingham taken his place.

April 12: No decrease in guards or duties. Nearly 100 of the 97th dead of fever and the rest weakly. The first of our gunboats has been launched. Six shiploads of enemy soldiers, said to be two regiments, disembarked at Algeciras and marched round the bay to their camp. The jetty at the Orange Grove is being lengthened.

April 14: David Eliott Conquy's 1st birthday. Miriam is determined that he shall be a Teacher when he grows up. It is the same they all hope for me. Abigail says I would make a wonderful teacher.

May 20: The Governor is determined to get a battery on the point of rock above the cliffs here. It is too steep for a path, but Sergeant Major Ince of the Artificers says he can make a tunnel to the place. He has begun. The Spanish are cutting the masts and upper decks off some ships of the line in Algeciras. No one knows what it means.

May 27: One hundred and fourteen enemy ships came this week, and 7,000 soldiers landed. Their tented camp spreads and looks like a great city. The sergeant says, with many oaths, that the enemy must be 20,000 men there, French and Spanish. They are estimating us at our true value at last. Personally, I feel strangely empty in the stomach when I look at that vast array and consider how few we are and how many sick and how many disaffected. But the Governor keeps us all in even greater fear, and respect, of him.

June 10: Captain Witham has fought a duel with Lieutenant Burleigh . . . to decide which is the biggest coxcomb of the fortress? The infantry battalions are changed about regularly, so that after a time in the front they spend a time in peace, except from the gunboats, at South Barracks or Windmill Hill. We of the artillery are always facing the enemy. We are the best gunners in the world. Practiced preparing and firing red-hot shot yesterday. Sergeant Major Ince's gallery proceeds slowly with much blasting and noise.

June 12: It is said the enemy are preparing great pumping engines with miles of hose and will soon undermine the foundations of Gibraltar with continuous powerful streams of water.

June 17: Another 60 enemy transports into the bay, with 5,000 Frenchmen. The Spanish General Alvarez, who replaced General Mendoza, is himself dismissed and his place taken by the Duc de Crillon, a Frenchman in the Spanish service. The Duc was the capturer of Minorca.

June 19: It is universally rumored that the enemy are going to assault on August 25. They have ceased bombarding us altogether, as though saving their ammunition. Smugglers report that civilians are coming from all over Europe to watch the spectacle. All the inns and houses that can see Gibraltar, to a distance of twenty miles, are booked up. We'll give 'em their money's worth, the sergeant says. Captain Witham admits now he has no notion what the enemy are preparing in Algeciras. A sailor I met says they are making more gunboats, but bigger. He says there are now 14 admirals' flags flying in the enemy fleet.

June 20: The 97th have put their first picket in the field! Improper and lustful dreams of Abigail continue to trouble my sleep. Emily says I am in love with someone and she can guess who. She has a sharp eye and knows everything, though only 20. She has been a strumpet here since twelve.

July 4: Sergeant Major Ince's gallery is now 82 feet long. It is 8 feet high and 8 feet wide. They blast the rock with powder, clear out the rubble, and so the same again. They also crack the rock with fire and water. Lieutenant Kohler has invented a gun carriage that can be loaded, aimed, and fired quickly at great depressions, which is the way ours are mostly fired.

July 15: The enemy fired a few shells and hit a small expense magazine. Sergeant Major Ince's gallery advances a yard a day. They are going to blow a hole out toward the cliff face now, because there is much delay whenever they fire a charge from the smoke and fumes that linger long after in the gallery. The hole will cause the fumes to be blown away and thus speed the work.

July 25: A band of Corsicans have arrived, being volunteers to help in our defense. Complaints of lazy and ignorant surgeons increase on all sides. The sergeant says if we ever let him get into a surgeon's hands he will cut our ***** off. More experiments with gun carriages and shell charges. The enemy are reported to be filling a thousand giant ballons with poison gas. When the wind is favorable, the balloons will be launched over Gibraltar and the poison released to kill us all.

August 16: The Governor was here when I awoke, his visage very grim. When I looked down, I understood why. The Spanish have performed a miracle under our very noses. In the space of a single night—in barely six hours of darkness—they have built a wall of sandbags some 1,500 feet long, about 10 feet high and as thick. Beyond this there is another wall, made of what appear to be casks, presumably filled with earth or sand. That is much longer, near three quarters of a mile, and 6 feet high. The sergeant says it is to give protected passage from the rear to the new works. He is so awed he has forgotten to swear. The Governor's aide-de-camp says there must be half a million sandbags in the first wall and as many casks in the second. All this less than 1,000 yards from the North Face. The aide-de-camp also says that they must have put out several thousand infantry in front of the working parties, even closer to us, as protection in case of another sortie. Captain Witham is very subdued, and with reason: last night *he had the batteries.*

August 17: A deserter says the French king's brother, the Comte d'Artois, and his cousin, the Duc de Bourbon, are come to watch our annihilation. The sergeant says two Mounseer princes aren't going to p*** us away through hoses nor poison us with their f**ts, because Old Von B. will b***** them both before breakfast and do as much for the Duc de Crillon afterwards. We have many sick, and some dead, of the grippe. It is said that the enemy are preparing 10,000 cork horses in Algeciras and their cavalry will use these, instead of their flesh-and-blood mounts, to charge upon us. With so great a force and so wily an enemy as the French, one must expect anything.

August 20: The Comte d'Artois has sent the Governor a rich present of food. The governor has sent an even richer one back, which will make the enemy wonder whether we are as close to starvation as they think. The two French princes spent an hour on board one of their battleships, moored 100 yards offshore, but then had to be taken ashore from seasickness. All the civilians have gone from New Jerusalem to Europa in fear of the assault. Some strange ships crept out of Algeciras Harbor, fired back at the land on that side, then returned to harbor. No one can make head or tail of them. It is very hot and dry, and the air is dense, day and night, with a purple-gray pall of smoke from Spain, where the peasants are burning the heather and gorse off the hillsides. At night the fires make strange signs—crosses, circles, animal heads—in the sky. I have seen it every year, but this year, so close to the day of reckoning, it turns land, sea, and sky into different parts of a ghostly and menacing inferno.

August 25: Midnight. The day has come and gone. Nothing happened. Sergeant Major Ince's gallery is 165 feet long.

August 28: Have been working three days to replace all our guns along the seafront with guns captured from Spanish men-of-war. A useless waste of time and sweat.

August 30: We all, except gun sentries, went to watch the sailors practice infantry drill, for the Governor has ordered that since our ships are blockaded the sailors shall form a special brigade under Captain Curtis. We laughed till we thought we would do ourselves a mischief as they rolled about the parade ground out of step, in no lines, bellowing, "Belay there," "Avast," "Steer two points more a-lee," and the like. The Governor has inspected Sergeant Major Ince's gallery and says that the ventilation holes will also make good gun positions. We are to drag guns up there tomorrow. Captain Witham says the guns on the sea front were changed so that when the enemy ships fire at the batteries there, we can recover the balls and fire them back, since they will be of the same sort and caliber. It is not wise to doubt the Governor, however unreasonable his orders may seem.

August 31: Sat up late talking to the sergeant, who asked a thousand questions about the Jews. Did we eat Christian babies? Did we drink blood in the synagogue? And many others as ridiculous. He asked because he could not believe such things of me, whom he has come to know. I told him of the strictness of our laws and observances and tried to explain what it means to be a Jew. I believe I made him see that our punishment is usually in ourselves, for the Jewish conscience never sleeps. A Jew can destroy himself where none other has been able to.

September 1: Captain Witham called the battery together and told us that the Governor has long had intelligence about what the enemy are preparing in Algeciras. It is a sort of floating battery, a ship which has been stripped and cut down so that it can fire to only one side. On that side wooden armor has been added, some of it 5 feet thick. Layers of sand lie between layers of timber, and there is a system of water pipes to water any part of the armor and so douse any red-hot shot that might penetrate. They have sails but can move only slowly. They are unsinkable and unburnable, and at this time they have built 10 or 12. It is these that we saw last week, firing their guns for the first time. I cannot see how we can protect ourselves against such hellish devices. The men look a little anxious, but the Governor will think of something to save us.

September 4: Dreamed that I watched Abigail undress and bathe herself.

September 6: Today the floating batteries are moored off the Orange Grove. We saw crews going aboard. With the spyglass the sergeant shouted he could see they were being escorted by marines with fixed bayonets. If the vessels are impregnable, why are they afraid?

September 8: All our northward batteries fired red-hot shot on the new works which the enemy put up so secretly last month. They soon caught fire, and we did great execution as the enemy tried to repair the damage and put out the fires. The sergeant says the only good Mounseer or Don is a dead one, but the gunners down there are very brave fellows, and it is a mark of man's stupidity more than his wickedness that we have to kill them.

September 9: Heavy fire against us all day. The Governor came up early and told Captain Witham to plot the exact position of each gun now unmasked. The Governor peered a long time through his telescope and said, "There is the duke, and those must be the two princes beside him. That explains this foolish bombardment." The sergeant began to lay a gun on where the duke and the princes were standing, but the Governor said very coldly, "That will do, Sergeant. Gentlemen do not snipe at each other like assassins." Spoke to Abigail through a window, as I was passing. She has asked me to come soon. I cannot resist any longer.

September 10: Ten enemy battleships sailed up and down off the front today, bombarding all our positions from the North Face to Europa Point. We set one of them on fire, but it limped back to Algeciras. Our battery had to send a detachment to man some guns below Windmill Hill and then back here later; but the Governor came here in the evening, rubbing his hands, and said, "They have shown us another card. A poor whist player, the duke, I think."

September 12: I have counted 150 enemy warships of all sizes in the bay. The sergeant says there are 35,000 soldiers in the enemy camp, and a deserter says there are 35,000 sightseers on the hills of the Campo. We shall have a very public funeral—or triumph. The palisadoes protecting the approaches to the Main Gate were burned last night.

September 14: Yesterday will go down in history. It began at dawn, when the sergeant called us all to arms. In the dim and smoky light we saw 10 floating batteries sail slowly from the Orange Grove toward us. They anchored about an hour later in an irregular line 1,000 yards off the town and opened fire. We heard our sea-front batteries return the fire. The cannonading became steadily heavier, but without any signs of damage to the ships. Near 11 o'clock I was sent down with the sergeant and 20 others to help the sea-front batteries. We found the gunners and matrosses there suffering from heat and exhaustion more than from the enemy's actions, though I saw some wounded men, and blood splashed over a gun, and several big pieces of facing stone had been dislodged. A lieutenant said that our hot shot was having no effect. "They are unsinkable," he added. The Governor was passing close, unknown to him, and rebuked him sharply, saying, "Sir, another word like that and you shall face a firing squad. Our shot are not hot enough yet." It was true, and we piled more driftwood and timbers on the fires, which we were burning furiously in the angles of destroyed houses and walls, to make the shot white hot. The floating batteries fired steadily, overturning one of our guns, but I noticed that only two were in a position to hit us. The others were either too far to the south, and so not opposite any of our positions, or appeared to be fast on a sandbank and out of range to the north. This led us to concentrate our fire on those two, and what a cheer arose near 3 o'clock when we saw smoke coming out of the sloping roof of one of them—this was an hour after the shot were pronounced hot enough to use. Enemy sailors ran out on the roof to put out the fire, but the smoke continued. Small boats came from Algeciras later, and some went back heavily loaded with men from the batteries. But I at least—and I suppose every one of us—was awaiting with the customary mixture of dread and expectation for all the other enemy to join in the action. For there was the huge fleet, there were the 35,000 men— our palisadoes were gone, our men scattered and tired. Yet by nightfall, still, of all that vast force bent on our destruction, only two of the floating batteries had engaged us. Then we could no longer see the targets and stood down in the gun positions. I drank water from the buckets we had been sponging out the guns with and had never tasted anything so delicious. I slept until we were awakened after midnight. I saw then that several of the floating batteries were burning like torches. We reopened fire with furious energy. The flames grew until the ships were outlined by fire, and at last they seemed to be made of fire. For an awful moment I thought I saw men, hundreds of tiny dark figures in silhouette against the flames, and heard their pitiful screaming; but I closed my eyes and served my gun the harder. The sergeant shouted like a madman every time we fired, "Walk up, walk up, any more for the show?" About 3 o'clock all our sailors came running from the south under Captain Curtis and became sailors again, setting out in small boats to rescue whom they could from the burning ships. Shortly before dawn the powder magazines began to blow up in each ship with dreadful explosions and a rain of wood and iron upon us all. As light began to spread after the most awesome 24 hours of my life, I saw Captain Curtis's boat coming toward shore. Some of the sailors rowed like mad men, for the boat was very low in the water, while others were stuffing rolled jackets and shirts into two large jagged holes below the waterline. A dozen naked Spaniards sat dazed and numb in the water in the bottom of the boat. Captain Curtis, white and handsome, sat in the stern, a sailor lolling dead in the crook of his left arm, and in his right, waving in the reddish light, the Royal Standard of Spain. He came wearily up the steps and gave the standard to the Governor, saying, "This was to fly over Gibraltar, sir." The Governor said, "Let it . . . under our own, there!" And it was done at once. The light soon began to reveal other more dreadful sights— the hulks of the enemy ships sticking out of the water, some still burning; the surface of the sea foul with wreckage and litter; and close below us, hundreds of corpses rolling along the rocks— some clothed, some naked, some smiling, some contorted in agony, some mangled, some whole, some white, some charred. The sergeant danced on the parapet shaking his fist across the bay and crying, "Roll up, roll up. Plenty of empty seats!" Being released from duty for a few hours, I went to the synagogue, gave thanks for my preservation, and said prayers for the dead.

September 15: We have won a mighty victory. No one can take this Rock from us except by treachery or guile. It is learned that we lost 16 men killed and 68 wounded in the battle. We hold 950 Spaniards prisoners, all rescued from the floating batteries, where not less than 1,400 others were drowned or burned. It is an act of God. The soldiers are beginning to celebrate in the usual manner.

Later: Abigail came to the battery and asked me to come to the house. Her eyes were bright and her lips parted. My uncle is in the hospital with the grippe, and she is alone. How did she know I had made up my mind? I said I would come the day after tomorrow, for I am on sentry duty tomorrow.

September 16: Every soldier in Gibraltar seems to be incapably drunk. This always happens after a victory, and all the world knows it. This would be the best time for the enemy to renew the attack. Perhaps they have thought of it but do not have the stomach anymore. The sergeant has come and said, "Finish your writing and have a drink with me. You're a damn soldier now, Moses." I shall obey. I have made up my mind.

September 18: All is finished, but I do not know what has happened. I am in the guardroom with a black eye and many bruises, and my head aches worse than I have ever known. The sergeant says grimly I am lucky not to have had the lash. I remember drinking with him and singing, and I remember Abigail staring down at me and a woman's body . . . but what else?

September 21: I am docked three days pay for drunk and resisting the guard. . The sergeant says he did it because he didn't want my Jewish conscience to make me kill myself, and perhaps he is right. He has told me all. After we had taken some drinks the other night, I began to talk of Abigail. I told him everything that I have written in this journal and more. It was a powerful relief, like release from a dungeon, to tell someone so much after holding it so secret for so long. At the end I told him that I had made up my mind to enjoy her, however bad I felt after, as I knew I would—on account of the sin I would be committing against my uncle, who was like my father. The sergeant congratulated me and said she was indeed a beautiful, lovely woman. We went on drinking until I fell down drunk. Then they took Emily—she was there—and me to a little rock overhang above the Moorish Castle where Emily often had men, wrapped us in blankets, set a lamp beside us, and sent a man to Abigail to tell her I wanted her to come at once to that place. She came up, and by chance I had half awaked from my stupor, and feeling a naked woman beside me who began to sigh and fondle me, I set upon her to couple with her, and it was thus that Abigail came upon us. She cried out, and I remember hearing Emily scream, "Go away, you slut! He's mine, always has been." Next day I began to remember more and set out to run to the house, but they prevented me, and when I fought them, the sergeant had me put in the guardhouse. Someone smuggled more rum in to me there, and soon I was drunk again. Now I am too tired to go to the house and explain. I will go tomorrow.

September 22: I tried to get into the house today, but the door was locked and no one answered. Yet I am sure Abigail was there.

September 23: My uncle back from the naval hospital and Abraham home too with the grippe. I am not sure that I want to go there now.

October 10: We and the enemy alike are as though in a trance, neither quite believing what has happened and neither knowing what to do next. It is said that when the news of the battle reached King Charles in Madrid he turned gray and could not speak for a week. My uncle says that the peace negotiations in Paris will now go forward more rapidly, for it must be obvious to all that they will never take Gibraltar by force. But he fears we may be sacrificed to the Spanish after all for other advantages to England elsewhere, as in the Indies, or in exchange for Minorca. Abigail did not appear. A terrible hurricane last night but little damage, as few houses are left standing.

October 19: Lord Howe has arrived with a fleet, the third since the siege began. A civilian passenger in the fleet, a Jew returning from London, told Captain Witham that Lord George Germain and others would dearly like to exchange Gibraltar for some other place, but the public will have their heads if they do, so great an impression has our defense made, especially when considered against the universal defeat and disaster elsewhere. Two more regiments, the 25th and 59th, came with the fleet, but without their baggage, extra clothes, or wives. Also many more military artificers, who are sorely needed. An ensign of the 97th tried for defrauding a Jew inkeeper.

October 20: The fleet sailed yesterday, with Captain Curtis aboard to carry the Governor's own account of our great victory to London before anyone else can; and of course this will result in honors and advancement to the captain. Dysentery prevalent. Saw Abigail at New Jerusalem today, and we spoke normally, though carefully. I think the siege is over and want to get out.

October 21: Two soldiers have killed each other in a quarrel. They were not drunk, which is a bad sign. Three dogs suspected of hydrophobia shot. All stray dogs to be shot—the Governor's order. The enemy fleet sailed after Lord Howe, but though 47 to his 33, they failed to engage him in the strait. Half the garrison were on Windmill Hill watching and saw the Spanish Admiral Córdova manage to avoid battle: a remarkable feat of seamanship on his part, a naval lieutenant beside me growled. The French have struck camp, leaving only the Spanish.

October 26: A Spanish colonel taken at sea, and much wined and dined by the Governor, has revealed much that was mysterious to us about the recent assault. The floating batteries were the invention of a French engineer called d'Arcon, who submitted the idea years ago when it was known all over Europe that King Charles would give the richest rewards to any who would help him recover Gibraltar. His plan was approved by the kings of France and Spain near two years ago now, and the building began last February. But this was before the Duc de Crillon was appointed to the chief command. As soon as he was apprized of the plan, the noble Duc saw that all the honor and glory attending the fall of this fortress would go to M. d'Arcon, and not to him. So before leaving Madrid to come south he inscribed a letter recording that M. d'Arcon's plan was disastrous and that he, the Duc, was only putting it into effect because the king ordered him to. Of this letter he left several copies with friends in Madrid, with instructions to make it public the instant that the attack with the floating batteries had been made. The Spanish colonel showed the Governor a copy of the Duc's letter, and indeed in it the Duc clearly stated that all the glory —or, of course, all the blame—would belong to M. d'Arcon. It is now clear why the floating batteries were left on their own, without help from the fleet or army: because the noble Duc and the Spanish admiral were interested only in seeing M. d'Arcon fail. . . . The colonel also said that the naval arrangements had caused much ill feeling. Admiral Barcello, who has borne the brunt of the war here for many years and has dedicated his life to returning Gibraltar to the Spanish crown, was left with only his gunboats. Admiral Moreno, in command of the floating batteries, complained that he was no more than a hired boatman for M. d'Arcon. Admiral Córdova, commander in chief, much resented M. d'Arcon's attempts to force him to engage his ships in a battle against the British. When the *Talla Piedra,* one of the floating batteries, caught fire, the Prince of Nassau at once took its only boat and rowed ashore.

October 28: More news from the captured colonel. The enemy had designed special boats with prows that could drop down so that infantry on board might run ashore dryshod with small cannon. But these were never used. In Spain when the news of the defeat spread, people were saying, this is as bad as the defeat of our Invincible Armada. King Charles' throne is shaking.

November 3: The rest of us may consider the siege over, but not the Governor. He has ordered experiments with shell fillings and fuses to continue in Poca Roca Cave, which has been a military laboratory for many months now.

December 4: More than 900 sick in hospitals and quarters of scurvy, flux, and unknown fevers. Without the excitement of battle the soldier's life is an empty one. Sickness or death, even self-inflicted, are a welcome change.

December 23: It is rumored that peace was signed between England and the American colonists last month. One hundred and fifty wives of the 25th and 59th arrived yesterday, and 17 of them straight to the venereal sickness ward. A soldier of the 72nd dead by throwing himself off the Rock Gun, a dreadful fate. Five more deserted. I have the trots and am sick and weary. No house but ours showed Chanukah lights this year, though three or four others are standing and there was permission. Abigail did it.

A.D. 1783

January 6: Riots in the hospital, officers were beating some women, supposedly for not discovering to them that they had the sickness before accepting relations. Two officers in arrest. The gunboats have begun their attacks again.

January 14: Sergeant Major Ince's gallery is 370 feet long. Parties of the enemy have been driven away from the foot of the North Face. Sergeant Major Ince says they are trying to find an old tunnel made there long ago, to blow us all up. How long is this going to go on?

January 19: The officers have put on a play. It is said to be very amusing and well performed.

January 22: The officers' play closed by order of the Governor. He says he will not have his officers dressing up like women. The sergeant says Old Von B. likes them better in tight trousers.

January 30: My uncle has heard from Lisbon that England is to retain Gibraltar. The French are secretly delighted. We Jews must be heartily thankful, too. Parliament voted thanks to all of us of the garrison last month, though General Ross tried to have old General Boyd excluded—a disgraceful thing. General Eliott is to be made a Knight of the Bath. The sergeant says, now we'll have to call him Old Von SIR B.

February 2: The Spanish soldiers in their forward works began to wave white flags at noon. Some came forward shouting, *"Ya somos todos amigos"*—we are all friends now. We are ordered not to let them close and to be ready to fire at all times.

February 5: It is confirmed. Peace has been signed. The war is over. No one is drunk.

February 11: All prices down by half. Inhabitants' houses not to be used without their permission. Inhabitants not allowed to dig lime or employ soldiers to rebuild their houses.

February 12: The Governor sent for me and told me I am to be mustered out as soon as I have compiled figures for the sick, wounded, died, and killed throughout the siege, also the quantities of ammunition fired. Cousin Abraham is out already, with a house and premises to hold for 21 years, this as a reward for volunteering. I am to get the same, the Governor says. I shall sell mine and go to England, perhaps to study, perhaps to become a merchant there.

March 2: My work is done. Among a host of other figures I have given to the Governor, I have calculated that we fired 205,000 shot and shell during the siege, using 8,000 barrels of gunpowder. The Spanish and French fired 260,000 missiles back at us. From first to last we suffered 333 killed and 1,008 wounded in battle, only 200 of these last severely. Sickness was a much more dangerous enemy, for 1,000 of the military died of sundry diseases, of which scurvy accounted for over half. No figures were kept for the civilian population, and their sufferings are hard to estimate, since so many left the Rock; but the president of our synagogue and I myself think it was nearly 1,500 dead from all causes, in particular scurvy among the elders and smallpox among the children.

March 3: Abigail is arranging a marriage for me with Renana Toledano. As soon as we are married, I shall take her to London.

March 4: Drunk last night with the sergeant, half the battery, and Emily. At midnight we filled a gun with hardtack and cheese and fired it toward the Spanish in case they were hungry. Captain Witham came, and we told him it went off by accident.

He drank with us for an hour and said we were all rattling good fellows. We gave him three cheers when he left. The sergeant called me Mr. Hassan and said I was to count on him and the battery for anything I wanted here or in London—a house built, military stores stolen, anyone I don't like done in on a dark night. He cried, we're gunners, sir, British gunners, and we fought at the Great Siege of Gibraltar! A Scotchman of the 72nd crept in when he smelled the rum, and he shouted a toast in his dialect, which, when we understood, we all drank many times —"Here's tae us! Wha's like us? Damn few . . . and they're a' deid!"

Awoke with fearful head this morning, the others the same, but on parade at 10 o'clock and mustered out at 11. All the soldiers shook my hand and congratulated me, as a result I have lice again. I am released from bondage at last and cannot understand why I am weeping. It will pass.

Book Nine

∞∞∞∞∞∞∞∞∞∞∞∞∞∞∞∞∞∞∞∞∞∞

Nelson's Port

The Jewish years 5539–5564
AUC 2532–2557
A.D. 1779–1804
A.H. 1193–1219

THE unharnessed herd of dukes, counts, and mad scientists had lost, and the fairy John Bull had won. It only remained to comply with the formalities. Crillon and Eliott paid reciprocal calls, with much fulsome mutual congratulation. Crillon explained that it had all been d'Arcon's fault. The British Army pay office was said to be considering the authorization of pay for Eliott's extra staff for the first half of 1780. King George III ruled that Eliott should be made a Knight of the Bath in Gibraltar, and appointed as his representative for the investiture the lieutenant governor, Boyd . . . who hated Eliott's guts, and vice versa. The ceremony was conducted under conditions which could not have been bettered in England. Continuous rain ruined the ceremonial arches and dripped down the spectators' necks, and everyone got drunk. The wonderful diarist Captain Spilsbury recorded:

> Never was a worse salute performed by the Artillery they not being able to fire a salute of 21 guns from 6 they had in the field, two of them being so neglected as to have a shot in each, left at the bottom before their loading was put in, and their

tubes were in general too long; a worse feu de joie fired by troops, worse weather, worse musick, worse fireworks or worse entertainment. . . .

The soldiery reverted to peacetime habits. Rape, murder, adultery, suicide, venereal disease, drunkenness, and indiscipline increased. The inhabitants trickled back from all over Europe. Abraham Hassan (a historical figure: Gamaliel Hassan is not) exchanged his house-and-premises-for-twenty-one-years for another property in perpetuity (but his collateral descendant Sir Joshua Hassan, chief Minister of Gibraltar from 1964 to 1969, has not been able to trace just where it was).

Smuggling began again, full swing. The Spanish seized a Gibraltar boat laden with goods being smuggled into Spain; the

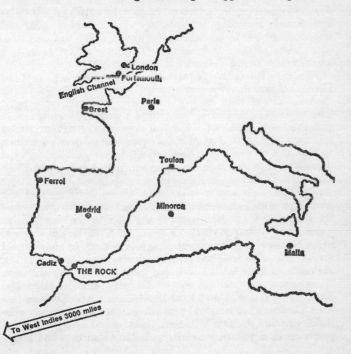

governor demanded, and got, the boat's release. Spanish deserters and refugees from an unpopular regime crowded onto the Rock. The situation was again fully normal.

There was now, however, a new factor in the Gibraltar equation. Strategy, commerce, politics were still there. The bitterness at Britain's usurpation was still there among the Spanish governing and aristocratic classes. But now there was also the Gibraltar Legend; for the place name had become synonymous in the hearts of the British people, and in all languages, with *impregnable, defiant, reliable, unconquerable.* After 1783 the cession of Gibraltar would have been regarded by most Britons as a cession of those qualities in themselves, that is, as a collapse of the national character.

Most members of Parliament shared the general view, but a few held exactly to the contrary. In a single debate on Gibraltar one member declared: "Gibraltar . . . is the most valuable and important of all the foreign territories belonging to Great Britain," while another claimed that "Gibraltar always hung like a dead weight round the neck of Great Britain."

The siege faded into history. Sir George Eliott became Lord Heathfield and in 1790 died of palsy. Admiral Sir Roger Curtis died in 1816 without adding to his already considerable fame. The three Hanoverian regiments which went through the siege took the battle honor *Gibraltar* and the motto *Mit Eliott Ruhm und Sieg:* and this led to much astonishment in later wars when British soldiers met the descendants of these regiments, by then incorporated in the German Army, in battle and found them wearing *Gibraltar* on their sleeves.

Gibraltar itself was a wreck, few houses standing and the ground so thick in cannonballs that they were still being picked up a century later. But by 1787 the population was back to 3,400, and by 1804 it was over 6,000, with the largest element being Genoese, and after them Jews and Spanish in about equal proportions. The Jews had built another synagogue, the Nefusot Yehudah on Line Wall Road, and some were among the most prominent and influential men in Gibraltar, notably Isaac Cardozo, Judah Benoliel, and Abraham Hassan the Volunteer. Just what Cardozo's business was remains a mystery; yet he was very rich, organized the first Gibraltar police, acted as agent for the governors in negotiating treaties with Moroccan beys and kings, and after the Spanish rose against the French, supplied their armies with money and clothes. Benoliel was known as the King of Gibraltar and was a friend of the priest who later became Pope Pius IX.

If there was boredom, a sense of letdown after the Great Siege, the governors did their best to alleviate it. One, General O'Hara, nicknamed the Cock of the Rock, kept two mistresses in different establishments in a feeble attempt to outdo his father, a previous governor, who had had three, and fourteen illegitimate children by them. O'Hara also believed that if he could stand just a few feet higher on the high point of the Rock he could see into Cádiz Harbor (65 miles to the northwest). Military surveyors assured him he was mistaken, but he built a large tower up there anyway. The surveyors were right, he was wrong, and the tower was called O'Hara's Folly.

Then in 1802 the Rock received its first and only royal governor, the Duke of Kent, fourth son of George III. He had been there once already, when he was banished to Gibraltar at the age of twenty-two for running away from his military training in Germany, to the fury of his father. He soon drove the regiment of which he was colonel, the 7th Fusiliers, to mutiny; but he went with them to Nova Scotia and stayed there nearly nine years, consoling himself for the Arctic exile with a Mme. de St. Laurent, who became his great and good friend for the rest of his life. She accompanied him in 1802 when the king appointed him to govern the Rock. They sailed from England in the *HMS Isis*, commanded by Captain Thomas Hardy, who started by grumbling about all the royal hoopla but ended much taken with the duke's charm.

The duke discreetly installed Mme. de St. Laurent in a farm in the Guadarranque valley below San Roque, for many years known as the Duke of Kent's Farm. He visited her there when he could spare time from his work in causing more mutinies among the soldiery. The trouble was that the duke had a considerable sense of duty but no sense of proportion. His brothers, the heir apparent and the Commander-in-Chief, had told him to restore the shattered discipline of the garrison. He saw at once that the trouble was due to excessive drunkenness—there were ninety wine houses in operation—and took direct action. He closed the wine houses. The soldiers, who had no release but drink and no charming mistresses to keep their minds off the lack of alcohol, mutinied. The duke's deputy, General Barnett, was delighted— this would get the duke dismissed, he thought; and he was right. The duke was recalled "for consultation" but never replaced, so that until his death in 1820 the men actually bearing responsibility in Gibraltar were lieutenant governors. (All the Duke's elder brothers being without legitimate offspring, he was finally compelled to marry and did so in 1818, marrying a depressing German princess called Victoria Mary Louisa, sister of King Leopold I of the Belgians. They had one child: Victoria.)

In these its last few years the eighteenth century's interminable war game was swept away by a genuine conflict, the French Revolution; and that outburst of fervor was soon harnessed to the ambitions of Napoleon Bonaparte. Spain, still tied to France's chariot wheels and without a strong king (Carlos III had died in 1788) was dragged into the wars on France's side, although, as usual, it was in her national interest to treat France as an enemy, not a friend.

It is unnecessary to describe here all the maneuverings and countermaneuverings, all the treaties and breaking of treaties, all the combinations and machinations of each side. It is enough to note that the war was fundamentally between England and France; that France at one time or another persuaded, conquered, cajoled, or threatened the whole continent of Europe onto her side; and that with this overwhelming land power, Napoleon only needed to gain control of the Channel for a short time to destroy the one nation that stood between him and world hegemony. The Rock was, as always, in a position to hinder or prevent French and Spanish naval combinations. On this depended England's existence.

It is proper, then, that the outstanding personalities of the period should not be eccentric or royal governors but sailors. Three in particular dominated the sea war and Gibraltar.

First in point of time was Sir John Jervis, "Black Jack" Jervis, later Earl of St. Vincent: disciplinarian, organizer, driver of men and ships. As admiral at Gibraltar he was always up at 2 A.M., made the rounds of every ship, then went to the dockyard to see that the workmen clocked in on time, then checked the supply of fresh water. Jervis won one great sea battle, trained the Mediterranean fleet into an image of himself—iron, tireless, ruthless —and made Gibraltar an efficient naval base.

Second was Sir James Saumarez, who with a small force attacked a French squadron that had taken shelter under the guns of Algeciras. The Rock scorpions had a grandstand view (July 6, 1701) of Sir James getting rather the worst of it, as was to be expected. The French admiral ran his ships aground, and Saumarez took a hammering from the shore batteries, with one ship grounded and taken, another put out of action, and a third, his flagship, severely damaged. Saumarez limped back into Gibraltar and began a frantic refit, as the enemy would obviously try to take advantage of the British setback. Sure enough, the French refloated their ships, and a few days later *HMS Superb* flew in from watch off Cádiz to report that six Spanish ships of the line were on their way. They sailed into the bay soon after and next day sailed out again, escorting the French squadron. They were now also carrying many women and children from Algeciras who had thought this an easy and comfortable way to return to Cádiz.

Saumarez had only four ships partially ready, and with these he set sail in pursuit later that day; but unrepaired battle damage slowed all the ships of his squadron except *Superb*. Saumarez sent her on ahead, alone. She caught up with the enemy in the night off Trafalgar and, unobserved, put three broadsides into the *Real Carlos* at 11 P.M. The *Real Carlos*—where the officers were at dinner with their lady guests and passengers—opened fire in all directions, notably on the *Hermenegildo*, her companion ship. After an hour or two of furious battle with each other both Spanish three-deckers blew up, with a loss of 1,700 lives. Meantime the *Superb* slipped on ahead, captured the *San Antoine*, and took her back to Gibraltar. Quite a night's work . . .

When the report of what had been done to get the ships ready after the first battle reached the old perfectionist St. Vincent, by now First Sea Lord at the Admiralty, he wrote: "The astonishing efforts made to refit the crippled ships at Gibraltar Mole surpasses everything of the kind within my experience, and the final success in making so great an impression on the very superior force of the enemy crowns the whole." It was perhaps the most lavish praise Black Jack Jervis ever bestowed in his life.

The third sailor was Horatio Nelson, probably the greatest sea commander of history, a man who combined fantastic courage with a woman's gentleness (to all except Frenchmen or republicans). Nelson was commander-in-chief of the Mediterranean fleet when Napoleon put in motion the vast plan aimed at gathering, in the Channel, sufficient naval strength to force a passage across for his invasion army.

As a first step the French admiral in Toulon, Villeneuve, succeeded in escaping from the Mediterranean. He passed through the Strait of Gibraltar into the Atlantic on April 8, 1805. It was only by chance that his ships were seen at all, and the news passed by frigate to Nelson, who was at the far end of the Mediterranean. Nelson arrived a month later, guessed that Villeneuve's destination was the West Indies, and though considerably smaller in force, sailed after him. Nelson was right, but Napoleon's plan was precisely to lure the British fleets westward while the French and Spanish, having drawn them out, doubled back, concentrated, and forced the Channel crossing before the British could regroup.

Alas for the landsman's calculations—Nelson was there and back before Villeneuve, having started a month later. Villeneuve did indeed combine with the Spanish admiral, Gravina, and bring a British fleet to action off Brest, but the action was a draw. The grandiose plan having fallen to pieces, the combined fleets returned first to Brest, then to Ferrol, and finally to Cádiz, where they holed up, ready to rot, while their imperial master in Paris furiously ordered them to get out and fight.

Before this, on July 18, Nelson stepped ashore at Gibraltar, the first time he had set foot on land for just over two years. He stayed only the inside of a day, then returned on board; but first he gave a gold medal commemorative of the Battle of the Nile to his friend and admirer Aaron Cardozo, patted him on the shoulder and said, "If I survive, Cardozo, you shall no longer remain in this dark corner of the world." Gibraltarians are not quite sure how to take that remark. . . .

Nelson returned to England for a much-needed leave. He had a month, and then on September 14, with rumors of Napoleon planning fresh combinations, he was recalled. He said good-byes to Lady Hamilton and little Horatia, whom he never directly acknowledged as his own, and took carriage to Portsmouth. There he boarded, as his flagship, the old three-decker *Victory* (Captain Thomas Hardy). She had worn St. Vincent's flag, too, and had first arrived in Gibraltar in Rodney's fleet during the Great Siege. Nelson did not go to Gibraltar but met his fleet at sea off Cádiz, sending a frigate ahead to order that no salutes should be given to him. He was vain but not modest, and he well knew that Villeneuve would think a long time before leaving Cádiz if he knew that Nelson was waiting for him outside.

Villeneuve may have heard from other sources or suspected: but a motive stronger than fear was driving him to sea. As so often before, the spur to fatal action was the news that a replacement was on the way. Napoleon had named Admiral Rosilly to supersede Villeneuve in supreme command. Rosilly reached Madrid on October 18: that day Villeneuve held a council of war in Cádiz, at which all his admirals vehemently disagreed with each other and with him. Villeneuve ordered his combined fleet to sea. It took it nearly thirty-six hours to get out of the harbor and bay, but it was finally clear at 8:30 A.M. on Sunday, October 20. The wind was slight from the east-southeast. Later the wind freshened and veered into the southwest. The huge fleet of thirty-three ships, French and Spanish muddled together, sailed slowly southeastward. Nelson's frigates signaled to him, where he waited over the horizon with twenty-seven ships of the line, that the enemy were out. During the night he moved slowly in. At dawn on Monday, October 21, 1805, the two fleets saw each other. . . .

But let us go back now to the previous year: August 3, 1804, was the one hundredth anniversary of the British seizure of the Rock. It was about to face the most severe test of its history—far worse than Caramanli's raid, or the storm of 1776, or the Great Siege. . . .

The Education of Eliott Conquy

"I close now," Old Joe the publican growled. "You go." He rattled his keys menacingly. Eliott Conquy rose to his feet, stifling a yawn. His table companion cried, "Stow your blather, man, d'you think I'd be staying where I'm not wanted?" He rose, weaving, and fumbled in his fob. Eliott said, "It's paid for, Mr. O'Brien." He swept several pieces of paper off the table, stuffed them into his pocket, and left the tavern at O'Brien's heels.

They started along Engineer Lane, O'Brien continuing his discourse from the tavern as though he had not been interrupted. "So ye see, me boy, that stuff I'm telling you about the heart and the spleen and the kidneys is just what we know now, and if that's all we know, that's all we can teach, isn't that right? But because it's what we teach doesn't make it right, d'ye see? Because . . ." He stopped, teetering, and pointed. "There! That's disease. That's where it's bred." Eliott started, for they were at the corner of Bell Lane, and O'Brien was pointing at the Shaar Ashanayin synagogue. Old Mr. Aboab's scandalized face, under a nightcap, was peering down at them from an upper window.

"I'm not pointing only at your religion, Eliott," O'Brien said. "Mine's as bad . . . worse . . . I mean that in religion, it's a matter of *believing*. In medicine it's a matter of *not* believing, but of finding out. But why do I tell you, who want to be a rabbi?"

"I don't know what I want," Eliott said.

"Well, you're young. Holy Mother of Mary, I want to piss."

"Here," Eliott said. They were by Mr. Pitt's new Garrison Library. Behind it, the garden sloped steeply uphill under scattered trees. O'Brien went up a few paces, and Eliott waited, looking into the garden and listening with amused affection to the torrential sound of Mr. O'Brien's relief. O'Brien was a square, short man with a big mouth and ears and a trembling hand.

He was surgeon to the 54th Foot and in his forties: he might have been great and rich, but for the curse of the Irish.

It was a night of the levanter, mid-August, hot, close, the gray cloud mass stifling the town. Eliott was sweating, though wearing only a thin shirt, cotton trousers, and sandals. The moon gave a hazy dispersed light, shining through the cloud, and by it he now saw a dark shape under a fig tree in the library garden and two more beside. They were men, one lying and two standing.

"There's a man ill there," he said.

"Ill or drunk," O'Brien said. He staggered a few steps up the garden. One of the men came down at once, stopped a few paces off, and said, *"Para, para, señor. No se acerca mas."*

Eliott saw by his leather leggings, deep sash, and the Huelva hat perched over a bandanna that he was an Andalusian. He answered in Spanish, "We thought we saw a man down. This gentleman is a doctor."

The Andalusian said, "Our friend has drunk too much, nothing more."

"What's he saying?" O'Brien demanded. Eliott told him and moved away. O'Brien joined him a few moments later. He said, "I wonder where those fellows come from."

"Spain," Eliott said, for of course the men were smugglers; that is, they were agents of Spanish merchants come to buy tobacco. England was at war with Spain, and the land frontier was closed, but the Gibraltar merchants saw to it that the smugglers could come in and out of the garrison at will, war or no war, regardless of what orders the governor gave.

"Does it not worry you that these men come and go as they please?" O'Brien said.

"It's not our business," Eliott said.

"Ah, you scorpions!" O'Brien said. "Nothing that does not happen on the Rock exists for you. But man, there's a world outside, and you're tied to it, for better or worse, in a hundred ways. If you're to be a physician, you have to think always, ask yourself, why is this happening? where has this come from? where is it going? . . . But you're not going to be a physician, are you?"

"I don't know, Mr. O'Brien," Eliott said. "Good night, Mr. O'Brien." He turned up Forty Steps and a minute later let himself into the family house on Flat Bastion Road and crept up to his room as silently as the creaking stairs would allow. He drew the curtains, lit the lamp, and sat down at the table. A copy of Albo's *Book of Principles* lay open at the section denouncing heresy, with on one side a torn volume of Maimonides' *Guide for the Perplexed* and on the other the *Book of Criticism* by Abraham ben David of Posquieres. Pages of notes in his own careful but ill-formed Hebrew, written with a scratchy quill and spotted with ink where the quill had spluttered, littered the table. Every time his Teacher came in, the old man shook his head sadly to see the word of G*D so disfigured and said, "If it weren't for the spirit in you, David, I'd think you had no respect for the Word"; and he'd stoop and pick up the sheets that had blown to the floor.

From his pocket David Eliott Conquy pulled the sheets he had swept up from the tavern table and spread them over the Hebrew texts. Here was a diagram of the heart; Mr. O'Brien must have had half a dozen glasses of brandy by the time he drew that, for it would not have been very clear even in a good light. Even so, it was hard to imagine just how the heart functioned. He would have to see a heart, a real one, to know what these muscles and arteries looked like. He turned to the next sheet: the digestive system . . .

He looked at the medical drawings and the half-hidden texts. Which was it to be? Sometimes the Word of G*D filled his thoughts, sometimes the formation and function of the human body. Or should he give them both up and learn to be a merchant worthy of his employer and future father-in-law? But did he want to marry Esther, or was he doing it only because the fathers had arranged it . . . ?

The lamp was guttering when Nahum Conquy quietly opened the door two hours later, at three in the morning, and came in. He looked down at his son, head on the table, arms spread, asleep. He looked at the medical drawings that covered the sacred Hebrew books and the copied sections of the Torah and raised his eyes to heaven. Then he touched his son's shoulder and said, "Come, David . . . it is time you slept. What will Mr. Matania think if you appear before him red-eyed and haggard?"

David Eliott stumbled to his bed, flopped flat, and returned at once to sleep. His father noticed that there was no smell of alcohol on his breath. That craving, at least, he had not learned

from the Irish surgeon. He looked again at the medical drawings, muttered, "Blasphemy", and pushed them all into a drawer,
leaving the religious works displayed on the table.

Eliott sat on a high stool in Baruch Matania's counting house
on Bomb House Lane, looking out the window. The blue water
danced in the sun. The wind blew gustily, and he watched a
young woman's light dress blowing about her as she walked
along the Line Wall. The dresses of the officers' ladies scandalized his mother, for they wore only a single thickness of muslin,
often damped, and now the wind was pressing it to their bodies.
He yawned.

The familiar sharp nasal voice aroused him with a jerk.
"Would it not be more comfortable if I were to provide you
with a bed here, Mr. Conquy?"

Baruch Matania was small and hunchbacked and heavily perfumed. He wore a black wig to hide his thin gray hair and held a
silk handkerchief to his lips when in the presence of young
women to catch the saliva that then dripped, uncontrollable,
from his jaws.

Eliott stood up. He said, "I'm sorry."

Mr. Matania limped to the window, his gold-handled cane
tapping. "Sit down, David. I know why you're tired. Your father's told me. . . . Let us make a bargain. I will release you
from this clerkship if you will promise to give up the medical
studies and concentrate on the rabbinate. And marry Esther at
once, as soon as the Teacher gives us a date. I'll settle five hundred pounds a year on you. I have made all the money I need,
and it is time I paid some back to bring forth a respected Teacher
in Israel. You shall be that Teacher, David."

"Thank you, sir," Eliott muttered. " 'Tis most generous of
you. I'm not worthy."

"I often have doubts myself, on that score," Mr. Matania said
testily. "Well, consider my proposal carefully."

He tapped out. Sighing, Eliott returned to the ledgers . . .
bill of lading, tobacco, Wilmington, North Carolina . . . Sight
draft, Navy Victualing Commissioner, £13,000 . . . His head
drooped.

Theodore Whittle, master of the Schooner *Partridge*, shifted
his quid from the left cheek to the right and shot a stream of

tobacco juice over the side into the harbor. "Come aboard, Eliott," he called, "—always welcome."

Eliott hesitated. He had been getting manifests from a ship at
the New Mole and was on his way back to Mr. Matania's; but
Mr. Whittle was an old friend, English, an ex-navy boatswain
settled now on the Rock and doing well by running cargoes between Gibraltar, Moroccan ports, and England.

Mr. Whittle called again, and Eliott went on board. Mr.
Whittle knew better than to offer him liquor but gave him lime
juice instead. Mr. Whittle settled himself on the upturned
dinghy and looked up the gray-green slope of the Rock to the
levanter cloud hiding the crest. He shook his head. "It'll be
worse tomorrow. I hate the levanter—masters run their vessels
aground, husbands and wives fight. . . . Do you have the fever
ashore?"

Eliott said, "Not that I have heard. Why?"

Mr. Whittle said, "Three days ago *Dido* stopped a xebec, but
the crew shouted they was from Málaga, and the fever was killing off three hundred people every day there, so the captain said
shove them off, don't touch them."

Eliott said, "Why would he do that?"

"Because there's some believe the fevers and pestilence is
passed from one man to another, contagious-like, and doesn't
breed by itself."

Eliott thought, that would mean the fever could come here
from somewhere else. From Málaga. And if it could come by sea,
then it could come by land. Mr. O'Brien's interest in the smugglers in the library garden of two weeks ago suddenly became
understandable, as also his upbraiding of Eliott's insularity.

Mr. Whittle said, "Mind, I don't know about this contagion,
myself. I think there has to be conditions that the fever likes,
and then it comes of its own accord."

Eliott wondered whether Mr. O'Brien had heard about the
pestilence in Málaga. He thought he ought to tell him and after
a few more minutes' gossip excused himself and hurried along
the mole. On reaching the shore he did not go to Mr. Matania's
establishment but to Town Range Barracks, where the 54th
Foot was quartered. He found O'Brien in his little room off
the sick ward. Fifty men of the regiment were drilling on the
tiny square inside the buildings, sweating profusely in their

heavy scarlet coats and high leather stocks. O'Brien glanced up from a thick book he was writing in and said, "Eliott, me boy! I was just going to ask you to come. I'm thinking we have some cases of the Bulam fever, and I'm thinking, if that's true, I'm going to be terrible short-handed. I was going to ask, could you come and give me a hand an hour or two a day? Ye said once ye'd give an eye to work with me, so . . ."

Eliott felt the manifests in his pocket. The hard edges of them suddenly made up his mind for him. He gave them to O'Brien and said, "Just send a man with these to Mr. Matania, and I'll stay with you as long as you need me."

O'Brien clapped his hands eagerly. "That's me boy! Now I want you to help me get a full record of everything we can about the patients. Everything! I wish we had time to put down all about their fathers and mothers and where they spent every hour of the past thirty days . . . and that's what we're going to have to do one day . . . but with only you and me and Thompson the hospital mate . we'll just have to do what we can." He gave Eliott the book and went into the sick ward. "Now write this down, Eliott . . . 'Private Richard Tamlyn, 54th. Born Haworth, Yorks. Age twenty-four. Town Range Barracks, in Corporal Lindwall's room. Admitted August 31, 1804, ten A.M.' . . . Got it? Now write that Tamlyn was in here with ophthalmia from the seventh to the fourteenth of August. We've had a deal of ophthalmia in the garrison, and there just may be a connection with the fever. We don't know. We don't know *anything*, Eliott, always mind that. Now let's go and see the man. He's in the end bed there. I'll speak, and you write down."

The ward was an ordinary barrack room, with ten beds on either side. The floor was of stone paving, well scrubbed. One sick man slept, a couple of others sat on the edge of their beds in trousers and shirts, playing cards on an empty barrel between them. The thud of the drum beating time for the drilling soldiers echoed loudly between the whitewashed walls.

The man in the end bed was tall and lantern-jawed, with thin, lank brown hair. "Write that down, how he looks," O'Brien said. He turned to the patient. "Now, Tamlyn, how d'ye feel?"

"Bad, sir, bad," the man replied in a scratchy voice. "Sir, am I . . ."

"Where's the pain now?"

"All over . . . like I'd been beat, doctor. Ooh, ooh."

O'Brien laid a hand on his forehead and said, "Chill . . . write it down, Eliott. . . . August 31, eleven A.M. Chill. Violent pains back and limbs. Throat sore . . . Stick your tongue out. . . . tongue furred, whitish. You look queasy. . . . Head, stomach? Both. When was your last stool? . . . Shit, Tamlyn. Last stool yesterday, can't remember what it was like, didn't look . . . but we have to, Eliott, it's very important, especially in fevers. . . . Urine—piss?"

"I wants to, but I can't. I wants to now."

"Under the bed. Hold it for him, Eliott. There. Let it go. . . . Hm. Not much. Write, 'Wants to urinate often but with little success; urine produced is thick, high-colored. Pulse—one hundred, full.' "

"Doctor, am I going to die?"

"Of course not. Cheer up, man. Holy Mary, let's have some air to breathe in here." He walked down the ward to the far door and opened it. The thudding of the drum and the yelling of the sergeants burst in louder. "That noise won't disturb *our* patients," he said. "They'd think they was dead without it. Write in Tamlyn's report, 'Very nervous.' That's a common symptom in the beginning of this fever. Depression, nervousness, fear."

Eliott said, "I see."

O'Brien poked a finger into his chest. "Don't you want to know what the treatment is? Ask, ask, Eliott, or you'll never be a physician. . . . And now I'll tell ye, we have no idea what the treatment should be. Some of us do one thing and some another. The first thing I do, if the patient's not too weak, is to purge him. This is what we'll give him." He took the book and wrote: *Ordered ipecac. gr xv. antimon. tartar. gr j to be wrought off with 2 quarts of water.* "Now take that to Thompson, watch him make it up, then you give it to the patient. I have to go to a soldier's wife who I'm afraid . . ." He hurried away, shaking his head.

Hospital Mate Thompson was a thin rheumy soldier who seemed to fear that Eliott was after his job, but when Eliott insisted, he grumblingly allowed him to watch the mixing of the ingredients. Eliott then took the medicine to Private Tamlyn, who had hardly swallowed it before he was sitting up, retching and straining, convulsed. Just in time Eliott got the bucket out from under the cot.

O'Brien returned as Eliott was taking the pot out to the latrines. He said, "Stop there, boy. What's in it? . . . Just his porridge, beer, tea, bread . . . Write it all down. Now listen. There's two soldiers coming in complaining of pains and don't feel well and their heads splitting open. You take all particulars. I must go back to Mrs. Cropley. Aye, she has the fever."

Eliott took off his coat and hung it on the wooden peg behind the door in the surgeon's little office. . . .

Pvt. Tamlyn, 3 pm. Emetic operated well. 2 copious fetid black stools. Body heat increased, tongue same, pains in back and loins worse, stomach easy. Face flushed, pulse 104, weak. Ordered oatmeal gruel with a little wine.

There were four other soldiers in the ward by then, and Mrs. Cropley in her married quarters behind. The lieutenant colonel of the battalion came and walked the ward with O'Brien. They stopped near Eliott, and the colonel said, "If it gets worse, I'll speak to the governor about taking the men out to camp."

Pvt. Tamlyn, 6 pm. 1 black stool; urine free, slight pain forehead. Thirsty, eyes red, tongue more furred, mouth dry. Took tea and toast. Pulse 108, moderately full. Ordered 1 gr James' powder, at once, and if no effect another in 6 hours.

Eliott followed O'Brien to the next bed. And the next. And the next . . . At midnight he was asleep on the floor of the surgeon's office, a blanket under him, when he heard his name called. "David, David?"

He awoke, groaning, trying to unstick his eyes. It was his father. "David, what are you doing here? We've been searching all the town and the ships for you. I feared you'd been pressed into the navy. Come home now."

"I can't, father."

The groans and sighs and mutterings of the ward sounded like low laughter in a charnel house. The smell of vomit and sickness and feces lay thick and sweet under the acrid stink of the feathers Thompson had burned in the evening to kill it.

"This is my place," Eliott said.

"Ay, *que miseria!*" his father groaned. "It's safer with us, son. None of *us* have it."

> *Pvt. Tamlyn, Sep 1, 8 am. The dose of James' powder operated violently as emetic and purgative; now easy but thirsty; face swelled. Took tea and toast, drank toast and water. Fearful of not recovering. Pulse 104 but very soft. Ordered 2 gills wine in gruel through the day.*

O'Brien said, "Ye recall that night we saw the Andalusians in the library garden? 'Twas August ten. Now a merchant called Bresciano—ye know him?—has come forward to tell that the priest of the Spanish church here, Don Francisco Hoyera, was dining with him that night and was called out to give the last Sacrament to a dying man. He found the sick man under a fig tree in the library garden, and as soon as he was dead his friends buried him there. They were smugglers from Málaga, but before they smuggled the tobacco out, they had smuggled death in. Aye, death, and ye see that what we have to thank this cursed fever for is greed. . . . How many more cases in the night? None? Well, 'tis early yet to say one thing or another. Now, Eliott, I'm going to do a very improper thing here. I'm going to experiment with these wretched men's lives. I'll give Tamlyn and the fellow next to him the regular treatment, but with others I'll try out different ideas. Ye've heard of the vaccination against the smallpox, which is giving the person a dose of a similar but less dangerous disease? Now the remittent fever's like the Bulam, but it's not so strong. So I'm going to give two patients a vaccination of urine from that man Hallam, who has the remittent fever. And we'll vaccinate volunteers who have no fever, ye see, to learn whether that protects them from getting it later. And I'm going to boil the stool of a patient who has recovered from the fever, and . . ."

> *Pvt. Tamlyn, Sep 1, 6 pm. Took 1 gill wine, tea, toast; vomited; head well, back and limbs painful; tongue very furred. Pulse 100, weak; feels chill, but body heat moderate. Ordered 1 gill extra wine before morning, and to take every hour 1 large spoonful of R. Decoct. Cort. Peruv. zviij. Tinct ditto. zj. spt. aether. vit. c. zjtinct. op ii. gr. xl. M.*

> *Pvt. Tamlyn, Sep 2, 8 am. Slept very well; 2 fetid black stools, vomited a little early; tea and toast since, which is still sitting*

in him; some pains in limbs and throat. Pulse 100 moderately
full but feeble; forward half of tongue toward tip clear and
shining. Ordered medicines continued and to have 4 gills wine,
with sago and tapioca.

"Eliott, there's a message for you here, to go to Mr. Matania's
place of business at once. Me boy, are ye still supposed to
be . . . ?"

"Tell him I'm sorry. I'm busy, I can't come."

"Aye, but listen to me, boy, you know 'tis dangerous work
looking after patients with the Bulam fever?"

Eliott nodded without speaking. He knew, too well. Fear of
the disease sometimes paralyzed him, now that he was seeing its
course at close hand and knew that all the surgeon's treatments
amounted to no more than a pious wish; but that was only when
he was not actually in the ward—once there, he became ab-
sorbed in his task of recording the symptoms and the treatment.
Several times, feeling an onset of panic, he had gone to the ward
to calm himself.

Pvt. Tamlyn, Sep 2, 3 pm. Thinks himself well; free of pain;
vomited much, ate 1 oz meat (given him without leave by a
soldier friend), face pale, tongue not so shiny, hawks bloody
slimy matter, eyes clearer. Pulse 106, rather feeble. Has had 2
gills wine. Ordered 4 more, and to continue medicine.

"Ah, Eliott, come in, come in. I've asked the surgeons of the
other regiments to have a look at our ward here, and then we'll
have a talk, and I'm hoping we can speak with one voice to the
garrison surgeon and he to the governor. This is Mr. Ashland of
the 2d, Mr. Greatorex of the 10th, Mr. MacKenzie of the 13th.
Gentlemen, this is Mr. Eliott Conquy, my assistant. Now, if
you'll follow me . . . This patient was admitted—read from
the book, Eliott. . . ."

They went down the ward and an hour later crowded into
O'Brien's office, all standing, for there was only one chair. O'Brien
said, "There you are, gentlemen. D'ye not agree that we must
urge the garrison surgeon to go to the governor and declare an
emergency? By God, we are at war! If the fever strikes us very
heavily, the Spaniards could walk in and seize the fortress."

"Quite right," Greatorex said. "We should fumigate the whole of Gibraltar immediately. The air is foul, and the pestilence is breeding in it. There should be fires in the streets, especially at night. Find the most pestilential areas and move the troops from those areas out into camp. Or into caves. St. Michael's Cave would make an excellent site for several hundred men."

MacKenzie said, "By your leave, your proposals are nothing short of disastrous. The only help is isolation. The Bulam fever is contagious and is passed by physical contact, or breathing common air, between the fit and the sick, in which I include those in whom the disease is not yet fully incubated, that is to say, persons whom we have no means of knowing are about to become stricken. Everyone, therefore, is a potential danger, and everyone must be prevented from giving the disease to others."

"What evidence do you have, pray, that the fever is contagious? It is well established that this fever is spontaneously generated in certain climates and places, such as that very island of Bulam off the Guinea Coast."

"Rubbish, Mr. Ashland."

"Mr. Greatorex, fiddlesticks to you, sir."

"Sir!"

"Gentlemen, gentlemen, can we not agree on one thing, just one recommendation?"

"Provided it is agreed that contagion is not . . ."

'Contagion must be treated as the one, the only . . ."

Pvt. Tamlyn, Sep 2, 6 pm. Vomited, continues easy. Tongue not so shiny, pulse 102, feeble. Ordered continued wine and medicine.

Pvt. Tamlyn, Sep 3, 8 am. Bad night, delirious, 1 stool; vomited twice, comatose, tongue dry, very weak, no appetite. Pulse 90, feeble. Ordered bottle sherry wine, and to continue medicine with aether vitriol zj to ziv of the bark, M.
3 pm. No alteration.
7 pm. Vomited about one quart of matter resembling coffee grounds; no pain, delirious. Pulse 102, v feeble. Ordered continue wine and medicine with a tablespoon of water, strongly acidulated with elixir of vitriol, every half hour.

Sep 4, 8 am. Slept little, was delirious, feels easy, vomited black fluid very often, had half hour of hiccups; took medicine regu-

larly, also 2 bottles white wine; pulse hard to perceive. Ordered
continue all medicines and apply sinapisms to feet.

"Eliott, you look like a ghost walking."

"Yes, Mr. O'Brien."

"Yeoman's well on the way to recovery. The other three . . ."
O'Brien took another swig from the rum bottle on his desk. His
skin was gray, and his breath rank with liquor. "Mrs. Cropley
died last night."

Pvt. Tamlyn, Sep 4, 2 pm. Died an hour ago. Bled profusely
from nose and mouth.

Eliott drew a line under the entry and looked at O'Brien.
"Next patient," O'Brien said harshly. "How do you feel, sergeant? Vomit? Stool . . . ?"

Eliott usually enjoyed Succoth, the Feast of Tabernacles, more
than any other religious occasion of the year. But today he felt
nervous and uncomfortable.

The cantor and the rabbi led the service, their three-cor-
nered hats bobbing and bowing. Eliott took the pointed palm
and the citrus offered to him by his neighbor and stepped into
the side aisle to find space. He bowed his body forward and began to thrust out the palm and citrus . . . but should he be
here at all, with Mr. O'Brien's certainty that the fever was contagious? Should any of them be here? Surely the Parnassim
should have canceled the service and closed the synagogue? But
could they?

Twice to the east, twice to the south, twice to the west, twice
to the north: then twice upward and twice downward. He gave
the palm and citrus to another. The singing became more
intense.

> "Hosha-na, Hosha-na,
> Save us, we beseech Thee
> Save us, we beseech Thee,
> For Thy sake, if not for ours, save us,
> O Lord, save us we beseech Thee, we beseech Thee."

The president drew back the curtains of the Ark, and the Levantadores went forward, brought out two Torah scrolls, raised

them, and carried them down the steps. Eliott bowed his head, carried out his prayer shawl, touched the case of a Torah with it, and kissed its fringes where they had touched.

When they had carried it slowly all round the synagogue and were again in front of the Ark, the Levantadores faced the congregation, suddenly raised high a heavy Torah, and unwound the scrolls so that three columns of the Word showed. In front of Eliott Mr. Matania half stretched out his arms, tears rolling down his cheeks. He believes, Eliott thought, so he is not a hypocrite, even though he is an unscrupulous old lecher. My father and young brother Hillel here beside me believe. But I? I am here, I perform the functions laid down, carry out the appointed rites, but do I *believe*? If not, how can I become a Teacher?

He glanced up at the balcony where his mother and three sisters watched intently, their faces half covered, wigs hiding their hair. Three hundred deaths a day in Málaga. What if the Law said one thing and medicine another? The Teachers were calling for a Cohen to read the Word, as was his right. Old Jacob Cohen hobbled up and read. When he had finished, the Teacher beckoned to Eliott, and he went up. He read from Leviticus 23, carefully, for he always found the unpointed Hebrew difficult to read:

"These are the appointed seasons of the Lord, even holy convocations, which ye shall proclaim in their appointed season. . . . And ye shall offer an offering made by fire under the Lord, seven days: in the seventh day is a holy convocation, ye shall do no servile work."

Afterward Mr. Matania met him outside the Tabernacle set up in the synagogue garden. He said, "You read well, David. But then you go and 'do servile work' in the soldiers' hospital. . . . Are you ready to come back to the counting house now? Or to start serious study?"

"There are still many sick among the soldiers," Eliott said. "It is getting worse. Afterwards . . . when it dies down . . ."

"All *our* people are well," Mr. Matania said. "None has taken the fever. It breeds in dirt, and to avoid it only cleanliness and clean living according to the Law are needed."

But it was not true. Succoth fell on September 23 that year. On

October 3 Eliott's father was stricken with fever, and the same day, Esther Matania and five other Jews. The pestilence continued among the military but now also moved full force upon the civilians. It crept out of the soil and shook down from the sky. It was breathed in the air, drunk with the water, eaten with the food. Day followed night followed day in a slow procession of nightmarish unreality of fear that spread and grew like cancer in the body, bursting out in sudden blossoms of violent pain and, worse, despair. There was a certainty of being unwanted, doomed. Twice Eliott saw men hurl themselves from upper windows and twice into the sea and make no attempt to swim.

Eliott left the 54th and moved out to the fever "ward" of tents and shelters set up on Windmill Hill. His daily hours of sleep dropped from six to four to two. In succession he nursed, and buried, five members of his family—all except his mother. The rich of all religions left Gibraltar, the Jews to Morocco, the rest to Genoa, a few to England. The poor stayed and died with the garrison.

Toward the end of the year the pestilence began to abate. In the first months of 1805 those who had fled began to return. The narrow streets of the town had become silent corridors, the houses silent but for the squeaking of rats. On Windmill Hill and by Black Town hundreds of vultures feasted on the ill buried bodies.

Eliott Conquy returned to work for Mr. Matania because he needed money to support his mother and because Mr. Matania, who had lost seven out of nine clerks, begged him to. In the evenings he studied medicine with O'Brien or the Law with the Teacher of the congregation; but more and more now, when he finished for the night, it was the sacred books that lay on top, obscuring the medical notes below. Many who had known him for all the twenty-one years he had lived before the pestilence did not recognize him; for he had lost thirty pounds in weight and developed a stoop, so that he looked like a black-avised heron, the dark blue eyes deep-sunk under the bony overhang of his forehead. He believed that YHWH had shown him His terrible face and commanded him; for Eliott had turned away from Him and now his father, his brother, and his three sisters were dead, taken in agony. Eliott knew he must obey YHWH . . . yet he had come to hate Him.

O'Brien rocked back in his chair, the grog glass shaking in his hand. He had not been able to drink heavily during the epidemic but had made up for it in the ten months since. Eliott did not think he would last much longer. It was a Friday—October 18—four o'clock in the afternoon.

"Do you have a shilling to spare, Eliott?" O'Brien said. "The navy officers here are having a sweepstake on how long it will take the new governor to discover about Signalman Dacres. D'ye not know about that? Well, there's a post for a common sailor to be naval signaler on the Rock that's been filled and the pay drawn for the past twenty-four years by Admiral Dacres, and him retired in England since 1788! Old Tommy Trigge never did find out!"

Eliott did not smile. The minor rascalities of the Christian military seemed very unimportant against life's permanent background of death and fear and the menace of YHWH, as real and as toweringly present as the Rock above these barracks.

O'Brien cleared his throat nervously, "Well, I mustn't be wasting your time, must I? . . . I've been making out a summary of the epidemic from the regimental reports and the civilian figures you gave me. Take a look at that, me boy. . . . Well, Jasus, I shouldn't be calling you 'me boy' anymore, should I?"

Eliott picked up the paper. On it was written:

	(Rank and File)	
Corps	*Admitted Hosp.*	*Died, all causes*
Artillery	462	201
Engineers	229	123
Military Artificers		15
2nd Foot	300	131
10th Foot	419	22
13th Foot	479	130
54th Foot	456	100
De Roll's Regt. Hanoverians	414	187
Officers, all corps		54
Military women and children		164
Civilians, all		4864
Total		5991

O'Brien leaned forward and tapped the paper with his finger. "Two things stick out like a sore thumb, Eliott. We had four thousand, eight hundred and sixty-four civilian deaths. That's about half the civilian population of before the epidemic. But many civilians left Gibraltar, so the mortality among those who stayed must have been near eighty-five percent . . . compared with fifty percent in the Engineers and only thirty percent in the infantry. And the infantry is the worst disciplined, the most crowded, and the dirtiest of all. What do you think of that?"

Eliott said nothing. O'Brien was a good man, but blind.

O'Brien went on quickly. "The other item is this—look at the figures for the 10th Foot. They have as many admissions as the others . . . but barely one fifth of the mortality! Now what can that mean? That the 10th have acquired a resistance? Where? They've come from India. Is that it?"

Eliott stood up. He said, "None of these things matter. I cannot be interested in your medicine any more, Mr. O'Brien. Thank you for what you have done, but I shall not be back."

O'Brien stared up at him open-mouthed. The glass rattled on the table. Eliott turned and went out, hearing one baffled, hurt cry behind—"Eliott!"

He went straight to Mr. Matania's house, where the merchant now lived alone with his only surviving daughter. He was in the parlor and stood up carefully when Eliott entered. "David," he said formally, "what can I do for you?" His manner to Eliott had changed greatly since the epidemic; but then, everything had.

Eliott said, "I have decided to become a Teacher."

"The Lord be praised," Mr. Matania exclaimed.

"I have come to accept your offer. I shall go to England to study."

"The Lord be praised!" Mr. Matania cried again. "David, this is wonderful! When are you leaving?"

"As soon as I can get passage."

Mr. Matania hurried out, calling, "Wait there." His cane tapped away and in a few minutes returned. "There's fifty sovereigns for your passage and to fit yourself out in London," he said, "and here's a banker's order on Mr. Rothschild for twenty pounds. If you need more, you have only to ask your Uncle Gamaliel. And . . . you'll come back to us, to be our Teacher and guide?"

He looked up, anxious and subservient.

"I shall come back," Eliott said somberly. He went out, the merchant's final "The Lord be praised" still echoing in his ears. Now he had to tell his mother. She would faint for joy, for she had been pestering him to take this step ever since the end of the epidemic.

He bumped into someone, and a voice cried, "Hey, hey, look where you're going, you walking beanpole. . . ." It was Mr. Whittle. He recognized Eliott. "Why, Eliott, damn my eyes, I haven't seen you in an age, and now I'm off again—but there's just time for a quick one afore we sail."

"Where are you going?" Eliott asked quickly.

"Bristol."

"I'll come." He looked at the sun—still an hour or more before the beginning of the Sabbath. "I'll be on board in half an hour." He ran away down the street, the tails of his black coat flying.

"Sail ho!" a sailor at the bow cried. "Two points off the port bow."

Mr. Whittle leaped nimbly into the portside rigging and peered forward. "Thank God!" he said. "It's one of ours." He jumped down and glanced astern, where a brown-sailed, black-hulled sloop was hauling up fast on the *Partridge*. A few minutes later the sloop's captain saw the new sail and put down his helm. Two puffs of smoke blossomed on his flank, two columns of water leaped out of the sea, far short, and then two thuds of cannon. The sloop, a Spanish privateer, turned and headed back for Cádiz, just out of sight over the eastern horizon.

Mr. Whittle laughed and cocked a snook after her. To the helmsman he called, "Steer for the man o' war, George. We'll sell 'em some vegetables."

The ship bore down upon them, all sail set before a northwest wind. When the black hull and yellow gunports and waving ensigns seemed to be right on top of them, sailors scrambled like squirrels up the rigging, and she backed topsails. A boat smacked into the water almost simultaneously, and Mr. Whittle said, "It's the *Ark Royal*. Best-handled ship in the fleet. She was fitting a new mainmast in Rosia till a few days ago. But . . . hold hard!

What do they want to send an officer and marines for? Put up the helm, George, quick!"

An officer on the poop of the warship shouted through a speaking trumpet, "Put down your helm, master, or I fire." Eliott saw that half a dozen guns on that side had been run out to the ports.

The boat rowed alongside, and a lieutenant came aboard. "Captain Burleigh's compliments, and he must press any able-bodied men aboard for the king's service."

Mr. Whittle shouted, "You can't press my crew, lieutenant."

"Oh yes, he can, master. It's Mr. Whittle, isn't it? He sailed forty short, and now we've lost ten more down with fever. And the enemy are reported to be warping out of harbor."

Red-coated marines scrambled aboard the sloop, and Mr. Whittle called up resignedly, "All right, Captain Burleigh. But leave me five sailors."

A marine jogged Eliott's arm and pointed to the boat. Eliott said, "I'm a Jew."

The marine said, "All right, Moses, into the boat."

"But . . . this is not my business. This is nothing to do with me," Eliott cried. "I'm a passenger, going to England for rabbinical studies."

Two marines seized him and dragged him, struggling and shouting, to the boat, "Go along easy," Mr. Whittle called anxiously. "It can't be helped, Eliott. The fleet needs men. . . . He's a doctor, lieutenant."

Twenty minutes later Eliott stood on the deck of the battleship with a dozen other sailors and passengers taken off Mr. Whittle's ship. The *Partridge* herself was just beginning to make headway toward the northwest, on the starboard tack. A tall, dark-jowled man in blue, with much gold lace, stood in front of them and said, "Seamen, one step forward. Mr. Trott, distribute them. . . . Bos'n, take charge of the rest. Give 'em some gun drill at once."

Eliott said, "I want to go to England."

A nearby group of sailors began to titter. The lieutenant said, "The master said this one was a doctor, sir."

Captain Burleigh said, "Ah, then down to the orlop with you, and report to Surgeon Halford."

Eliott said obstinately, "I am not a physician. I want to go to England."

Captain Burleigh glared at him, the dark eyes snapping. They stood alone on the poop, for everyone else had gone about his business. Two marine sentries, guarding the companion up from the main deck, stared woodenly ahead.

The captain said, "You speak very good English for a Rock scorpion. You are a Gibraltarian, aren't you?"

"Yes."

"Try saying, 'Yes, sir'."

"Why? I am not in the military."

Captain Burleigh said, "You are now. . . . You are an educated man or you wouldn't speak English. And yet, you seem to know nothing. . . . This ship is about to rejoin Lord Nelson's fleet. Tomorrow that fleet will fight the French and Spanish, somewhere near here. Do you know what will happen if we lose?"

Eliott shook his head. It was none of his affair, this business of fleets and armies and battles.

"The enemy will be able to invade England. And Gibraltar will go back to Spain."

"Gibraltar?" Eliott exclaimed. "Here?"

"Here!" the captain said.

Eliott looked out over the heaving tumbling waste of blue and white. Specks of sails had begun to show along the western horizon. If Gibraltar became Spanish, what would happen to the Jews? It seemed unbelievable, and unjust, that such a question should be decided miles away, upon another element, by men from other countries. But so it was. And the movements of these forces, which he had lived with all his life but ignored, would now also decide his own career and his fate.

"Take me to the surgeon," he said. "I will do what I can."

The next morning was Monday, October 21. Shortly after dawn a sailor found Eliott killing cockroaches in the orlop and told him the captain wanted him. "Bring a sharp knife, captain says," the sailor added. Eliott worked his way up narrow ladders, through long, low-roofed spaces crowded with chattering men and silent guns, to the open air. Captain Burleigh was sitting on a barrel on the poop. The rising sun shone on his worn blue coat and tarnished gold lace. He thrust his hand out. "See that splinter? Cut it out." The splinter was at least an inch long and had been driven hard into the palm of the captain's hand. Eliott said, "But . . ."

"From Commander-in-Chief, sir—form order of sail in two columns," an officer nearby called out, the telescope still to his eye.

"Acknowledge, Mr. Ponsonby. . . . Don't 'but' me, surgeon, do as I say."

Eliott took the hand, and probed gingerly with his scalpel. He began to sweat, and his own hand became slippery.

"From Commander-in-Chief, sir—course east by south. Masthead reports enemy fleet wearing in succession from rear."

The sun shone on blue heaving water, the sweat glazed in Eliott's eyes, his wrist trembled.

"From Commander-in-Chief, sir: prepare for battle."

Battle, Eliott thought. Soon, and he was to be in it. His trembling stopped; he gripped the captain's hand firmly with his left and cut deep along the line of the splinter with the point of the scalpel. The hand tightened but did not move. Blood flowed freely as he slipped the scalpel under the splinter and eased it out.

"Water, someone," the captain said. "Wash it. Didn't you bring a bandage, surgeon? Think, man, think!" He peered at Eliott more closely, meanwhile wrapping his own handkerchief around his hand. "By God, you look as if you need a tot more than I do. And I certainly do." He prized up the lid of the barrel, dipped in the ladle hanging at the side, and gave it to Eliott. Eliott drank, coughed, choked, and drank again. The captain clapped him on the back. "Sit down a minute, man. If blood affects you that much, are you sure you wouldn't rather serve a gun?"

"No, sir," Eliott muttered, "I've never worked with the wounded or hurt, only the sick. It's different."

"It is indeed," Captain Burleigh said. "Take a look round while you can."

Eliott looked ahead and saw in the eye of the low sun a long line of sails, stretching across from horizon to horizon. The Andulusian mountains rose hazy behind them. "That's the enemy,"

Captain Burleigh said, "about fifteen miles away. They're turning to try to get back to Cádiz before we can cut into them, but they won't do it."

A column of ships stretched ahead and astern of the *Ark Royal*, and a mile to the left there was another column, the two heading for the middle of the enemy line. "That's the Commander-in-Chief's column," the captain said. "He's in the van, in *Victory*."

"From flag, sir—course east by north."

"Acknowledge. . . . You'd better get below now, surgeon. Mr. Halford will need your help. Tell him we'll probably engage about noon—say, in four hours—if the wind holds."

Eliott took a long look around the circle of sea and sky, filled now with ships. From all the English ships huge white and red ensigns streamed out ahead in the breeze. Then he went below.

The orlop deck was a part of the third deck down on the port side, forward. It was below the water line and had no ports. Flimsy wood partitions shut it off from the rest of the deck, which contained powder magazines, huge water butts, and bins of 32-pound cannon balls. Oil lanterns swung from the beams, and there was a mixed smell of tar, rum, and sweat. Mr. Halford, the surgeon, was gaunt and harried, with pale eyes and gingery whiskers. "Set to, set to, Mr. Conquy," he said. "Arrange, put out, stack. . . ." There were four or five seaman-mates, and with them Eliott began to get ready. In the orlop "prepare for battle" was a grim business indeed: scrubbing a heavy table for operations, laying out knives, saws, pincers, and a padded hammer; broaching a small cask of rum; setting out buckets of pitch, buckets of water, and just buckets—several of them, empty; a wooden bin, for legs and arms; miles of bandage. . . . Eliott worked with his jaw set. He felt uneasy in the pit of his stomach but hoped it would go when the firing actually began.

They finished at last. Halford sat down on the table with a sigh and helped himself to a mug of rum. He drank, shaking his head. "There'll be a big butcher's bill today, if Lord Nelson gets his teeth into them." He drank again.

At half past eleven the pipes shrilled, and Mr. Halford said, "All hands on deck." Eliott followed him up through the decks— empty of men now, the guns standing in long rows on either side, to the top. There he gasped, for the line of enemy ships seemed very close. The lead ship of the *Ark Royal*'s column must be no more than quarter of a mile from them. Eliott, from the sixth ship of the line, felt he could almost recognize men's features in the enemy vessels.

Captain Burleigh stood on the break of the *Ark Royal*'s poop, the crew massed below, a few officers behind. Eliott climbed into the rigging close to the poop, the better to see, and looked out over a sea of blue, white, striped jerseys, and black bandannas of the sailors, mixed with the red coats and cock-aded black top hats of the marines.

The officer with the telescope said, "From Commander-in-Chief, sir—intend to pass through enemy line, make all sail with safety to masts."

Captain Burleigh said, "Acknowledge," and turned to face the crew. "Men," he began, "on this auspicious occasion, I feel it is my duty to address a few words to you. We are about to engage the enemies of God, of the king, and of mankind. Let it never . . ."

"From Commander-in-Chief, sir—" the signal officer interrupted.

"God damn it!" Captain Burleigh exploded. "We don't need any more signals!"

"England expects that every man will do his duty."

The captain's raised, bandaged hand sank. After a long pause he turned to the crew and said quietly, "Did you hear that, men? There's nothing more to be said."

"From Commander-in-Chief, sir—close action! . . . The signal is being kept flying."

"Except that!" Captain Burleigh cried. "Three cheers, men, then to your action stations. Hip, hip . . . !"

Eliott found himself cheering with the rest, and though all the hundreds of mouths were open, bellowing lustily, the sound came out thin in the open air against the creak of the masts and the slat of the sails and the surge of the sea. The upper deck began to empty. Eliott gazed ahead, fascinated, as the leading ship of the column suddenly vanished in a huge cloud of white smoke. Seconds later a thunderous booming reached him. Very quickly the thunder was repeated, and Captain Burleigh shouted to his signal officer, "Eighteen seconds between broadsides! *Royal*

Sovereign's outdoing herself. . . . Can you see who we're likely to draw, Mr. Ponsonby?"

"*Bellerophon*'s going to get *Monarca*, sir. I think the next ship is *Covadonga*, seventy-four. That'll be ours."

The white smoke ahead billowed higher and wider. More and more of the center of the enemy line was vanishing in the smoke. Over to the left smoke began to hide the head of the other English column, as it too engaged. Ahead of the *Ark Royal*, ship after ship sailed steadily into the white murk, all but their topsails vanishing. One by one Lieutenant Ponsonby muttered their names as they went: *Royal Sovereign, Belle Isle, Mars, Tonnant, Bellerophon*. . . . The thunder of cannon grew into a continuous battering.

"Our turn now, sir," Ponsonby said.

Captain Burleigh said, "Good luck, Mr. Ponsonby. . . . Good God, surgeon, what in hell are you still doing up here? Get to your post!"

Then they were in the smoke, the fumes caught at Eliott's throat, a great bow loomed over, and pair by pair the guns on both sides of the ship began to fire, from bow to stern. The deck jumped, the masts groaned, the whole ship shook. Eliott ran for the ladder, filled with a wild, fearful exhilaration.

They started coming into the orlop at once—men with chests crushed, knees smashed, arms gone: thirty-two-pound cannon-balls fired at a range of forty feet or less made no small wounds. *Crash . . . crash . . . crash . . . crash . . .* the explosions of the guns never paused, and under them there was a heavy, hollow rumbling. "The guns recoiling and being run back, sir," a sailor with a pulped left hand told him. "Can I have a little water please, sir? God bless you, sir. Thank you, sir." *Crash . . . crash . . . crash . . .* The ship jarred and grated. . . . "Rammed someone," a seaman-mate said. *Crash . . . crash . . . crash . . .* The minutes accumulated into hours, the pile of legs and arms grew in the bin. The operating table and the deck all round were red and slippery. Every few minutes the mates carried off men who had died, to throw them through a port, and came back staggering under new cases. Powder burns, amputations, disembowelings, deep gouges from flying splinters, Eliott saw them all, wept inwardly over them all, and did his best for all; and below the sadness at the horrors men were inflicting on each other he recognized a steadily growing assurance, a contentment of discovery. Whether he liked it or not, he *was* a surgeon. It was, and must be, in this way that he would serve his God.

Crash . . . crash . . . crash: and always the faint voices—Water. . . . Thank you, sir, God bless you. . . . I'm all right, look after my mate, sir. . . . Those he heard louder, in his mind, than the helpless screams and groans.

"Are we winning, sir?" a sailor asked, pale as death with a splinter clean through his body.

"I don't know," Eliott said.

Captain Burleigh stooped under the beam beside him. "Yes, we're winning, Muggeridge," the Captain said, speaking loud so that all in the orlop would hear. "The *Covadonga*'s struck to us, and *Monarca* to the *Bellerophon*. But we're badly holed below the water line. Get everyone on deck, Mr. Halford."

He left, and Eliott realized then that the ship was tilted slightly to starboard. He began to support and carry the wounded men to the upper deck. The noise was as great as ever, though only the port side guns were firing. When he returned to the orlop after his second trip, the list had increased visibly. On deck the masts were only stumps, and all the sails were hanging over the side. Sailors were cutting loose spars and barrels, anything that would float. Eliott went down once more to make sure no one was left in the orlop. It was empty, the buckets and barrels beginning to slide down the tilted deck and legs and arms rolling out of the bin after them. He started back up. As he passed the empty lower gun deck he looked down it and stopped, gripped with a paralysis of horror. He had not paused in the gun decks as he ran up and down with the wounded. Now he was seeing one after battle for the first time. He thought the sight would remain burned onto his eyes for the rest of his life, a permanent background for all else that ever passed before them.

The deck was only empty of the living. The dead lay in drifts and piles, a hundred, two hundred, mixed red, white, blue, yellow. Heads rolled in scuppers awash with blood and tripes. Under the bodies the teak deck was inches deep in blood, ears, fingers, entrails, and eyes. The thick bulwarks of the ship were smashed and splintered the whole way down both sides. Many of the square gun ports had become gaping raw-edged holes.

Several of the upper deck beams had been smashed, to fall angled across the deck. Some of the cannon had broken free from the restraining ropes. One by one they thundered down the slope, mashing the bodies under their wheels, to stop with a deafening crash against the lower bulwark, or smash through a huge hole into the sea.

Eliott muttered a prayer, then went slowly up the last ladder. A few minutes after he reached the upper deck the *Ark Royal*'s list increased suddenly, and as she went over, he jumped into the sea. Ten minutes later he found himself almost alone on the water, sharing a spar with three sailors. It was late afternoon, the sea was rising, and the warring ships were fading to the west.

One by one the three sailors slipped, exhausted, off the spar and vanished into the sea, their mouths open, but Eliott heard nothing. Near dark the waves became shorter and steeper, and he felt sand under his feet. Holding to the spar, swimming, trying to walk, being knocked down, rising again, he struggled at last to the shore. On hands and knees he crawled up the beach till he felt sharp reed grass and the slope of a high dune. There he fell, lay down, and slept.

He awoke screaming, for in his sleep he had seen the sand covered with dead men, and others rolling in the waves, and men on land hacking each other with swords and spears. He staggered to his feet, for an elderly man in a torn and soaked uniform was coming toward him barefoot. A river ran into the sea on the right, and beyond there was a low sandy cape and a steep green hill behind. Dead men, mostly naked, did indeed cover the sand, and others rolled in the waves; but of the warriors with swords there was no trace.

"You cried out?" the other man said in classical Castilian. "You are wounded?"

"No," Eliott said. "I was deafened yesterday, but now I can hear. . . . I was going to England to study to be a rabbi."

"You are a Jewish priest?" the gray-haired man said, still polite but obviously baffled. "Spanish?"

"I was. I thought I was," Eliott said. "But I'm not. I'm a physician. Gibraltarian. I was assistant surgeon on *Ark Royal*."

The other's face cleared, and he bowed. "You have won a

famous victory, sir. I am Luis Santangel, Count of Grazalema and lately Captain of His Catholic Majesty's ship *Covadonga*. I own an estate near here. We will go there, and . . ."

"Where are we?" Eliott interrupted.

The count pointed. "That low cape is Trafalgar. This is the River Barbate. You must be my guest for as long as you wish. I shall be honored to show you . . ."

"Thank you, sir, thank you," Eliott said, "but I must get back to Gibraltar at once. I have to start all over again, properly."

Book Ten

~~~~~~~~~~~~~~~~~~~~~~~~~~~~~~~~~~~~~~~

Victorian Heyday

The Jewish years 5564–5662
AUC 2557–2655
A.D. 1804–1902
A.H. 1219–1320

NELSON was killed in the battle. They cut off his hair to give to Lady Hamilton, put his body in a large barrel, filled it with brandy, and lashed it to the *Victory*'s mainmast below decks, with a sentry over it. On the slow stormy voyage back to Gibraltar the body rose and lifted the lid in the night. The sentry's thoughts are not recorded. In Gibraltar, alongside at Rosia Bay, the brandy was drawn off and replaced by less volatile spirits of wine. The *Victory*, her wounds patched, sailed for England with her much loved admiral, neither ever to see the Rock again.

The four chief admirals at Trafalgar were Nelson; Cuthbert Collingwood, who succeeded him and died at sea five years later, without ever again setting foot ashore; Villeneuve, who committed suicide before reaching Paris; and Federico Carlos de Gravina, the Spanish commander—he died of wounds received at Trafalgar. On his deathbed he said, referring to his conqueror that day, *"I go now to join the greatest hero the world has ever known."* Over 8,500 men were killed, wounded, or drowned in the battle.

But the glory must be shared by others. There were Black Jack

Jervis and the nameless officers and boatswains who had forged the weapon that Nelson so terribly wielded. It took Spanish ships of the line twenty-four hours to unmoor—a British ship as many minutes; when Spanish ships had to cross their yards for a harbor ceremony they started the day before—the crew of a British man-of-war did it in one minute from the deck. After Trafalgar a tremendous storm blew up, but Collingwood stayed on his post, reporting: *"I kept the sea after the action with the least injured ships. I had another view in keeping the sea at that time (which had a little of pride in it) and that was to show the enemy, that it was not a battle or a storm which could remove a British Squadron from the station they were directed to hold."*

And there was the common sailor, the brutalized, press-ganged subhuman who yet at such times became superhuman. During all that week in 1801 when the Gibraltar dockyard maties were working night and day to get Saumarez' squadron ready for action again, there were no drunks and no desertions in the fleet —except several wounded and sick sailors who "deserted" from hospital to rejoin their ships. During and after Trafalgar the sailors not only did their duty, as the famous signal expected of them, but in their conduct toward each other and toward wounded and defeated enemies they lived up to the far more severe standards Nelson had set in his noble and moving prayer before battle (written into his diary an hour before action was joined): "May the Great God whom I worship Grant to my Country and for the benefit of Europe in General a great and Glorious Victory, and may no misconduct in anyone tarnish it, and may humanity after Victory be the predominant feature in the British Fleet."

The only permanent relics of Trafalgar at Gibraltar are the so-called Trafalgar Cemetery, where among victims of other battles and fevers lie buried two men who died of wounds received at Trafalgar, and the huge figure of Sir Augustus Eliott in the patio of the convent. This was carved from the bowsprit of the *San Juan Nepomuceno*, one of the four prizes which reached Gibraltar (the other sixteen were all wrecked or driven ashore in the storm). Captain Churruca fought the *San Juan Nepomuceno* until she was a shattered hulk, her decks in the state described of the imaginary *Ark Royal*. When dying, he was asked which of the six ships engaging him he wished to surrender to, he said, "To all, for surely no one of them alone could have brought us down." His ship was a prison hulk in Gibraltar Harbor for many years, the captain's cabin locked and left as it was in memory of Churruca's gallantry.

By Trafalgar the epidemic in Gibraltar was just past its worst but by no means yet over. Its effects were so shattering that the Spanish general Francisco Javier de Castaños had arranged a conference of French, Spanish, and British medical officers on the neutral ground outside Gibraltar to discuss measures that might be jointly taken to prevent a recurrence. Nothing seems to have been decided except the usual arrangements for quarantine, which the Spanish had used and were to use so often for non-medical reasons; and the failure is not surprising when there was as yet no knowledge of the cause of the disease. This particular epidemic finally faded, having killed some 6,000 people in four months, as against the Great Siege's loss of 300 in four years.

The war continued, bringing Gibraltar an increased prosperity. One chief cause was the establishment of an Admiralty Court there, which enabled merchants based on Gibraltar to buy—often at bargain prices—ships and cargoes seized by British warships and privateers operating in the western Mediterranean and central Atlantic. This prosperity increased still more when on May 2, 1808, the Spanish people rose against Napoleon. There was now plenty of scope for legitimate trade, but that was never enough for Gibraltar, and on July 12, 1808, we find the governor issuing a proclamation:

> "His Excellency [the Spanish governor of Algeciras] having complained that much smuggling of tobacco and other goods has been carried on between this place and Algeciras and St. Roque by inhabitants of Gibraltar: This is to give notice that any persons so transgressing against the laws of Spain are not to expect any Protection from the passport granted them by [the British Governor]; nor are they to suppose that His Excellency wishes to screen inhabitants of this place who have made so unworthy a use of the indulgence granted them. . . ."

Three years earlier, replying to London about some Gibraltar merchants' complaints against the imposition of quarantine, the then Governor-General Fox (brother of Charles James) had written:

> "About the letters from Messrs Faulkner and Turnbull, I will pay great attention to the matter, but I am much afraid Mr. Turnbull and the merchants and traders of Gibraltar are inclined to expect such Facility to their Commercial Intercourse as is inconsistent with the Safety of the Garrison either with regard to the Enemy or the prevention of the return of the Disease; and are more indifferent than they ought to be to the King's Service where there is a possibility of its interfering with their smuggling goods into Spain."

The previous chancellor of Spain was Godoy, who had taken the unusual title of "Prince of Peace," which is usually reserved, in England at least, for Jesus Christ. He had worked out an ingenious scheme to get back Gibraltar by arranging for it to be attacked by an Irish army while Irish regiments were serving in the garrison; in return Spain would back and guarantee the setting up of an independent Irish state.

But that was all past, and now Spain and England were friends on the surface. Forts San Felipe and Sánta Barbara, which had guarded the isthmus for so long, were leveled and the fortifications between them razed. Spanish armies were supported and supplied from Gibraltar, and British soldiers went out from there to fight against the French invaders. Particularly heroic actions were fought at Tarifa and Barossa. Yet it was, alas, only a surface friendliness. England's aim was certainly not the emergence of a free and powerful Spain, nor Spain's the strengthening of England's grip on Gibraltar; and when the histories came to be written, the English consistently underrated the enormous sacrifice of the Spanish people in the war against Napoleon, while the Spanish, going farther, gave the impression that no English troops fought in their war of independence at all, whereas all but one of the successful actions were fought with a majority of British troops and British casualties.

When Napoleon fled from Waterloo in 1815, the Victorian Era began, though she herself was not yet born. It was the century of the Pax Britannica, the British Empire, and laissez-faire. Peace reigned, with the usual unsettling effects on Gibraltar's role as a trading entrepôt, for there was now no need for ships to change or pick up cargoes there, as there had been when most of Europe was under blockade. Politically, England was steady as another rock, Spain unstable as a weathervane. Time and again through the century Gibraltar was to give shelter to victims of failed or successful coups of the right, left, and center.

In the town itself the population rose steadily from about 7,500 after the effects of the fever had been overcome to 17,000 in 1831 (nearly 2,000 Jews) and stayed close to that figure to the end of the century. Spaniards began to enter as the Napoleonic Wars ended, until by the end of the century there were 1,900 of them out of a total population of 19,000. The largest single group of Spaniards were females, who came in as servants to prosperous Gibraltarians. The prosperity seems to have been based on cigar making. There were only a handful of cigar makers in 1800, but 2,000 by 1900; and cigar making was an excellent cover for tobacco smuggling.

There was also much work at the dockyard, but it did not benefit the Gibraltarians directly. The headquarters of the Mediterranean fleet moved to Malta in 1833, but at the same time plans were made to enlarge the facilities at Gibraltar, and this work was put in hand about 1842. For some unclear reason convict labor was imported for the job. Barracks for 1,000 convicts were built, and soon 600 were actually at work. They worked with notable inefficiency, and they had an effect on the Gibraltarian outlook that has not yet died: an association of manual labor with degradation. When convict labor was ended in the 1870's, it was not Gibraltarians who filled the vacancy but Spaniards.

About the middle of the century the population of some 15,-500 was occupied as follows:

Local government	132
Professions	72
Commerce	681
Trade	1297
Agriculture	28
Miscellaneous	5565
At school	2633
Unemployed	4994
Paupers	60

As for revenue, Gibraltar was still nominally a free port, and most of the local government revenue came from wine and spirit duties, liquor licenses, and the like. A considerable number of ships passed through Gibraltar—about 3,300 a year in the 1850's—but they cannot have caused a general prosperity when the figures for unemployment are considered. When the high prices of food, rent, and clothes (endemic in Gibraltar) are thrown in, the Rock is seen as a depressed area for the poor; yet —and this must never be forgotten—it was a paradise of luxury compared with the Andalusia that bordered it. There, entrenched in their latifundias, the Spanish rich could starve whole villages into accepting sub starvation wages by leaving acreage out of cultivation until the peasants surrendered.

In 1869 the Suez Canal was opened, and Gibraltar's strategic and mercantile importance still further increased. Though individual fortunes were being made, there was still no general prosperity; but a stable government and at least a chance of something better than most of Europe knew kept the immigrants coming—Dutch, Belgian, Russian, and Maltese. These last started arriving in 1871 and were particularly unwelcome to the resident Gibraltarian, for their skills and ways of life were in direct competition with his own.

The Jewish population reached its height about the middle of the century and then declined. The great families began to go; by 1900 there were no Benoliels and no Cardozos (of the latter some had gone to London, some to Portugal, and thence to the United States).

But one famous Jew had visited Gibraltar, the twenty-five-year-old dandy Benjamin Disraeli. He went there on part of a "Grand Tour" in 1830. His letters to his father are as informative as a contemporary print:

"This Rock is a wonderful place, with a population infinitely diversified. Moors with costumes radiant as a rainbow or an Eastern melodrama: Jews with gaberdines and skull-caps; Genoese, Highlanders, and Spaniards, whose dress is as picturesque as that of the sons of Ivor. . . . We were presented to the Governor, Sir George Don, a general and G.C.B., a very fine old gentleman, of the Windsor Terrace school, courtly, almost regal in his manner, paternal, almost officious in his temper. . . . His palace, the Government House, is an old convent, and one of the most delightful residences I know, with a garden under the superintendence of Lady Don, full of rare exotics, with a beautiful terrace over the sea, a berceau of vines, and other delicacies which would quite delight you. . . . Tell [Washington] Irving he has left a golden name in Spain. . . ."

And two weeks later:

"After dinner . . . it was the fate of Meredith and myself to be lionised to some cave or other with Sir George. What a scene and what a procession! First came two grooms on two barbs; then a carriage with four horses; at the window at which H. E. sits, a walking footman, and then an outrider, all at a funeral pace. . . . In spite of his infirmities he will get out to lionise; but before he disembarks, he changes his foraging cap for a full general's cock with a plume as big as the Otranto one; and this because the hero will never be seen in public in undress, although we were in a solitary cave looking over the ocean, and inhabited only by monkeys. The cave is shown, and we all get into the carriage, because he is sure we are tired; the foraging cap is again assumed, and we travel back. . . . Meredith, myself, the Governor, and the cocked hat, each in a seat.

A little later (in 1844) another famous man visited it—William Makepeace Thackeray. His comments, too, are sharply evocative, particularly of the "feel" of Gibraltar to a civilian:

"If one had a right to break the sacred confidence of the mahogany, I could entertain you with many queer stories of Gibraltar life, gathered from the lips of the gentlemen who enjoyed themselves round the dingy table cloth of the club-house coffee-room, richly decorated with cold gravy and spilt beer. . . . All the while these conversations were going on, a strange scene of noise and bustle was passing in the market-place in front of the window, where Moors, Jews, Spaniards, soldiers were thronging in the sun; and a ragged fat fellow, mounted on a tobacco barrel, with his hat cocked on his ear, was holding an auction, and roaring with an energy and impudence that would have done credit to Covent Garden.

" 'All's Well' is very pleasant when sung decently in tune; and inspires noble and poetic ideas of duty, courage, and danger; but when you hear it shouted all the night through, accompanied by a clapping of muskets in a time of profound peace, the sentinel's cry becomes no more romantic to the hearer than it is to the sandy Connaught-man or the bare-legged Highlander who delivers it. . . . Men of a different way of thinking, however, can suit themselves perfectly at Gibraltar; where there is marching and countermarching, challenging and relieving guard all the night through. And not here in Commercial-square alone, but all over the huge rock in the darkness—all through the mysterious zigzags, and round the dark cannon-ball pyramids, and along the vast rock-galleries, and up to the topmost flagstaff where the sentry can look out over two seas, poor fellows are marching and clapping muskets, and crying 'All's Well.' . . . The young men in the coffee-room tell me he [the Governor] goes to sleep every night with the keys of Gibraltar under his pillow. It is an awful image, and somehow completes the notion of the slumbering fortress. Fancy Sir Robert Wilson, his nose just visible above the sheets, his nightcap and the huge key (you see the very identical one in Reynold's portrait of Lord Heathfield) peeping out from under the bolster. . . ."

On Gibraltar, the sense of community was only now slowly beginning to develop. Below and alongside the governors, officers, staffs, troops, and sailors, all of whom were on passage, Gibraltarians began to merge as a people; and the town, or colony, began to compete and conflict with the fortress. Civil rights and a civil magistracy were granted in 1830 (Jews were put on the jury lists in 1878); and the governments in London and on the Rock began to exercise themselves over a problem which they should have tackled a hundred years earlier. Now the Maltese immigration forced them to ask, and answer, the question: What is a Gibraltarian? That is, who has the right to live on the Rock, and under what terms?

From the beginning, governors had influenced the answer by the way they had attracted one sort of person and discouraged another, given some certain rights and denied them to others. The census of 1871 showed a population of 18,700. A couple of years later an order-in-council made "better provisions to prevent the entry into and residence in Gibraltar of unauthorized persons not being British subjects and to prevent the further increase of the overcrowded condition of Gibraltar." This was the thin end of a wedge, though London does not seem to have realized it, for if you define whom you can keep out, you define who has the right to stay in—thus creating something which is separate from the military complex. The governor in 1849, Gardiner, had already seen this and represented to the government that Gibraltar was and must be solely a fortress. The present problems would be much simpler if his opinion had been taken—but it aroused an enormous outcry from people whose human and financial interests were threatened, so the report was shelved and Gardiner removed.

Town and garrison together became the parents of the institutions British take or found wherever they go. First, of course, a pack of foxhounds. When the last British regiment (24th, South Wales Borderers) came out of Cádiz in 1814 at the end of the Peninsular War, it brought with it a pack of foxhounds belonging to the Real Isla de León Hunt (this is the old name of San Fernando, the military town at the head of the Cádiz peninsula.) The pack, descended from hounds originally brought from England by the Duke of Wellington to while away the time between battles (see Conan Doyle's marvelous exploit of Brigadier Gerard, "How the Brigadier slew the Fox"), was taken to Gibraltar to found the Calpe Hunt and so give Spanish peasants and landowners the privilege of watching the unspeakable pursue the uneatable over their crops and through their cork oaks and olive groves.

After the hunt, the ornithological society, the horticultural society, the philosophical, the Garrison Library—a most important and permanent addition to Gibraltar's facilities this. Founded by Captain Drinkwater, historian of the Great Siege, and financed by Pitt, it is a fine building with a fine garden and provides the garrison not only with books, but many of the attributes of a quiet club. The Gibraltar *Chronicle*, later published by the library, in its early issues seldom bothered itself with local happenings—its eyes were focused on far places and imperial themes—but every now and then a snippet of news reveals more about life on the Rock than a thousand statistics.

June 8, 1805—Captain Fuller of the 20th Light Dragoons is drowned sailing behind the Rock when his boat capsizes. This was in the middle of the Napoleonic Wars, which obviously did not seriously interfere with the normal amenities. . . . July 6, same year—a woman of bad character drinks herself to death in a shed near the castle; the shed, furniture, and clothes are destroyed by the authorities "as a useful lesson to the lower Classes for them to obey the regulations of the Board of Health respecting cleanliness of homes and persons." . . . After 1806 there is a dentist advertising himself, Peter Seminara: before that the blacksmith? . . . The *HMS Beagle,* the ship in which Darwin later sailed, serves from Gibraltar. . . . There is a fire in Mr. Israel's house in Engineer Lane: it was a Friday night of course, for Sephardic housewives put the Sabbath *adafina* in the oven before sundown on Friday and do not touch it or look at it before noon the next day. So, frequently there are runaway ovens and "Jewish" fires on Friday nights. . . . The venereal hospital of San Juan de Dios, which has become first an ordinary hospital and then a British barracks (Blue Barracks) is now pulled down and again becomes a hospital, successively called the Civil, the Colonial, and St. Bernard's. . . . A naval captain on his way to China with his ship bets a friend, after a late night, that he can knock down O'Hara's Folly in three shots. Next dawn he sails and, hangover notwithstanding, hits the tower with his third shot.

The most important event of Gibraltar's century was not much remarked at the time. In 1848 in the course of normal operations at Forbes Quarry, a smugglers' rendezvous at the foot of the north face, a human skull was found. It seemed to be of great antiquity and so was shown to the Gibraltar Society (this was one of those societies which in a small place keep forming and fading according as interested personalities come and go). The society thought it was "an old skull" and as such sent it to the Royal College of Surgeons. The College did not show much interest in it, either, although it had features markedly different from those of modern man or of any known previous race of man.

In 1859 German archaeologists—the science was in its infancy —discovered a skull and parts of a prehistoric skeleton which they could attribute to no known race of man. They therefore named this newly discovered race after the place where the remains were found—Neanderthal. Now the Royal College of Surgeons took another look at the Forbes Quarry skull and found that it was of a woman of the same race, the race driven to extinction by Cro-Magnon Man. If the Gibraltar Society in 1848 had numbered even one archaeologist, that race would now be called Gibraltar Man, not Neanderthal. Whatever we call him, he certainly used Gibraltar for a long time.

Cave exploring became fashionable. Two officers set out to explore St. Michael's Cave. They never came back, nor has any trace of them ever been found, though St. Michael's Cave has since been explored to a distance of 1,700 feet from the entrance and to depths of 600 feet below the entrance, which is 937 feet above sea level. But as to the vanished officers, some believe that they had troublesome wives or debts in England which a judicious "disappearance" would have much eased.

The most devoted cave explorer and scientist of the period was a Captain Brome, who was in charge of the convict labor. The prisoners did not work well for the navy, but they did marvels for Brome in helping to find and explore caves. His most notable find was a series of four, separate, on Windmill Hill Flats. They were later named Genista One, Two, Three, and Four in honor of their discoverer (*genista* is the Latin for "broom").

Genista One, of which Brome released full details to the Gibraltar *Chronicle* on January 23, 1865, is 200 feet deep and full of animal fossils, including rhinoceros, horse, pig, deer, aurochs, leopard, hyena, innumerable kinds of birds, fish, and shells, and man. Genista Two is a small cave at the foot of a steep ramp, which the reader may think he has already seen.

Brome's work soon received its just reward from a government always alert to reward scholarly initiative: he was fired.

Militarily the fortress attained its zenith of usefulness about 1870 when enemy artillery could hit, but not shatter, its defenses, while its guns could reach nearly across the strait. The largest gun installed, at the end of the muzzle loading era, was called the 100 Ton Gun. It is still there, on a semicircular railed mount near Rosia Bay. It fired a one-ton shell about eight miles, at the rate of one round every four minutes. The traversing, elevation, and loading were worked by steam, but the firing cartridge was electrical—the first in the world. It was never fired in anger and seldom in play. At a visit by an artillery general in 1902, a full-charge practice was arranged. The electric cartridge fired, but the main charge, of God knows how many hundredweight of powder, did not. After the compulsory wait of half an hour under cover, the general asked for a volunteer to extract the shell.

This meant sliding head first down the barrel (about eighteen inches in diameter) and attaching a rope to the ring in the nose of the shell. Behind the shell was all that powder. The general's request evoked a clamorous silence. Finally a thin trumpeter volunteered, and the general, who was probably thirty inches in diameter, said, "There's no danger." The trumpeter replied, in an excess of military effusiveness, "If you say so, sir!" slid down, and attached the cord. The general, in one of those scenes beloved of Victorian lithographers, pointed to him when he came out and cried, "This man's promotion to bombardier is to appear in orders tonight!"

It was a beautiful gun, but of course by the thin trumpeter's day quite useless. The time for a testing of Gibraltar's defenses was not yet at hand, fortunately. The British Navy was modern, reasonably efficient (though far from being the terrible instrument of Nelson's day), and enormously numerous; but by the end of the century the ground defenses were out of date and faced with an insoluble problem. The main line of defense had been drawn back from the sea wall to halfway up the Rock, where several modern big guns were installed; but other batteries looked like something left over from the American Civil Wars and in some of the galleries cannon and cannonballs which had seen service in the Great Siege were still in position and on the books. Still, the fortress could throw a powerful weight of metal onto attacking ships or the Spanish mainland. The insoluble problem was that the Spanish mainland could now throw a powerful weight of metal back, not at the fortress' guns—they couldn't harm them much—but at the harbor.

To question the impregnability of Gibraltar at this time, after all it had been through, was, as someone said, equivalent to speaking disrespectfully about the equator. There is little doubt that it was in fact impregnable; but if it could not be used as a naval base and port, its impregnability was of no value. Nevertheless, when the Royal Navy surveyed its worldwide position in 1890, it decided to put larger and more modern facilities into Gibraltar to service and repair warships and to protect ships in harbor against mines, torpedoes, and submarines. As soon as the plans for the new dockyard on the western side were announced and work begun in 1895, anxious critics pointed out that the facilities and any ships using them would be subject to the direct fire of Spanish guns mounted in the semicircle of hills all around and now all within easy range. Parliament appointed a committee under Admiral Sir Harry Rawson to investigate. The committee concluded that the new dockyard was wrongly sited and that another one must be built at once on the east side of Gibraltar, where the mass of the rock itself would protect it from everything except perhaps high-angle howitzers. The government took careful note of this view and went on with the western site, the work being done by Spanish laborers under the supervision of British technicians. The only concession to the "western" threat was to put the oil fuel tanks on the east side and run a rail tunnel clear through the Rock near sea level, linking them with the harbor.

The critics now raised again the general question of Gibraltar's real value to England, and there were again discussions about exchanging it for Minorca, one of the Canary Islands, or Ceuta.

Nothing came of any of it. The New Dockyard was completed —308 acres of sheltered anchorage, coaling facilities, three dry docks, all kinds of cranes, shops, forges. In view of its total vulnerability to Spanish fire, one must assume that its defense, in 1902, rested on a tit-for-tat threat, i.e., if Spain bombarded Gibraltar, the British fleet would bombard Santander, Cádiz, Cartagena, Barcelona, Bilbao, San Sebastián, Málaga, and a dozen other cities vulnerable to sea power. In other words, Gibraltar was to be protected by the general power of England, not the other way round.

In 1902 the Boer War—a focal theme for much of the long-massing anti-British sentiment in Europe—came to an end. England was again at peace. In Gibraltar officers, soldiers, merchants, traders, laborers, and petty bourgeois lived their ordinary lives in an extraordinary place. Though there were still brothels on the Rock, many favored the more open and *alegre* atmosphere of the establishments in La Línea, a city grown up, just across the Neutral Ground, for the sole purpose of feeding off, and on, Gibraltar's needs. Some of the girls of La Línea were public and cheap. Some were private and expensive. From there one got an extraordinarily clear view of Gibraltar, close up, seen from below. . . .

A View from La Línea

The ivory figurine of a naked woman, which hung over the head of her bed where the devout often had a crucifix, blurred and enlarged before her eyes. It always did in these final seconds of ecstasy, seeming to bless her lust. She spread herself, crying out, took him into her heart with a convulsion of her muscles, wrapped arms and legs about him, and immediately began to come in shivering transports. She felt his teeth in her neck, a sharp pain, and held him tighter. Minutes, hours later, the spasms calmed into long trembling waves. He was rolling off her. She held him, whispering, "Stay," but he got up, lit a cigarette, and inhaled deeply.

She could see him, back and front and side, in four full-length mirrors on the wall, and herself in another on the ceiling. He plucked her dress off a chair and slowly swirled it around him in a *paso natural*. He was insolently graceful, with narrow hips and long gypsy hair. Her neck hurt where he had bitten her.

"I need money, Dolores," he said.

"Again?"

"I have no work now. The count dismissed fifty of us. He needs more money to serve the king, he said, so he could not afford to pay us."

She sighed and slipped out of bed, found a key in her purse, and opened a drawer of the ornate escritoire. "I will give you a hundred pesetas," she said.

"Make it two hundred," he said. "I have to live."

She shrugged and gave him the money. He was pulling on his trousers. She stood naked in front of him, wishing he would touch her breasts or enter again into the aching emptiness. But he sprawled in a chair, the cigarette dangling from his lower lip. "Put on my shoes," he commanded.

She knelt before him and slipped one battered, cracked brown shoe onto his bare foot. "You should go to Pablo Larios' stables," she said. "I heard he needs a man to look after the English hounds. You are good with dogs."

She picked up his other foot.

"I might," he said, "just to get a little money so I can leave La Línea for good." He put his foot on her shoulder and pushed hard, sending her flying over backward. "I'm going to be a *torero!*" he cried, striding away from her with the exaggerated, mincing walk a matador uses in the ring to show his dominance over the bull. "*El Gato Moreno*—the Black Cat."

"You're nothing but a gypsy," she said.

He brought the lighted end of his cigarette close to her nipple, so close that she felt the heat of it. She did not cringe, and he suddenly stooped, kissed the nipple, and swaggered out.

She went slowly to the window, pulled back the edge of one long velvet curtain an inch and watched him leave the front door. She heard him calling his dog. "Cabo? Cabo! Come!" Beyond the lights of the last houses of La Línea, beyond the lights at the frontier, Gibraltar glittered like a magic city in the sky.

She drew the curtain and said in an ordinary speaking voice, "Who's first, Juana?" She looked at the calendar: January 8, 1902. It would be . . .

The old maid waddled in from a side door. "Tomás Lopez. He's waiting."

"Ten minutes, Juana." She douched herself in the ornate bathroom, using a herbal concoction an old gypsy woman had recommended to her. It had not failed her yet, either with disease or pregnancy, and she had been at this trade thirteen years now—just half her life.

She dressed again and then went through the side door into another bedroom identical to the first, even to the maroon curtains and the precise pattern of the heavy frames of the mirrors. Juana set to cleaning the bathroom and remaking the bed in the first room. These details cost money and took trouble, but they marked the difference between a whore and a courtesan.

Tomás Lopez was solid, square, about forty, a little grizzled. He liked a glass of wine and a little conversation before attending to business. Dolores did not mind humoring him, as his more particular demands, unlike those of most of her clients, were very simple.

He sipped the wine carefully. "That Court of Inquiry the English sent out are said to think that the dockyard could be made useless by our Spanish guns. That is a serious matter."

"Yes?" she said. "You mean they have wasted all that money?"

"Of course, yes. But perhaps they will close it. We will lose our positions. Not everyone can say, 'I work in the English dockyard, I receive so many pounds a week,' you understand."

"Naturally," she said. Tomás Lopez was Andalusian and poor, so the appearance, the position, mattered more to him than the reality.

"It is from my wages, and the goods I smuggle out every day, that I am able to visit you once a month. And that is known to all the men, of course. It is not everyone who can afford your kindness."

"You are generous. All know it."

"A man's position, his wife's virtue, these have value. The Gibraltarians look down their noses at us because we work with our hands and go home dirty. To them it is only valuable that the wife should employ a cleaning woman. A Spanish woman, naturally, for *their* women won't demean themselves."

He got up and took off his coat. He had to have the lights out and would only approach her from behind. She pulled off her drawers, flipped up the back of her skirt, leaned over the bed, and waited.

Afterward he paid and gave her a bottle of Scotch whisky, his usual gift, smuggled out of Gibraltar. She poured him another glass of wine.

"I shall win the dog show," he said. He saw her look of mystification and said, "The English prince and princess are visiting Gibraltar to attend a dog show. The important class is for smooth-haired fox terriers. My Manolo is of pure race, and he will win. Unless the Freemasons rob us. Father O'Callaghan of the Gibraltar church says the Freemasons are at the bottom of all our troubles. He says they sent out the Court of Inquiry to do away with our positions. . . . The prize is fifty English pounds."

"Enough to buy a nice little bit of land," she said.

"Yes," he said. "And to improve the situation still further, my wife is going to seek work as a cleaning woman on the Rock. Unfortunately, my dog Manolo has not been well. There is time for him to recover. Nevertheless, I am looking for another dog, in case Manolo should still be showing the effects of his sickness. And there is the judge to be taken into consideration, of course."

She said, "But the judge is Don Pablo Larios. There's not enough money in the world to bribe Don Pablo, especially in anything to do with sport, or the English."

"Money is not the only value in a gentleman's eyes," Tomás said. "Indeed, with a rich and great *caballero* like Don Pablo, it is the least. . . . But what is Don Pablo's passion? Rare books? A new plant? Old wine? I must find out. But my position in the dockyard does not throw me much into his company."

"There's a young fellow called Paco Santangel who's going to work quite closely with him, at the hunt stables," she said. "I imagine he could find out, for a consideration."

Tomás Lopez shot her a shrewd peasant look, "I see. Well, perhaps. Though I am not a rich man." He drained the wine, got up, and bowed formally. "Señorita, a thousand thanks."

She said mischievously, "If the English prince and princess are coming to Gibraltar, perhaps it is to close the dockyard and give the Rock back to Spain."

"No, no, they are coming for the dog show," he said firmly.

Señorita Falcon was a superb-looking woman, the deputy chief of police thought—high-bridged aquiline nose, strong eyebrows, oval face, good lips, and intense, deep blue eyes. He'd seen her naked, too, when duty had made him burst in to "surprise" her with a man they wanted—her breasts were high and a little small, but some liked them that way. Her hair was dense, strong, almost blue-black. When it fell to her shoulders, it looked like black wine on the thick, creamy white of her skin. The same with her pubic hair, a thick black pelt, clearly limited, and the strong tufts in her armpits, all amazingly definite against the skin. If she had not chosen this profession, she could have married almost anyone in Spain. Well, "chosen" was a cruel word. No one knew her past or where she came from, but there would certainly have been a seduction, a child perhaps, banishment, disgrace. That was, sadly, the way of the world.

He rose to go, saying, "You are a very beautiful woman, señorita."

"Not that it ever stirs you," she pouted, tapping him with the envelope. He took it and dropped it into his pocket. His hand was on the door. "By the way, young Paco Santangel is not, how shall I say? Threatening you, is he? He has no money. He visits. One wonders. . . ."

"No," she said. "He is a friend."

The deputy chief of police bowed himself out. Poor woman. They all had one, usually six or seven years younger, like this half-gypsy lad. It was, sadly, the way of the world.

Dolores yawned. She knew who was coming—Carlos Firpo, the Gibraltarian—because Juana had reminded her to drink an extra two glasses of lemonade and not relieve herself. Juana showed him in five minutes later. At once he started to pant and slaver and undo his trousers, as he always did. And she, as always, held out her hand and waited. Only after he gave her the money and she had put it away did she respond to his urgency. She spread a heavy towel on the tiled floor at the foot of the bed, and he lay down quickly on it, naked, holding his erect penis in one hand and muttering obscene words in Spanish and English. She took off her drawers and danced around him, holding up her skirt. His eyes glazed, and he spoke louder, his hand jerking on his penis. She knelt over him. . . .

After a time he sighed, "Marvelous!"

"I try to please," she said.

He went into the bathroom and began washing himself with great energy, as though to eradicate any trace of what, so recently, he had craved for. "I've got a job," he said. "Crewman on one of Mr. Torrenti's fast new steamers."

She said, "Doesn't your brother the shopkeeper still support you?"

"Oh yes, but with the new child my wife needs a cleaning woman, and now we can afford it. We got one today. A woman called Maria Lopez."

He came out and began to dress. He was short, with a long nose and wide mouth and a little potbelly, though he was only thirty-three. He spoke Gibraltarian Spanish, with many English words. He always seemed aggrieved and ready to take offence.

"Mr. Torrenti used to play safe," he said. "Just import the tobacco in bulk from America, and sell it to the shippers—"

"You mean the actual smugglers?" she said, smiling.

"They're not smugglers when they buy the tobacco," he said with a little heat. "Just merchants. The Spanish can call them smugglers if they catch them taking the tobacco into Spain. . . . Well, you'd think Mr. Torrenti was making enough money with that and his cigar factory, but no, he wants to send his sons to Eton and have the Governor invite him to tea, so he's going into the shipping end as well. He'll be richer than the Jews soon."

He paused in the act of pulling on one sock. "You know what some of the young fellows are going to do this Easter Saturday? . . . throw a dummy with a top hat over the wall into the synagogue. Only it will be on fire, see. A good joke."

"Don't people get hurt?" she asked.

"Sometimes. A Jew girl got burned a bit last year. . . . How about a little champagne, eh? Put it back in so it can come out again!" He gave her a nudge in the ribs.

She called, "Juana—a half of champagne."

Carlos Firpo was dressed now. He fumbled in his pocket and gave her a small box of cigars. "Brought them out for you," he said.

Juana opened the champagne and poured expertly and disappeared. Firpo sat back, glass in hand. "Did you know the prince and princess are visiting Gibraltar? In March. There's going to be a dog show. I'm going to enter my fox terrier, Fido. He won't win the first prize, but as long as he does better than Mr. Torrenti's, that's all I ask."

"It will be a great honor for Gibraltar," she said. "The prince and princess visiting."

Carlos Firpo shook his head. "Perhaps. But you know what I think"—he lowered his voice—"England's finished. Look at the Boer War. Couldn't beat a few Dutchmen. Every country in Europe hating her. If you ask me, we should get someone else to take over Gibraltar."

"Spain?" she asked.

"Mother of God, no! We're not Spaniards."

"A great many of your mothers are," she said.

"No, no. What we want is someone like Germany. They'd take it like a shot. Father O'Callaghan says it's the Freemasons and the Jews behind it all."

"Behind what, Señor Firpo?"

"The Boer War and England going downhill. My wife's sister's walking out with an English private, a fellow called Tamlyn. When it began we were all congratulating ourselves, because although he's only a private, he's *English* and would take her to England. Now we don't know." He drained his glass and pulled out his watch. "Time to go, or the wife will be wondering where I've got to."

Juana said, "He doesn't speak any Spanish. He just says, 'Dolores' and holds out money."

"Enough?"

"More than your lowest, much less than your highest. I think he is a soldier." She squared her shoulders and indicated a short haircut.

"Is he drunk?" Dolores asked. "Alone? Show him in then."

He was a tall man, nearly thirty, with a long, sad, bony face, dull red hair, and big, horny hands. He stood, awkward but determined, in a cheap brown suit and huge ammunition boots, in the center of her little reception parlor.

"You speak English?" he said. His voice was deep and accented, but she did not know enough about England to be able to place him.

"Yes," she said. "My mother taught me. You are a soldier, aren't you?"

"Private Richard Tamlyn, Royal Berkshire Regiment," he said.

"How did you get this money? It is a lot for a simple soldier."

"Stole a dog," he said. "There's to be a dog show, and a Spanish dockyard workman gave me ten pounds for it. The prince and princess are going to give the prizes for that show, did 'ee know, miss?"

"Perhaps they'll give all you soldiers extra pay in honor of their visit."

"Nay, miss, they'll never do that. Just extra parades, drill, and such. We did three hours today."

"Goodness, and the visit nearly two months away still. You must get bored with it."

His pale, distant blue eyes looked down into hers. "Tis better than sitting in the barrack room staring at the wall," he said.

"Hours on end. Aye, soldiers go mad here. No one wants us. No one speaks to us. 'Cept to take our pay on Fridays. I hate 'em."

"The Rock scorpions?" she said.

"Aye, that's what they are. . . . I got one of them into trouble, she says."

He sounded almost pleased. What a life it must be on that gaunt rock for such as these, she thought. He spoke as though he had got the girl "into trouble" not out of love but out of boredom, almost as an act of revenge.

"Before I stole the dog I got drunk, thinking of you. What I heard about you, miss. The colonel gave me fourteen days C. B. and said he'd a good mind not to let me go on the parade for Their Royal Highnesses."

"And you would have minded that?" she said, fascinated.

"Aye, miss. I'm the flank man of Number Three Double Company."

"Oh . . . Do you find people unpleasant to you because of the Boer War?"

"All the Niggers and Frogs and Wops are yapping, miss. The colonel says the whole lot of 'em's not worth a pint of 49th piss . . . begging your pardon, miss."

"49th?"

"That's us. The 49th Foot. The Royal Berkshire Regiment, miss, though I'm from Yorksheer, myself."

She was feeling a little dazed, so she held out a hand. "Come."

He took her firmly and manfully. If any of her clients could arouse her, she thought, he might, when they came to know each other better. And he, to her surprise, rapidly passed from a stolid lust to an almost poetic rapture of passion.

He had hard, strong muscles and the outdoorsman's sharp color lines at neck and wrists, brown on one side, white on the other. He had reddish hair, a man's good phallus, and a bullet scar in his right shoulder.

Long after he had spent his strength in her he kissed her breast and lay on his back and said, "I wor a shepherd when I wor a boy. On the dales, by Haworth. Sometimes, when I'd been alone a long time, and it wor cold, and a full moon, and all the sheep around me, I'd feel I knew what we wor all doing here on earth. . . . It's the same now, miss. You'll not go away from La Línea?"

"No."

"Then I'll not go away from Gibraltar. Not as long as I live."

George Torrenti, Esquire, was in his mid-forties: rather short, plump, swarthy, big nose, of a very Italian appearance except for the flowing silky moustache, which might have been borrowed from a caricature of a British Guards officer.

He was nervy, jumpy, fiddling with his glass of whisky (never touched anything else). He always was, through the half hour it took him to shed the layers of convention and shame separating him from what he really wanted.

"I thought my Baron would win the dog show," he was saying, "until some swine stole him. A soldier, I'll swear. Those animals will do anything. . . . But the dog show's a minor matter, really, even though the princess will be giving the prizes in person. The really important thing is the dinner party at the Convent. By the time you have counted the two admirals, the general, the brigadier, Lord Howard Kingsley, the Colonial Secretary, the artillery brigadier, the judge, the priest, the chairman of the city council, and their wives . . . there are only four places left. Two couples!" His prominent eyes bulged, and he had begun to sweat. "One must be Haroldson, the lawyer. The other must be either me or Joseph Aboab."

"Oh, surely they would give you precedence over a Jew," she said gravely.

"Of course, they *should!*" he said vehemently. "But King Edward loves Jews. Father O'Callaghan says they're strong in the Freemasons, and you know the prince is a Mason."

He drank some whisky and eyed her obliquely, licking his lips. He was uncomfortable on her chair, but she knew it would pass. "Aboab's been made an honorary whip of the Calpe Hunt," he went on. "How can I compete with that? I hate riding. And then yesterday I shot a bird, and it turned out to be a Barbary partridge female, which was out of season. And the Governor's a keen ornithologist. . . . What can I *do?*"

"Make a big contribution to some fund the Governor is interested in," she said. "Money is very persuasive."

"I'll think about it," he said. "But I have very heavy expenses just now. I'm fitting out three fast new trading steamers."

"Surely the syndicate must have borne a share of that?" she said.

"What do you know of the syndicate?" he said, suddenly suspicious. "Well, it is not really very secret, is it? Old Bawltrum's the official owner of the ships, but he's only a dummy. The syndicate really owns them—myself and three Spanish gentlemen."

"Spaniards?" she said. "Engaged in smuggling from Gibraltar?"

He laughed without humor. He got up and began to pace the floor. It was getting close now. "Lord Howard Kingsley's in charge of the invitations to the dinner. He'd give his eyes to be made comptroller of the Royal Household in London. Looks the other way while the admiral here sleeps with his wife. If King Edward wanted her, good God, he'd guide the royal cock in himself. But how can I help him to become comptroller?"

"I don't know," she said.

"Nor do I. But he's taken to greeting me very cordially in the street. I think he's going to ask me for something. I wish I knew what."

His eyes were glazed, and he stopped pacing. He suddenly undid his fly.

She got up. "Disgusting man," she said and slapped him on the cheek. "For that you must be punished. Go into the bedroom, sir!" She pointed imperiously.

He hurried through. She followed, and while he undressed, she selected a few canes. Juana was tying him expertly, head to knee, in the middle of the floor. "Kiss my boot," Dolores said, thrusting it into his face. She took a cane, stepped away, and gave him a swishing blow on the buttocks as hard as she could. "Disgusting," she cried. "Kiss Juana's stinking foot. Lick her shoes." Swish! Swish! The red weals leaped up across his buttocks. "No, no!" he cried. "Enough. Let me up!"

Swish! Swish! She wondered how he kept his wife from seeing the marks. Swish! They had probably never seen each other undressed.

"Oh, oh! Mercy!"

The cane whistled more fiercely.

The next visitor would not arrive for half an hour. Dolores put her feet up on the couch and rested—the whipping always tired her, though Torrenti was in many ways so despicable that she rather enjoyed it. When Juana signaled that the next client had arrived, she undressed and put on a man's suit. Then she lit a cigar, stuffed her hair under a bandanna, and waited, legs crossed, puffing nonchalantly.

Lieutenant Colonel Lord Howard Kingsley, Grenadier Guards, was tall, broad-shouldered, narrow-hipped. His fair hair was wavy and touched with gray, he had level gray eyes, a square jaw, slightly cleft, and an easy, effortless grace of movement. The first time he visited her she saw what he really wanted and sent for a beautiful young public pederast; but the Oscar Wilde scandal had bitten too deep into his world, and she soon realized that he dared not admit to himself, let alone to anyone else, the true nature of his need. So he came to her to prove that he was the same as other men; and she did her best.

They went into the bedroom and he undressed at once. In one respect he was not at all like most men: he was endowed with enormous sexual equipment; more like a horse's than a man's, she had thought, almost quailing, the first time she saw it. She had no fear now, for it would never serve her, or any other woman. She used her wiles, as always. As always, nothing happened.

"I'm afraid it's no use, m'dear," he said. "I'm a little tired. Been overdoing it on the tennis court a bit."

He rolled languidly over on the bed and closed his eyes. She slipped out of her trousers, strapped on a large dildo, and climbed up onto the bed behind him. He began to quiver. . . .

When it was done, she retired, washed, and dressed as a high-class courtesan—expensively but a little garishly.

He wandered in a few minutes later, drank manzanilla, and talked of his brother, the Duke of Devizes; of his master, the Governor of Gibraltar; of his friend, the Count of Grazalema. "Do you know him?" he asked.

"I've seen him," Dolores said.

"A really delightful man," Lord Howard said. "His daughter's staying with us now, as a matter of fact. She and my own daughter are thick as thieves—both mad on horses—tireless—spend the nights dancing with the young officers and the days galloping all over Andalusia exercising their horses."

"The young ladies ride out unaccompanied?" she asked.

"Oh no. Pablo Larios lends them a stable lad as groom. . . .
You know, the count's very fond of England. Between you and
me, he's hoping to become the next ambassador to London. All
he has to do is manage a little affair to King Alfonso's satisfac-
tion, and it will be arranged. There's a damnable amount of
smuggling goes on out of Gibraltar into Spain, y'know. A lot of
these Gibraltar tradespeople are up to their necks in it. Well, King
Alfonso's asked Grazalema to do something about it—in a way
to help England, y'see, because it'll stop the anti-British complaints to his government. The count doesn't have any official
position, of course, but he's the largest landowner round here—"

"He can ride thirty miles in a straight line without leaving his
land," she said.

"Just so. Well, in a way it's better for him not to be in an official position because so many of them are in it, too." He rubbed
thumb and forefinger of his right hand together. "Rotten with
corruption, Spain is, y'know. Oh, by the by, there's a little
present for Juana." He gave her a parcel he had brought. "Five
yards of Harris tweed. I had to slip the customs chap twenty
pesetas not to see that. . . . Did you know our prince and princess are going to visit us?"

"I had heard something."

"M'dear, you should see the intrigue that's going on among
the tradespeople to get invited to the big dinner. There's a Jew
who's pouring money into the hunt. Torrenti's frantic. So frantic that I *think* I can get him to cut off his own nose for us."

"Cut off his nose?"

He laughed. "Only metaphorically."

"Is there not to be a dog show, too, for the prince and princess?"

"Is there? Oh yes, I recall now, I asked Pablo Larios to be
judge. I have a pedigree fox terrier bitch that will win that class.
I didn't think it was quite cricket to enter her, but H. E. said,
'No, no, let the best dog win.' Ha ha."

He waved his hand around the magnificence of her drawing
room. "I've only had the honor of visiting you four times, m'dear,
but you intrigue me. Such . . . splendor! Dare I ask, how did
you achieve it? By what path did you attain these rarefied if,
ah, a trifle *scandalous* heights?"

She looked surreptitiously at the grandfather clock in the corner. She'd give him the half-hour story. She dabbed a small handkerchief to her eyes and began:

"I was born . . ."

One of the mirrors on one wall of the bedrooms was not a true mirror but a glass through which one could watch the next room without people in there knowing they were under observation. She stood in front of that mirror now, naked, her breasts cushioning the back of the head and neck of the client, who sat, also naked, in an upright chair close to the mirror. He was Don Pedro de Santangel y Barrachina, twenty-eighth Count of Grazalema, a grandee of Spain with a tremendous lineage and a tiny penis.

In the next room a man and woman performed acts of sexuality with slow deliberation, always ensuring that an observer behind the false mirror would get a good view of their sexual organs and the details of each act. The man was a powerfully built young fellow, available for any service Dolores would pay for; the girl was Juana's daughter, plump, large-breasted, and large-eyed.

Dolores raised a hand to her hair. From concealment Juana would see the sign and whisper the word to the couple next door —"Go to it now."

The young man half rose, pushed the girl's other leg aside, and rammed into her. The count began to breathe deeply. Dolores guided him quickly to the bed and pulled him down on top of her. After a few rapid, trembling jerks, he burst into tears, and that, she knew, was the sign. She patted his head and murmured, "There, there! Lie still. . . . You have exhausted me." With the count there was no sense of hurry, for on a day when he was to visit her he required that she see no one else.

Later, he took coffee in her big drawing room. Through a gap in the curtains they could see the lights of Gibraltar. The count pointed. "Do you see those lights, Señorita Falcon? Not the town —in the bay. Those are twelve British battleships. Twelve! Spain owns three, altogether. No, we shall never regain our Rock by force, but by generosity I think we might. That is what I shall try to achieve in London."

"You are going to London, Count?"

"As ambassador, I hope." He was quite tall, slender, rather dark-skinned, with large sad, black eyes, the classical long Spanish face, and long hair going gray.

"Do you pay to become an ambassador?"

"After," he said, smiling slightly. "Not usually before. A man of no family might have to buy the place. But many noblemen have had to pay considerable sums, under some other pretext of course, to persuade the king *not* to send them to such places as Siam or Paraguay or Ethiopia." He shuddered delicately. "I for one cannot tolerate heat, or black men, or brown men—or Jews for that matter, but there is no Jewish capital, God be praised. . . . In this matter of the ambassadorship—well, I will tell you —Don Alfonso has asked me to produce some spectacular success against the smuggling from Gibraltar. As you know, many agents of the Tobacco Monopoly and the police and customs are involved in it, so to achieve success one must go outside them. I am particularly interested in some fast steam vessels recently built for the trade. I believe I am a member of the syndicate owning them, but of course it would not do to make any direct inquiries in that capacity, so I have approached an important English officer to obtain precise information about their proposed activities for me. Then, with a little threatening and bribery on my part—we shall strike. There will be a great success, just as Don Alfonso asked, and I shall go to London. . . ."

"More coffee, Count? A cake? . . . Have I not seen your daughter riding through La Línea with Miss Kingsley, the daughter of the governor's military assistant, and a groom from the Calpe Hunt stables?"

The count's eyes flickered in recognition of her subtle method of indicating that she could guess who the "important English officer" was.

"Yes," he said. "Kitty is staying with Lord and Lady Howard for a week or two to hunt with the Calpe. My wife is not entirely happy about it."

"Lady Howard Kingsley is not as discreet as she might be."

"Precisely. She will set Kitty a strange example . . . but I do need Lord Howard's help, so we could not refuse the invitation."

Pleasantly the talk drifted on. The count's occasional visits were always oases of calm for her. His yellow Daimler in the driveway, the chauffeur and postilion sitting outside a nearby tavern, guaranteed that there would be no interruptions.

The hands of the clock came back to twelve, the pages of the calendar to one. It began again . . . Paco her lover, a drunken *juerga* with a half a dozen gypsies clapping and singing and herself dancing on the table, no drawers under her flaring skirt, and finally Paco taking her there, on the table, in front of all of them . . . Tomás Lopez, the dockyard laborer . . . Carlos Firpo, the contraband crewman . . . Private Tamlyn of the 49th . . . George Torrenti, Esquire, importer . . . Lieutenant Colonel Lord Howard Kingsley of the Guards . . . Don Pedro de Santangel y Barrachina, Count of Grazalema . . .

The hands of the clock came back to twelve, the pages of the calendar to one. . . .

"I've been staying with the count," Lord Howard said. "Very pleasant, except that it was unseasonably hot. The count can't stand heat, y'know. But that was the only fly in the ointment. Excellent partridge shooting, though not up to Yorkshire grouse, of course . . . good riding . . . came down for a day with the Calpe once . . . rattling good day, too, with a five-mile point, which is rare in this country. Kitty Santangel fell into a ditch. That gypsy groom, Paco, was up with the second horses for her and Clara, that's my daughter, and pulled her out."

"It was fortunate he was there," she said.

"Fortunate for him, too—the count gave him a hundred pesetas."

He was silent, puffing on his cigar.

She opened a newspaper she had kept on the escritoire and handed it to him. The headline was *British Smuggling Steamer Sunk. Captain killed, 2 crewmen wounded, 4 tons tobacco seized.* She said, "How did you get the information?"

"Just asked Torrenti. The reward to be a place at the royal dinner."

"It was a great success then, just as the count needed."

Lord Howard did not seem very cheerful. "Not really, I fear. No one was supposed to open fire, but the Spanish had artillery ready and sank the ship. Some tobacco she had already landed was seized, the rest went down with her, not far off shore. But

too many people have been offended. The success may have been
too spectacular. The Spanish politicians are crowing, but our
admiral is threatening to bombard Málaga. And the count has
had to spend a vast sum of money in bribes. . . ."

"I feel sorry for the wife of the poor man who was killed," she
said.

"Great pity, that, because the gutter press in England's taken
it up. . . . The ship should never have been lost, either. That
was the captain's fault, backing off when he was holed instead
of running her farther ashore. Then we could have got her back."

"Even though she was caught in the act of smuggling?"

"Good heavens, yes, m'dear. We just send a strong note de-
manding the return of our ship and have a battleship steam out
of harbor. And the owners see that a suitable sum is passed to
whoever's responsible for releasing the ship. . . ."

She listened, thinking, perhaps I could hire two *maricons*
to do it to each other in the little room and get Lord Howard to
watch through the secret mirror. If at the time he could be
drunk, or could pretend to be drunk, then he could tell himself
he was not responsible for what followed when the two men came
in to join them. There'd be an orgy of sodomy. She would have
to be there at the beginning, then she could leave, and Lord
Howard could discover his true love.

". . . Pablo Larios wants me to get Aboab into the royal
dinner because of the hounds he gave, but I can't squeeze him in
unless I squeeze someone else out."

Yes, there'd be a fine bout of buggery. Lord Howard would be
deliriously happy, and the next day he'd shoot himself, and
everyone would say he'd just discovered he had cancer. The
English acted as though the fat writer Wilde had invented
mariconeria.

She looked surreptitiously at the clock, keeping her smile
alert and interested.

"It was insured!" George Torrenti shouted.

"Against theft? Oh, you mean the ship, not your dog."

"Of course! But the particulars weren't correct. You can't get
insurance if you say what the ship's really going to be used for,
and now . . ."

"A man killed," she said.

". . . Lloyd's won't pay. Do you realize how much we'll each lose? Thirty thousand pounds! And do you know who the papers say was behind the whole thing? The Count of Grazalema!"

"He is a great lord here," she said.

"Yes, but I've also just found out that the 'Pedro Perez' who's a member of our syndicate, and who we all thought was the cover name for a group of officers in the Tabacalera headquarters in Madrid, is not other than the Count of Grazalema! The rotten, lying intrigue of the Spaniards!"

"And the man killed," she said.

"But Lord Howard Kingsley's the one who's responsible for the loss of the ship and cargo as far as I'm concerned. Worming confidential information out of me and then passing it to the Spanish! Oh God, I should have stayed in the customs house side. . . . And he promised he would get the ship back, but she's sunk!"

"And the man killed."

"Well, I'm sleeping with Lady Howard! That'll teach him. I approached her the next day. He was still up in Ronda with the count. I was terrified, because, well, she is a duke's sister-in-law, but I was so angry that I could do it."

"Does she—punish you?" Dolores asked.

"She'll do anything as long as I make love to her, too. . . . And I'm getting half a dozen of us together, the most important merchants in Gibraltar, and we're going to write an official letter to the Admiralty in England, hinting that Lord Howard gave away British naval secrets to the Spanish. And we'll send a copy to the *Times*. The scandal will break while the prince and princess are here. He'll never be made comptroller at Buckingham Palace."

"And you'll never be invited to the Convent," she said.

"Oh God, I suppose not," he said, relapsing into uncertainty. "It's a . . . a *damned bad show* all round."

"Especially for the man killed," she said.

Today her caning of him served as a release for a sudden venomous hatred of men in general and George Torrenti in particular. Further, she felt physically queasy. So she whipped with tight-lipped, precise force, the cane whistling, the livid welts springing up exactly superimposed. She broke a cane and took another. Torrenti's moans and prayers for release grew louder.

She aimed carefully low and hit his testicles twice as he was ejaculating. He began to writhe and scream like a trapped animal then, but she took another cane and kept up the savage, whistling cuts until his buttocks were purple and white and dripping blood all the way across. Then she flung the cane away, rushed into the bathroom, and vomited.

Dolores Falcon was not looking well, the deputy chief of police thought. That young Paco Santangel had been beating her, probably. And her request was an unusual one. Still, it was not for him to inquire into the secret life of high-class courtesans, and on general grounds her request should be granted. She had been good to the police—paid well and punctually, given extra presents when there was sickness or a new baby, never caused scandal or noise except sometimes when Paco took his friends to the house.

"As long as it is no important official of the British government who could make trouble for us in his turn . . ." he said.

"No. It's a merchant, very rich," she said. "But that must be forgotten."

"Perfectly. We shall hear from you?"

"In a week or so."

The police officer smiled, pocketed the envelope—it was a good deal thicker than usual—and bowed out.

Private Tamlyn came half an hour later, and Juana brought beer. "I've asked for my discharge," he said, almost before he had sat down. "The colonel says he wouldn't stand in my way even if he could. I've done me time, and nobbut a week to go before I could sign on again, but I won't. An' the colonel says he'll recommend me for policeman in the dockyard. They like old soldiers there. They can't hire the Gibraltar folk because they'd never arrest each other. I saw the officer in charge of the police, and he said if I applied when I was discharged, he'd take me on if the colonel recommended me."

"So it's all arranged. When are you getting married?"

His long face set into a remote hardness. "Next month," he said.

"Did the colonel give you his blessing?"

"Lor' no! He called me everything but 'darling,' miss. Offered to send me back to Blighty sick. Said these Gibraltar women were useless to man or beast. But I said I had to stay. He thought it was to do right by Luisa and shook my hand and said I was only a private soldier but a natural gentleman." His voice softened. "But it's to be near you I'm staying, that's the only truth on it."

She thought, that poor woman he marries is going to have a really dreadful life. She had partly brought it on herself, but still . . .

"I was telling you about Tofrek last time," he said. "About the fuzzie-wuzzies and how they couldn't break our square. . . ."

"When was this?" she asked, a little dazed.

"I don't know, miss. Not long, 'cos there's plenty of long service men now was there. But it's the Frogs I'd like to fight. Wish I'd a few in front of my bayonet right now, that I do. I'd teach 'em to stick out their dirty tongues at England, and the king and queen, and . . ."

She put out her hand to him and said, "Tell me later. . . ."

But later he said little, only looked at her with his pale blue eyes glowing and his bony face fallen into a deep calm. When it was nearly time for him to go, he said, "Will you see me at the dinner? There's to be a guard of honor outside the Convent. I'm the left flank man, front rank."

"I'll come," she said, "just to see you all."

Carlos Firpo's right arm was in plaster of Paris from the elbow down, the whole carried in a sling. He was even more frantic than usual, as though his brush with violent death had reemphasized the real values in his life.

Later, he was more subdued. "Smashed my arm," he said, over and over. "A shell splinter, it was. Another killed the captain. Blew his brains all over me. And that dirty, stuck-up swine Torrenti's refused to give me a pension or a bonus or anything."

"What can have happened?" she asked. "Juana, the champagne."

"Someone got paid a lot of money, that's what happened," he said bitterly. "Probably Torrenti. He's capable of anything."

"But it was his ship."

"Yes, but . . . I don't know. Father O'Callaghan says it was the Freemasons fixed it, because everyone on the ships, and in the syndicate, is Catholic. . . . And I promised Luisa, that's my wife's sister, twenty pounds for a wedding present, and now I can't give her two. And she's having hysterics because the fellow she's marrying, this Private Tamlyn, is not going to England at all but staying here as a dockyard policeman. Well, that'll be worth something to the family, I suppose."

He got up moodily. The effects of the sexual therapy were wearing off fast.

"And your wife?" she asked.

"Bad backache, she has. And very upset, because the woman who was working for us left. María Lopez. She and I were on the bed. Her husband came in, unexpected, from the dockyard. My wife came back at the same time, because she'd forgot something. So . . ."

"I understand perfectly. You could find another cleaning woman. Uglier or older, perhaps?"

"Yes. But I can't afford it any more."

Tomás Lopez sat on the edge of the straight-backed chair drinking red wine, very correct in his gray cotton suit and white shirt buttoned up, with no tie. "My wife, unfortunately, cut her nose quite severely. The end cut off, in fact. Only a few days ago. Yes, she is recovering, thank you."

He'd do that, she thought, the old Andalusian, Moorish way. There was a position to hold, a seat to be sat in, straight.

"The English Prince and Princess arrived yesterday for the dog show," he said. "The soldiers lined the route when they paid a call on the Governor. They are living on the royal yacht in the harbor. It is all done properly, with much *señorío*."

"And the dog show? Are you still confident your Manolo will win?"

"I am confident, señorita. As you suggested, I paid Paco Santangel one hundred pesetas to inform me what was Don Pablo Larios' passion, or, as you might say, weakness; but after nearly a month he told me only that Don Pablo craved to own a full-blooded Arab stallion. I am not in a position to present Don Pablo with such a horse. That young man is, perhaps, a scoundrel, señorita."

She sighed and said nothing.

"In the end I gave Don Pablo a perfect yellow rose. I could see that he recognized in me a person who knows the correct values."

"Indeed yes."

"It will not influence his judgment of the dogs . . . but it will cause him to look very carefully at Manolo. A man who could select so perfect a rose . . ."

". . . would naturally have a perfect dog," she finished.

"Precisely. Manolo is not perfect, but he is good. Very good. Indeed, his appearance and posture have changed, that is, improved, immensely in the past few weeks. Well, tomorrow at two thirty of the afternoon is the 'moment of truth' as they say in the bullring."

She refilled his glass. He lit a "black" cigarette and drew on it cautiously. "There has been a considerable scandal in Gibraltar over the arrest of Mr. Torrenti, a prominent merchant, the evening before last, in the house of a professional lady of La Línea. Many believe that the misfortune befell him because he shot a female Barbary partridge out of season, which is well known to be almost as fatal as catching the eye of our king, Don Alfonso." The shrewd eyes surveyed her. "It is said that the lady was yourself, though it has not been published."

"That is so," she said, nodding at the memory. The police had come while she was whipping him. She had wondered whether he would keep his appointment after the way she had beaten him the last time. If he failed to appear, she had only to apologize to the police. But he had come, begging for more whipping —"only let me loose when I ask you to."

"Father O'Callaghan says it is the Freemasons who caused his arrest, in order that he should not be able to dine with the English prince and princess, for now, it is understood, he has been requested to return his invitation."

When the police burst in, she recalled with pleasure, he had thought it was some exciting new continuation of the whipping that they were going to do. Then when they arrested him, he began to rave like a madman. She had to bury her face in the curtains and pretend her laughter was sobbing to see him shaking his fist, his potbelly quivering, his silky moustache puffing out. When they took him away, he could no longer speak.

"What was the charge against him, that the police should follow him and enter here? It must have been serious," Lopez said.

"Yes," she said. "It was smuggling. They found a packet of English cigarettes on him that he had smuggled through the frontier."

Lopez said, "A serious matter, indeed. It is certainly true, then, about the bad luck that will follow anyone who kills a Barbary partridge, for it was surely a very ill stroke of chance that reporters from the Gibraltar newspapers, and even the representative of Reuters, happened to be with the police when he was arrested."

"Yes," she said. "Otherwise he might have persuaded the police, on the way to the jail, that there had been a mistake."

"God preserve us all from such mistakes, Señorita Falcon," he said meaningly. He gave her money and the usual bottle of whisky. "I trust the police will not break in on account of this bottle, which certainly has not been seen by any customs officer."

"There is no chance of that, Señor Lopez," she said and led the way to the bedroom.

The day of the dog show dawned, waxed, waned. She heard nothing. She had no clients and went to bed early.

The clang of the front door bell awakened her. She sat up, wondering whether it could be day yet. But it was not. It was three o'clock in the morning. She heard Juana's shuffling feet, then distant murmuring. Shoes clattered up the marble stairs, the door burst open. She jumped out of bed, her arms wide. "Paco!"

Juana waddled in and lit the lamps, grumbling, "Send him away, señorita. Before he causes any more trouble."

He was wearing an expensive gray worsted jacket, incongruous over the patched blue cotton trousers. There was a big bulge inside the jacket. He dived in his hand and pulled out a fat, sleepy puppy. He pressed it into her hands. "A foxhound bitch," he said. "I stole it for you. It'll be a good guard dog when it grows up. Good-bye."

He was going. She grabbed his arm. "Paco!"

"Let him go," Juana said. "It'll be best."

"Paco, what are you doing? What do you mean, good-bye?"

"My Cabo won the dog show, because he's really a pup of the count's pedigreed bitch that I stole when I birthed her two years ago. So I won fifty pounds and I'm running away with Kitty, the count's daughter. She's waiting in the carriage outside."

"But . . . but . . ."

"The count's been appointed ambassador to Ethiopia. Tomás Lopez was arrested and fined five pounds for dog stealing, right in front of the princess, because his dog wasn't his but Torrenti's that he'd stolen and painted."

She sank onto the bed, looking at him as though he had come from another planet.

"We'll be married in Cádiz, then we're going to Peru. I'll come back when the excitement's died down. The count will want to see his first grandson. Then I'll be a *torero* . . . *El Gato Moreno!*" He pirouetted on his toes and ran out.

"Good riddance," Juana said. She bustled over and fluffed up the pillow. "You get back into bed."

She said, "The girl's going to have his baby."

"Naturally," Juana said. "The English girl, also, I wouldn't be surprised. He will leave them all over the world." Dolores felt pale and ill. Juana looked at her keenly. "You, too?"

Dolores nodded. "I'm sure."

"It was that *juerga*. You were drunk."

"Perhaps. But it might be anyone."

"Well, we can get rid of it."

"No, Juana. I'll keep it."

"You're mad!"

"Perhaps. Good night."

She had a good position near the front of the crowd opposite the Convent to watch the ceremonies preceding the great dinner. She was wearing black, with a heavy veil. The sergeant of the police next to her was one of the few people in the world who knew her and her whole history; but he did not recognize her under the veil.

In the hiss of the gas lamps she watched the redcoats march down, the band playing, and take up their positions to the left of the main entrance. She saw Private Tamlyn and thought that his wandering eye—his head and neck remained ramrod stiff throughout—detected her. In the crowd she saw Tomás Lopez and his wife, with a bandage over her nose; and Carlos Firpo, his arm in a sling, with his sour wife and depressed sister-in-law.

And when the guests began to arrive she saw Father O'Calla-ghan, looking every which way to make sure his flock appreciated that he had been invited; and Mr. and Mrs. Joseph Aboab, Jews, invited at the last moment to take the place of the Torrentis, un-happily indisposed; and Don Pablo Larios and Pepita, who were warmly applauded by all; and Lieutenant Colonel Lord Howard Kingsley and his thin, blond, hungry-looking lady.

Finally the sound of cheering rolled up Main Street from the direction of Casemates, and the Governor came out to stand under the arch outside the Convent. Beside him a red-coated, spike-helmeted sergeant held a velvet cushion, and on the cush-ion rested three huge, ancient keys, the Keys of the Fortress.

The royal carriage rolled up, and the crowd surged forward, cheering. Dolores was left against the wall. She pushed up her veil and stood on tiptoe, trying to see. The sergeant of police turned, stared, and said in a low voice. "What are you doing here, Leah Conquy? What concern of yours is such an affair as this?"

Book Eleven

⬦⬦⬦⬦⬦⬦⬦⬦⬦⬦⬦⬦⬦⬦⬦⬦⬦⬦⬦⬦⬦⬦⬦⬦⬦

The Grey Diplomatists

The Jewish year 5662–5696
AUC 2655–2689
A.D. 1902–1936
A.H. 1320–1355

STORM clouds were gathering over La Línea, over Gibraltar, over all Europe, the sun of a brilliant, selfish young century already fading. In the chanceries the candles burned late as the politicians wove and rewove the alliances for the "inevitable" conflict. In the shipyards arc lights sputtered and oxyacetylene torches glared twenty-four hours a day as ship after fighting ship joined the swelling navies.

Gibraltar showed its teeth in October, 1904, when battleships put out into the Atlantic to intercept a Russian fleet heading from the Baltic clear around the world to fight Japan. The Russians, steaming down the North Sea earlier, had fired on a number of British fishing vessels. Britain demanded apologies and compensation—and sent out the Gibraltar fleet to enforce its demands. The Russians, who must indeed have been stricken with panic to imagine that British trawlers were Japanese destroyers, quickly made amends, and Lord Charles Beresford steamed back to Gibraltar. The Russians sailed on to annihilation at Tsushima.

In January, 1906, the representatives of the major European powers met at Algeciras to divide up the Moroccan empire and so complete the absorption of all Africa except Ethiopia. The

convention being arranged was a piece of skulduggery of dubious antecedents and more dubious promise. Its main purpose
was to keep out Germany. In return for concessions in Egypt and
elsewhere, England was to agree to a French takeover in Morocco, except that a part directly opposite Spain—and Gibraltar
—should be allotted to the weakest and most ailing of the powers
concerned—Spain. If it came to vote, Germany would stand almost alone, backed only by Austria and Morocco itself. The British plenipotentiary, Sir Arthur Nicolson, was grave and anxious.
The proposals held enormous possibilities for future disaster.
Still worried, he went over and spent the night in Gibraltar.
Harold Nicolson tells in his biography of his father what happened:

> The Atlantic and Mediterranean Fleets were there—thirty
> battleships, innumerable cruisers, countless destroyers. He dined
> with Lord Charles Beresford upon the flag-ship. Those great
> grey shapes lay around him under the great Rock: *Illustrious,
> Indefatigable, Implacable, Indomitable.* Clearly there was no
> reason to be frightened of Count Tattenbach. [He] decided that
> at the very next meeting he would put things to the vote.

The battleships, which at that time many Englishmen called
"grey diplomatists," had signed another treaty, and the Rock had
witnessed it. The thoughtful observer would be tempted to
quote Lord Rosebery's remark of half a generation earlier: "Till
I saw Gibraltar I never fully realized why we are so hated in
Europe."

The Edwardian period in Gibraltar itself was perhaps the
finest heyday of snobbism. Queen Victoria had sent her third
son, the Duke of Connaught, there for six months in 1875. The
reason for his posting has escaped history, for he had no
responsibilities and wasn't studying anything. As he was twenty-
five and a bachelor one might suspect that the queen sent him
away from some petticoated menace in London. The duke's
elder brother, Edward, visited the Rock briefly as Prince of
Wales and again the year after he was crowned. He dined with
the governor and ordered that the name of the latter's official
residence should be changed to Government House; it didn't
seem right for a Governor to live in a Convent: all those nuns
. . . (The name was later changed back again).

Queen Alexandra came: King Alfonso XIII came to Algeciras (not to Gibraltar, that would have been too much for a Spanish king): the new Prince and Princess of Wales (King George V and Queen Mary) came. . . . The link between the upper echelons of Spanish and Gibraltar society was the Larios family, Spanish landowners and aristocrats who also owned estates and houses in Gibraltar. It was Pablo Larios and his wife who escorted the kings, queens, and princesses through the cork woods of Almoraima, it was he who introduced the Spanish gentry to polo, it was he who became Master of the Calpe Hunt in 1890 and was still master in 1906 when King Edward and King Alfonso honored it with their patronage, and its title was changed to the *Royal* Calpe Hunt. The exaltation in royalty-worshiping Gibraltar knew no bounds.

More prosaically, the water problem was at last overcome. It had been so bad that Nelson once came out from England with a warship loaded with nothing but water. Of old, convoys and fleets had to go over to Tetuán or Tangier to water. Jervis had inveighed furiously that he would eject all women from H. M. ships (many were then permitted on board) as *they would insist on washing.* Between 1898 and 1961, in three main spasms, thirteen reservoirs with a total capacity of 16,000,000 gallons were constructed. All but one of these are deep inside the Rock and are fed and serviced by a tunnel and railway of their own. Some of the water is collected on cemented-over outcrops of limestone on the west face, but the main catchment area is 34 acres of corrugated roofing material spread over the steep aeolian sand slope of the eastern side. It is this huge expanse of grayish white, the sheets screwed firmly into timbers driven into the sand, which every traveler from the east now sees before anything else of Gibraltar emerges from the haze.

Archaeological research continued, and the first formal scientific exploration of a Gibraltar cave was made by a Mr. Duckworth in 1910. He explored Cave S, at the top of the east face water catchment area, and found many bones and artifacts, confirming that Gibraltar is an inexhaustible mine of material for the study of early man in a certain definite and plainly limited environment. Later Gibraltar also attracted the attention of the father of modern archaeology, the Abbé Breuil, but he made no remarkable discoveries.

Smuggling continued, limited only by the primitive means then available—sailing cutters and a few steam pinnaces for sea work (though the invention and use of radio at sea was soon seen to provide an excellent means of communicating between the smugglers and the *Tabacalera* operatives so that unfortunate encounters between them might be avoided). On land, dogs wearing tobacco belts continued to trot back and forth across the neutral ground from the caves under the north face, where the tobacco was stored, to their waiting masters in La Línea, until, at the request of the Spanish authorities, a dogproof fence was built from sea to sea across the isthmus.

In 1914 Gavrilo Princip shot Archduke Ferdinand of Austria at Sarajevo, and the lights began to go out over Europe. War began. Spain remained neutral, though her royalty and court had strong ties to both sides—the queen was English, the queen mother German—so Gibraltar did not have to face direct attack from the mainland. Gibraltar's situation made it an excellent place for gathering and "mating" of convoys and escorts, when that system of antisubmarine defense was introduced. But it had remarkably little effect on the German submarine campaign in the Mediterranean. The first U-boat passed through the strait in May, 1915, and from then on shipping losses in the Mediterranean were very heavy. Submarines came and went almost at will, and to cock a final snook, one of them surfaced off Trafalgar two days before the war ended and sank the battleship *Britannia*.

The guns of Gibraltar were fired in anger for the first time since the Napoleonic Wars against submarines. One, spotted on the surface on December 31, 1915, was engaged and probably sunk by the Levant batteries on Windmill Hill; another was engaged in Gibraltar Bay during 1917 by the Devil's Gap Battery. Some say this submarine was sunk, some say it wasn't, some say it never existed. What is certain is that a number of shells ricocheted into "neutral" Spain, which protested. Spain had no cause for complaint, as her official class much preferred Germany to England, and several damaged U-boats had secretly been repaired in Spanish harbors.

The war ended in November, 1918, bringing a bad combination of circumstances for Gibraltar—the world was at peace but depressed. The British forces, particularly the navy, were ruthlessly cut down; and once again the value of Gibraltar had to be considered anew, for the four-year war had seen the birth, infancy, youth, and early manhood of a new force, air power. When it began, pilots in fabric wings tied together with string fired pistols at each other, and strong headwinds caused the machines to go backward. When it ended, England had four-engine bombers capable of flying from London to Berlin and back, nonstop, with 4,000 pounds of bombs. Similar bombers could fly much more easily from Madrid, Mallorca, or Morocco to Gibraltar. . . .

A postwar governor assured the populace that they had nothing to fear from aircraft. He had frequently sailed around the Rock in his little boat, he said, and all seafaring men would agree that the air currents were very treacherous and unreliable, far too much so to permit the operation of flying machines. Nevertheless, as the smelly things seemed to have come to stay, a landing strip would be cleared in the middle of the racecourse. This racecourse was on the disputed area between the north front and the sites of the forts of San Felipe and Santa Bárbara. The Spanish said the land was not part of Gibraltar, it belonged to them. They had built the old forts that far back, as it was customary not to put up any defense work within gunshot of a fortress (they were well within gunshot, even when built: about 450 yards from the north face). They had permitted the British to use the land solely as an act of courtesy, first to build barracks for the care of fever cases after 1808, later for gardens and recreation purposes for the cooped-up garrison; but an airfield . . . no! The British, naturally, said the land was theirs and always had been.

In the ruins of the old Europe, like poisonous glittering weeds, the tyrannies of Communism and Fascism flowered—Salazar, Lenin, Mussolini, Stalin, Hitler. . . .

Internal disease had wracked and rocked Spain throughout the nineteenth century. There is an old Spanish legend relating how God, when allocating the virtues and qualities to the nations, asked each patron saint what he wanted for his country. St. George asked sea power for England and got it; St. Denis, good food for France and got it; but when it came to Spain's turn, Santiago wasn't there. He was off converting the heathen in Galicia (where some say he obviously never had a chance to finish the job). God sent a messenger to fetch him and meanwhile went on with the allocations. When Santiago arrived, panting, God asked him what he wanted for the Spanish people, and he replied, "Just one thing, Lord—good government." And God looked into his depleted sack and shook his head and said, "You can have the swiftest horses, the most passionate women, the bravest men, the clearest water, the most glorious sun, but what you ask . . . never, never, never."

The nineteenth century was one long demonstration of that legend: anarchy, revolution, coup, countercoup, counterrevolution; the monarchy overthrown and a republic established in 1871; the republic overthrown in 1873; bloody civil wars between followers of the regular and the Carlist lines of succession from 1833 to 1837 and 1870 to 1876; a bomb thrown at Alfonso XIII's wedding coach, many killed, blood spattering his bride's face and dress; in the 1920's military disaster in Morocco against Abd-el-Krim and ignominious rescue by the French; a public clamor blaming the king, causing him to hand over power to a dictator, Primo de Rivera; the collapse of Primo de Rivera; the elections of 1931 won by left-wing parties who set up another republic; the flight of Alfonso and his family (his eldest son escaped through Gibraltar).

The left-wing parties in the Republic held a paper-thin national majority, which its actions did nothing to increase. It was beset by riots, separatism, risings by the still-further-left in Asturias and the gradual coalition of all the interests in Spain which it had made its implacable enemies.

On July 12, 1936, the right-wing leader Calvo Sotelo, who had consistently spoken out in Parliament against the regime, was murdered in Madrid by men of the Guardia Civil, acting on the orders of the government. Six days later the right rose from end to end of the country, and all that had been hidden, all that had been deeply felt but unspoken, five centuries of repression on one side and five years of personal insult and national and religious degradation on the other, burst out into civil war. . . .

Sanctuary

"The shame of Spain, I agree," Señor Porras said. "But how can we get it back? England is much too strong for us to take it by force."

"Even if that were legal," Susana's father said. "No, force will get us nowhere."

"It's getting Mussolini what he wants in Abyssinia—in spite of the British."

"Negotiation," Susana's father said. "A socialist government, with whom we can talk like reasonable people . . ."

Susana, leaning over the parapet and gazing toward Gibraltar, switched off her attention. Her father always called it "the shame of Spain," but she thought of it as the Red Prince's castle. Especially after dusk she liked to look at it, for it glittered then like a magic city hung in the night, and there, in the middle, among the brighter lights, the Red Prince had his palace. By day, just before dawn perhaps, a wizard came and transformed it all, taking the palace into the sky, while huge secret doors opened and the rest of the castle vanished inside the mountain, and instead the town came out, so that by day no one would know about the castle or palace.

". . . I know well that you are not of our socialist camp, my friend. That is your privilege. But grant me that in this one matter of Gibraltar, which lies equally close to the heart of every Spaniard, royalist or socialist—the socialist attitude is more likely to achieve success. After all, we have had kings of England arguing and fighting about it with kings of Spain for two hundred years now, without result. . . ."

She yawned and was reverting to her daydream when her pigtails were sharply pulled from behind. She cried out, pleased but pretending to be angry. José Porras had left her brothers to come and play with her. She rushed shrieking round the rooftop after him, flailing with her arms at his back, until her father said, "Susana, José, run out into the street now."

The streets of Castellar were wonderful for playing, narrow, crooked, and full of sharp corners and hidden arches, and she played with José and her brother David until it was time for supper. Her father did not come to the table, and they could all hear him fiddling with the radio in the sitting room. She heard men shouting, screeches in the radio, music, more voices. Her father put his head round the door. "There's been a military rising, Leah. In nearly all the capitals. I knew there'd be trouble when those bloodthirsty fools had Calvo Sotelo murdered, but this . . ."

"Eat. Drink," her mother said. "Be quiet, boys. Your father is worried."

"Don't worry, Papa," Susana said and stood up to kiss him. She sat next to him at the table and was his favorite, she knew, because she was a girl.

He hugged her tightly with one arm. "It'll be all right," he said. To her mother he said, "I'll go and see Paco as soon as I've eaten, and I'll talk to the *cabo* of the Guardia Civil, too. One report said the government is arming the people in Madrid to fight the army. . . . Perhaps we ought to do that everywhere. Otherwise, what hope does any civilian government have against the military?"

"Don't go interfering," her mother said, "Paco's the mayor. Let him talk to the *cabo*."

"I must," her father said. "Otherwise, perhaps nothing will be done."

Susana slept in a bed in the passage that was like a big drawer and was turned up against the wall during the day. In Madrid she had a little room of her own, because she was a girl, but she liked the summers in Castellar better. When she felt sleepy she took Prince's cage down from its place in the patio and hung it on the hook over the foot of her bed. Prince was a baby bird her eldest brother, Saul, had found with a broken wing just after they came down a month ago. He was still wild, really, but he would eat from her hand—pecking at her finger sometimes—and her father had set his wing. He said Prince was four months old and was a Barbary partridge, and when he grew up they'd use him as a decoy to attract others, which they would shoot; but Susana cried, "No, no, you shan't!"

She talked to him in whispers and then said, "Good night,

Prince. Sleep well," and lay back to sleep. The door of the living room was close, and she heard her father saying, "I don't like it, Leah. Paco seems terrified. The *cabo* said he'd had no orders; in any case they only have their own arms here, for the four of them. I'll go to Jimena soon and see what I can do there. Or Algeciras. If we moderates don't show we're determined to support the elected government, the extremists will take over, and then. . . ."

Susana yawned mightily and heard no more.

On the third day after that she made a dress for her doll and a hood for Prince. It was a very hot day, and her next older brother, David, didn't eat any dinner. He was always dreamy and had longer eyelashes than most girls. He was twelve, and Susana was ten. José Porras was eleven, but he didn't come round today.

Her father came in late to supper. They heard him wheeling his bicycle into the hall and then shutting the door. Her mother's head jerked up. He was bolting the door, though no one had gone to bed. He came in, and her mother got up at once. "What is it, Simon? What's happened?"

"Quiet," he said, "lower your voice. Keep calm. You children . . . No, stay. You'll have to know. I've been shot at."

"With a rifle? Or a machine gun?" Saul, the eldest, asked. He was sixteen and like her father but taller, and he didn't have a droopy mustache.

Her father said, "As I was coming up from the river. Wheeling the bicycle, of course. Someone fired two shots from the bushes, quite close. . . . I heard them running away, so I kept on up the road."

"Have you told the *cabo*?" her mother said.

"Yes, and that's the worst part of it. He said he had other things to do than worry about the safety of Jews and Communists. My God, I'm not a Communist and never have been and never will be." He tore off a piece of bread and went into the sitting room, calling, "Saul, bring me some wine." The radio was clicked on, and soon the air was full of squeaks, shrieks, and shouts.

She was asleep, but a tapping on the side window nearly opposite her bed awakened her. Her father and mother were talking in the living room, but in low voices. They stopped. The tapping came again. Her father came out and muttered, "Who is it?"

"A friend." Susana, listening intently now, recognized Señor Porras' voice and wondered why he didn't knock at the front door and come in. "Listen. They are going to kill you tonight. Take your family and leave Castellar at once."

"But . . ."

"Don't ask questions. Do you think I'm not risking my neck for you? Not because of your politics, God knows. Because you've spoken up for Spain. Don't go south, the road's picketed. But go!"

She didn't hear him leaving then, but he must have. Her father and mother stood in the passage, almost over her. The light from the living room slanted across the floor and up the wall behind them.

"It's . . . it's unbelievable! That was Fernando Porras! Who's 'they'? Why . . . ?"

Her mother said, "Someone shot at you, didn't they? I'll get the children up. Where are we going? And take some money, hidden."

Her father repeated, "Where are we going? With Spain become mad? People you've known all your life shooting at you from the dark? There's only one place to go. Only one sanctuary —the Rock!" He burst into a terrible laughing, until she jumped out of bed and said, "Move, papa, you're standing on my shoes."

She was ready in three minutes in her best dress, in spite of dressing in the dark, but then her mother made her change into her oldest and wear her worst, raggediest shoes. She heard her telling the boys the same and understood that it was like a game, they were all to dress up like tinkers, and then her mother called her, and she helped pack bread, onions, and sausage into little sacks.

Her father came into the living room. She nearly cried out, putting her hand over her mouth, for he had shaved off his mustache. Then they all dirtied their faces, and her mother let out her hair from the pigtails and shook out her own.

They gathered in the parlor. Her father began to speak, choked, tried again. He said, "We must be brave. Keep together. Make no noise. If anyone asks, our name is García, and we are a poor family, laborers, from Ronda, going to join relatives in Algeciras, where we hear there's work. Our identity papers were burned in our house by a mob. Now open the back door, Saul. No, leave the lamp. Someone may be watching to see when we put it out."

Ruy, her middle brother, who was red-haired and gawky, because his voice was breaking, said, "Susana can't take the bird cage, can she?"

Susana cried out, "I will, I will! Prince shall come to the Rock!"

Her mother began to argue with her, but her father said, "Leave her be. She can free him when she gets tired. He will be no worse off than he will be here."

Then they left the house and the village, and after a short pause at the orchard where their hired man kept the donkey, on northward along the ridge top, on a broad path now, Ruy leading the loaded donkey.

Susana looked over her shoulder. Castellar was dark; beyond it Gibraltar glittered and sparkled, the enchanted castle and palace of her dreams. And now she was going there at last, even though they had to start out in the wrong direction. Prince in the cage would meet the Red Prince of the Rock: and the Red Prince would talk to her. She felt thrilled and frightened together and muttered to the bird, "Be brave, Prince."

They walked all night, slowly, along the sierra, curving steadily left-handed until when light came they were nearly level with Castellar but on the next ridge to the west and facing Gibraltar. They crept in under the bushes, tethered the donkey, and lay down to rest.

The sun rose, and her father said in a troubled voice, "It's going to be hot, Leah." Her mother didn't like the heat, nor did David.

The sun climbed. It was always hot in the middle of July, but this was the hottest day she remembered. By noon her mother was beginning to moan, and David said he had a headache. Her own tongue hurt, and there was no water or spit in her mouth.

"Water, Papa," David croaked. "I want water."

Later in the afternoon her father said, "Load the donkey. We must go down to the river." They started down the side of the ridge, among the holly oaks and gorse, but came to a cliff the donkey could not get down, so had to go back. Then Saul thought he saw men with guns, and they waited, keeping still, till it was dark, then tried again. At last they came to water, and though it was still and rank, they all drank, then lay down. Susana gave Prince water and then slept.

In the morning she did not feel well, but her father said, "None of us do, little daughter. But we must get up to the ridge again." They started back up, and soon Gibraltar climbed above the middle hills, and she looked at it longingly, set there in the blue and silver bay; but it did not seem any closer, for all the hours they had been struggling. Then she felt a gripe at her belly and rushed into the bushes and pulled down her underpants. In a moment she was vomiting, too, and crying, for she had dirtied her clothes.

When she had finished, they moved a hundred paces, then her father had to go. A hundred paces on, and it was David. The next time it was her mother, and herself again. Her mother said, "We must stop here, Simon, until all this is over. It was the water."

"We can't stop here," he said. "We must go on, or we'll never get there." He was looking very tired. He was not fat, but he did not go out of doors much, either here or in Madrid, and he was not used to the exertion.

They moved on thus all day, southward, stopping every few minutes for one or another of them to strain at their empty bowels or retch and moan at an empty stomach. It was as hot as the day before. By afternoon Susana felt strangely light and stumbled sometimes, though she thought she had raised her feet high. Her mother could not walk anymore and rode on the donkey. Her father walked very slowly, his face shiny and white. Sometimes they would stop because one or another of them saw trails of dust moving along the roads in the valley floor below or men going out to the fields, for her father said, "We can trust no one now—after a lifetime of trusting everyone!"

Darkness came before they had found any more water, and they stopped. Gibraltar shone there ahead, and Susana cried, "Let's go on, Papa. I'm not tired."

"You're fainting, little daughter," he said. "We must stop."

"I must have water," her mother said. "There's water in the valley just down there. That's where the river comes in."

Her father hesitated, but her mother began to moan, so he said, "Very well. Lead, Saul. I will hold your mother secure."

They moved on. For the last hour clouds had hidden the sun, and it was close and dark. They wound downhill, over uneven rock, over steep-sided water runnels—but dry—and along the side of a hill with lights below; and suddenly something jumped out of the gorse and dashed through the line of them. Susana thought it was a fox or a wild pig—but by then the donkey had snorted and broken free and vanished with her mother in the dark. Her father ran after it. Saul cried "Stop!" and there was a crashing, thump, repeated, another crash. Her mother screamed, cut off like a hiccup.

She went forward and found the boys on the lip of a quarry. She heard faint sounds from below. They hurried round the side and down. Her mother was lying on her side in the quarry, making a strange noise as she breathed. The donkey lay twenty feet away, and Saul said it was dead.

Her father crouched beside her mother, whispering to her, but she did not answer. After a time Saul said, "Take the food off the donkey. We must carry it now. The water jar is smashed."

Then they huddled together under the cliff and ate a little. Susana went to sleep, and when she awoke it was daylight. David slept beside her. Her father, Saul, and Ruy were coming back from a group of bushes at the far side of the quarry. All three were crying.

"Your mother's dead," her father said.

Susana jumped up and hugged him. Her own tears mingled with his on her cheek, but she did not truly feel sad, for this was all too strange, too different from the time when Granny had died, slowly in bed. Then she had cried every day for many days. Now she said, "I can cook for you until you marry again, Papa."

Her father sat down, and she curled up in the crook of his arm. Saul said, "We can't stay here, Papa. We must cross the valley and get onto the sierra the other side."

"Very well," her father said dully. They moved off, but now it was Saul who gave the orders, and her father walked like a man in a dream, holding Susana's hand.

A rough road, used by the stone carts, led from the quarry out to the road a quarter of a mile away. Before they reached it, Saul crept on ahead and came back to tell them that they could cross safely, as no one was in sight. When she reached the road, Susana saw that it ran straight in both directions for a long way, the hill on one side and a forest of cork oaks on the other. Opposite the track from the quarry a footpath led into the cork forest, and Saul took that, saying, "This is going the right way, Papa."

Susana liked it among the corks, for there was a good shade, and there were no bushes or thorns under them. Prince in his cage had felt very heavy yesterday and had made her arms stiff from carrying him; but now he felt light, and she talked to him as they walked along. At noon her father fainted, and Saul said, "He is tired. He didn't sleep all night. We must rest here until the evening."

They rested where they were, and Prince ate some bread, and Susana slept some more. Then her father sat up, saying, "I can go on now," and they started walking again. After sunset, in the dull twilight, Ruy said, "This path is coming to a cork factory, Saul," and her father said, "Better turn right."

Saul said, "But that's the road again. It's curved round, and we've gone straight. We're going to join it just before a bridge and . . . soldiers!"

He stopped and turned. Her father said, "They've seen us . . . keep on . . . remember what I said."

Susana saw the soldiers clearly; two men in brown and black with rifles and fixed bayonets. "They're not real soldiers," her father muttered.

The path left the cork oaks and led up a little bank to the bridge. The other side of the bridge there was a roadmen's hut, with half a dozen more men lounging about outside and smoke curling from the chimney. The nearest sentry held up his hand. "Stop!"

Her father said, "What is this? We are going to Algeciras." He spoke in a thick imitation of the accent the ordinary people of Castellar spoke in.

A man from among the loungers outside the hut came across the bridge to them. A few of the men were really boys, no older than Ruy or Saul; the rest were as old as her father. They wore ordinary clothes, but mostly good, not peasants'; and they had ties on, and all wore a red and yellow armband on the left arm. The new soldier, who had a pistol, said, "This is a Falange picket. Have you seen any bands of Reds? Where are you going?"

Her father began his story. She and the boys stood close together, a little behind him. The men outside the hut had gone back to their cards, but another man had come out and was standing in the doorway, staring at them and listening.

"We have no papers," her father said. "They were burned. We lost everything, everything. . . . Because we are churchgoers! What can one do with such a government?"

"Well spoken," the interrogator said. "All right, move on. Keep your eyes open, and if you see or hear of any bands of Reds, tell the first army or Falange picket you come to. *Arriba España!*"

"*Arriba España!*" her father responded. He beckoned to them. "Come." They walked out onto the bridge. It was almost dark now. The man from the hut doorway was standing there, waiting for them. He was wearing a military uniform, but it hung loose on him, as though he had been bigger when it was made. He was tall, old, with gray hair and dark eyes and a very long, mournful face.

As they came up to him, he peered closely and said, "It's Señor Toledano, the lawyer and journalist, isn't it?"

"Toledano?" her father muttered. "No, no—García. A laborer with no labor." He made to pass by.

"Wait!" the officer said. "You have shaved off your mustache, but I know you. We were on the platform together two years ago at the Gibraltar Protest Meeting in Madrid. I am the Count of Grazalema."

The sergeant had joined them by then. "Did you say this man was Señor Toledano, Count? The Jew Communist from Castellar?"

"I'm not a Communist," her father shouted.

The sergeant drew his pistol and said, "We won't bother to . . ."

A shot cracked out by her ear. She jerked round and saw that Saul had grabbed the rifle from one of the bridge sentries and fired. The sergeant's brains spattered the road, and his body lay half over the parapet. "Run!" Saul shrieked. "Into the woods!" He fired again, and the other sentry collapsed. By then she was running hard and did not look round till she reached the edge of the cork woods beyond the roadmen's hut. Her father and Saul were coming, running. It was too dark to see where the soldiers were, but a flurry of shots exploded around the roadmen's hut, and she heard bullets clattering overhead and slamming into the tree trunks. Beside her, David gasped, "Someone hit me!" Her father stumbled out of the dark, crying, "Where are you?"

"Here, Papa."

"Run," he said. As he ran he gasped, "Saul's dead. . . ."

David said, "My side hurts, Papa. . . . It's numb. . . ."

"Can you move, son? Just a bit farther."

They stumbled on for twenty minutes, all sounds died behind them, and then, deep in the cork forest, David groaned and fell.

They crouched beside him. Her father felt David's body and muttered, "He's bleeding from the belly. . . . Oh God . . . I must give myself up. Though to whom, and for what crime, I don't know. We can't go on."

Ruy said, "We could carry David back to the soldiers."

Susana burst out, "We are going to the Rock! You promised!"

From the ground David said, "It doesn't hurt, papa. But . . . I just can't walk. . . . Don't go back. That man was going to shoot you. He would shoot me, too—all of us!"

Her father said, "Very well. We'll stop here. In the morning we can look at your wound and make up our minds then."

When light came they found they were on the edge of a small stream that trickled through the cork woods toward the Guardarranque. The ground was uneven, and at the foot of a small hill nearby there were leaning rocks which, though they did not form a cave, gave shelter from view. They carried David there, and after Susana had washed his wound—it was in his back, low down, with another larger hole at the front—her father tore off his shirt and made a bandage. Then they waited.

They waited the rest of that day. At first Susana sat by her brother's head, watching his every movement, ready to run to fetch him water when he asked, while her father and Ruy slept. Then her father awoke, and Susana left Prince and his cage in Ruy's charge and went up the hill above the rocks. From the top, as she had thought, she could see Gibraltar. It was much closer now, and seen in a gap between the lacing tops of the trees, its head again crowned with cloud, it seemed to be staring back at her and whispering, "Come. Why are you so slow?"

They waited all that night and the next day. She asked her father who the Count of Grazalema was. "A nobleman," he said. "Very rich. Very conservative. He served a few years in the cavalry as a young man. He and I would have nothing in common—though his estates surround us—but that we were at that accursed public meeting together to protest the British occupation of Gibraltar. . . . Intellectuals, military, landowners, church, merchants. I sat next to him on the dais and spoke for the legal profession."

"Who are the Falange, Papa?"

"A political party, child—very much opposed to mine."

She looked at David, dozing now a few feet from them, and said, "Is David going to die, Papa?" Her father sank his head between his hands and began to sob silently, and she knew it would be no use trying to comfort him.

They waited all that night. Before dawn David began to talk, and when the light came she saw that his skin was dull gray and his lips blue. Soon he died. Her father knelt and began to say a prayer in Hebrew, but Susana slipped away and hurried up the hill to see the Rock again so that they would know which way to go when they moved on. The cloud had gone, and the face shimmered pale gray toward her. "I'm coming," she whispered; and then she saw the soldiers, a line of about twenty of them coming round the base of the hill on the side farthest from the Rock. She ran quickly down the hill, bounding from rock to rock under the boughs. A bullet cracked over her head, and she saw her father and brother run out of the rock shelter where David had died.

"They're coming!" she screamed. "Soldiers!" She reached them, scooped up the birdcage, and started to run back up the hill. Her father said, "Stop, Susana. It's no use."

She saw that he and Ruy had raised their hands, and the soldiers were coming. It was the same ones from the bridge, in the ordinary clothes, with the Count of Grazalema in the middle.

"If you have arms, lay them down," the count said.

"We have none," her father said.

"Shoot the whole brood now, and have done with it," a man muttered, glaring at her with a bloodshot eye.

"None of that, now!" The count's voice was sharp. "That's the way the Reds behave. That's what we're trying to wipe out in Spain. . . . Can you walk, Señor Toledano? You must come along with us, then."

"Why?" her father burst out, "By what right? In whose name are you acting? For what government?"

"For the soul of Spain," the count said. "This is a rising of the old spirit, Señor Toledano. We have tolerated the filth of the republic long enough. . . . Besides, your son killed my sergeant. He is—was—a prominent wine merchant of Algeciras."

"He was going to murder me in cold blood," her father said.

The count said, "Come, please. It is no use talking here. A court-martial in Algeciras will see that justice is done to you."

They started back through the cork woods then, the count in front, then some soldiers, and then her father, Ruy, and herself, followed by more soldiers with bayonets fixed on their rifles. At the bridge there was an old motor bus, very small and battered, and more soldiers cooking food. Susana's mouth watered, and when a soldier gave her a plate of beans, she ate greedily, but Prince would not touch them. He looked tired and small, and she said to cheer him up, "It won't be long now, Prince"; but she did not think the soldiers would take them to Gibraltar or let them go there. She heard her father saying, "My son, Count . . . ?"

"Buried," the count said, "under that tree. I am sorry. I will send men to bury the other, too, as soon as . . . Soon."

"And our mother," Susana said. "She is dead in a quarry."

The count shook his head. "Terrible . . . I will speak to them in Algeciras about you, Señor Toledano. My word may carry some weight, although . . ." He shook his head again. "When the men hear what is being done in Madrid, all over Spain, it is hard to hold them. And we have had five years of this, this . . . rape, arson, murder, anarchy. If you will get into the bus now."

They got into the bus. By the time her father and Ruy had got into the back with half a dozen soldiers to guard them and a few more who wanted to go to San Roque, Susana had to sit in front with the count, beside the driver.

After several swings the engine started, the driver jumped in, and they bumped off down the road, southward. The railway line was on the left, cork woods beyond it, and a river close to the right. After a few minutes they turned a corner, and there was Gibraltar straight in front, seeming to rise up out of the woods.

At another corner, the driver slammed on the brakes, and lurching forward, Susana saw a tree across the road. She saw men, too, and before the bullets came knew what was going to happen. The bullets came in a wild crackle, glass shattered all round her, and the driver began to cough blood over the steering wheel. The bus ran into the tree and stopped with a crash. "Out!" the count cried, trying to clamber over her. She reached up her hand, took his little automatic pistol out of its holster, pressed the muzzle into his side, and pulled the trigger. The door swung open, and he fell out, head first. He was looking toward the wood, where men were coming, running. Then he saw Susana, the automatic in her hand and a wisp of smoke still curling from the muzzle. "Spain!" he gasped, "Oh, my God. My poor country."

A short, square, grizzled man wearing peasants' gray cotton, rope-soled shoes, and a black cummerbund was standing over her, a rifle in his hand. "Shall I finish this one off?" another asked, pointing at the count.

"Don't waste a bullet on him," the square man said. "This little beanpole of a *Pasionaria* did his business. Get rid of the rest and set fire to the bus."

"My father and brother are in the back," she cried. "Prisoners. That one's my father." She pointed. "Where's Ruy, Papa?"

"Killed," he said. "Killed in the first burst."

"I'm sorry," the square man said gruffly. "We didn't know there were any of ours with them. No more, though?" He waved a hand. His followers raised rifles and revolvers and began to fire. In a moment six of the militiamen lay sprawled in the road amid pools of blood. Two more and Ruy were dead in the bus.

The bus began to burn. "I'm Manuel Susarte, once a shepherd, till I saw the light," the square man said. "Now I'm an Anarchist. I have three brothers. One's a Communist, one's a sergeant in Africa, and one's a priest. Can't be more Spanish than that, can you?" He laughed bitterly. "Time to be going. They will have heard the shooting. Do you want to come with us? Though it's a hard life, and we'll have to farm out the little girl with some of our people. And it may go on a long time." Thick clouds of oily acrid smoke enveloped them.

"We're going to the Rock," Susana said, pointing. "Papa and Prince and I."

"Oh, you are," Susarte said. "Well, maybe that'd be best, if you can just get over the border. Or swim." He pointed down the road. "San Roque railway station's about two miles down— you know it? San Roque's on the hill above, a mile or more back. If I were you, I'd keep between the two, work down to La Línea, and try to steal a boat. Or get to the British wire in some sort of disturbance." He raised a hand—"*Que siguen bien!*"—and soon disappeared into the cork woods, his ragged band on his heels.

Her father looked at her and the distorted corpses and the wide-eyed count. "He was right," he said. "Poor Spain. Come, child, or they will find us here."

They moved off in the direction indicated by Susarte. Half an hour later they saw soldiers marching along the road toward the scene of the ambush and crouched in a thicket until they had passed. Then, walking on again together, they breasted a hill, and the woods ended. Before them lay the white houses of San Roque—and beyond, a narrow neck of land; and at the end of it, the Rock. They sat down side by side and stared. She saw a row of black holes high in the face of the Rock and thought they must be windows of the inner castle. The palace clustered at the foot of the slope, washed by the sea. Her father interrupted her. "That town close under the Rock, on our side, is La Línea. It will be full of soldiers. But do you see on the right where the river flows into the bay? There was a famous city there before anyone lived in Gibraltar. Now there are a few fishermen's huts. We shall go there and buy or steal a boat. God knows what we will do when we get to Gibraltar. The only man I know is a jeweler called Conquy. I met him at a Freemasons' meeting in Algeciras a few years ago."

"Shall we start now, Papa?"

He shook his head. "Not until dark, Susana. It is . . ." A crackle of gunfire interrupted him. It seemed to be coming from San Roque, barely half a mile away.

"Look!" Susana pointed. Bands of men and women, some with firearms, some with billhooks and kitchen knives, were running across the heath from the left toward San Roque. The firing increased, and a few bullets smacked over their heads.

"Those aren't soldiers or Falangists," her father muttered. "They must be peasants, workers . . . they're attacking San Roque."

Susana grabbed the birdcage and stood up. "Come then, Papa! To the boats! That's what Señor Susarte said we should do."

"Get to the British wire in some sort of disturbance," her father said. "Very well . . . You're braver than I am, Susana." He struggled to his feet, and they started diagonally down the slope, leaving San Roque on their left.

Gradually, very slowly, the white town swung past, from in front to the side to behind. They saw soldiers at a distance, but running away from San Roque; and others, further on, walking toward it. They saw big guns, at a distance, and two dead men, close to. Women passed carrying babies, hurrying aimlessly. All the time the rattle of firing sounded from the town, irregularly—long periods of silence shattered by a few minutes of frenzy.

They came to a wide river. "The Guadarranque," her father muttered and walked down the bank toward a clump of tall trees that sheltered half a dozen houses. They reached the trees in the middle of the afternoon, and her father knocked on the door of the first house. No one answered, and when he tried the door, it opened. They went in, and he said, "We'll rest here till dark, Susana." There was water in the jar and half a ham hanging in the kitchen, and Prince ate better than he had for two days. She stroked his head with her finger through the bars and said, "Look, Prince, out of the window. There's your castle!" Then she curled up on a bed in another room and went to sleep.

Her father was shaking her, and it was dark. "We have a boat," he said. "I wanted to buy it, but the man said, 'What good is money now—take it.' Are you ready?"

She felt a real excitement for the first time, and as she slipped down a narrow, dusty lane with him, her heart pounded so loudly she could hear nothing else. There was the boat, under a tree on the sandy bank, where the river flowed into the sea. They pulled it out, and her father went away and came back with oars, then they launched it, and he started to row, while she sat in the back looking toward Gibraltar, Prince's cage on the floorboards between her feet.

It was a dark night, and the pyramid of lights in the Red Prince's castle and palace shone more brightly from the blackness of the land—not a light in San Roque behind or La Línea beside or Algeciras to the right. The water made small, oily lapping sounds, and even in the darkness some sparkle of light fell from the ends of the oars when her father pulled them out of the water.

Her feet began to get cold, and she put her hand down to them and found it wet. "There's water in the boat, Papa," she said.

"Bail with your hands," he gasped. "We're halfway." He began to row harder, the oars creaking ever faster in the oarlocks. Susana put Prince's cage on the seat beside her and knelt and began to scoop the water over the side as fast as she could. The magic city towered ever closer, and she thought she heard the Red Prince's bands playing in it, but the water kept rising, and the boat went slower, and her father's groaning, frantic efforts became slower. Suddenly, they stopped. His head hit her knee as he fell forward. He was ill and could not speak. A bright light bathed them, and she saw that the water was only two inches from the top of the sides. She scrambled over her father, pushed his body aside, and took the oars. A motor chugged close as she began to row. Then the sea was flooding in, and men were shouting in a foreign language. She leaped for the birdcage and seized it just as a strong arm pulled her out of the boat, and it vanished, with her father, under the black water, the oars floating free on the surface.

The motorboat went slowly around and around, its searchlight weaving back and forth over the water. Then someone gave an order and it turned toward the lights and increased speed. The tall, grizzled, blue-uniformed old man with the big hands who had pulled her out of the boat said, in poor but understandable Spanish, "Was that your father?" She nodded. "I'm afraid he's drowned."

She nodded again. Her father had fallen forward before the boat sank. He was very tired and had to row so hard. The lights were very close. Soon she would step ashore with Prince, onto the enchanted land. To the old man in blue she said, "Conquy?"

He said in surprise, "Me? No. My name's Tamlyn, little miss —dockyard police, on special patrol, and lucky for you we are. But I know Conquy, same Lodge as me. He'll see you're looked after."

Book Twelve

◅◅◅◅◅◅◅◅◅◅◅◅◅◅◅◅◅◅◅◅◅◅◅◅◅

Between Wars

The Jewish years 5696–5700
AUC 2689–2693
A.D. 1936–1940
A.H. 1355–1359

THE fighting which enabled Susana Toledano and her father
to slip past San Roque took place on July 27, 1936, when
a Republican column about 3,000 strong arrived from Málaga
and retook the town. Troops from Algeciras and La Línea, who
had joined the rebellion, soon drove them out, and the Campo
de Gibraltar remained under the Rebels' control until the end
of the war.

Gibraltar saw many refugees those early days. Many more
tried to get in than it could hold or than was safe for its security.
Throughout the war it was also used as a handing-over point for
prisoners condemned to death by one side or the other and here
exchanged instead. It saw a little action, too, since the Republicans held control of the sea until near the end. Republican destroyers harried a Rebel troop convoy all the way across the strait
from Ceuta to Algeciras on August 5, 1936, and next day the battleship *Jaime I* and the cruisers *Libertad* and *Miguel de Cer-
vantes* bombarded Algeciras. Toward the end of 1938 the heavily
damaged Republican destroyer *Jose Luis Diez* limped into Gibraltar for repair. She crept out on the night of December 30-31,
hoping to evade the Rebel ships waiting for her; but someone
"accidentally" fired a rocket from Gibraltar, and she was at-

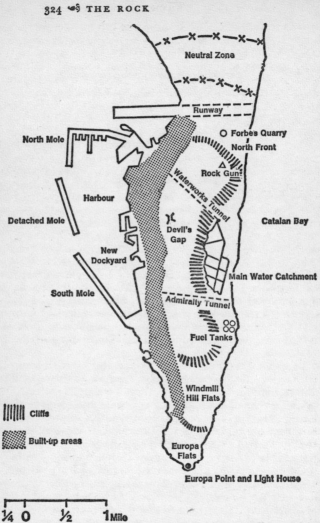

Neutral Zone

Runway

North Mole

Harbour

Detached Mole

New
Dockyard

South Mole

O Forbes Quarry
North Front

△ Rock Gun

Waterworks Tunnel

Catalan Bay

Devil's Gap

Main Water Catchment

Admiralty Tunnel

Fuel Tanks

Windmill
Hill Flats

Europa
Flats

● Europa Point and Light House

|||||| Cliffs

Built-up areas

¼ 0 ½ 1 Mile
Scale

tacked round the back of the Rock and driven ashore at Catalan Bay. The British later refloated her and interned her till the end of the war.

Most of the rest of the world had signed a pact of nonintervention, but the pact was observed only by the democracies, which alone had the power to save the Republic from its internal and external enemies. The pact was ignored by Hitler, who wanted to test war theories and also attach an ally; by Mussolini, for the same reasons plus a wish to humiliate the British, who had organized sanctions against him for his Abyssinian aggression of the year before; and by Stalin, who wanted to ensure that the Republic should not be democratic or anarchist but Russian Communist. These helping hands strangled Spain, slowly, until on April 1, 1939, Generalissimo Franco, who had early succeeded generals Mola and Sanjurjo (both killed in air crashes) as the head of the rising, was able to announce that the war was over.

The new nationalist Spain was a country bankrupt, split, and shattered. It had suffered more casualties, proportionately, than England was to suffer in the coming Hitler's war or than the USA had in its own Civil War, and incomparably more material damage. It needed enormous foreign aid, capital investment, and above all, peace . . .

Hitler armed, planned, and maneuvered with ferocious efficiency. France of the Third Republic staggered from one political crisis or scandal to the next. England dithered. The United States looked the other way.

The inhabitants of Gibraltar were in for a rough time . . . but let us pause now and examine the apes. Later we shall not have time.

As already mentioned, these beasts must have been imported into Gibraltar by the Moors. History does not record the origins of the legend that the British would leave Gibraltar when the rock apes did, but it sounds like a not-so-subtle Spanish joke. From the beginning of this century the huge new dockyard, increasing population, urbanization, and mechanization all worked to restrict the areas where the apes could live and to reduce the plants on which they fed. Their numbers fell drastically, until in 1924 only four apes could be found on the whole of Gibraltar. These had taken to raiding down into the town, fouling roofs (always used to collect drinking water), and stealing vegetables from barrows and backyards. The year before —whether moved by concern for the apes or for the people—the Secretary of State for the Colonies applied for permission to have the remaining apes transported back to Africa. This was refused on account of the legend, and more attention was paid to the preservation of the surviving animals.

The "head keeper" was the artillery general in Gibraltar, who appointed one of his officers as Officer in charge of Rock Apes. A master gunner was appointed to see that they had enough to eat, supplementing their natural food with scraps and leftovers begged from military kitchens and civilian institutions. At last the Colonial Office was persuaded to make an allowance for their care and feeding. The master gunner's post became that of cageman-cum-storeman. The "cage" part of the title came in because by then covered cages had been built to provide shelter for the apes, who now consisted of two mutually hostile packs, one at Queen's Gate and one at Middle Hill.

When Winston Churchill began to take a personal interest in the apes, during Hitler's war, the numbers were again very low. By 1943 there were only seven, even after imports from North Africa. Gradually, with the devoted attention of the famous cageman Gunner Portlock and his successors, the numbers increased. Now the apes have assumed an importance which makes a look at the *Ape* files like a glimpse into the mind of Edward Lear. . . .

Telegram from the Secretary of State for the Colonies to the Governor of Gibraltar, February 3, 1951:

> "Parliamentary question, APES: Following is text of question down for oral reply February 7: To ask S of S for the C if he is satisfied that subsistence allowance of 4d a day paid out of civil funds for maintenance each Barbary ape at Gibraltar is still sufficient; when amount was fixed at 4d; and to what extent the ape population has increased or decreased since the end of the war. . . ."

And in May, 1953, after the queen made Winston Churchill a Knight of the Garter:

> "After careful consideration the Commander Royal Artillery has decided not to authorize a change in the name of the ape

'Winston'. Winston Churchill himself is still called Winston, even though now knighted."

About this time, with the population in the low thirties, apes were offered to zoos all over the world, with free transportation by Royal or United States navy, although a monkey expert thought that to keep the pack going needed a strength of about one hundred. The reason for this apparently reckless generosity was that the Gibraltar civil government, which had taken over financial responsibility for the apes, announced that it would not pay the subsidy of fourpence a day for more than thirty apes.

The humorless Hitler, caring not a fig for the havoc he would cause in the files and among the apes and their keepers, invaded Poland on August 31, 1939. At this point Neville Chamberlain became suspicious of his intentions, and preparations were hurriedly made to teach the bounder a lesson. Gibraltar's days of leisure, hunting, and upper-class dalliance were over forever, and Pablo Larios had died with them.

Nothing much was done until the fall of France in June, 1940. Then, with a thunderstroke of astonishment, Whitehall realized that only Spain lay between Hitler's armies and the Rock; and Spain's ruler owed his position in part to Hitler's help.

Between July and November, 1940, all male civilians, except about 4,000 engaged in vital work, and all females, to the total number of 16,700, were evacuated. To be more precise, they were evacuated twice, first to Tangier and French Morocco, whence they soon had to return owing to the hostility of the Spanish and Vichy French governments installed there; and then reevacuated to Britain, Jamaica, and Madeira. Those who went Home found it less homelike than it had seemed from the Rock; the Jamaican climate and landscape, which some have thought idyllic, were too lush and tropical for the Gibraltarians; only those who went to Madeira found anything to rejoice over—as much as anyone can rejoice uprooted from home and/or separated from husband, lover, family. The only women in Gibraltar were nurses, a few in the services, and the señoritas who still came every day to work from Spain and could sometimes, by a well-worded offer to carry their bags, be persuaded to spend the night in the fortress.

The civil population had been about 20,000. Britain now put

in that number of troops. And the troops laid barbed wire and sandbags and installed guns, mortars, machine guns: and above all, under all, they dug, like fear-crazed moles. Under the personal omnipresent drive of the governor, Field Marshal Lord Gort, V.C. (recently defeated at Dunkirk) the engineers tunneled and bored. Rock began to be thrown out by thousands of tons. At first all the excavated stone went to make a runway, for when Hitler defeated France, it was considered that even the racecourse would have to be sacrificed for the making of an all-weather airfield large enough to take modern fighters. While this runway crept out westward into the bay from under the north face (the Spanish protesting all the time that Gibraltar had no territorial waters and no right to build out from the isthmus), the tunnelers hammered and blasted and gouged deeper into the bowels of the Rock. . . .

Inside

1941

"Who are you?"

The man addressed started out of his study of the sheet metal ventilation ducting running along the side wall of the tunnel. It was a good question. What should he answer? The late assistant manager of Coggeshall Colliery, Yorks? Samuel Chaddock, B.Sc. (Notts)? The only son of Joseph Chaddock (né Crapp), Esq., and of Mrs. Margaret Chaddock (née Akers-Carr), of Darley Court, near Pewsey, Wiltshire?

"Well, speak up, man."

He stared at the speaker, a tall thin brigadier in well-cut khaki battle dress, a row and a half of ribbons, and a thin, grayish mustache. Chaddock's company commander was at the brigadier's elbow and now cut in, frowning. "This is Captain Chaddock, sir, my new second-in-command."

The brigadier stuck out his hand. "I'm Hamilton, Chief Engineer. Sorry I couldn't see you when you arrived. I was laid up with gippie tummy. . . . What were you looking at?"

Chaddock said, "The metal ducting. It's full of leaks, and it's very difficult to take down and put up for blasting. I was wondering whether rubberized canvas could be used."

"Put in for some. Try it out. In your own time, of course. Make a report. In quadruplicate," the brigadier said. They were walking fast along the tunnel now, the brigadier in the middle, Chaddock on one side, Major Hughes, commander of 177 Tunneling Company, Royal Engineers, on the other. The racket of drilling increased. The colonel shouted, "Remember, that's for development heads only. We have natural ventilation in the main shafts. . . . What are you? Coal?"

Chaddock nodded. "Yorkshire."

"This is quite different. Hard rock. Tunneling, not mining. I keep asking for more hard-rock men. Quarry men. University?"

"B.Sc., Nottingham School of Mines, sir."

The brigadier glanced at him curiously and yelled, "School?"

Chaddock tensed. Why the hell couldn't a man who wanted to get out of some place he'd been put in be allowed to move without being pestered, reminded, firmly slammed back? "Eton," he said, "and King's. I have a B.A. of a sort, too."

"Thought so," the brigadier shouted. "Well, I won't hold it against you as long as you get your yards in. Four hundred and forty cubic yards per platoon per week."

They were close behind the men drilling charge holes in the face now. The nearest drill coughed to a momentary stop as the colonel shouted again, "Four hundred and forty yards!"

The man at the drill bellowed in a powerful Geordie accent, "Ah fucking know it's four hundred and forty fucking yards, but we have to do it one fucking yard at a time!" He turned his head and saw the red tabs. "Ma Goad!"

Major Hughes said, "Sergeant, take that man's name."

The brigadier waved his hand. "No, no. What's a few kind words between miners? Keep that bloody thing going, sapper, so we can't hear what you want to say next."

They edged back from the clamorous work face and walked back down the twin sets of rails to a row of waiting empty tubs. The noise faded. The brigadier said, "You've come in at the beginning of a great game, Chaddock. Before this war began, there were less than four miles of tunnel in the whole Rock. We plan to put in over twenty. We're going to make the Rock absolutely, finally, totally impregnable to any assault, no matter how great the firepower. The Royal Engineers' motto is *Ubique*, 'everywhere,' as you know. Well, here in the tunnels we have a little extra motto. *Four hundred and forty* or . . ." He jerked his thumb. "Off to the infantry you go." He indicated the row of men sitting along the tunnel wall. "4th Black Watch, acting as muckers to save our chaps for the technical jobs. We're getting some Eimco-Finlay loaders soon, though." He slapped his swagger stick into his hand for emphasis. "You've got to get the feel of this rock, Chaddock. This limestone is not like coal. It's hard as hell, but it's absolutely honest. No deception. No tricks. It'll give you fair warning, and then if you ignore it—wham! You've got to break it, but you've got to respect it . . . love it, *I* think."

He strode away, tapping his leg with the swagger stick. When he was fifty feet away, Hughes brought his hand down from the salute. "You are supposed to salute, too, Chaddock," he said.

"I know," Chaddock said. "I was thinking of something else."

"It's better to concentrate on the work in hand," the major said, "and safer, too."

"Yes, sir," Chaddock answered formally. Hughes was Welsh, a colliery manager in peacetime, careful, anxious to please owners or seniors. He said, "By the way, Tunneling H.Q. Mess is inviting all the army nurses to drinks tomorrow." He nodded and hurried off.

Chaddock began to walk back toward the face. The drills were making a lot of dust, yet they were drilling dry. Limestone was much safer than silicas, but he must find out whether X-rays were being taken and how often. Surely they could wet-drill here, using seawater? Safety was poor all round. No one wore miner's helmets except the drillers. The infantry muckers didn't even wear their steel helmets.

The section sergeant fell in beside him, and he remembered the name—"Gaffer" Farley, small, fiftyish, a coal-mine foreman in peace. Chaddock started asking questions . . . were they using hole directors for the easers? What about the dry drilling? The helmets? How much air was reaching the face? What was the maximum capacity of the pump? How about exhaustion of fumes? The little sergeant answered patiently in an accent Chaddock could barely understand.

The blast master came and asked permission to blow the round. Chaddock walked back behind the safety line, his brow furrowed. "Four hundred and forty cubic yards a week is a lot, sergeant," he said. "There's no allowance there for little errors. Corners are being cut, safety precautions are not being observed, in order to reach that figure, whereas we ought to be tightening up and . . ."

The sergeant said, "It's not easy, sir, but . . . Look, the army's a game, see, and it's best just to play the bloody game. It's not like trying to earn a living in Dipton in the depression. That's serious, see."

Chaddock said, "We've got to win the war, sergeant."

"Aye, we will, but it'll be a long tram. For drills we're using these twenty-five-pound jackhammers that the oldest colliery in County Durham would 'a thrown out twenty years back. Half a dozen portable hundred-cubic-foot compressors that sound like my Aunt Jane dying of the pneumony. Then the bloody Eyeties drop a bomb slap on the R.E. stores depot and bang goes half our steels, cable, pulleys, clamps. . . . You have to take it easy, captain, or they'll carry you out in a straitjacket."

The sharp regular cracks of the exploding round echoed down the shaft.

In the saloon bar of the Star & Garter the flight sergeant had a large audience of army corporals and sergeants. His RAF Harrow-and-Stepney accent filled the room. "This Jewish fellow goes to the magistrate and says he wants to have his name changed, see. The beak fixes him up and out he goes, Clarence Fauntleroy, Esquire, instead of Joe Levy. A couple of months later, back he comes and says he wants to change his name to Thompson. The beak scratches his head and says, aren't you the chap was in here a few weeks ago, changing his name to Fauntleroy? Don't you know who you are? Yes, your Honner, the Jew says. Then why do you want to change your name again? And the Jew answers, Vell, your Honner, ven someone asks my name I say Thompson, and they vill look at me and my nose—he has a real Jewish conk, see—and they vill say, Ah, but vat vas your name *before* it was Thompson, and I shall say, Fauntle-roy!"

The soldiers laughed, the ape corporal frowned. Mr. Wardrop and old Sergeant Tamlyn stared into their glasses without expression. Chaddock took a draft from his glass. It was a filthy hot muggy Levanter day, and the beer was heavy and livery, but that was what they had at the Star & Garter, and that's what you had to drink.

A naval petty officer said, "And now we're fighting for the Jews."

Joe Morello behind the bar spoke, half aside, to the ape corporal. "They not fighting for Gibraltar, *claro*. Sometimes, before war, *sometimes,* maybe they ask us what we want, ask whether they can take this, blow down that. Not now. Just take. War on, they say. And no bloody civilian allowed into a service concert. They think we don't need amusement, too?" He murmured a Spanish obscenity.

Mr. Wardrop said, "You scorpions would be on a better wicket about the service concerts if you'd ever raised a finger for the redcoats in the old days. You kept 'em out of *your* dances and bunfights, didn't you?"

The petty officer said, "I'm not fighting for no fucking Jews, I tell you straight. I'm fighting for fucking England."

Mr. Wardrop raised his gin glass. "That's what I like to hear —patriotism. Talking of which, listen to this. This'll bring a lump to your throat, friends. Silence for Mr. Disney-Roebuck's poem, which many connoisseurs consider the worst ever written:

> 'Watchful and silent, wakeful and stern
> Frowns the great fortress . . .
> High o'er the sea in the midst of the Rock
> Gray guns point threateningly over the bay
> Keen eyes peer into the fringe of the night
> Gunners are patiently awaiting the day.' "

"What the hell is this?" the petty officer muttered.

"Poem," Joe behind the bar said. "Mr. Wardrop often speak it. It's about when Devil's Gap Battery fired at a German submarine, 1917 or 1918, about then."

"Did they sink it?"

Mr. Wardrop paused in his declamation and said, "No. But they did at least try to, which is more than the navy did when the French fleet passed through the straits in 'forty."

The petty officer sprang to his feet. "Now, look 'ere. . . ."

But Mr. Wardrop was off again:

> " 'Governor's Lookout with a shattering roar
> Hurls its vast projectiles into the black:
> Shrieking they rush on their way overhead
> Woe to the target they meet in their track.' "

"Sit down, chief," Joe said. "Mr. Wardrop don't mean any harm. He not sure what he say this time morning."

Morning, Chaddock thought. What morning? How could anyone tell? He must be on the first shift, then.

"We're the only people doing any fighting now," the petty officer said belligerently. "Us and the R.A.F."

"It's going badly at sea," Flight said, shaking his head. "The shipping losses are much worse than we're being told, you mark my words."

"It's going badly everywhere," Mr. Wardrop intoned, speaking with the unnatural precision of the permanently drunk. "On land, on sea, and in the air we are being thoroughly defeated. . . . You were arguing just now about this war being fought for the Jews. Well, Corporal Pember here will tell you that's a damned lie. The war is being fought for the apes."

"You will have your little joke," the corporal said sullenly. "But everyone in the world knows about that prophecy, about when the apes go, we'll lose Gib. The pack's down to ten now, and still the fucking civilians complain about them. There's this fellow . . ."

"Some fucking civilians think they have more rights than fucking monkeys," Joe the owner muttered.

The Ape Corporal swept on: ". . . Pasarelli on Lopez's Ramp. An ape on his roof, he reports, and will we get it off because it's making messes on the roof where he collects his drinking water. So I go. To see on the roof they has to open a trapdoor and I stand on a toilet. The ape's there, it's Tony, one of the young males who's been kept off the females by Monty. . . ."

"Don't talk to me about females," Flight groaned. "How many

are there on this bloody Rock, not counting the señoritas? Twenty-seven, to twenty thousand men. All nurses, all look like the north end of a tram going south, and all bloody military. And even with that, every time I see one I get a hard-on you could hang your hat on."

Joe said, "Our women all sent away 1940—two years. You go back England this year, next year. Not us."

"So Pasarelli claims I broke his toilet bowl with my hobnail boots, but I was wearing P.T. shoes, see?"

"Wouldn't matter what Pasarelli say," Joe said. "He only bloody Gibraltarian."

"Rock scorpion," Mr. Wardrop said. "Great name. Be proud of it. Sting!"

The petty officer said, "You bloody Brylcreem boys don't have much to boast about, come to that. The Jerries are dropping bombs on England just where they fucking like, and . . ."

". . . so the Governor replies, no, in principle he has no objection to the next male apelet which is born to be called Anthony, after Anthony Eden. But the C.R.A. says . . ."

1942

". . . never saw so many ruddy airplanes in one place in all my bleeding life. The ruddy airfield's full of them. You couldn't fit another in with a shoehorn." The infantry sergeant drank thirstily.

"You're not supposed to see them," Flight said, brushing up his gingerish R.A.F. mustache.

"I'd have to be blind, man! My platoon's on the Upper Galleries, and we're looking straight down on them. They've been flying off all day today."

"No Spanish laborers in town. First time that happen, ever."

"What! No señoritas, either? Christ. I've been saving up for a month to carry a bag tonight! Christ, I was going to fill one of them señoritas up to the ruddy brim tonight!"

"It's the invasion of North Africa," Mr. Wardrop said.

"Here, here, *cuidado*," Joe said, pointing to a sign tacked up behind the bar: *Loose talk costs lives.*

The Ape Corporal said, "I knew it was coming. Had a Yank

general up day before yesterday to inspect the apes. Didn't look too much different from one himself, if you ask me."

Chaddock drank up. The first ten minutes every day in the Star & Garter were like a foreign holiday, a breath of fresh air, a dramatic change from the harsh tunnel and his barren quarters. But soon a sense of unease would begin to possess him, and then it was time to drink up and get out. Whatever it was they talked or fought about here was unreal; the people themselves were unreal—they didn't exist, and being among them made him wonder whether he did. Only rock was real. He lit another cigarette, paid, and went out. He was smoking too much. God, how long, how long?

Inside the Rock he tramped along the drive under the lights. Gradually the pub and its sounds faded into dream. A little diesel loco puttered past on its way to the spoil box with half a dozen tubs. Lieutenant Glass passed on his way out. "We made eight feet on the shift," he said triumphantly.

Major Hughes was watching the shifts hand over at the face. He came back to Chaddock and said, "Glass's lot made eight feet."

"I know," Chaddock said curtly. "He just told me."

Hughes said, "You've got to increase your yardage overall, Chaddock. Tunneling H.Q.'s on my back all the time. We've given you the loaders, and the yardage ought to go up fifty percent, but you're only up twenty-three percent."

Chaddock's head ached, and he wanted to shout in the other's face, but he controlled himself and said, "I'll improve the figures."

"For all our sakes," Hughes said, a little more gently. "The C.E.'s biting Tunneling H.Q., and the Governor's biting the C.E., and Winston's probably biting the Governor. You're just the chap at the bottom of the pile."

He left, and Chaddock went to look at the men working on development head No. 42, Black Watch Raise. What the hell could he do to increase the yardage? . . . Train the men to work the new loaders more efficiently. Keep the drills sharper. Place and fire the charges more quickly. Hughes had said he was at the bottom of the pile, but he wasn't—that man there was, the man with the drill at the face, the mucker, the loco driver. . . . Those diesels cleaned their own exhausts of everything except carbon monoxide. That was okay for the face men as long as the ventilation, natural or artificial, was working well; but for the loco drivers, sitting right behind the exhaust, it must be different. And the ventilation *wasn't* working well, especially in the development heads. The metal ducts were not doing the job, and how the hell could man or machine work without air? At 300 feet from the air pump, rubberized canvas increased ventilation by 400 percent. Quite apart from that, it could be taken down before blasting and put together again afterward in a quarter the time of metal. How long since he had put all this in his report? Four months, three months? And still no canvas ducting.

"You look as though you just swallowed a dose of paregoric, captain."

Sergeant Farley's face was dim under the helmet lamp. "We had two men go to hospital yesterday," Chaddock said, "and the medical report says bronchitis for both of them."

The sergeant said, "It's just a chill on their chests."

"Are you sure the doctors aren't lying?"

"Captain, what are you saying?"

"I'm saying they're so bloody keen to win their bloody K.C.B.'s that they may have told any doctor who finds a trace of silicosis in our men to say it's something else so they won't have to start wet-drilling."

The sergeant chuckled. "Ee, that's a booger of a notion! . . . P'raps ye'd better be taking a holiday, sir."

Chaddock said, "We've got to increase our yardage, sergeant. Come to my office after shift." He walked back to the main drive. Some rails needed replacing before a loco got derailed. The concrete floor of the spoil box was getting damaged. It ought to be relaid before the rails came loose and caught a tub load, or they'd have hell's own job freeing it.

At the end of the drive he turned left, strode into the company offices, knocked on Major Hughes' door, and walked in without waiting. "When are we going to get the Meco rubberized ducting?" he snapped.

Major Hughes looked up frowning from a pile of papers on his table. He took off his glasses, and his Welsh accent was strong. "When we are sent it from U.K.," he said. "And, Chaddock, it is customary to call your company commander 'sir.' "

"Fuck that," Chaddock said. "The C.E. told me to investigate the rubber ducting. I did. You saw my report. You saw the Tunneling H.Q.'s forwarding letter saying we must have the Meco at once. Why haven't we got it?"

"Because there isn't any for us, yet," Hughes said. "We have been allotted a priority below . . ."

"Below what, for Christ's sake? Are they tunneling in the desert? . . . Another thing, here we are trying to improve our yardage a few percent by cutting safety corners, fiddling about with old-fashioned methods. Is anyone investigating what we could do with diamond-drill techniques?"

"That's only suitable for blasting big chambers."

"That's what is said now, because that's what the Canadians did. But who knows what the limitations are? Who's been working to find out? Give me a diamond-drill team and I'll . . ."

Hughes stood up. "Look you, Chaddock, I have work to do, and I bloody know you have, too. When you have done your own work, it is time to think about taking on other responsibilities, eh? Now get back . . ." He peered more closely at Chaddock. "Look, man, I'm sorry. We are all tired. I have bad news, you know. My wife . . . well, that's war, too."

"I'm sorry," Chaddock muttered, because it was a reflex response to the other's tone. He had no idea what Hughes was talking about.

"Why don't you take a couple of days off? Sit on the beach behind the barbed wire, eh? Have your batman bring you tea in bed. Go along now."

Joan was waiting for him when he arrived at the door of the nurses' quarters. It was a levanter day, sun shining everywhere but on Gibraltar. She was in Q.A. uniform and examined him critically. "You look tired. Are you suffering from night starvation?" She giggled and said, "All you men are, really, aren't you?"

He tried to smile but couldn't manage it. Her energy sometimes wearied him. They had met soon after he arrived in Gibraltar, and something had clicked between them at once. Two or three times they had even managed to make love in the dark on the hillside, but it was not important for either of them, and Chaddock sometimes wondered why.

She rested her hand on his sleeve and then took it away. "Oh dear, officers mustn't walk hand in hand, must they?"

"You look a little down yourself," he said.

Her mouth tightened to the professional calm, cool feeling. "Oh, we had some merchant seamen brought in," she said, "rather badly burned. There was no room for them in the naval hospital. . . . It was quite exhausting, and several of us were on extra shifts. . . ."

He had heard a badly burned man once, for two days, and said, "I don't know how you can . . ."

She interrupted brightly, "Isn't Lower St. Michael's Cave marvelous?" They fell into step together and started down the road to Europa Point. She was tall, well made, and blond, rather like his mother. "The sapper officer who took us in said there are hundreds of caves on Gibraltar."

He said, "There must be. It's all Jurassic limestone, and limestone gets eaten away by water—chemical reaction. There are a few minor faults, but nothing we can't get through, except one in there"—he nodded at Windmill Hill—"where we've run into trouble, but . . ."

She said, "Now don't talk shop, Sam. Look at the flowers. Look at that funny little cucumber." She stooped to pick a furry green cucumber three inches long. It leaped into the air with a sharp pop, and she jumped back with a gasp. A blob of creamy white liquid lay in her palm. She blushed and wiped it on the grass. "Goodness, that gave me a turn. What is it?"

"I have no idea," Sam said.

They walked on around the level Europa flat. "Well," she said, pointing, "*that's* an autumn crocus. You know, if you dry those stamens, that's saffron."

He smiled, more easily now. She smelled of soap and water, not very feminine, but at any rate different from miners' sweat and limestone dust and gelignite fumes. She was about thirty and definitely in the marriage market. If he married her she'd be Mrs. Chaddock. Or should it be Mrs. Crapp? Perhaps she'd mind that as much as his mother had. He frowned, remembering the flight sergeant's story in the pub. Could his father have changed his name twice?

Joan said, "You're not listening. You're always daydreaming, Sam. What is it now?"

He said, "I was wondering who I am."

"What? . . . Are you feeling all right, Sam?"

"My father changed his name right after he came to England from South Africa. Mother says she refused to marry him unless he did, but I think he may have done something disreputable in South Africa."

"What was his name before?" she asked, suddenly suspicious.

He said, "It took me ages before he'd tell me—Crapp."

She laughed, obviously relieved. "I thought for a moment he might have been a Jew. I can't stand Jews."

"Nor can my mother," he said. "That's what makes me wonder."

They walked on, round and round. Joan was fit and brave and clean and honest. She would face up to the Nazis come hell or high water. She was indomitable, admirable.

"Wonder what?"

He said, "Whether my father had changed his name twice. Who he *really* is, in other words. So, who *I* am. One reason I think my father did something bad in South Africa is that he's always been a maniac for respectability, for doing the right thing. Of course my mother may have caused that. . . . He made his pile in gold and diamonds, but my God, he's turned himself into a country squire. He reads books but pretends not to so the fox-hunting crowd will take to him. I was to inherit everything . . . Darley Court, the squiredom, Joint Master of the Ted-worth, the lot. I went through Eton and Cambridge, then I wanted to do something real . . ." He was talking to himself now. "Real, with my hands. With my brain. I went to mining school. I became a mining engineer. Father nearly died of chagrin. And, do you know, until I got my degree I didn't even know he had made his loot in mining! Am I me or my father over again? Or someone else?"

They walked round and round. After two hours they returned to the quarters. When he kissed her good-bye, she said, "I think you'd better take a good dose of Epsom salts, Sam, and ask for a couple of days off. I'll take two days at the same time, and we'll play tennis all day. . . ."

Sam went to his quarters. Constipation as the root of all disquiet. It was an old female shibboleth, and Joan was female to the tips of her toes, in spite of the outward severities.

He sat down at his table and found his writing pad. He had to know. The doubt had been drilling into his mind all day— through the talk with Farley, through the scene with Hughes, all the time with Joan; especially with Joan. After what she had said, if he cared for her, he must get down behind the face, tunnel through the dark, reach the open.

"Dear Father," he wrote, *"What was your name before it was Crapp?"*

1943

" 'Swift is the flash that lights up the obscurity
Sudden in answer the echoing roar
Where ye light hearted ones now your security
Mind ye tonight the world is at war?
Thunder the monsters aloft on the Ridge
Echo the pop guns below on the Moles,
Jews, Buffadero, Levant . . .' "

"What's that about Jews?" Chaddock snapped, thumping his tankard down on the counter and half-standing.

Mr. Wardrop eyed him owlishly. "Name of a battery, my boy. Jews' Battery. Joe, another gin for me, and a pint for Captain Whatsisname here. You're looking a mite distray tonight, captain."

"I've got things on my mind," Chaddock said shortly.

"Wouldn't you find it more congenial, shall we say, in the Piccadilly? That's the officers' pub."

"I came here first with some Canadians, officers and O.R.'s together," Chaddock said. "They didn't give a damn for this separate officers' pub business, and nor do I." He turned his back.

"I hear you're importing apes from Morocco," a petty officer said to the Ape Corporal.

The Ape Corporal nodded. "Yes, we are. On Winston's orders, express. Though mind, getting the ones already here to accept the new ones so they can settle in, that's another kettle of fish. We put them together in threes, the ones from Morocco, 'cause their coats aren't so thick as ours, and they can huddle together for warmth. . . ."

"It wasn't warmth I saw two of 'em huddling together for," the petty officer said. "It was you know what. So Gibraltar's safe again."

Old Sergeant Tamlyn said, "Those monkeys are nobbut a damn nuisance. It's the Barbary partridge we ought to be saving. There are too many people on the Rock, so the hens can't sit."

A sergeant-major of signals turned to the petty officer. "Had a little trouble with the Italians, haven't you?" he said.

The sailor said, "No."

"I see a ship's mast and funnels sticking out of the water outside the Detached Mole. What happened?"

The sailor ostentatiously turned his back. Flight said, "Eyetie frogmen. It took our noble bluejackets rather a long time to find out."

The petty officer said "Fuck you," and stalked out, slamming the door behind him.

Mr. Wardrop said, "Seeing that you Brylcreem boys can't fly a Polish general a hundred yards without killing him, I don't think you've got much to boast about."

"Thank God for our allies. Look at the Russians! Look at Stalingrad!"

"What about Alamein?"

"What about Arakan?"

"Eighteen months and I haven't seen a bit of skirt."

"Three and a half years for us," Joe said. "But things looking better, maybe. Today the army asked me if okay to strengthen my roof, to put anti-aircraft Bren gun up there. Last year, they do it, don't ask. Someone smell the end of war, maybe."

"This is not the beginning of the end, but it is the end of the beginning."

Mr. Wardrop said, "This is better than any female in the world." He raised his gin glass. "What woman could have written

'Down in the city, lights are a-twinkle,
Hums the close hive with the evening's affairs . . .'"

"And they're *tough!* We had to put Monty down. Three bananas loaded with nembutal. Another shot full of cyanide. He just acted a little sozzled. A couple of days later . . ."

Chaddock slammed down his tankard so hard that it shattered. Beer splashed his tunic and Joe's face and Flight's feet.

"Shut up, shut up!" he yelled.

"Here, here! What the . . ."

"Hey!"

The lights swung in front of Chaddock's eyes. "Apes. Skirts. Stand here filling your bellies with beer. We are in the presence of EVIL," he shouted. "This . . . Hitler . . . this is not a war for glory . . . not a cup final. We are fighting the most evil thing in the history of the world. Until it's burned out, it affects us all, we're all unclean because we're all human, too, like him."

He stopped, his hands clenched at his side. Joe was mopping up the counter. Flight said awkwardly, "We're all with you, sir. . . . I mean, none of us want to invite Hitler to tea, you know. Here, take a seat."

Chaddock stared at them, their faces wavering. The lights grew bright, dim. He ran for the door and out.

Chaddock felt a little more solid on his feet as soon as he entered the tunnel, and the gradually growing stutter of the drills acted to settle his jangling nerves. By the time he came near the face he felt sure of his balance and did not wonder at every step why he was not falling.

The round of charges were set, and the explosives were being tamped in. Three men were dismantling the last hundred feet of the ventilation ducting. He glowered at the work, for it was still the sheet-metal type.

"Who are you?"

The voice was in his ear. He wheeled round. "Conquy," he said.

Major Hughes frowned. "This is Captain Chaddock, sir. My second-in-command."

"Is your name Conquy or Chaddock? Or do you mean conky, C.O.N.K.Y? . . . I'm Greenway, the new C.E." Chaddock saluted.

The whistle blew for the safety check. Everyone started to move back behind the safety line. The new chief engineer was round and youngish and popeyed. "What delays are you using?" he asked.

"Zero in the cut, one-second easers, two top outers, three side outers, four bottom outers."

"It works well? Leaves a clean advance?"

"Clean enough. There's no need to have the walls smooth as a house corridor, is there?"

The C.E. poked out a thick forefinger. "What you civilian mining engineers have got to understand is that the basic principle of military mining is exactly the opposite of what you have been brought up in."

"It's the time that matters, not the cost," Major Hughes said, quoting the previous chief engineer's favorite dictum.

Chaddock said, "Hole not string."

"Eh? By God yes, that's it. In normal mining, your object is to extract a valuable substance—coal, ore, whatever. The shape of the hole doesn't matter, *per se*. In military mining your object is to make a valuable hole. The shape or value of quantity of the extract doesn't matter, *per se*. . . . Hole, not string, like a net. Very good."

A whistle blew again, and Sergeant Farley intoned, "Blasting. All clear?"

"All clear."

Farley pressed the firing plunger. A series of cracks echoed sharply down the tunnel, followed by a short, heavy rumble. A cloud of gray dust and fumes hid the face. "Nineteen fired," a voice cried.

"Fuck!" Sergeant Farley said.

" 'Twas one of the easers missed, gaffer."

Chaddock lit a cigarette. Now they had to find the misfired detonator in the mass of fallen rubble and extract it and after it the actual charge.

"The detonator's in the top of the charge?" Hughes asked anxiously.

Chaddock said, "That's where we always put it."

"This is the sort of thing that makes six hundred cubic yards a week hard to keep up," the C.E. said.

"There'd be fewer delays if we had electric detonators," Chaddock said.

"We've asked for them."

A miner standing close by, dragging at a tiny stub of cigarette, said, "It's nothin' to do with the bloody charges, man. It's the ghost."

"Ghost?" the C.E. said cheerily. "What ghost?"

"There's a naked woman runs about with her mouth open," the miner said. "She's the one who fucks up the drillpoints and derails the tubs and snuffs out the fuses."

"Does she have a name?" the brigadier asked.

"Aye. The ghost of Thompson's Raise, we call her, 'cos that's where she were first saw. The officer had a dog with him, and suddenly the dog started whining and whimpering as though he'd seen . . . a ghost. Since then that bloody woman's been seen in every raise and winze and drive in the Rock."

Chaddock said, "It's not a ghost holding us up. It's unnecessary delays. Spit and polish. Old-fashioned methods. Nondelivery of what we need. Look at these ventilator ducts. I put in a special urgent report in January, 1941. The air flow at three hundred feet from source was six hundred thirty cubic feet a minute with this stuff, and *two thousand six hundred cubic feet* a minute with rubberized canvas. How the hell can the men be expected to work without enough air?"

"Chaddock!" Major Hughes said warningly.

"No, no, I like an officer to speak his mind," the C.E. said. "I've got to go now. Walk back a little way with me, Chaddock."

They started down the tunnel. Chaddock kept talking, because he could not stop. He was aware that the brigadier was looking at him under the passing lights, rather than listening, though every now and then he murmured Yes, or No, or Quite. "One size rip bit only, one and a half inch diameter," Chaddock babbled, "No steel transport, use the drill sharpening shop only for reshanking the rip rods. . . . Hand drills, Holman SL 9 or something like, instead of the sledges . . . compressors in banks, three point five gallons diesel oil per hour for the Ingersoll Rand . . . drifters . . . two fans in parallel, short Y junction . . ."

"Are you a regular?" the C.E. said. "I thought I only had three in Gib. Where were you at school?"

"Eton!" Chaddock shouted. His hands were shaking violently, and he could not hold them still. "What the hell does it matter where I went to school? We're in the presence of Evil! . . .

That's the ghost of Thompson's Raise—Evil, Evil! And all you can do is ask where I went to school. And in the pub, about monkeys . . . the . . . the . . ."

The brigadier took his arm. Chaddock felt hot tears running down his cheek. "Been overdoing it a bit, eh?" the brigadier said. "Come along, old chap. Here, Fanshaw, give me a hand. There. Sit back."

He sat in the back of the staff car, his hands held tight between his knees. A green room. Two years, three months, twenty-one days. Tunneling all the time? Yes, sir. Tunneling Company? Of course. Airplanes roaring overhead continuously. Must be imaginary. One hundred and seventy-five feet, 7/8-inch riprod, climax stopers and 1-inch steel, 4.9 tons, cubic yards, rock, rock . . .

The window was open, and there were red flowers in a box outside. He sat in an armchair. They ought not to keep books away from him, surely? A man's mind couldn't be stopped turning by depriving him of books. That would only make it go round and round, instead of along the lines of the author's thought. The Spanish hills were brown across the bay. A coastal steamer had just cleared Algeciras Harbor, heading outside Europa Point, the Spanish colors of red and yellow painted huge on its side. The sky was still full of aircraft, and their droning went on day and night.

Joan came in and sat beside him. "Don't get up. . . . How are we feeling this afternoon? Good. You look better, too."

She was nice, strong, no nonsense, everything clear: black, white—good, bad—us, them. Impossible to imagine her wondering who, or why, she was. Perhaps if you lived with her, you wouldn't worry either, because she would tell you, and you'd believe.

"Everything's going well," she said, "except at Casablanca."

"Eh? What's that? . . . Oh, the African invasion."

"You poor dear, there's a war on, you know. They thought that's what was on your mind. You were gabbling a lot about evil, you know."

"Not the kind of thing one talks about," Sam said. "Sin. Crime. But not evil."

She said, "You've been working too hard. You didn't even know your own name, the nurse who admitted you told me. She said you kept telling her it was Conky."

"It is," he said. "Or should be. C.O.N.Q.U.Y. An old Jewish family of Gibraltar."

Her voice rose. "You're joking."

"You remember when I told you my father changed his name? I wrote that same day asking him what it was before that."

"And it was . . . Conquy? I've seen the name on one of the houses here. Why didn't you tell me? Where's the letter?"

"I don't know," he said. The light was growing bright, dim. "Months ago. I . . . thought I had the letter, but then I couldn't find it. Must have torn it up, burned it, at once. . . ."

She said, "So that's why you've been so odd. And I thought it was just overwork."

His brain was missing its gears. He said, "Overwork, yes. Turning my world, my views, upside down. Listening to all the talk about Jews, but I *am* one. Hitler. What happens if we lose . . . Suddenly, Joan, I began to understand, to feel, evil."

She was surreptitiously wiping tears from the corner of her eye with a handkerchief. "Mustn't excite you, Major Borthwick told me," she said. She got up to go.

He said, "I'm not the same man I was, Joan, but I feel the same about you as I did before."

She ran out of the room.

Patriotism is not enough, Sam repeated to himself. Nurse Cavell, 1915. I say unto you . . . Blood toil sweat tears. Not enough either. Vengeance is mine saith the Lord. Suppose we tried wedge cuts instead of pyramid? Easers have a burden of three feet, yet they fall, so . . .

1944

Chaddock nodded, and Joe refilled his glass. Chaddock took the letter from his pocket and read it again. It was plain enough. His father had many faults, but he'd never known him to lie. So it must be the truth.

"D Day at last!" a corporal of the Devons shouted. "Now we'll show 'em."

"Up the 49th," shouted old Sergeant Tamlyn, whom no one had ever seen drunk.

"*Roll out the barrel, we'll all have a barrel of fun.*"

"Hoo-bloody-ray, same again!"

"Make more quiet please, or M.P.'s come."

"Fuck the M.P.'s. Another pint, Joe."

Mr. Wardrop said, "Perhaps within my life-span on this accursed Rock we shall be getting some decent Holland gin again, the best, the only *real* gin, my friend. Where was I?"

" '*Death to the submarine . . .* ' "

"Ah, yes.

> 'Death to the submarine out in the night
> Death to the crafty piratical foe
> Swiftly we bring you the murderer's fate
> Death to the slayer of mother and babe
> Death to the Hun who has taught us to hate.'

How's that for a lambasting? They ought to recite that in the synagogues, eh, captain?"

Chaddock smiled faintly. He had told them all that his real name ought to be Conquy, though the Conquys in Gibraltar hadn't made any rush to claim him. In his only effort to establish contact, Mr. Conquy the jeweler had indicated politely that there was no trace of any member of the Gibraltar clan who could possibly have been his father, in South Africa or anywhere else. Well, that again tended to confirm this second letter. But what about the first? Had it not existed?

The Ape Corporal said, "So you will all be glad to hear that the apes are increasing. We shall win the . . ."

"We '*ave* won!" a private yelled.

"Must have," Joe said sourly. "Yesterday an officer say he recommend me for medal. And Mr. Carlotti pay me back two pound he owe. Must be going to be an election soon."

"These apes have got brains. On New Year's Eve last year you know what one did? A young male called Pat. He tried to cross the boom that blocks the entrance to the Admiralty dockyard."

"Must have been a skirt on the other side."

"Gawd, that word's like a spanner. Every time someone says 'skirt' me nuts tighten."

"'The navy's better at keeping the ruddy apes where they belong than the ruddy French. . . .'"

His words ended in a yell. "Here, what do you . . . ?" and that in turn cut off by a fist smashed into his nose. The bar was full of bluejackets. Fists flew, glasses smashed, tables overturned. "You dirty pongo," a sailor near Chaddock snarled. His fist flashed out. Behind the bar Joe picked up the telephone and spoke a few words in it.

> " 'Narrows the circle of flashes and flame
> Closer and closer the columns of spray,' "

chanted Mr. Wardrop.

> " 'Whitey gray monsters from out of the deep
> Ghosts of dead mariners claiming their prey.' "

A voice in Chaddock's ear shouted, "Here's another of them bastards in the shit-colored suits." A hand gripped his shoulder, then the voice said, "Christ, it's a fucking officer."

Chaddock felt suddenly hilarious. This was ridiculous and childish and atavistic, but it wasn't evil. He jerked out of his battle-dress blouse and said, "Now I'm not an officer, you bloody matlo. I'm a Royal Jewish Engineer. Take that!" He landed a good solid blow on the sailor's nose. Then the M.P.'s burst in.

Chaddock walked through the portal, went to the pick-up station, and waited. Half a dozen miners were waiting already for the lorries that shuttled up and down the subterranean Great North Road carrying men to their shifts. They talked and smoked quietly. More came in from the open. Chaddock read his letter again under a bright bare bulb, shook his head, and put it away.

He looked around. There was something strange about tonight. Coming into the tunnel had not made him feel secure, that was it. For weeks, months, years, entry into the Rock had been recontact with reality, escape from an airy false world of emotions, of loyalties and jealousies, envies and fears, hunger and greed, hope and despair, all equally unreal.

Here inside the Rock—this very rock he leaned against, touch-

ing with his fingers—there were only air, light, heat, rock—
reality, he had thought. But today it was the tunnel that seemed
unreal, a glittering, beautiful, visionary elfland, and the lusts
and angers and hilarity of the pub that were real. What was reality? Take the first letter from his father. Was that real or not?
Had he imagined it? And if he had, did that make it unreal, for
had it not changed his manner of living, his posture of being?

"Are ye no' coming, sir?"

The lorry was here and he climbed up into the back. He recognized Sapper Tim Althorne, a long cut over his right eye. Tim
held up his hand, showing raw knuckles. "That were a good fight
in the Moon and Bloomers," he said grinning. "Best I seen since
I left Blaydon. . . . I saw you gi' that sailor something to remember you by!"

Sergeant Farley was already at the face, marking out the next
round. Lieutenant Glass came away, lighting a cigarette. He was
a tough capable young officer now. "You'll reach daylight, Sam,"
he said. "The brass hats will be here in strength to watch."

The drills started stammering, and Sam made a cursory tour
of inspection. Methods had changed for the better, and he could
take credit for a little of it. Holman hand drills instead of jackhammers; rip bits and studs, so the power tool could be worked
longer hours: power loaders instead of picks and shovels: compressed air winches on the loaders when the gradient permitted,
and static winches beyond that: and of course diesel locos instead
of hand tramming to and from the spoil boxes—he could hear
the steady chugging of one of them behind him now; electric
detonation instead of fuse; good ventilation . . . that had been
his real baby, the thing he had fought for all his time. He
glanced up at the canvas ducting; that was the stuff, and to some
extent he could take the credit. He coughed and mopped his
face. It was hot here, near the surface. The drillers were resting
more often than usual, too.

The telephone bell down the tunnel rang, and a voice
shouted, "Captain Chaddock, Sergeant Farley, the major wants
you both."

Farley joined him with a cheerful, "The buggers can only
shoot us, sir." They set off together down the long tunnel. The
company offices were in a deep bay off the Street, designed for

use as headquarters for combat commands under full siege conditions.

Major Hughes stood up as they came in. He smiled and put out his hand. "Good news for both of you. You're both going on repat, on the next boat. They never say when that'll be, but between ourselves I hear a convoy'll be in the day after tomorrow."

Chaddock shook the proffered hand automatically. "Is that all?" he said. Had Hughes brought them away from the face just to hear this?

"No," the major said with a little frown. "You've been awarded the M.B.E., Chaddock, and sergeant, you've got the B.E.M."

Sergeant Farley made a comic face. "Gaffer Farley, B.E.M.? The buggers'll laugh me out of the cage, back home."

"Thanks," Chaddock said absently. It was becoming more unreal every moment.

"You deserve it," Hughes said. "It's for your work to improve our methods here, of course, particularly in ventilation. Now, I want to go through the company stores list and a few other things with you while we're waiting for the C.E. and the tunneling adviser. You'd better get back to the face, sergeant."

They sat down and set to work.

After a couple of hours the telephone rang. Hughes picked it up. "Company commander. Yes. All right." He said to Chaddock, "They're ready to blast. I told them you'd be right along. But wait till we arrive before you fire."

A couple of hundred yards before he reached the face Chaddock passed the diesel loco that trammed the tubs. The engine was running, but he could see no driver. Glancing back after he had passed, he stopped, stared, and ran.

The driver of the loco had fallen from his seat. His head was on the ground, his feet up on the machine's side. It was Tim Althorne. The diesel fut-futted steadily on. Four hundred feet away the rest of the shift sat near the face, smoking, talking, and laughing animatedly.

Chaddock felt the man's heart. It was beating, but faintly and irregularly. His own heart pounded painfully, for he knew at once what had happened. He yelled, "Farley, send two men back to the loco, at the double. Phone for the oxygen crew."

A voice spoke over Chaddock's shoulder. "What's happened?"

He looked up. It was the brigadier, with Colonel Baines, the tunneling adviser. "Carbon monoxide," he said.

Farley ran up. "They're sending the oxygen right away, sir."

The C.E. said, "Turn off that damned thing." The diesel puttering stopped. "Don't move him for a moment, just lie him down properly. Disconnect those ducts, there, and let's have some air."

They waited. A truck engine raced in the Great North Road, then they heard boots, running. The stretcher team with the doctor and the oxygen arrived.

The C.E. said, "You'd better start an investigation as soon as we've blown, Hughes."

Chaddock walked ahead of them toward the face. At the forward fans he said, "Help me get these down, Farley."

"But, sir . . ." Farley began.

Chaddock shook his head wearily. "Thanks, sergeant, but I don't want to be protected." They brought a fan down. Chaddock looked at it, knowing what he would find. It was clogged with dust and grease. The other one was the same. He showed them to the C.E. "These fans have to be cleaned every forty-eight hours if there's to be proper ventilation at the face," he said. "I proved that in forty-two. I had it written into the regulations here. I'm responsible for seeing that it's done. Last time, I forgot. Everyone trusted me, because I'm the expert on ventilation. . . . If Althorne's dead, I've killed him."

It was the business of the letter, he thought, that had made his mind wander; but that was no excuse.

The C.E. said, "You haven't killed anyone, Chaddock. You made a mistake, perhaps. We'll find out. Now blow the round. I want to see daylight."

The others crowded round the exploder. Farley stayed behind with Chaddock. "Don't take it so hard, sir," he said. "It's a bugger, but these things happen, tha' knows. Tim'll pull through."

"No thanks to me," Chaddock said.

The tunnel shook and shivered and rumbled. A current of strong, fresh air began to move up from behind. The miners raised a ragged cheer.

"Come on, Chaddock. Let's take a look. After fifteen thousand seven hundred twenty-nine feet, that's the least we deserve."

Chaddock crawled on hands and knees over the pile of rubble. The dawn light was spreading, and the sun was close below the rim of the violet sea. The drive had reached the open air.

"Look at this," a miner said. "The poor wee bugger." He held up a small skull. "A bairn. It's been here a long time, any road."

"That's the ghost's baby," the C.E. said jovially. "Give it a decent burial and you'll have no more trouble."

He held out his hand to Chaddock. "Congratulations. I'll be sorry to lose you. . . . You've got to *care*, Chaddock, but not worry."

The sun burst out of the sea, and Chaddock yawned mightily.

At Jews' Gate, when the sentry was checking their identity cards, Chaddock said, "We're going to look at the cemetery first."

"Very good, sir." The soldier handed back the documents and saluted.

The flat tombstones were jammed together so tight that there was no path between. To get through the cemetery you had to walk on them. He peered down at the eroded Hebrew lettering, and Joan said, "Good heavens, have you learned to read those squiggles?" He did not answer. The cemetery had been abandoned nearly thirty years earlier, the Conquys had told him. It lay on the hillside above Windmill Hill Flats, looking toward Africa. Autumn crocus flowered in the crevices, and thorn bushes and scrub were creeping in to cover the stones.

After a time she led impatiently out of the cemetery and back onto Martin's Path. They walked one behind the other around the slope, past the deserted, ancient gun of the Levant Battery, past tangles of rusty barbed wire, past empty sentry posts and unoccupied machine-gun positions, dandelions and coarse grass growing in the torn sandbags.

"It looks as if they think it's all over," he said to her back, "but it may be a long time yet."

She said, "Last Tuesday the matron asked me whether I wanted to go on repat. I'm past due, if I want to take it."

He said, "I'm going home."

"Oh . . . You didn't tell me."

"They only told me this morning. . . . On the next boat. The day after tomorrow, perhaps."

She led up the narrow ledge to Martin's Cave and turned. Her face was deep red. She said, "What do you mean, you're going home? Isn't Gibraltar your home? Aren't your people here?"

He said, "No, Joan, but—"

She said, "I . . . I . . . said I'd stay on in Gib . . . because . . . oh damn . . . because of you . . . and now, and now . . . you're going away. I might have . . . expected it from a, a, a . . . dirty Jew!"

He said, "Will you marry me, Joan?"

She turned her back violently. He took her shoulders, holding her gently and making no attempt to turn her to face him. "Look, darling," he said, "if I've learned anything inside this Rock the last three and a half years, it is that if you're going to stay human, you have to hold onto what's good, even if it's stupid and isn't working out right, and you have to reject what's evil, however well it works, however easy it is to take it or let it take over. I think we love each other, or can, and that's good. I think we have had, and still have, fears and prejudices, and that's bad. Let's work out the good."

He swung her round gently and lifted her chin. She was a big woman, and he knew she was surrendering because he couldn't have pulled her round or lifted her chin if she hadn't wanted him to. She looked past him at the vertiginous eight-hundred-foot drop at his heels and jerked him to her, snapping, "Come back, Sam!"

He turned and looked down. There was the mouth of Arow Street, and there, just inside, was the end of the tunnel he'd been working in all the war; or should he say trapped in all his life?

They kissed, long and delicately. She was warm and experienced. He released her and gave her the letter from his pocket. "Read it."

She read it, holding it up to the light; and again. "I don't understand," she said. "Are you or not?"

"Probably not. Does it matter?"

"Not the way it used to, but everyone ought to know who he is. I suppose that first letter you told us about, from your father, just didn't exist? It was part of your nervous breakdown?"

He pulled her to him and said, "If that was a nervous breakdown, then any time we look at misery and evil and say, 'That's *them*,' not 'That's *us*,' then it'll be time to have another one.''

She hugged him with a bone-breaking eagerness that made him laugh, and they went slowly back to Jews' Gate.

Book Thirteen

❖❖❖❖❖❖❖❖❖❖❖❖❖❖❖❖❖❖❖❖❖❖❖

Foreign Fortress? Puppet Colony? Free People?

The Jewish years 5700–5730
AUC 2693–2723
A.D. 1940–1970
A.H. 1359–1390

DURING World War II the military tunnels in the Rock were increased from a total length of 4 miles to over 25 miles. The biggest single work was the driving of the Great North Road, which runs the length of the Rock from northwest to southeast, about 400 feet above sea level. It is, like all the recent work, a vehicular tunnel, with passing places, light, power cables, and water pipes. It is the spine of Gibraltar, with other tunnels (adits, winzes, raises, and galleries, in the delightful mining jargon) taking off on both sides, some to the open air, some to other tunnels at upper or lower levels, some to form great or small bays.

The object of these works, of course, was to enable Gibraltar to withstand a siege by modern weapons. To that end the engineers excavated sites for barracks, storehouses, magazines, power stations, headquarters, hospitals, offices—everything that would be needed under full siege conditions. The hardness of the limestone enabled very large galleries to be excavated without roof supports. One, containing vehicle workshops, is some 400 feet long by 80 feet wide. Inside these places it is hard to believe one is in a cave, because the engineers found that it paid to put up conventional walls, roof, and floor inside the tunnel—to keep out the damp and to enable all the wiring, plumbing, lights, power outlets, and so on to be hung, put, or fastened on something easier to work than the rock.

The names bestowed on these works often give a clue to their history: *Jock's Balcony*—built by the Black Watch: *Jellalabad Tunnel*—built by the Somerset Light Infantry (Jellalabad is their chief battle honor): *Arow Street*—which is not a misprint but is named after an engineer officer, Lieutenant Colonel A. R. O. Williams, who is also commemorated in *Williams' Way*.

Together with the water tunnels, the Admiralty tunnel, and the old North Face galleries, these works make Gibraltar the most formidably honeycombed place on earth. And these are only the works of man. The number of natural caves seems to be without limit, and the only boundary to the discovery of new ones is the number of man-hours Gibraltarians are disposed to put into the task. One of the finest was revealed by chance in 1940, when it was planned to use St. Michael's Cave as an emergency hospital. A new operating theater with its own exit tunnel had to be blasted out below. While making the tunnel, the engineers found that they had blown in the roof of another huge cave system, hitherto unknown. The new cave, Lower St. Michael's, is a miracle of softly tinted limestone, shaped into a thousand forms. At the far end there is a pool of soft, still water. The rock walls plunge sheer into the water, but just below the surface there is a hidden ledge of rimrock extending around the pool, by means of which one can reach the last secret grotto. It is a marvelous place, both in itself and to see one's companions walking on the water!

A recently formed Cave Research Group of the Gibraltar Society is setting about its task with considerable scientific skill and boundless enthusiasm. It is systematically mapping, exploring, and recording full details of the caves, categorizing them as Cavers' Caves, Archaeologists' Caves, or Anyone's Caves (meaning anyone who wants them is welcome). The full report on each cave is pages long, with plans, elevations, and detailed descriptions of the cave's geology, biology, and history; but the brief notes are racy, to the point, and tell the interested person as much as he initially wants to know, thus:

*Boathoist Cave. At sea level, and just north of Governor's
Beach. Access from Boathoist Tunnel, Arow Street. Explored.
Small. High roof-hole needs looking at.* [This cave was prepared
for use as a launching place for VIP's in case they needed to get
into or out of Gibraltar by submarine.]

*Diesel's Pot. Behind the fuel storage tanks in Glen Rocky Dis-
tillery. Explored. Large and Deep.* [Deep indeed . . . it has
been explored to 100 feet below sea level: the mouth is about
250 feet above sea level! Glen Rocky Distillery, alas, distils
nothing healthier than fresh water from seawater.]

*Devil's Dustbin. In the foot of the North Front Face. Extension
in West Chamber. West wall not explored.*

The Cave Researchers achieved their finest hour so far on May
30, 1966, when they went to have another look at Cave S, first
scientifically explored by the archaeologist W. H. Duckworth in
1910. The cave is now extremely difficult to get at, being under
a cliff at the head of the east face catchment area, but the group's
surveyor, George Palao, managed to climb up and found prehistoric engravings on the cave wall. There were representations of
men, fish, boars, and other living things, some covered by a thin
layer of sinter. Precise dating of this art has not yet been done,
but it has been tentatively assigned to between 30,000 and 40,000
B.C.

Perhaps one day the spelunkers will discover a bone statuette
of a naked woman. . . .

But the Cave Research Group and its activities were still in
the future while Hitler's war raged. The raging was mostly at a
long distance from Gibraltar, although the Germans had an
invasion plan, *Felix,* which depended on Franco's cooperation;
he never gave it. Gibraltar's war role was as a way and staging
station and a headquarters for task forces, such as Force H. This
small carrier-battleship-cruiser group was the force which re-
located and crippled the *Bismarck* in April, 1941. When the old
Swordfish torpedo biplanes took off and landed on that operation, the *Ark Royal's* flight deck was rising and falling 60 feet in
heavy seas.

General Eisenhower's headquarters for the assault on Vichy-
held North Africa on November 8, 1942, was at Gibraltar. In re-

turn Gibraltar suffered three air raids, two by the Vichy French and one by the Italians. In anticipation of air raids a little booklet was prepared, giving both the English and Spanish names of streets, for use by fire wardens and others (few Gibraltarians had much English at the time). The booklet shows not only different names, but different ways of thinking. City Mill Lane is the *Calle de los Siete Revueltos* (Street of the Seven Turns), Flat Bastion Road is *La Cuesta de Mr. Bourne* (Mr. Bourne's Ramp), Fraser's Ramp is *Escalera de Benoliel* (Benoliel's Steps), New Passage is *Calle del Peligro* (Street of Danger), and Castle Steps is *Calle de Comedias* (Street of Comedies)—these last two were the brothel areas!

Gibraltar's most interesting war was that fought in secret, under water, between the Italian and British navies, personified by Prince Valerio Borghese on one side and Commander Lionel Crabb on the other. Three times between October, 1940 and September, 1941 Borghese took his submarine into Gibraltar Bay and from it launched piloted torpedoes. One of the torpedoes narrowly failed to get the battleship *Barham* inside the inner harbor, and later efforts did sink three ships, including a large armed motor ship. From mid-1942 Italian frogmen launched from submarines or from Spain placed limpet charges on the bottoms of merchant ships marshaling into convoys in the bay. Several ships were sunk. When the Italians swam ashore in Spain, to be captured by the Spanish police, they were at once released to repeat their gallant but not precisely "neutral" feats.

The previous year the epic of the *Olterra* had begun. She was a small Italian tanker scuttled in Gibraltar Harbor at the outbreak of war, later raised, bought by a Spanish firm or "front," towed across the bay, sold to an Italian firm, and moored alongside the long outer mole of Algeciras. The Italian Navy, with great ingenuity, now turned her into a fitting-out basin and home port for their midget submarines. On December 6, 1941—one day before Pearl Harbor—the *Olterra's* midgets set out for Gibraltar, where the battleship *Nelson* and the fleet carriers *Formidable* and *Furious* were in harbor. But Crabb had devised a system of random firing of depth charges into the harbor approaches twenty-four hours a day. One of them hit a piloted torpedo, killing its crew; the other attackers ran into bad luck; and the operation was an expensive failure for the Italians.

Midget attacks were made from the *Olterra* through August, 1943; all this time, Crabb and his small team were also fighting the frogmen and their limpet charges. Then Marshal Pietro Badoglio took Italy over to the Allied side. The underwater team in Algeciras, like their countrymen at home, were split down the middle in their loyalties and broke up. By then Crabb and Intelligence had guessed that the derelict *Olterra,* apparently manned by a watch and ward crew of half a dozen scruffy Italian merchant seamen, was really the headquarters of the operations, which had been carried out under the noses of the Spanish authorities. Those noses began to be a little more aware of bad smells after Alamein and Stalingrad, but by then the worst was over. (Crabb died as he had lived. He vanished mysteriously on April 19, 1956. He was last seen swimming in Portsmouth Harbor near the Russian cruiser *Ordzhonikidze,* which had brought Khrushchev and Bulganin on a state visit to England.)

In 1945 the United States dropped nuclear bombs on Japan, and the war ended. Britain had already started to repatriate the civilian population of Gibraltar, but so slowly that the people began to stage mass protest meetings for the return of their families. The snail's pace of the repatriation was probably due to the British government's need for time to reassess its attitude to Gibraltar in the light of new conditions. It was not only the weapons of war that were changing. Britain led the way in a worldwide process of decolonialization. Gibraltar had been one of a number of strongpoints and fleet bases guarding the route to India, Australasia, and the Far East. But now India became independent, Australasia turned toward America, and China dominated the far East. England was still a great power, but clearly she was less powerful relative to others than she had been, and a combination of economic and political factors was hastening her decline. She had to consider whether she still needed Gibraltar, whether she could still afford it.

The first consideration was strictly military. What was Gibraltar's worth in the atomic age? In case of actual nuclear attack, the Rock must surely have been classified as "livable but unusable." Men and installations could probably survive inside the limestone, and rockets could be fired out; but no ship or aircraft could survive. This, as we have seen, was the situation even with conventional weapons, that is, that Gibraltar could be held, but not used, against the enmity of Spain or some other power holding the Ceuta-Tangier area. To *use* Gibraltar a large area of Spain and Morocco would have to be cleared.

Provided Spain were neutral or friendly, then, Gibraltar still had a role. By electronic gadgetry it was possible for Gibraltar to detect and prevent all sea passage, both submarine and surface, through the strait. Modern aircraft could fly comfortably from Gibraltar to, say, Israel or Turkey, thus enabling Gibraltar to be used as a staging base for operations throughout the Mediterranean and also in the Canaries-Azores-Morocco area, which has always been a focal point of world shipping lanes.

But if Spain were neutral or friendly, all these operations, and more, could be better carried out from Spanish bases. The key phrase was thus *Spain friendly*.

The dominant Spanish concern with Gibraltar was not military but, as always, political. As Britain had gone relatively downhill, so Spain had come up. She could hardly have moved in any other direction. From the start of her own war in 1936 to the end of World War II in 1945 she had for practical purposes been without external trade or aid. Her matériel was falling to pieces, her morale was shattered. Francisco Franco was able to begin at the bottom, with no opposition. Although antagonism to his regime gradually strengthened as the years passed, the Spanish people at first accepted him and his policies without question. They would have accepted anything rather than face even the faintest chance of such another trauma as the Civil War. The United States' need for air bases out of reach of Russia's then rocket capacity, plus tourism attracted by Spain's starvation-level prices, plus this imposed stability, enabled Spain to climb from a shattered and bankrupt wreck to a reasonably powerful and austerely solvent power of the second class.

In due course Franco decided to tackle the Gibraltar question. Given England's weariness, Spain's desire, the Rock's dubious strategic significance, and the powerful commercial ties between the two countries, there is no doubt that the return of Gibraltar to Spain could have been negotiated but for the intrusion of a third factor into the equation: the people, the Rock Scorpions, the Gibraltarians.

They had had a bad war. The summary evacuations had brought home to them what a century of peace had made them forget: that they were chattels of the military, slaves of the fortress; but it had also given them a new sense of unity and identity.

Gibraltar had changed. We have seen the growth of the civilian population—first the families of the military and the craftsmen and tradesmen to service their needs; then the burgeoning of other industries and trades; a steady increase in numbers; servicing and trading not only for the military, but with each other and outside—until a part of the colony did not depend economically upon the fortress. The form of government had changed correspondingly, though more slowly. In the last resort the Governor retained his autocratic power to do almost anything he judged necessary for the safety of the fortress. In practice his nonmilitary powers had for years been gradually passing to various forms of council, at first wholly nominated, later wholly elected; and today only a nuclear emergency could cause a Governor to use his full powers without reference to his council or to London.

When at last given the chance, the Gibraltarians showed a considerable political maturity. Not many towns with a 95 percent Roman Catholic Italian and Spanish majority would elect and reelect a Jew as Mayor and Chief Minister, as they did Sir Joshua Hassan. (Incidentally, there were only two Queen's Counsel—senior attorneys—in Gibraltar: Both were Jews.)

Demilitarization had extended into every area. There were fewer soldiers, and those much less visible. Gun salutes to visiting warships and foreign admirals were no longer fired from King's Bastion, right behind City Hall, but from a battery at a discreet distance. The admiral still lived in a big house with acres of beautiful gardens, but more and more War Department land was being given, leased, or sold to the elected government, which kept clamoring for still more and for the cession of still more military facilities . . . and for Britain to continue responsible for the defense of the Rock.

And the Gibraltarians? Who *were* they, now? At the last census (1961), the civil population comprised 19,044 Roman Catholics, 1,632 Protestants, 654 Jews, and small numbers of other religions. Most of the Roman Catholics were ultimately of Italian origin, though with a very strong Spanish strain, since for generations Gibraltarian males had been marrying Spanish girls.

Most of the Protestants were of British origin. The Jews had come—or come back—from Barbary, Minorca, and Genoa and other parts of Italy.

The ordinary language was Spanish, strongly Andalusian-accented (indeed, there was to the expert a recognizable Gibraltar accent called *llanito*). The language as actually spoken might be called Engañol or Esplish, for one heard things like "*Faltan tres* quarts *de* engine oil" or "*He perdido un* six-inch bastard file *en la casa del* water commissioner." The use of English was increasing greatly, aided by snob value and growing anti-Spanish resentment. Nor was the Gibraltarian "spirit" at all Spanish. It was considerably more tortuous, more darkly "Italian," less *alegre,* than the Spanish.

The Gibraltarians had a very British respect for law, which in Gibraltar was generally sound and well and honestly administered. Judge, counsel, and clerks all looked as though they had been borrowed from the Old Bailey; the police wore British bobbies' helmets, acted with the bobby's vaguely bored patience, and went unarmed. The people drank strong tea and heavy beer and worshipped Manchester United, an English soccer team. The upper classes were always snobbish, and their attitude toward the royal family would have done credit to a third footman in the days of "God bless the squire and his relations and keep us in our proper stations." Wherever royalty has stopped, looked, or visited in Gibraltar, the fact is recorded in fawning brass and concrete. Yet several old-time visitors and non-Gibraltarian residents have insisted that the general sentiment of the Gibraltarians—except for that uppermost crust—was anti-British; and this should surprise no one.

How these fascinating people, flotsam from the wreck of an empire, lived, apart from taking in each other's washing, was something of a mystery. The official report stated that "Gibraltar has no agriculture or other natural resources and apart from small coffee, tobacco-processing and garment-making industries, opportunities for employment continue to be provided mainly by the Official Employers (the Government of Gibraltar, the [British] Ministry of Defence, the [British] Ministry of Public Building and Works, and the City Council) and by the wholesale or retail trades, the hotel and catering trades, shipping services, the building industry and private domestic service."

"Retail trade" covered the sale of many goods to ships' crews, particularly Russians, and cruise passengers. Sometimes there were seven or eight Russian freighters and tankers anchored in the bay at one time, and the streets were full of square-faced men carrying huge brown-paper parcels. They would clean the stores out of one or two items, for example, blankets or shoes, caring nothing for size, style, color, or quality. It was rumored that when they returned to Russia they held public auctions on the quayside.

There was a fair amount of tourism. Foreigners came to see the famous Rock, and Gibraltar was also home base for many English who retired to the Costa del Sol. It combined two qualities which many British regard as essential for a foreign holiday resort: it must have sunshine, and it must be as unforeign as possible. The weather was usually good, the pubs just like those in a small English town, and the restaurants the same, but even worse. The more sophisticated tourist tended to avoid Gibraltar, for he could get much more for his money in Spain, where the truly foreign atmosphere was for him not a drawback but an inducement. Gibraltar had the added attraction of being inside the sterling area, so a visit there did not bite into the Briton's tiny allowance of foreign exchange when currency restrictions were in force.

To increase tourism gambling was permitted and a casino built. Some members of the Gibraltar administration wanted to restore the eighteenth-century fortifications (the galleries) and run *son et lumière* productions there. Others thought that the money should be put into more and better hotel accommodation, esplanades, boat marinas—anything to mitigate Gibraltar's overpowering claustrophobia, which had strengthened as the civil population grew to near 25,000.

And there was smuggling, the export or re-export of goods knowing or suspecting that they will evade payment of legal duty in their country of final destination: one can call a spade a spade or a bloody shovel. There was always a small amount of smuggling *into* Gibraltar, mainly brandy, wines, and spirits, which were always much cheaper in Spain; but the principal direction, of course, was into Spain, and by far the most important item was tobacco. This had been going on for a long time, and so had Spanish complaints against it to the governor or to London.

The British were in general unhelpful. Anthony Eden minuted on one of these protests that it was not the responsibility of Her Majesty's Government to protect the revenues of foreign states; but there is no doubt that if the French or the Dutch had asked for British help in preventing a huge traffic, contraband according to their laws, into their countries, they would have got it. The Spanish did not get it, and they must take part of the blame. As far as Gibraltar is concerned, their attitude had always been noncooperative or worse, from the punitive quarantines of the 1700's to the affair of the *Olterra,* and they had no right to expect any friendly help from the Gibraltar British.

Further, the root of the problem was in Spain, not in Gibraltar, and this was particularly true after Hitler's war, when a number of fast war surplus navy patrol launches were put on the market in the Mediterranean. The organizers and principal beneficiaries of the syndicates which bought and operated these launches for smuggling were Spanish. Their bribes and payoffs—indeed, smuggling as a fact of life—penetrated every level of Spanish society and government. The commissioner of police of La Línea was a frequent visitor to Gibraltar; his chauffeur was soon able to buy two blocks of flats and a bar. The military and municipal authorities of the Campo had a daily shopping list, and a man with a horse-drawn cart went into Gibraltar every day to fill it. An intelligence officer of the military government also went to Gibraltar every day, possibly in the line of duty—but he took with him a shopping list for high-ups in Madrid. One senior official publicly stated that the smuggling was necessary because it enabled Spain to provide American cigarettes to tourists without having to buy them with hard currency. The same could be said of streptomycin and penicillin, which were also heavily smuggled in the early postwar years.

In the face of this situation, British measures against the trade would have hurt Gibraltarian revenues and made no difference to Spain, for the stuff would have come from Tangier or Italy, as much of it did in any case. Nevertheless, the blatant operations of the smuggling launches based on Gibraltar (to claim British protection and status they had a British subject as nominal owner) began to embarrass the Gibraltar government, and in the mid-1950's it set about harassing the trade in various ways. This caused much of it to leave Gibraltar to work out of other bases under other flags. Gibraltar also offered the Spanish authorities means of identifying the crewmen of the smuggling boats, all of whom lived in or near Algeciras; but the Spanish never took action.

Most telling of all is the fact that Spain and Gibraltar are both members of Interpol. When the Italian government earlier mounted a great investigation of the smuggling into its country, it asked for and received information from all other Interpol countries, including Gibraltar. The Gibraltar government later prepared a list of the names, functions, and addresses of everyone it had traced in the organization of smuggling in the western Mediterranean. This list named 4 Latvians, 3 Dutchmen, 1 Swede, 4 Austrians, 5 Canadians, 4 Cubans, 41 Italians, 195 Portuguese, 4 Albanians, 3 Swiss, 20 West Germans, 12 Danes, 61 French, 9 Belgians, 134 Moroccans, 3 Americans, 158 British (including Gibraltarians), and 1,013 Spaniards. The Spanish government never asked Gibraltar for this list of names, because every country in Interpol would then have known that the smuggling was connived in and actively supported by some of the most highly placed men in the nation.

By 1963 Gibraltar's measures had reduced the number of potential Gibraltar-owned smuggling boats to 13, as against 42 of other flags in the area, mostly at Tangier. In this year General Franco decided that negotiations would not bring Gibraltar back to Spain and chose contraband as the point of his attack against the *status quo*. Because of the smuggling, he said, Gibraltar was a cancer in the Spanish economy. In using this line he obviously had to ensure that no investigation could implicate the Spanish government or its senior officials in the continuance of the disease. So thousands of police, guards, agents, and Tabacalera employees who had routinely been receiving payoffs for years were told—fingers out of the pie, *finis!* The Spanish state security is extremely tough and efficient when it wants to be, especially if the Generalissimo himself has given the word. The crackdown began. A few old hands like Juanito el Canario, who hadn't got the message or didn't believe it could apply to them because of their previous special connections, found themselves in jail. In a very short time the smuggling was stopped cold.

To give an idea of what it had been worth, note that in the previous year the Tabacalera had legally imported 12,000,000 packs of U.S. cigarettes for sale in Spain. The year after, they imported 97,000,000. The difference—85,000,000 packs, at a sale price in Spain of about $40,000,000—was what the smugglers used to supply. With the great flow of tobacco, the crackdown also dammed the lesser streams of whisky, luxury cars, refrigerators, carpets, and British wool cloth which used to pass through Gibraltar. Small amounts of hallucinatory drugs are still occasionally seized and publicized as being from Gibraltar, but the evidence seems to be that they are not.

So today the contraband business is dead; and with it, one might add, the "Gibraltar as a cancer in the Spanish economy" argument. General Franco had shown that a strong, tough government which meant business could reduce smuggling to negligible proportions. But of course the use of the argument as political ammunition continues, because as long as Gibraltar is not Spanish the smuggling *could* start again . . . if this or a subsequent Spanish government were to permit it.

From the "cancer" policy, Spain progressed by gradual stages to the imposition of a blockade against Gibraltar, which can be called the Fifteenth Siege. Her justification has been a series of motions in the United Nations accepting Spain's position and calling upon Britain to hand the tiny peninsula back to the great peninsula of which it is physically a part. The effects of the blockade are various. Gibraltar imports food from Morocco and wine from France and Italy, whereas both would naturally come from Spain. Prices are high, and much that ought to be readily available cannot be had at any price. No Spaniard is now allowed to enter Gibraltar to work, so Moroccans have to be imported—again underscoring Gibraltar's historic dependence on a friendly Morocco—but this has also forced Gibraltarians to learn trades and professions which they used to consider beneath them. The worst effect of the blockade has been to increase the claustrophobia, for each one of the 25,000 inhabitants seems to own a car, with which he used to stretch his spirit in the vastness of Andalusia; but now he drives it endlessly round and round, up and down, the narrow streets and roads . . . and there is no escape.

Since Spain has cut off all land and sea communication between herself and Gibraltar, the Rock's only links are by sea and air with other countries, notably Morocco and England. From Gibraltar's point of view, therefore, Spain's most dangerous threats are concerned with air rights and territorial waters. Briefly, she claims that Gibraltar has neither, since they were not mentioned in the Treaty of Utrecht or any other agreement; but Gibraltar obviously must have territorial waters and air rights if its ships and civil aircraft are to operate. Spain keeps pushing— today anchoring tall-masted ships practically at the end of the airport runway, tomorrow complaining that British aircraft fly over prohibited areas. And day in and day out, the gray hull of a Spanish man-of-war slices through the waters of the bay, observing and menacing all maritime activity. This vessel is about 40 feet long, has a maximum speed of 5 knots, and apparently last had its flues cleaned about 1933. For obvious reasons it is universally known as *Smoky Joe*.

Stick in one hand, carrot in the other . . . Spain set out to persuade the Gibraltarians that happiness and prosperity awaited them in the arms of the fatherland. This needed major engineering, because for centuries the Campo de Gibraltar—the semicircle of about 20 miles' radius centering on the Rock—had been as poor as any area in Europe. There were, and are, men who work on the estates of great lords for *el cubierto*—four pennies and a bowl of pottage—per day. In all the Campo few but went to bed hungry, and some, starving. Few, that is, except those who worked for the English on the Rock: *they* had a good wage, regularly paid, and the customary right to bring out a little something each day without paying duty on it.

To remedy this Spain announced, in 1965, a Plan of Development for the Campo. The plan involves spending $60,000,000 a year until 1990 to convert the Campo into a highly industrialized zone of great technical efficiency. A huge petrochemical complex has already been built, factories for plastics, cellulose, and the like are going up, modern roads and a sports stadium are under construction. All this the Gibraltarians can see over the closed fence on the isthmus. "Come out," Spain wheedles, "you'll never have it so good."

To put a final dressing on the carrot, it has also been announced that a new Spanish province called Gibraltar is to be formed. It will consist of the Campo, somewhat enlarged; and the eventual capital, when it returns "home," will be Gibraltar. There are a lot of jobs and money in a capital. People have to go there for all kinds of ceremonies, licenses, passes, permits. . . .

So far, the Gibraltarians have refused to be cajoled. At a referendum held in 1967 after Spain took her case to the United Nations, the people were asked whether they wanted the British connection or an association with Spain. The pro-British response to this referendum (which Spain denounced as illegal and invalid) was over 99 percent. Pro-British or perhaps, according to the old residents before quoted, anti-Spanish. If Spain were as rich as the United States, these say, the Gibraltarians would have clamored to become Spanish. The sneer has some truth in it, but not much. Spain has never known liberty or responsible government. After two and a half centuries of military dictators of their own the Gibraltarians are enjoying the pains and pleasures of democracy far too much to consider risking them. Gibraltar Jews particularly fear any surrender to Spain's rigid and anti-Semitic Roman Catholicism.

Only one country promises any hope of protection against Spain. So the visiting Briton finds himself warmed, perhaps slightly embarrassed, and as surprised as would be an American in Paris if confronted with placards proclaiming *Yankee, stay, we love you!* On the poorer back streets, if he looks British enough, he is liable to be greeted with a murmured "God bless you!" Whole streets are painted red, white, and blue, including the sidewalks and gutters. The Union Jack is the favorite decorative pattern for window frames, doors, house ends, and old jalopies. Everywhere the hand-printed signs shout *British 265 years, British forever . . . God Save Our Queen! . . . Born British, we'll die British . . . To hell with Franco!* When Manchester United, which has become the personification of Britain abroad, played and beat Real Madrid, the personification of Spain, the score was chalked all over the streets and walls, with triumphantly disparaging remarks added for the benefit of the Spanish workmen who, in those days, were still going in and out of the dockyard. (This chauvinistic crowing was misdirected. All Spaniards are patriotic, but different classes place their emphases differently. It is not the peasant or laborer but the aristocrat and professional man who cares most deeply about British Gibraltar.)

But there are at least two sorts of Gibraltarian who would like to see an accommodation with Spain. First are the people called *palomas* (doves, passenger pigeons). Born Gibraltarian, the typical *paloma* married a local Spanish girl, bought a cottage and a little land in the Campo, and lived there but worked in Gibraltar. Then the Spanish made him apply for Spanish papers, thus forcing him to admit that he was not a Gibraltarian but a Spaniard from the Spanish city of Gibraltar. Next they closed the frontier altogether, compelling the *paloma* to make a final choice. Thus families have been split, wives and children abandoned—or pride swallowed and the Rock deserted.

Many of the Indians and Pakistanis whose shops are so prominent a part of Main Street also want accommodation with Spain, to the considerable disgust of the true Gibraltarian. Because they came from countries of the British Commonwealth they were admitted without limitation; but none of them *lives* in Gibraltar. A family buys a store and sends some member from India to run it. It never hires shop assistants but just sends over some more young members to work for nothing. All the money they make gets sent back home. (And they make plenty, for they ally industry and shrewdness: one merchant always travels through Russia on his journeys back and forth so that he can see what consumer goods the Russians lack most: it is these goods he stocks, from Japan or Hong Kong, for the benefit of the Russian seamen).

These factors, plus their aloofness, had already cut the Indian-Pakistani community off from the other Gibraltarians before General Franco's recent moves. But many Indian families and firms also have branches on the Spanish mainland or in the Canaries. In order to improve their status there some of the Gibraltar firms cabled the United Nations in support of the Spanish case. This did not increase their popularity with their neighbors.

So we come out of history into the continuing "now"; yet "now" is always, too, a continuation of history and cannot be separated or considered apart from it.

The Gibraltarians want to be independent but protected by Britain, or they want to be welded onto the British state. They declare that they cannot be handed like a chattel to anyone, least of all to a Spanish dictatorship.

Britain defies the United Nations mandate to hand Gibraltar

back to Spain on the ground that a people's right to self-determination is paramount, taking precedence over treaty commitments made in the distant past. Whether Britain needs or wants Gibraltar is doubtful; whether she would or could hold it in the face of a Spanish attack, even more so.

Spain declares that Gibraltar was taken, and has been kept, by naked force; that the Gibraltarians do not have the right of self-determination because they are not a true "people" but a British importation, a puppet; that Gibraltar cannot be handed over to the Gibraltarians because the Treaty of Utrecht rules that if Britain ever gives it up, it must be offered to Spain *before all others*; that Gibraltar cannot be politically united with Britain because, under the same treaty, Spain retains sovereignty.

And behind all this loom huge shapes, giant flares from the past, none the less powerful for being purely spiritual: the Sacred Reconquest . . . the Spanish Inquisition . . . the Gibraltar Legend . . . the Holy Crusade. . . . It is not law and logic, it is these, and the ways in which they have molded the human spirit, for greater or smaller, that will decide the fate of Gibraltar's inhabitants.

The Rock itself will journey on, unmoving, through time.

1985

The old man paced slowly up and down the cave, his feet in the ragged shoes making no sound in the deep powdery soil. The morning sun glittered brightly on the sea, sending flashes of light deep into the cave. Half a mile out, two fishing boats sat like birds on a painted tray. The warmth of the sun on his skin made him turn back quickly. The fishermen were not likely to notice or care, but any needless risk was one too many. He raised his wrist to glance at his watch, but it was not there. He remembered that he had removed his own for this mission and had had no time to find something more suitable to the clothes and station he had temporarily adopted.

It must be near nine. She had been gone about an hour and a half. Nearly three hours in hand. He retreated into the back of the cave.

This was Gibraltar all around him now, at last. A strange feeling. It was . . . Holy Mary, it must be seventy-five years since his grandfather the old count took him up to the battlements of Castellar and pointed to the great Rock in the sea below and said, "There it is, Rafael. *El Peñon. La Vergüenza de España,* the Shame of Spain, we call it." It was nearly fifty years since he had stood under the sheer north face arranging for Republican refugees to escape into the British enclave. Then the Legionaries had come. He could see the sheer limestone cliff now over their dark faces, over their rifle barrels leveled at his eyes. . . . Well, they had not fired, and here he was, on Gibraltar at last, in a cave.

Smoke of ages darkened parts of the roof. How many boats had come here by night, as he had? How many sailors had slept on this dark soil? How many had sheltered here for their lives? How many lovers had worked here that other wonder of God?

An isolated stalagmite, almost human in shape and size, stood on guard by the entrance. A beercan-pull glittered in the powder at his feet. Frowning, he bent slowly and dug with his fingers to bury the ugly little object. He found something hard and took it to the light. It was a small bronze scarab brooch—a woman's gewgaw. He dropped it into his pocket.

He heard the girl's voice calling up from the beach. "Don Pedro, is all well?" Her Spanish was of the American Southwest, Mexican-accented. The old man answered to the agreed name, calling down, "All is well, Dolores," and adding the key words to indicate he was not under duress. "I am alone."

She came up then, followed by two men. One was tall, clean-shaven, about sixty-five, aristocratic, his eyes watery and blue. The other was short, heavily built, black-haired, olive-skinned, his mouth wide under a defiant, fleshy nose.

The woman said, "Cardinal, this is Admiral Sir Lionel Kingsley, the British High Commissioner in Gibraltar. And this is Mr. Hillel Conquy, the Chief Minister. Gentlemen—Cardinal Rafael Santangel y Santangel-Barrachina."

The admiral extended his hand with a breezy "How d'ye do." The cardinal looked about seventy, he thought, though Hillel had assured him he was eighty-three. He was tall, stooped, and dark as a gypsy. In the dirty old clothes he *was* a gypsy.

The Chief Minister spoke curtly in Spanish. "Honored to make your acquaintance, Excellency." The cardinal looked just as he had in the old pictures, he thought. It was fortunate that the Revolutionary Council's sea patrols had not picked up the boat, for that face was impossible to disguise.

The cardinal said carefully, "I speak English. Not well, but enough, perhaps. Unless the admiral speaks Spanish . . . ?"

The admiral shook his head, "Sorry . . . And Hillel, now that we have met His Excellency, couldn't we translate this discussion to your house or the Convent, where we have coffee, food —even tables and chairs?"

The cardinal said, "Also, agents of the Council are on watch outside, I know. . . . I will not take up much of your valuable time, gentlemen. I must not, if I am to save a man's life. And, I believe, the future of Spain. Also, I hope to convince you, the future of Gibraltar."

The young woman stepped back, leaned against the rock wall, and took out her notebook and pen. The Chief Minister eyed her thoughtfully—American, about thirty, black hair, amazing deep blue eyes, intelligent; and, perhaps, dangerous.

The admiral said, "Miss O'Brien told us you came here in a smugglers' launch. I did not know that there was much of that traffic since Spain and Britain entered the Common Market."

The cardinal said, "It is engaged in the heroin traffic and is owned by Moroccans. On this occasion we hired it for this special trip. It will return for us after dark. . . . The reason we . . ."

The Chief Minister interrupted. "And Miss O'Brien is of your party?"

"She has been with me ever since I escaped to Morocco," the cardinal said impatiently. He collected himself. These people did not mean to let him hurry them. They owed him nothing. He must guard himself and remember what he had learned in his years in prison: be patient, watchful, impervious.

He said, "She found out where I was hiding—I do not know how—contacted me, and persuaded me that we, the Loyalists, need true reporting if we are to have good public relations, particularly in the United States."

Dolores caught the Chief Minister looking at her. She broke in before he could speak. "I have promised the cardinal to publish nothing without his permission. I give the same promise to you."

The Chief Minister said, "We have little faith in promises made by journalists, especially American journalists."

She said, "I am also an officer of the Central Intelligence Agency. If you want the President to know what you have decided, and why—fully and fairly—I will ensure that he does. Or even if you do not wish it, as long as I am here."

The Chief Minister frowned at her. He looked like a Jewish Churchill, Dolores thought as she stared back. He said suddenly, "Very well. No publication without the written permission of the Chief Minister of Gibraltar. And now, cardinal . . ."

The cardinal said, "The Count of Grazalema is returning to Spain on the weekly Algiers boat today."

The admiral glanced at his watch. The Algiers boat was due to dock at Algeciras at noon. Two and a half hours from now.

"Has he made his peace with the Revolutionary Council, then?" the Chief Minister asked.

The cardinal shook his head. "The opposite. He has gathered his forces, completed his preparations, and is returning to lead the counterrevolution."

"He is coming incognito then?"

"Yes. As you know, they have put a large price on his head."

"For the murders in Granada, isn't it?" the Chief Minister said.

The cardinal said, "Those people were secret agents of the Council. They were responsible for the deaths of over two hundred people in and after the Communist rising—including many women and priests. The charges against the Count are purely political."

The admiral thought, they are fencing: Hillel was an astute politician and would have made a good lawyer, like all Jews. Like all Gibraltarians, come to that. They were a dark, secretive lot. He hadn't liked them when he first stepped ashore from, let's see, the old *Ark Royal* in thirty-nine, and not much better when he was the admiral here ten years ago. Still, there were good ones, no use denying it.

Hillel Conquy was saying, "And the Count is going to lead this counterrevolution of the Right?"

The cardinal said, "Of the Right. And of the Center. And of all the Left who are not Communists. *My* credentials are not of the Right, Señor Conquy."

Hillel Conquy said quickly, "Of course not." The old man was as good to meet as his reputation would have led one to expect. He had been one of Hillel's heroes all his life for his long fight against Franco and the succeeding dictatorship and because it was he, above any other, who had persuaded the king to introduce a responsible democratic government into Spain. He had even fought for religious tolerance . . . but there was Gibraltar to think of. He must not let his personal admiration warp his judgment. Rafael Santangel was a great man, but a Spaniard, a Catholic, and a cardinal.

The admiral said, "Then what is it that . . . ?"

The cardinal said, "The Count was betrayed yesterday. The Revolutionary Council know he is on the ship. He is sailing to certain death. And our rising, to failure."

No one spoke for a long time. Dolores wrote the word *muerte* carefully on her pad: "death" in Spanish. She remembered, when she was a young girl, her great-grandmother, old Mrs. Falcon, lying in the great bed in the Santa Fe house, whispering, "*Voy a la muerte y estoy contenta.*" How old could she have been then? Ninety-seven, ninety-eight? She was from Spain originally, she said—but what part? No one seemed to know. She was the one who had insisted that Dolores be named after her.

The admiral said, "You mean . . . there is no other leader?"

"None other whom the people—all the people—trust and will follow. Like me, he was imprisoned by Franco. But I am a churchman; he is a fighter. He fought, leading the guerrilla war against the dictatorships. He was not a secessionist like many of the Basque and Catalan leaders, so all Spaniards could follow him. Like Franco he believes in a Spain *una, grande, libre*—but truly so. Above all, the young believe in him."

"We know," the Chief Minister said.

The cardinal said, "I fear that no one else can lead us to overthrow this murdering Council. But the Russians are supporting them, and we cannot afford to lose, for there will be no second chance. Nor, I suggest, can Gibraltar—or England—or the United States—afford to see us lose."

"Our relations with the Revolutionary Council have been excellent," the Chief Minister said.

"Naturally," the cardinal said.

"They have guaranteed our freedom and independence, or our union with Britain, if that should be agreed on."

The cardinal said, "So I understand. You will, of course, know what value to place on these assurances if the Council win the present struggle, once they feel themselves secure in power."

The Chief Minister said, "Naturally. But the worst they *might* do is no different from what the Count of Grazalema has publicly announced that he *will* do. Except for the imposition of Communism."

The cardinal shook his head with a gesture of denial. The admiral's watch read ten fifteen. The sun was off the sand at the mouth of the cave. The cardinal said, "The count is the hero of Spain—all Spain, Señor Conquy. All Spain desires the return of Gibraltar. The Count says aloud what all think."

Dolores wrote "Gibraltar" on her pad. An imposing place, familiar to the eye and mind long before one actually saw it. Circled by the Spanish mountains. Sound of Spanish in the streets. Joined to Spain by that thin, unbreakable belt of sand. Separated by human emotions, human history. What God hath joined let no man put asunder. But the people were not joined.

The Chief Minister said, "Setting aside for a moment the Count's view on our future . . . would he care to face trial here for the murder of Charles Torrenti two years ago? It was done in the streets of Lisbon, but I imagine we could find a legal precedent for trying him in Gibraltar."

The cardinal said, "Your Minister of Information was murdered by Spaniards. By members of the party to which the Count and I belong. I admit it and regret it. But it was not done by the Count or on his order. As the guerrilla campaign . . ."

Hillel Conquy, not listening, looked attentive. The old man was tired but would not show it. It was ten twenty-five. The Count had lived by the sword, and he might as well die by it, like his grandfather murdered in the Civil War out there in the cork oaks of Almoraima. But there was something else present here, a

shudder from the past . . . or the future? A sense of history or
prophecy, an emanation from the great Rock in whose womb
they stood. The girl felt it, perhaps, staring up at the limestone,
out to sea, biting her lip. The admiral . . . no. He was not really
interested or involved. There had been a noticeable lessening of
British involvement here in recent years. And the few years of
liberal government in Spain between the military dictators and
the present Council had destroyed the Labour Party's special pro-
tective attitude.

". . . never authorized or ordered any violence against Gibraltar or Gibraltarians, let alone murder," the cardinal ended.

The admiral said, "The blockade of Gibraltar . . ."

"Was his idea," the cardinal said. "As I have said, he thinks—
as do I—that Gibraltar is a part of Spain, to which it must
return."

The Chief Minister said, "That is his privilege. But it does
not, of itself, incline the Government of Gibraltar to come to his
aid."

Government of Gibraltar, he thought. Taxes. More legislation
on unemployment and education. More jobs. But where is the
money to come from? Shipping. Tourism. Defense. No room, no
escape. But the mind would not be caged.

Ten thirty. It would take twenty minutes to get an order to
the guard ship; say twenty more for the ship to reach an intercept position.

The cardinal's hooded eyes glittered. He spoke with new authority, not as one supplicating: "If the Revolutionary Council
establish themselves, you will have a Communist dictatorship in
Spain, which cannot be overthrown without a major war. The
regime will sign a treaty with Russia, and Russian troops and
ships and aircraft will be stationed here at Spain's request. Gibraltar will find itself in the same position as Czechoslovakia or
Hong Kong . . . existing only at the convenience of the conti-
nental power, subject to harassment and humiliation at any or
no excuse . . . forced to comply with any demands made on it by
the Spanish government. You may be sure that the first things
you will lose are a free radio, press, and television and your right
to grant political asylum. . . . For the United States and Britain,
the door of the Mediterranean will be slammed in your face, and
it will not be Spain's weak hand on the bolt but Russia's. You

know as well as I what will be the fate of your friends and ours, shut in behind that door. They will be devoured at leisure. . . . In the name of God, gentlemen, do not make the same tragic mistake that the democracies made in 1936. The Revolutionary Council are receiving communist help and will receive more. Help *us*. As a beginning, a vital first step, rescue the Count from the Algiers boat!"

His upraised hand dropped slowly. Twenty to eleven, Dolores noted. And how much time did Gibraltar have? Or America?

The admiral said, "One thing I don't quite understand . . . why haven't the Council radioed the skipper to find the Count and put him in irons?"

"They do not know whether the captain is of their party—he is an Algerian," the cardinal said wearily. "For the same reason we have not tried to radio any warning to him, though it might be possible. . . ."

The Chief Minister said, "Admiral, what do you think?"

The admiral said, "It's no secret that H.M.G. are very worried about the possibility of Spain becoming Communist. The P.M. spent an hour discussing it with me last week. But the Russians have been pressing very hard for nonintervention. . . . They have kept their help to the Council very much under cover—no warships or bombers or anything obvious like that. . . . If there were an established government in Spain which we could help, then perhaps . . . but with the king and most of the Cabinet assassinated and the parliament in jail or hiding . . ." He shrugged.

"The Count will soon set up a government on Spanish soil with which you can deal," the cardinal said.

"How would the rescue actually be carried out?" the Chief Minister asked.

The admiral said, "H'm. Quite a poser, eh?"

The cardinal caught Dolores' eye. He felt very old and weak. Dolores burst out, "If you don't make up your minds soon, he will be dead anyway."

The Chief Minister said, "If we agree to rescue the Count, there should be no problem. H.M.G. have instituted a semi-blockade in persuance of their hands-off policy."

The admiral said, "I suppose I might get authority to search the Algiers boat on suspicion of carrying arms."

"And what if London refuses to give it?"

"Then we can do nothing."

"They will certainly ask what we advise," the Chief Minister said. "What *do* we advise?"

The admiral looked at the cave roof. Dolores thought, he is not a breezy sailorman really but a cautious and rather cold diplomat.

The admiral said, "I'm afraid I would have to say that this is an improper use of H.M. ships. We have no reason to believe that the Algiers boat is carrying arms. Rescuing the Count by force would seem to be a direct intervention in the affairs of a foreign country . . . in this case, too, in the civil war we have declared it our policy *not* to intervene in. I do not think I could recommend it."

The Chief Minister said, "The Count is your cousin, is he not?"

The cardinal nodded. "After a fashion. The thirtieth Count was my grandfather and his great-grandfather. That Count's daughter ran away with my father, a gypsy from La Línea. I am the result, without benefit of wedlock. The family have always treated me well."

The Chief Minister said, "What if we took the Count off the ship on condition that he refrained from all political activity for the rest of his life? That would also save the Council the embarrassment of executing him."

"They would feel no such embarrassment," the cardinal said. "They are Communists. . . . As for the Count, of course I cannot speak for him, but I am sure he would refuse your terms. . . . What is your decision? Time is short."

"A break with the council would be a serious matter for us," the Chief Minister said, as though to himself. "They can control our air flights—restart the blockade, and now we are so organized for getting our food from Spain that we would not easily change. We would be ruined. Many would starve."

The admiral said, "I don't think you need worry, Chief Minister. I am sure H.M.G. will find themselves unable to do what the cardinal asks. Of course we can press very strongly against the execution on . . ."

The Chief Minister said, "Yes." He stared into the cardinal's eyes. The old man was Spanish to the tips of his fingers, as he himself was Gibraltarian. But they were both more—the cardinal, through the Church; himself, through the Rock. He was at the same time a Jew, worshiping; an Englishman, holding; a Spaniard, yearning.

He said softly, "You want a base for the reconquest? A Spanish base? How would Gibraltar serve?"

The cardinal swayed in the stillness. Dolores stepped quickly to his side. "You are offering . . . to return to Spain?" he stammered.

Hillel Conquy said, "No. I am thinking of offering Spain the chance to return to us. . . . If we were to declare Gibraltar a part of Spain, ours would be the only legitimate, freely elected government in the country. Yes?"

The admiral said slowly, "Yes. I suppose so."

The Chief Minister went on, still tentatively, as though searching for words in a puzzle picture. "We could declare leased to Great Britain, for say ninety-nine years, all land she now holds here."

The admiral said, "Wait a minute. . . ."

"So an attack by the Revolutionary Council on us would become an attack on Great Britain. That should hold them a few days—long enough for the Count to start military operations. . . . We could proclaim that we will accept into our government those parties, those provinces—and *only* those—which adopt and guarantee to their people full free democratic process. . . ."

The cardinal said in Spanish, "Señor Conquy, if you will take the Count as your right hand, as the leader of the armed struggle, he and all Spain will accept you as Chancellor."

"Until there can be free elections," Hillel said.

The admiral cried, "Chief Minister, we must talk privately before . . ."

"Religious freedom for all Spaniards. Public and full," the Chief Minister said.

"I promise it."

The Chief Minister said, "The promises of your Church sometimes do not hold their value very long, cardinal. We remember some made in Granada in 1492."

The cardinal said, "For the Holy Pontiff, I cannot answer. For the Church in Spain, I can and do."

The admiral said, "On behalf of Her Majesty's Government, I must . . ."

The cardinal said, "Your thought is beyond words noble, Señor Conquy . . . as noble as this Rock which gave it, and you, birth."

The Chief Minister glanced at his watch. "We must run. . . . I will order an armed police launch out to stop the Algiers boat as it rounds Europa Point. Miss O'Brien, get word to Washington as soon as you can. A strong hands-off note to Moscow would be a help. *Shalom!*"

He turned and ran down the steep slope, his coattails flapping. The admiral began to run after him, stumbled, and slowed to a walk. At the beach the Chief Minister stopped, turned, and shouted up through cupped hands, "Stay hidden unless you need help. There'll be a security guard on watch above until your boat comes. He'll bring you food and something to sit on. Young fellow called Tamlyn. You can trust him."

With a wave he was gone, the admiral twenty yards behind. The cardinal, raising his hand in blessing, found he was holding up the scarab brooch he had discovered in the floor of the cave.

"Take this, child," he said to Dolores. "Keep it." He raised his hand again in blessing on the empty sand, the short beach, and the Rock.

Author's Note

The seaside cave mentioned in Book One is Gorham's; the one called Eagle's Nest in Book Three is Martin's; Rachel's Secret and the Hermit's (Book Four) are Genista Two and Glen Rocky Distillery, respectively. Lost Lamb (Book Seven) is Pete's Paradise, which must have silted up again before its recent rediscovery. The Great Cave, or similar wording, is always Old St. Michael's.

J.M.

Bibliography

The following books and articles have been of value to me in the writing of this book:

Air Headquarters, Royal Air Force, Gibraltar (Intelligence Section), *Flying from the Rock*. Gibraltar, 1945.

Ancell, S., *A Circumstantial Journal of the Long & Tedious Blockade & Siege of Gibraltar*. Liverpool, 1785.

Anonymous, *An Authentic and Accurate Journal of the Late Siege of Gibraltar*. London, 1785.

———, *An Enquiry into Pretensions of Spain to Gibraltar, as Founded on His Late Majesty's Letter*. London, 1729.

———, *Boletin de la Comision Provincial de Monumentos, Año IV, No. 15*. Cádiz.

———, *Gibraltar Society, Report of Sectional Activities and Papers*. Gibraltar, 1929-30.

———, *Jewish Encyclopaedia*. London, 1905.

———, *The Medical and Physical Journal*, Vols. 13, 14, 18. London, 1805-1807.

———, *Quarterly Publication, Cave Research and Rock Climbing Society*. Gibraltar, 1961.

Arraras, Iribarren, Joaquin, *Historia de la Cruzada Española*. Madrid.

Augusta, Josef, *Prehistoric Man*. London, 1960.

Bögli and Franke, *Radiant Darkness*. London, 1967.

Camon Aznar, José, *Las Artes y Los Pueblos de la España Primitiva*. Madrid, 1954.

Carrington, C. E., *Gibraltar*. Royal Institute of International Affairs, 1956.

Castro, Adolfo de, "Historia de Cadiz y su Provincia." *Revista Medica*.

Congregation of Spanish & Portuguese Jews, *Ascamot*. London, 1906.

Disney-Roebuck, Wyndham, *The Gateway*. London, 1937.

Dozy, R., *Spanish Islam*. London, 1913.

Drinkwater, Col. J., *A History of the Siege of Gibraltar 1779-1783*. London, 1905.

Duckworth, W. L. H., "Cave Exploration at Gibraltar in September 1910." Typescript.

Eley, D. M., "The Gibraltar Tunnels." Typescript.

Ellicott, J. T. and D. M., *An Ornament to the Almeida*. Portsmouth, 1950.

Ellicott, D. M., *From Rooke to Nelson*. Gibraltar, 1965.

———, *Gibraltar's Royal Governor*. Gibraltar, 1955.

———, *Bastion Against Aggression*. Gibraltar, 1968.

Fellows, Sir James, M.D., *Reports of the Pestilential Disorders of Andalusia*. London, 1815.

Frere, Sir B. H. T., *Guide to the Flora of Gibraltar and Neighbourhood*. Gibraltar, 1910.

Gallwey, Lt. Col. H. D., "A Hoard of Third Century Antoninioni from Southern Spain." *Numismatic Chronicle*, 1962.

Garratt, G. T., *Gibraltar and the Mediterranean*. London, 1939.

Garrod, D. A. E., *Excavation of a Mousterian Rock Shelter*. Royal Anthropological Institute of Great Britain and Ireland, 1928.

Gibraltar Garrison Library, *The Wild Flowers of Gibraltar and Neighbourhood*. Gibraltar, 1968.

Goodwin, Lt. E. G. M., *The Galleries, Gibraltar*. Gibraltar, 1927.

Graetz, H., *History of the Jews*, Vols. 1-5. London, 1892.

Griffiths, Arthur, "The Question of Gibraltar." *Fortnightly Review*, 1902.

Harden, Donald, *The Phoenicians*. London, 1962.

Hennen, John, *Sketches of the Medical Topography of the Mediterranean*. London, 1830.

Homer, *The Odyssey* Trans. S. O. Andrew. London, 1953.

Hort, Major, *The Rock*. London, 1939.

Howes, Dr. H. W., *The Gibraltarian*. Colombo, 1951.

Hudson, Derek, "Gibraltar, July 21-24, 1704." *Cornhill Magazine*, 1933.

Irby, Lt. Col. Howard, *Ornithology of the Straits of Gibraltar*. London, 1895.

James, T., *The History of the Herculean Straits*. London, 1771.

Jevenois, Pedro, *El Tunel Submarino del Estrecho de Gibraltar*. Madrid, 1929.

Jones, G. D. T., *An Outline of the Structure of the Rock of Gibraltar*. Archaeological Society of Gibraltar, 1956-57.

Kamen, Henry, *The Spanish Inquisition*. New York, 1965.

Kelaart, Dr. E. F., *Botany and Topography of Gibraltar*. London, 1846.

Kenyon, Maj. Gen. E. R., *Gibraltar Under Moor, Spaniard and British*. London, 1938.

Lopez de Ayala, Ignacio, *Historia de Gibraltar*. Madrid, 1782.

Luna, José Carlos de, *Historia de Gibraltar*. Madrid, 1944.

McGuffie, T. H., *Siege of Gibraltar*. London, 1965.

Mackenzie, Col. R. H., *The Trafalgar Roll*. London, 1913.

Madrazo, Pedro de, *España, Sus Monumentos y Artes (Sevilla y Cádiz)*. Barcelona, 1884.

Nolan, Comdt., *Une visite aux singes de Gibraltar*. Gibraltar, 1928.

Norris, H. T., "Ibn Battutah's Andalusian Journey." *Geographical Journal*, 1959.

————, *The Early Islamic Settlements in Gibraltar*. Royal Anthropological Institute, 1960.

Officer then serving with the Allies, *An exact Journal of the Taking of Gibraltar by the Prince of Hesse*. London.

An officer who was at the taking of Gibraltar, *An impartial Account of the Late Famous Siege of Gibraltar*. London, 1728.

Pasley, M. S., *A Few of the Wild Flowers of Gibraltar*. Portsmouth, 1876.

Pla, José, *Gibraltar*. London, 1955.

Poley, Antonio, *Cádiz y su Provincia*. Sevilla, 1901.

Pugh, Marshall, *Commander Crabb*. London, 1956.

Quennell, M. and C. H. B., *Everyday Life in Prehistoric Times*. London, 1924.

Quintero, Pelayo, *Cádiz Primitivo*. Cadiz, 1917.

Romero de Torres, Enrique, *Catalogo Monumental de España, Provincia de Cádiz*. Madrid, 1934.

Roth, Cecil, *The Spanish Inquisition*. London, 1937.

————, *A Short History of the Jewish People*. London, 1936.

Russell, Jack, *Gibraltar Besieged*. London, 1965.

Sayer, Capt., *History of Gibraltar: and of its Political Relation to Events in Europe*. London, 1862.

Scott, *A History of Tropical Medicine*. London, 1939.

Schulten, Adolf, *Tartessos* (Spanish translation). Madrid, 1945.

Serfaty, A. B. M., *The Jews of Gibraltar*. Gibraltar, 1933.

Servicio Informativo España, *Gibraltar: Historia de una Usurpacion*. Madrid, 1968.

————, *Gibraltar en el Pasado*. Madrid, 1965.

Sordo, *Moorish Spain*. London, 1963.

Spilsbury, Capt. J., *A Journal of the Siege of Gibraltar*. Gibraltar, 1908.

Stewart, J. D., *Gibraltar, the Keystone*. London, 1967.

Waechter, J. d'A., "Excavations at Gorham's Cave, Gibraltar" (proceedings of the Prehistorian Society). Gibraltar, 1951.

————, *Bulletin of the Institute of Archaeology* (Excavation of Gorham's Cave). Gibraltar, 1964.

Warner, Oliver, *Trafalgar*. London, 1959.

White, Anne Terry, *Men Before Adam*. London, 1949.

Wiseman, F. J., *Roman Spain*. London, 1956.